THE CHOICE

Claire Wade is the winner of the Good Housekeeping Novel Competition 2018. She was bed bound for six years with severe ME, trapped in a body that wouldn't do what she wanted; her only escape was through her imagination. She now writes about women who want to break free from the constraints of their lives, a subject she's deeply familiar with.

Her favourite things are books, baking and the WI. She's the founding president of a modern WI (Women's Institute) and runs a baking club for other cake lovers. You'll find her in her writing room, nicknamed Narnia because it's also home to a wardrobe and is the place where she escapes to other worlds. She's happiest if she's got a slice of chocolate cake, a cup of tea and a good book.

THE CHOICE

Claire Wade

ORION

First published in Great Britain in 2019 by Orion Fiction,
an imprint of The Orion Publishing Group Ltd
Carmelite House, 50 Victoria Embankment,
London EC4Y 0DZ

An Hachette UK company

1 3 5 7 9 10 8 6 4 2

A CIP catalogue record for this book
is available from the British Library.

ISBN (Mass Market Paperback) 978 1 4091 8774 5
ISBN (eBook) 978 1 4091 8775 2

Typeset by Deltatype Ltd, Birkenhead, Merseyside

Printed in Great Britain by Clays Ltd, Elcograf S.p.A.

www.orionbooks.co.uk

For Mum

From out of the darkness and into the light,
thank you for being there through it all.

Chapter One

It was impossible to ignore the Shame Box. The large transparent cube squatted on the tarmac to one side of the supermarket entrance. This morning it was occupied.

Olivia Pritchard unlocked her trolley and fought to push it in a straight line towards the store. Beside her, Alice kept up a stream of small talk, her best friend's usual distraction technique. It normally worked, Olivia desperately wanted it to work, but today she couldn't focus. Her full attention was drawn inexorably to the poor woman who sat hunched in the Box. Please don't let it be someone she knew, she thought.

Other shoppers gathered around the Box. Watching. Judging. Two little boys banged on the glass, leaving small, smeared handprints behind. Olivia winced. This was no place for children. Where were their parents?

The woman inside the Shame Box didn't look up. She just sat there, clutching the string of pearls around her neck, her fingers moving over the beads like a rosary; there was no prayer Olivia knew of that could make the situation any better.

She tried to see without looking, to know for sure if the woman was a friend, but the prisoner's dark hair fell forward, obscuring her face. Was there a hint of familiarity in the tilt of her head? The slim curve of her shoulders?

Seeing a stranger who had broken the law was bad enough, but a friend? Relationships changed for ever when

1

you saw someone in the Box, and Olivia had already lost too much; she couldn't lose any more.

Her footsteps faltered. Alice reached out to rest her candy-pink manicured hand over the top of Olivia's washing-up chapped skin.

'I don't recognise her,' Alice whispered, propelling Olivia forward. 'Keep walking.' She nodded towards the two men in dark suits standing by the sliding doors. Customer Service Agents. They stood ramrod straight, dominating and oppressive, and motionless except for their eyes. They scanned the shoppers, their gaze never settling for long. If you were lucky.

Steps heavy with a familiar lethargy, Olivia felt the prickling sensation of being watched, but Alice wouldn't let her slow. They passed through the intrusive body scanners and entered the fluorescent glare of the supermarket. First trial over.

Alice stopped to get a basket, so Olivia pulled her trolley to an abrupt halt. There was relief in the stillness, a moment to catch her breath before facing the next onslaught. Under the scrutiny of the patrolling Customer Service Agents, the surveillance cameras and – worse – the other shoppers, she took out her shopping list, going through the motions of innocence, anything to extend her brief respite.

Unfold the paper, read it, reread it. Make sure everything was there. She needed all the usuals: fruit, vegetables, a box of bran flakes, some brown rice, a tin of No Sugar, No Salt Baked Beans. Nothing exciting, not any more. Shopping for food wasn't what it used to be; nothing was.

'Ready?' Alice asked, with a hint of concern in her voice, and Olivia arranged her face into a smooth, practised smile. Anyone would think that the weekly shop was a pleasure and not something to be endured.

'I'm good, thank you.' For a second her smile became real, her gratitude for Alice's moral support flooded through her. Doing this together made the whole thing easier; well, slightly. 'Let's get this over with.' She nodded her readiness to Alice and together, they slipped into the carefully designed flow of the store and followed the other shoppers towards the fresh fruit and vegetables.

The produce was arranged in a rainbow of neat rows, the grown-up alternative to a sweet shop. Serene, smiling shoppers reached through the mist of dry ice to retrieve bunches of spinach, heads of broccoli and shiny, bright peppers. They held each non-rationed item aloft, just for a second, to ensure the overhead cameras captured a clear image. From the first item Olivia picked up, to the last, her compliance was tested. She had to sell her performance, but it was hard to get excited about buying a bag of potatoes; she settled for pleasantly neutral instead.

Alice stopped at the exotic fruit and reached up with ease to take a mango from the top shelf. Olivia stretched up on tiptoe, hopping to keep her balance. Why did they have to put them so high? Always at the back of the shelf. As her fingertips brushed against a smooth curving fruit, a draught on her back made her jump. She stopped to pull her top down, hiding the expanse of stretch-marked skin. Hopefully, nobody had noticed. Her stretch marks were old – two primary-school-aged children old – but she couldn't risk someone thinking her weight was fluctuating, not on Mother Mason's strict diet. There were absolutely no excuses.

'Here, let me.' Five nine and gorgeous, Alice easily reached the top shelf, another benefit of their joint shopping trips. Alice's willowy height balanced out nature's lack of generosity in Olivia's stature.

In the centre of the fresh produce section, a shop assistant was mid-demonstration, her face lit up with enthusiasm as she chattered to the shoppers congregated around her, all complying with the unspoken policy of unwavering adherence and devoted interest.

'This simple Little Gem lettuce can be transformed in just a few short steps.' The assistant held up a dark-green head of lettuce. 'It's delicious fast food, guaranteed to make you feel fantastic.' She sliced it, knife flashing under the bright overhead lights and the oppressive gaze of the small, black, domed camera mounted on the ceiling directly above them. The audience watched in silence, intense concentration stretched mask-like across their faces. One woman had her phone out, making notes on everything the assistant said. Olivia reached for her own handbag; it wouldn't hurt to be seen doing the same.

'It's so versatile, you can combine it with any of the fresh vegetables available in store.' The assistant was far more excited than any normal person should ever be about vegetables, but then the shoppers weren't the only ones under scrutiny. 'How beautiful are these tomatoes?' She held up two large, round tomatoes and received a collective 'Ooo' from the crowd.

Alice snorted and Olivia turned her head just a fraction to glare at her. Some things came easily to Alice, but biting her tongue was not one of them. They only needed to make it through a couple of minutes at the demonstration table, surely Alice could keep quiet that long.

Thankfully, nobody else seemed to have noticed her lapse in protocol; their expressions remained pleasantly blank, their polite English reserve had become their strongest survival skill.

'This is Mother Mason's favourite salad and we have the

ingredients on special offer today. All you need to do is slice ...'

Please, it was a salad, they hardly needed instruction on how to prepare it; Alice could manage a decent one when she was forced to venture into the kitchen. Even so, Olivia started typing out the 'recipe'.

'What are you doing?' Alice asked, her voice low but not low enough. 'You could turn those ingredients into a seven-course meal in under an hour; you do not need to take notes.'

'Shh,' Olivia hissed out of the corner of her mouth, glancing round at the nearby shoppers. The man closest to them didn't show any signs that he was listening but that didn't mean anything, he could be an undercover agent, or worse, a local busybody proving his loyalty to Mother Mason. There were far too many of those around and you could never quite tell who they were, or what you might do to get reported.

She glanced back up at the camera above them, the little red light watching and recording everything. She'd avoided the Shame Box and the Re-education Programme so far; there was no way Alice was going to ruin her perfect record today.

'Sorry,' Alice whispered.

'It's okay, I'll fix it.' She squeezed Alice's arm quickly and walked up to the demonstration, making eye contact with the shop assistant, who beamed as Olivia took two recipe cards from the display.

'It's truly delicious,' the woman said brightly, but there was a taught brittleness beneath her smile. 'Try sprinkling on some toasted sunflower seeds. You'll never taste better!'

'Will do. Thank you!' Olivia echoed the woman's high, energised tone.

She returned to Alice and handed her a card. They studied them for a moment, waiting the appropriate length of time for the cameras to capture their image and attendance, then walked on, their tension easing with each step. The jolly voice of the demonstrator followed them as they moved deeper into the store, away from the fresh produce and towards the unrationed store cupboard goods. Apparently, it didn't matter how much rice, pasta or tins of beans they bought, they could browse those sections in relative peace. Everything here was healthy; okay, technically if you ate them in vast quantities, you could tip over the daily calorie allowance, but nobody was stupid enough to do that now.

The restricted items section was a different story and Olivia's temptation to skip the dried fruit, nuts and seeds was almost unbearable. These aisles drew the most Customer Service Agents and double the number of cameras, but she couldn't get through the week without her packet of apricots. They were the closest thing she had to dessert now, and on days when the kids drove her mad, the rush of sweetness was her only escape.

'Can you pass me some cranberries?' Alice loaded her basket up with bags of dried apricots, raisins, pineapple and almonds, unconcerned about raising any red flags through buying in bulk.

'Are you sure?' Olivia asked.

When she didn't move, Alice leaned past her and retrieved her own. 'You worry too much.'

And you don't worry enough, Olivia thought, but that old argument could remain unspoken today. Just because she preferred to avoid the attention didn't mean Alice had to. It would be easier though.

The comforting smell of warm bread enveloped them as they entered the bakery section. Olivia's stomach rumbled and she pressed a hand to it, muffling the sound. Nobody should feel hungry on Mother Mason's carefully developed diet.

'Do you need one?' Alice stopped to get a loaf.

'No, I'm okay, I made some this morning.'

It was the only baking she was still allowed to do and it was relatively safe, so long as she followed Mother Mason's recipe. The colourfully packaged loaves stretched the entire length of the bakery aisle and Alice picked up one, seemingly at random. Not like the middle-aged woman who stood blocking the aisle, squinting at the label on a sliced granary. Reading glasses perched on the end of her nose, she scrutinised the list of ingredients. She was trying too hard, clearly wanting to prove to the cameras that she was committed to Mother Mason's Eat Healthy Directive. Everybody knew there was nothing sold in the shops that the prime minister didn't personally approve of. The woman was just trying to get extra brownie points.

Brownie points. Brownies. Rich, dark, chocolatey. It had been so long since Olivia had been allowed to bake some, to taste some. She swallowed the sudden rush of saliva. Right now, she'd even settle for one of the thick, stodgy ones they used to sell in plastic wrappers. What she wouldn't do for a brownie, a slice of cake, even a small square of chocolate.

She wouldn't break the law. Obviously. But still.

'Liv?' Alice nudged her.

'Sorry, what?'

Alice rolled her eyes. 'I said of course you made some this morning.'

'Made what? I didn't make anything, I wouldn't do that.' Panic made her voice shrill.

The other woman watched them, not even pretending to look at the bread label any more.

7

'What are you talking about? You just said you made some.' Alice was staring at her oddly too.

'I did?' If her voice grew much higher it would be beyond human hearing. Please say she hadn't spoken aloud, hadn't voiced her desires. Not here of all places.

'Yes, you said you didn't need any bread,' Alice spoke slowly, enunciating every word, 'because you made a loaf this morning.'

'Oh yes! Of course. Yes, I made some bread this morning. Good old, plain brown bread.' She raised her voice for the woman's benefit, smiling at her until the nosy stranger looked away.

'Are you feeling all right?' Alice asked.

'Me? Yes, fine, why wouldn't I be?' she bluffed, shoving her trolley into motion before Alice could interrogate her further. She strode past the woman, reached the end of the aisle and swung her trolley around the corner. A jarring shock tore through her body and a loud clash of metal screeched through the store.

'I'm so sorry,' she said to the man she had collided with, barely looking at him as she desperately tried to pull her trolley away.

'It's all my fault.' He checked over his shoulder and she followed his gaze, searching for any signs of Customer Services. They tried again to drag their trolleys apart, wrenching the screaming metal.

'I wasn't paying attention.' She tugged at the handle, but it was impossible to act sensibly when her focus was on the imminent arrival of Customer Services. How could she have been so careless? So stupid? All attention was bad attention and now everyone in the store was watching her.

'Here, let me.' Alice joined Olivia and together they fought to separate the two trolleys. Nobody else came to help. The nearby shoppers backed away from the commotion, taking alternative routes, unwilling to get involved in somebody else's drama.

The man gave a sharp kick to the interlocked wheels and with a final pull, the trolleys lurched apart. Without another word, they scuttled off in different directions.

'I didn't realise we were at the dodgems.' Alice caught up with her halfway down the cereal aisle. 'If I'd know, I'd have got a trolley too.'

'That's not funny.' She couldn't stop scanning the store, straining to hear the sound of approaching footsteps above the supposedly pleasant piped music.

Alice caught hold of her, anchoring her and the trolley, stopping her frantic rush. 'Liv, we've still got to get our rations, you need to pull it together,' she spoke in a whisper, then raised her voice. 'You know there are so many types of porridge, I just can't choose.' She reached past her, as if searching for something on the shelf. For a moment her body acted as a shield from the cameras. It was just long enough for Olivia to release her tight grip on the trolley.

Nobody from Customer Services had come for her. She'd done nothing wrong. She was safe.

'They all taste so delicious,' Alice continued.

It was okay, everything was okay. She could do this.

'Mother Mason gave this brand five stars.' Alice held the bag up towards the camera. 'It's got her seal of approval on it, so it must be good. Do you want one?'

Olivia arranged her face into her practised smile and stepped away. 'I'd love one, thanks, Alice.'

'You're welcome.' Alice linked arms with her. 'Come on, time to face "Ration Row".'

The Nutrition Distribution Centre, or 'Ration Row', lined the far wall of the supermarket. Silver machines hummed and whirred as they distributed the weekly rations of butter, milk and salt. Four unsmiling Customer Service Agents stood on guard, overseeing the process.

'Have you got your ID card?' Olivia asked Alice.

'I hope so.'

She hoped so too. They started the joint shopping trips after the rationing began, a way to take some of the fear out of what had once been a mundane activity. At first it helped, then it became routine, but now Alice was slipping, getting more blasé, at the very time when Mother Mason was cracking down on any dissent.

They locked their shopping in the security booths, hurried past the black refrigerated doors marked 'Authorised Personnel Only' and joined the long queue of silent shoppers. The only sounds were the low rumbling of the ten ration dispensers and the high-pitched squeak of shoes on the shiny linoleum floor.

The chill of the refrigeration units hit Olivia's exposed skin. She shivered, then gritted her teeth against it. Shivering looked far too much like shaking and she couldn't risk looking like she had something to hide.

A green light came on above Dispenser Six. A stooped old man left his place at the head of the line and shuffled forward with the aid of a walking stick. It was hard to watch his slow progress. He needed help but legally only one person at a time could approach the machines. It was a stupid rule, one of many, but not one she could do anything about. She forced herself to focus on retrieving her own identity card. It was always in the front pocket of her purse, she never failed to check before she left home, but it didn't stop the niggling doubt, the moment of panic, the increase in her heart rate as she opened her purse.

The sight of her horrific ID photo couldn't temper her

elation and relief when she saw it, exactly where it was supposed to be. Unlike Alice's. As per usual, her old friend dug through the contents of her designer handbag, muttering under her breath. 'I'm sure it's here. It must be.'

Ignore her, Olivia thought. They went through this every time; she'd find it in the end.

The old man collected his rations and a woman with bright pink braids took his place. Without flinching, she stepped onto the weighing plate in front of the machine.

Damn it. Olivia had meant to weigh herself this morning but there hadn't been time. It was always chaos trying to get everyone ready to leave, helping Danny find his car keys, encouraging Mia to eat her breakfast and Matthew to brush his teeth; if he got a cavity they would all be in trouble.

She'd barely had time to grab a bowl of bran flakes before rushing out the door. They now sat inside her stomach, an unwanted extra weight. What else had she eaten over the past few days? Everything she cooked was from one of Mother Mason's approved recipes, with regulated portion sizes and using the official measuring cups. Okay, she made a few additions to adapt the recipes to her family's tastes, but she never used anything forbidden.

There was absolutely no reason to think she was over the permitted weight limit, but she wished she could be sure. Her HealthHub on her wrist informed her that the trip round the supermarket had added four hundred more steps to her morning total, but was it enough?

There was a shift in the atmosphere of the queue. People around her tensed, becoming more statue-like, and Alice ceased her frantic searching. Something was wrong at Dispenser Three. A young man had drawn the scrutiny of the nearest Customer Service Agent. His movements were jerky as he tried to insert his ID into the card slot. The agent looked up to the overhead camera. He lifted his electronic notepad, slid a finger across the screen and looked back at the camera.

The customer's frantic motions stopped as the card disappeared into the machine and his posture relaxed. The shoppers exhaled a collectively held breath. There was a beep and a whir and his details flashed up on the dispenser's central display screen.

Olivia averted her eyes, following the unspoken etiquette, it was the only privacy they were able to grant each other. In trying to be discreet, she looked straight into the emotionless gaze of the agent. With well-worn practice she glanced away, registering only dark hair and small, deep-set eyes.

On the wall above him were brightly coloured posters of the Vitasan family, all smiling down on her. 'Healthy and Happy!' declared Mary Vitasan. The picture captured the stunningly beautiful woman playing in the park with her partner and children; the perfect family all grinned at the camera. None of Olivia's family photos ever looked that good; it was a miracle if they all looked in the same direction and she didn't have her eyes closed. Danny had to take a million pictures to get just one decent shot.

In the next poster Mary served dinner; with her glossy hair and perfect teeth, she was beautiful and serene as she dished out a bowl of peas. 'A good home and health are your best wealth.' There was none of the carnage Olivia expected at meal times. No arguments of wanting more of this, or none of that, or refusing to eat all together. What was the Vitasans' secret? It wasn't like they were a perfect TV family, just actors playing roles, following scripts. They were real people, chosen by Mother Mason to represent the ideal family, encouraging the nation to aspire to a better way of living. They always looked so happy, especially Mary; it had been a long time since Olivia had felt like that.

Alice had gone back to rustling through her bag and the clutter that accompanied her everywhere.

'Hurry up,' Olivia whispered, not daring to look to see if the agent was watching. She concentrated on the poster of five-year-old Isabelle Vitasan, looking wide-eyed and innocent. 'Be smart. Eat smart!' proclaimed Isabelle, her mouth open, ready to take a bite of a shiny red apple. Mia would want it peeled, cored and sliced before she'd even consider eating it.

Olivia tapped her ID card against her palm as she stared at the next poster, the largest. A friendly looking middle-aged lady, in a twin set and pearls, smiled down on the shoppers. Mother Mason had a warm, knowing look, her eyes motherly and benign behind her wire-rimmed spectacles.

'Eat the best, leave the rest! Remember: Mother knows best.'

Below her was a little red sign. 'Have you got your identity card? Shoppers without their cards will be refused rations and may face £1000 fine or disciplinary action. Please speak to Customer Services for assistance.'

'It's here, I know it is.' Alice gave her bag a good shake.

'Let me.' Olivia took it from her and sorted through the contents, collecting together the scraps of paper, the old receipts and empty food wrappers.

The woman in the queue behind them bent down and picked something up.

'Here,' she passed it to Alice who slipped it into her pocket without looking at it.

'Thank you.'

Someone further back in the ration line cleared their

throat. A space had opened up ahead and Alice nudged Olivia forward.

Olivia thrust the handful of rubbish at her friend and moved one space up, closer to the agent on the right. She slowed her motions but didn't stop. 'Is he watching?' she asked, feeling the cold metal of keys, a chewed biro and a soft leather purse.

'I don't think so, but hurry.'

She searched faster, her fingers raking the inside of the bag, scraping against a zip, catching crumbs beneath her nails, until she touched something wet and slimy and snatched her hand out.

'What is it?' Alice tugged on her favourite necklace, unravelling a little more of the pink tassel that hung from the gold flower.

Gritting her teeth, Olivia put her hand in again, extracted the remains of an apple core and held it out between finger and thumb.

'Oops.' Alice took the core and stuffed it into her pocket.

The woman behind them kept a few steps back, her head turned away, but there was a small pulsing vein in her neck that showed above the dark blue of her suit.

'Alice, it isn't here. You'll have to come back later.' Olivia passed the bag back, but a hard corner scratched her wrist. 'Wait a minute.' She grasped the smooth, plastic card sticking out of an inner pocket and withdrew it.

'Thank you.' Alice pressed the ID card to her heart. 'It won't happen again, I promise.'

Except it would, it always did. It had become as much a part of their shopping routine as the rations and constant scrutiny.

They had made it to the front of the queue; a balding man collected his packet of salt and walked away, relief clear on his face. The green light came on over his newly vacated dispenser; it was her turn.

'Think light thoughts,' Alice whispered.

Olivia drew herself up and stepped forward. Shoulders back, look straight ahead, don't slow, don't hesitate. She tried to ignore the Customer Service Agent but could feel his attention on her, a creeping, tingling sensation that spread across her skin. She bit her lip then forced her jaw to relax, forming her mouth into an almost smile.

The light glinted off the weighing plate as she approached. She should have skipped breakfast, gone to a drop-in Be Fit class en route to the supermarket. It was too late now. The scales were getting closer. Five steps, four, three. She drew in a deep breath, let it out in a rush of air and stepped in front of the dispenser.

It was part weighing machine, part vending machine, part parking ticket validator and it didn't matter how many times she collected her rations, it was always terrifying. She closed her eyes for a second and breathed a silent prayer: Let it be okay, let my weight be fine, don't let me get in trouble today.

The screen lit up and the words Insert Card appeared. A flashing green arrow pointed to a white illuminated card slot. Fingers shaking, she inserted her identity card into the machine. It sucked it out of her hand, disappearing without a trace. There was a beep and her name, photograph and ID code flashed up on the screen, with details of everything from her birth date to her body mass, followed a moment later by photos and files on Danny, Matthew and Mia. The machine processed their information, checking it against the Department of Nutrition and Health's national database, correlating their HealthHub data with their latest weigh-ins and health checks. It wasn't until she heard the first internal whirring noise of the dispenser in action that she allowed herself to relax slightly.

Four small, individually wrapped cubes of butter dropped into the bottom window and a light flashed to show the ration was ready. She reached into the opening, pushed past the clear flap, and retrieved them. There was a gushing sound of pouring liquid and a plastic milk bottle hurtled down the chute, to land with a thud in the metal rack. Two down, one to go.

As she closed her hand around the small packet of salt, a high-pitched siren shrieked. A red light flashed, a bright pulse that filled the store. She stopped, staring straight ahead; her throat tight as she waited for the dark shadows of Customer Services, to feel the strong hands that would drag her through the doors marked 'Authorised Personnel Only'. Her vision blurred with tears. This was the moment she had been dreading for the past seven years. What had she done?

The siren stopped but the silence that followed seemed louder and more painful.

'Name?' a male voice demanded.

'Oli—'

'Becky Hubbard.' A shrill voice to her right interrupted her.

Olivia kept her head down. Out of the corner of her eye, she saw the Customer Service Agents standing either side of someone two dispensers down. They shifted position, blocking the person's escape, and revealing the woman who had been behind Alice in the queue. The red light pulsed unrelentingly and Olivia looked up to check her own machine. It was a steady, reassuring green. Not her then; not this time.

'I don't understand. What's the problem, sir?' Becky cowered away from the men.

'Ms Hubbard, we need you to come with us.' The dark-haired agent took hold of her wrist.

'There must be a mistake.' Becky tried to pull away, struggling as they began to half-lead, half-drag her towards the black doors. 'I haven't done anything wrong. Please, let me go.'

The agents ignored her, their pace never slowing as she fought against them.

'Please. Help me,' Becky begged.

But the other shoppers had their heads bowed, focusing on the machines in front of them. No one stirred.

Becky struggled against the men and in trying to wrench her arms free her bracelet broke. Little silver charms fell to the floor, bouncing and scattering across the ground. A small sparkling heart rolled to a stop by Olivia. She bent down automatically to pick it up and her gaze locked on Becky's. The other woman's eyes were wide and desperate, far too large for her pale face.

'Please.' She reached out towards Olivia.

Olivia wanted to help, to do something, but her children were waiting for her to come home, they needed her to stay safe. She looked down, the charm falling from her hand. The scratched weighing plate blurred and faded as she stared at the ground, fighting not to cry. She had no right to tears, not when she was choosing to turn away, to protect herself. But what else could she do?

Becky's cries rose higher at the opening hiss of the refrigerated doors but cut off abruptly as they closed behind her, leaving the shop in silence. There was relief in the silence, in the peace, then came the sickening guilt. Just like that, another person taken, another person Olivia hadn't helped. Couldn't help, she corrected herself. She was safe, that was what mattered, wasn't it? She could go home to her family. But what about Becky's family?

There was a long pause and then at some unspoken sign the other shoppers came to life again, reaching to retrieve packages, pots and bottles. They kept their movements small and careful, before hurrying away.

Olivia started to tremble, the icy refrigerated air penetrating deep into her core as she extracted the packet of salt. She stepped over the fallen beads, the frayed and broken cord, and moving on autopilot, walked back to her trolley. Her hands were so cold she couldn't get the key into the lock, but Alice was there, Alice was always there. She took the key and unlocked their shopping. For a moment, she leaned against Olivia, their shoulders pressed together as they stood side by side, before they headed to the checkout.

Outside, the woman was still hunched in the Shame Box. Maybe she was one of the lucky ones. Becky's fate might turn out to be far worse.

Chapter Two

Six hours later and Olivia noticed that her hands were still trembling as she took the bottle of milk out of the fridge. Becky's face was a pale blur of a memory; the only part in sharp focus was her large, frightened eyes, desperate and then devastated when Olivia turned away. There was nothing she could do, Olivia reminded herself, nobody would have listened to her. She had absolutely no reason to feel guilty.

Except she did. It gnawed at her, turning her stomach so that every waft of smell from the bubbling casserole made her feel more and more nauseous. It wasn't her fault that Becky had been arrested. She must have done something wrong, something really wrong if she was taken away on the spot and not sent a letter demanding her attendance at a Shame Box or Re-education class. There was no way to help a woman like that, she was beyond anyone's help.

The chill air of the open refrigerator brought goosebumps up again and Olivia shivered. She couldn't risk getting in trouble too, she had a family to protect, a life she couldn't put at risk.

'Hello? Earth to Olivia.' Danny's voice pulled her back.

'Sorry?' She blinked, trying to focus on her husband.

'The troops are thirsty.' He nodded to Matthew and Mia sitting at the kitchen table, arguing over who had the most

19

peas. He took the milk from her and poured two glasses. 'Everything okay?'

'Fine,' she said, without thinking, without feeling. 'How was work?'

'Oh, you know, same old, same old. We've got a new set of scales in the staffroom, apparently the last one wasn't calibrated to the government standard.'

'That wasn't your responsibility, was it? You're not going to get into trouble are you?' She caught his arm, almost making him drop the glasses of milk.

'Relax, it was nothing to do with me, but I wouldn't want to be Dennis right now.'

'Did they arrest him too?'

'Too? Who else—'

'Mummy, Matthew's being mean,' Mia said.

'Am not.' Matthew stuck his tongue out.

'Am too.'

Olivia snapped. 'Not tonight! Can't we get through one dinner without a fight?'

The children fell silent.

'Mummy's right. That's enough,' Danny said, breaking the painful silence. He gave them their drinks and they took them without a word.

She turned away from their hurt expressions to put the milk back in the fridge, but the bottle felt too heavy and she held it up to check that Danny had poured enough.

'It's okay, I used the regulation glasses.' Danny was close behind her and she jumped, guilt causing her to flush. Of course he had, he knew how important it was to make sure the children got their daily calcium requirements. It wasn't fair of her to doubt him, but it was hard to trust anyone now.

'Sorry.' She tried to slip past him but he caught her hand.

'Are you going to tell me what's wrong?'

'What could be wrong?' She didn't sound remotely convincing. The suppressed tears built up, burning behind her eyes, and her throat tightened as she watched the children, friends again for now. The words pushed their way to the surface. 'This morning—'

There was a heavy thump from the kitchen table and Mia squealed.

Oh please, no. The same high-pitched sound from the supermarket. Not again. Please no.

Danny rushed forward to wipe up the flood of milk that raced across the table from Matthew's spilt glass but Olivia stayed motionless, replaying the morning's scene. Again Becky begged for her help, again she did nothing, the sound of that scream would never stop. Unless it had, possibly for ever.

'Liv, I could use some help.' Danny's request forced her into action.

'Matthew, why weren't you more careful?' She snatched up a towel and stepped over Kit, the cat, who entrenched herself beside the puddle, lapping up the mess. Just like that, Matthew's daily ration was wasted. What if it affected his next calcium test? They'd get one of those dreaded brown envelopes through the post demanding an interview. It would be the first step towards being put on special measures. She couldn't cope with that, not on top of this, on top of everything.

'It was an accident,' Matthew said.

'He can have my ration,' Danny said. 'I can have black coffee tomorrow.'

'He can have mine too.' Mia pushed her glass towards Matthew.

'Good try, young lady, but you need to drink your own.

Remember what Captain Fit says about strong teeth and bones.' Olivia tried to force some joviality into her voice, to hide her fear and frustration.

'Calcium, calci-yum!' Mia parroted.

'Sorry Mum,' Matthew whispered as she wiped the milk up from under his chair.

'That's okay, you didn't do it on purpose.' She gave him a quick, one-armed hug, the most contact she could get away with now he was growing up. Eight years old and already too cool for cuddles from his mum.

'I don't know about you but I'm hungry.' She kissed the top of his head and returned to her seat. Danny watched her as she sat down but she ignored him and picked up her napkin, unfolding the paper cloth, spreading it across her lap and smoothing out the creases. She hadn't eaten since the bran flakes at breakfast, unable to face food of any kind.

Mother Mason's chicken casserole was on the menu tonight: all traces of skin and fat removed, the dish was bulked out with plenty of root vegetables and she had added thyme and the smallest pinch of their rationed salt. It should be delicious, but her appetite was lacking. She picked up her fork, lowered it again, then raised it once more when she realised Matthew and Mia were watching her. She had no choice but to start. It was 'a mother's duty to set a good example at all times'; so said Mother Mason.

'How was school?' Danny filled the silence and drew the children's attention away. 'How was the spelling test, Matthew?'

'A, w, f, a, l .'

'That good, huh?' Danny laughed and Mia joined in, despite the joke going completely over her head.

'What did you have for lunch?' Olivia tried to keep her voice casual.

'Key-na again,' Mia gave a dejected sigh. 'It's yucky.'

Olivia laughed. 'Quinoa's not yucky, it's just not to your taste.' She had to give the school credit, they didn't give up on trying to get the children to eat the chewy seeds; she had abandoned her attempts years ago. 'What else did you have?'

Matthew scooped a hole down the centre of his mashed potato mountain. 'Stewed apple, I didn't like it.' His face puckered at the memory, as though he was sucking on a lemon.

'Was it too sharp?' It wasn't surprising, cooking apples weren't meant to be eaten without sugar. What they really needed was some custard or ice cream. In the past she would have cooked them into a crumble or made them into a pie with a lattice top, like she used to do for the bakery. With the tiny pastry flowers and delicate leaves, they were more art than dessert.

She scrunched up her napkin, balling up the memories and forbidden thoughts. 'How's the proposal for the new trainers?' she asked Danny, after forcing another mouthful down.

'Great,' he said. 'It's almost ready to submit. I think DoNaH are going to be impressed.'

'Who's Donna?' Mia looked up from her pile of peas, sending a few bouncing and rolling across the table towards Matthew. He flicked them back at her and they both giggled.

'It's not a who, it's a what,' Danny said. 'The Department of Nutrition and Health. I'm designing shoes for the government.'

'Spy shoes? That's so cool.' Matthew filled the mashed potato hole up with peas until they overflowed like a volcano.

'Matthew, that's enough building, time for eating,' Danny said. 'Mia, eat your carrots.'

'I don't want them.' She pushed them as far as she could to the edge of her Captain Fit portion control plate.

'You have to eat your vegetables or the men in suits will come and get you.' Matthew speared a carrot and waved it at her.

Mia's eyes filled with tears and her mouth formed a trembling O. She slid off her chair and rushed to Olivia, climbing up on to her lap.

'Matthew, that's enough,' Danny said. 'You mustn't say that, especially to your little sister.'

'What? It's true.' Matthew jutted out his chin and folded his arms. 'Ben said so. His dad said the men in suits take you away and you disappear. For ever.'

Mia wailed and buried her face deeper into Olivia's shoulder, her tears soaking through the thin cotton of Olivia's blouse.

'Shh, it's okay, Mia.' She looked to Danny for help, or reassurance – for something – but his expression of horror mirrored how she felt. They had tried hard to shield their children from the world they lived in, but it wasn't enough, the threat had found them here, in the safety of their home. What more could they do to protect their 'should-be' innocent babies?

'Ben said if I was bad he'd tell his dad and the men in suits would come and get me.' Matthew's voice wobbled and Danny went to him and pulled him into a tight hug. For once, Matthew didn't resist.

'No one is going to take you away,' Danny said, although knowing the Hook-Medwoods – Ben's family – they'd happily inform on anyone, even a child. Ben's mother Jenna was the president of the local Mother's Institute and his

24

dad Lewis worked for the government; they probably had DoNaH on speed dial.

Olivia's arms tightened around Mia, and she carried her over to join Danny and Matthew.

'Mummy and I would never let anyone take you. There's nothing for you to worry about.' Danny rubbed Matthew's back. 'You're a good boy and you do what you're told. Ben was just trying to scare you. I promise you're safe.'

'You know he sometimes says things that aren't kind, or true,' Olivia said, but her voice shook. 'Don't listen to him and if he says something mean you tell your dad or me, you understand?' She stroked Matthew's tear-stained face until he nodded in agreement.

'I think that's enough dinner for tonight,' she said. 'Everyone, look at your HealthHubs, how many steps have you done? Have we got enough to watch a whole film?' They each checked the bands on their wrists, but they were still below the number needed to power the TV. It was Mother Mason's way of eliminating couch potatoes, linking electronic devices to HealthHubs and only granting access based on the amount of physical activity you achieved. If they tried to watch a film, the screen would simply cut out after an hour. Mia started to cry again.

'It's okay, I've been at my desk most of today,' Danny explained quickly. More likely, he'd used his steps wasting time on social media.

'I'll go for a walk round the garden. Who wants to come? We can use the Round and Round the Garden app. Who can be the best teddy bear?'

Matthew and Mia cheered and raced to the back door. Danny reached for Olivia's hand and they followed the children outside, the real world held back for a little longer.

*

Olivia found comfort in the familiar routine of bath, story and bed, but she wasn't sure if it was her or the children who clung on a few moments longer during the last cuddle of the night. She and Danny took it in turns to tuck them in and reconvened in their bedroom, with the door pushed to.

She sank down onto the bed and Danny lay beside her, smelling faintly of sweat and freshly cut grass. Together they stared up at the ceiling.

'What are we supposed to say to them?' he said finally, voicing her concern.

'Isn't it more what we're allowed to say to them?' She rolled onto her side so she could rest her head on his chest. The rhythmic lub-dub of his heart could almost stop her racing brain, almost push back the memories of the day – almost, but not quite.

'Something happened today.' She spoke to the buttons on his shirt, unable to look at his face. 'A woman ...'

He waited for her to go on, not rushing her, willing to let her go at her own pace.

'A woman was arrested at the supermarket. Taken away by Customer Services. She was so close I could have touched her, helped her, but I didn't do anything.' It was easier to say the words if she separated the emotion from them, keeping that pushed down inside.

'You couldn't.' He kissed the top of her head. 'They wouldn't have listened to you.'

'I know, but I was so powerless. I am so powerless in everything. I can't help her, I can't protect our children, I can't do anything.'

He buried his face into her hair. 'That's not true, you're the most capable woman I know, but those things, they're not things we can change. This is the way life is, post-election, this is Mother Mason's world now. We voted for it, remember, so we have to accept it.'

For 'we', she heard the silent 'you'. She was the one still clinging to the past, the one refusing to move on and accept life now. It was easier for him. When Mother Mason came into power, his life had stayed pretty much the same. Sure, his diet changed and he had to go to the gym once a week, but he did that anyway. That was why he was so content to go along with things. Why he couldn't understand how she felt. He hadn't had to make the same sacrifices.

'I have accepted it. Why can't you see that?' She sat up and moved towards the side of the bed but he caught her waist and she stayed where she was, perched on the edge of the mattress. 'I've accepted the rations and the rules; I gave up everything: my bakery, my passion, my life. I know that things are different!'

'I'm sorry, I don't want to fight.' His fingers gently kneaded her sides, pushing against and releasing the tension that constantly kept every cell of her body rigid. 'I wasn't aiming that at you.'

She rubbed her hands across her face but with her eyes closed she could see the supermarket all over again.

'Have you thought about looking for something to do? A new project to distract you? With Mia at school you'll have more time.'

'You want me to get a job?'

'No, not a job, something to focus on, you're always at your best when you're working on a project.'

She stood up to retrieve his abandoned jumper from the floor. 'You don't think I'm at my best at the moment?' Bending down, her too long hair fell over her face and she felt small in her baggy jumper; it used to hug her curves

27

but now it hung around her, tent-like, exaggerating her too-angular shape.

Danny let out an exasperated breath. 'I'm not saying that either. I just think you might be happier.'

'Happier? So you think I'm not happy?' As if happiness was a choice and she just wasn't trying hard enough. Another thing she was failing at.

'You're not listening to me,' he dragged his fingers through his hair. 'I don't want to fight about this. I thought . . . never mind, I shouldn't have brought it up.' He picked up his electronic tablet, dismissing her as he returned to his constant scrolling through social media.

Online he wasn't "poor Danny", the long-suffering husband of the shunned baker. For a man who always went with the majority, hated causing a fuss, being married to her had been problematic. No wonder he spent hours on the internet: he could find anonymity and friends who knew nothing of their past. She hated to think what he was saying and to whom.

'What exactly do you think I can do?' she raised her voice to recapture his attention, to not lose him to random strangers, his 'other family'.

'I don't care. I mean,' he corrected himself at her audible breath of pain, 'I only want you to find something you love.'

'I'm not allowed to do the thing I love.'

'There are other things, baking isn't the only thing in the world.' He set his tablet aside but the screen remained illuminated, just a flicker of a notification away from stealing his attention back.

'It's the only thing *I* can do, I'm rubbish at everything else. Making cakes is all I've been good at and now it's illegal.'

'You can still cook.'

'It's not the same.' Her voice rose still further with frustration. Seven years later and he still didn't understand that. Cooking was a necessity, it could be interesting, but it was a daily requirement, like brushing your teeth. Baking was different. Cakes were purely for joy, for celebration. Her bakery's creations had been at the centre of thousands of special occasions, and it was like being part of each and every one. Making dinner, no matter how fancy, just didn't come close.

'Don't get upset,' he said, like her emotions were a genie she could stuff back in a bottle. 'All I'm saying is you're incredibly talented.'

'At making cakes,' she whispered the words.

'No! You needed more skills to run Sweet Temptations than just baking. You have so many talents, so many things you're good at. Why can't you see that?'

'You're biased. You don't really see me, you just see who you want me to be. Who society wants me to be, but I'm no Mary Vitasan.'

Pain sank deep into Danny's features, a pain she had inflicted on him so many times since the government closed her business, since the world ostracised her for making the delicious baked goods they used to praise her for. People always got excited when she walked into a room carrying a cake. Strangers became friends when there was a sweet treat to share, but after the ban they all turned against her.

'I wish you could see yourself the way everyone else sees you.'

'I do, that's the problem.' She was a pariah: her friends, her family, *her parents*, they all shunned her after the sugar ban came into place. They refused to acknowledge her presence, ignored her online and worse, in person. She had

29

never felt so alone, stuck at home with a small baby and nobody to talk to except Alice. Danny just wanted her to acquiesce to the new government's demands and do it with a smile. Anything to end the negative attention.

Her friends and family might have stopped speaking to her, but random strangers on the internet wanted to make sure she knew exactly what they thought. They seemed to think that by spewing their hatred, they could prove their allegiance to Mother Mason. The truth was, they were all terrified of guilt by association. Especially once the arrests started, once the trials went live and the defendants disappeared as soon as they were found guilty – because they were all found guilty, always. And maybe they were right, maybe she had been part of the problem, part of the reason that fat had been rationed, sugar had been banned. But then, was it her fault that people couldn't regulate the amount of food they ate?

'People weren't unhealthy just because of your cakes. That was on them, it was their responsibility,' Danny said, knowing what she was thinking after twelve years together.

She shrugged, too tired to carry on the argument. The bed suddenly looked so inviting, she just wanted to curl up and go to sleep, to sleep for as long as it took to feel better.

'You are so much more than this one thing you're good at, you have so much more to offer the world than baking cakes,' Danny said, his voice weary.

'That's sweet, but it's not true.' She gathered up the rest of his abandoned washing. 'I need to go and get the kids' stuff ready for the morning.'

She didn't rush to clean the kitchen or iron the uniforms for the next day, instead she rearranged the fridge, emptied the expired jars into the bin, and washed up the cans and bottles ready for recycling; she finished by wiping the worktops down, taking extra time to scrub at the stubborn stains she normally abandoned. Finally, with her back aching and her brain ready for sleep, she opened the top cupboard and reached in for the half-empty cornflour tin, or more specifically, the small brown bottle hidden inside. She cradled the precious vanilla extract, and with a glance at the kitchen door, she unscrewed the top and inhaled the sweet scent. Sponge cakes, fudge, custard: the memories returned with a flood of saliva that set her taste buds craving sugar, but the smell uncoiled the tension within her and she returned to the bedroom feeling lighter. Hopefully, Danny would be asleep and they could skip round two, or three, or four ... thousand.

As she climbed the stairs, a familiar scream for help left her paralysed.

'Becky Hubbard was shopping for groceries,' a distorted voice came from Olivia's room. She raced up the final stairs and found Danny lying in bed, his tablet propped up in front of him, another of the illegal viral videos playing in high-definition.

'Becky committed no crime. She broke no rules.'

Olivia swayed as dizziness swamped her. The scenes from the day no longer played out inside her head, instead they were right there for Danny to see.

'So why did Mother Mason arrest her? Where is Becky now?'

'Liv, are you all right? Liv?' Danny threw the tablet to one side and reached her before her legs gave way. They sank down onto the floor together and he held her tight, tight enough that she stopped feeling as though she might break apart and spin out into nothingness.

'Cut the Apron Strings!' chanted the voice. 'Join the fray. Bring down Mother Mason.' The slogans were infamous, the calling cards of the underground rebellion, the faceless, nameless protesters opposing their leader's suffocating control.

'Talk to me.' Danny's voice was calm as he stroked her back.

'I didn't help her, I didn't do anything; I just let them take her.' She rocked back and forth and he rocked with her, holding her together.

'There was nothing you could do. Nothing anybody could do.'

'That's not good enough, it can't be.' Her tears finally broke free. 'Somebody's doing something, I bet the video's all over social media.'

'For now, but they'll take it down. Mother Mason will make sure that every trace is deleted by the morning.'

'Does that matter? Isn't it better to try to fight back?'

'Not if it gets you in trouble, not if it doesn't make any difference.'

When they climbed into bed, Danny moved his tablet, trying to shield it from her, but she caught a glimpse of the final screen frozen on Becky's terrified face. 'Where's Becky?' asked the end titles. '#CutTheApronStrings #CTAS #JoinTheFray #DownWithMotherMason'

Chapter Three

The Fighting Fit Gym was the last place Olivia wanted to be the morning after Becky's arrest, but now more than ever, she had to follow routine and attend her enforced exercise class. It was the first of many items on her day's to-do list, compounding her exhaustion from her sleepless night.

The gym was busy despite it being mid-morning, the legal requirement of twice-weekly fitness sessions came with the benefit of Exercise Hours, allowing workers to take time off to attend. Everyone trooped in wearing their standard-issue red and blue tracksuits; some looked energised and pleased to be there but most walked with slow, plodding steps, and that was before they had been to class. The men tended to gravitate towards the Power Pro workout, which combined strength, cardio, and boxing components, while the women were encouraged to attend the Be Fit step aerobics classes. Either way, they were in for a punishing hour of intense exercise, all endorsed by Mother Mason.

Olivia checked the foyer clock. The second hand seemed to be speeding round the dial, getting closer and closer to ten o'clock. It wasn't unusual for Alice to be late, but she couldn't afford another absence, not if she wanted to avoid the Shame Box. It wasn't like this was a drop-in class; Alice's attendance was mandatory.

Olivia took out her phone, just as Alice strolled down the corridor opposite, already dressed in her tracksuit.

'When did you get here?' Olivia asked.

'A while ago. Are you ready for class?' Alice looked mildly flushed, her cheeks had a rosy glow.

'You've already worked out? Without me?'

A woman came out of a door at the far end of the hall Alice had emerged from; the scent of lilies and something darker, more earthy, lifted from the woman's perfume as she passed.

'It was just Barre Class. I would have invited you, but it's not your kind of thing. Come on, there's only a couple of minutes until our session starts.'

Maybe it's not my kind of thing, Olivia thought, but it would have been nice to be invited. Thanks to Alice's prior engagement, they only had two minutes left before entry to the class closed. They both risked getting a black mark and that meant being a step closer to the Shame Box.

As soon as Olivia reached the entry machine, she inserted her ID card and the light over the door switched from red to green. She didn't wait to see if Alice had her card ready.

Unsurprisingly, they were the last to arrive, so they sidled in with their heads down, trying not to draw attention to themselves. Carrie, their instructor, watched their progress from her position at the front of the class.

'Just made it, ladies,' she shouted, despite the microphone on her little black headset.

'Sorry, Carrie.'

They usually chose the middle row, where they could hide from the mirrors on all four walls, but they were too late to bag the best spots. Instead they had to settle for a place at the back, right in front of the vast mirror.

Although it happened at the start of every session, it was still jarring to hear Mother Mason's loud voice over the speakers. 'Welcome to your Mother Mason's Be Fit, Be

Active class. Are you ready to be fit, be active, and get happy and healthy?'

Three rows of people in matching red and blue tracksuits all pumped their fists in the air and said, 'Yes!'

'I didn't hear you. I said,' her voice was louder and cheerier now, 'are you ready to be fit, be active, get happy and healthy?'

'*Yes!*' they shouted.

'All right then, let's go.'

The music started and Carrie's strident voice carried over the top of the booming beats. 'Come on everybody, it's time to be fit, be active, get happy and healthy. Let's do this. You know the drill, start marching on the spot.'

They began the routine, their smiling faces bobbing up and down in the mirrors, expressions that would stay fixed no matter how tough the routine became. Olivia did her best to match the forced joy and enthusiasm. She had heard there were people behind the mirrors, that sometimes you could hear them laughing. You never knew who was on the other side of the glass, taking notes, keeping records. What else could you do? Just play your part and smile through the pain.

She did her best to keep in time, her limbs stiff and heavy as she tried to move with the rest of the class, hoping nobody noticed her mistakes, her stumbles and slips.

'And change, facing the back. No Bob, the other way,' Carrie shouted at one of the few men who chose the exercise class over a gym session.

Now Olivia's row was at the front of the class, all eyes on them. She sucked in her stomach and tensed, concentrating harder on the routine.

Must get this right, two, three, four. Don't slow down,

two, three, four. Everybody's watching, two, three, four. Think of the extra steps, two, three, four.

'Olivia – pick those feet up.'

She stumbled at the sound of her name but managed to keep upright. She tried hard not to glare at Carrie's distant reflection, to reveal how much she hated this.

As her temperature rose, sweat soaked into her T-shirt, dark patches that showed every time she caught sight of her reflection. Beside her, Alice looked gorgeous, slightly flushed, but that was all. How did she do it? Especially after barre class.

'People, this is not a warm-up.' Carrie stepped up onto her block and down again. 'One, two, three, four. To the side, two, three, four. And back.' She made it look effortless as she bounced up and down on her step box, her arms and legs moving in perfect coordination, her energy-enthused voice only getting higher and more cheerful the further into the routine they got.

At least Olivia wasn't the only one to struggle; Bob was always three steps behind, but it was a battle not to get distracted by him, to ignore his reflected actions in the mirror and focus on Carrie instead. If Olivia did get into a muddle, a quick look at Alice always set her right. Alice's long-limbed body seemed made for exercise, even if she did complain whenever they paused for breath. Fortunately, the music was so loud that only those closest to her could hear.

'She's trying to kill us,' Alice muttered during the brief respite.

'Can't. Talk.' Olivia bent over, her hands braced against her knees, desperately trying to draw in a couple of wheezing gasps of air.

'The sessions never get any easier, do they?'

'Harder. Much, much harder.' As soon as Olivia mastered one routine, they introduced a new one. She could never settle in and relax. Maybe that was the point.

'Not that Lena seems to mind.' Alice unscrewed her bottle of water and passed it to Olivia.

At the front of the class, in the spot nearest Carrie, stood – or rather, marched – a woman who was at every class they attended, no matter when they went to the gym. Lena was also a member of their Mother's Institute and all her conversations centred around fitness. Health was her sole focus and during the Be Fit sessions she never paused, never rested, not even during their allowed breaks. It was hard not to feel like a failure in comparison.

'She puts the rest of us to shame.' Olivia swallowed a mouthful of water and handed the bottle back to Alice.

'Yeah, but she'll have to be careful. There's a fine line between proving her dedication and pushing her body too far. They'll intervene if she's overexercising.'

'Ladies, this is not a coffee morning,' Carrie shouted. 'If you've got enough breath to talk, then I'm clearly not working you hard enough. Class, it's time to pick up the pace. You can thank Alice and Olivia for your extra exertion today.'

The eyes of the reflected class looked towards them. Their smiles remained, but there was anger behind their passive expressions, resentment that would not be forgiven. Then the workout intensified and it was all they could do to keep up.

Chapter Four

All the women in Bunham were expected to attend the monthly Mother's Institute meeting. Rain or shine, for better or worse, sickness or health, they obediently packed into the small village hall, ready for an evening of education and improvement.

Olivia dressed in her smartest ankle-length skirt and blouse and checked her appearance ten times before leaving, ensuring she picked off every cat hair and piece of fluff. Look good on the outside, feel good on the inside, that's what Mother Mason said. The Mother's Institute lived, and died, by her words.

She walked to the meeting, counting every step on her HealthHub, and checked her stats when she arrived. Alice was unusually early again; she stood by the Shame Box outside the hall, talking to a couple of women Olivia only knew by sight. They were watching something on Alice's phone, silent and engrossed. It didn't take three guesses to figure out what it must be. The video of the supermarket arrest had gone viral, anonymously popping up on social-media streams, websites and blogs. It didn't matter how fast the government cracked down on it; like everything that Cut The Apron Strings had posted before, the video was out in the world and unstoppable now.

Watching it in public, though, was beyond dangerous. 'Alice,' Olivia called, causing the group to scatter. Their dispersal revealed a young woman sitting on the floor of the three-metre-cubed box. She met Olivia's gaze but Olivia was the first to look away. It wouldn't help anyone if she was seen sympathising with a rule-breaker.

Thankfully, they didn't know each other, had only ever exchanged a few nods or a polite smile at meetings, but the woman always seemed to act appropriately. Not that it took much to earn a stay in the Box. From going over the permitted weight limit, to breaking the Decency Laws or even forgetting the night-time noise curfew, the list of potential "crimes" that could get you into trouble was extensive and seemed to grow by the week. Sometimes a local court summons was the first you knew of an infraction and by then it was too late. You could be sentenced to anything from a few hours up to a whole day depending on the severity of your crime. Just the thought of how easy it was to break the rules made anxiety fizz through Olivia's body.

'Liv!' Alice stuffed her phone into her pocket and came over looking flushed, her eyes bright. 'You're here.' She sounded breathless.

'I am, as are half the village.' Keeping Alice out of trouble was becoming a full-time job. 'We should go inside.'

The small, musty-smelling village hall was already full. Everyone looked familiar even if Olivia didn't know their names: there were mums from school, women from the gym, elderly ladies she had seen gossiping outside the post office. They greeted each other in loud, cheerful voices, and Olivia did the same, ensuring everybody saw her in attendance. She waved at Mia's teacher, smiled at their family GP and said a brief hello to two women she ought to know, but couldn't quite place.

Their chatter was light and bubbly, belying their awareness of the Shame Box, visible through the open front door.

The woman inside slouched against the wall, picking at her fingernails as the last of the night's attendees arrived.

'You know her?' Olivia asked Alice as they joined the back of the sign-in line.

'No, not really; she's from one of the new builds. I'm sure Madame President will tell us all about her terrible crimes. Knowing Jenna, she'll take pleasure in every gory detail.'

'Shh, don't let Mrs Flynn hear.'

The old woman sat at the registration desk, revelling in her power as treasurer. Olivia had the great misfortune to live opposite 'Eagle Eyes', the village's self-appointed overseer. She carried a little notebook with her everywhere she went, keeping track of MI members and villagers alike. It made you shudder to even consider what must be written in there.

They reached the head of the queue and Olivia tried to smile, but Mrs Flynn's stern expression didn't change as they handed over their ID cards. Mrs Flynn was the first person to shun Olivia and she still blanked her if she could. Unfortunately, her MI role meant she had to deign to inter-act with them. She inspected their photos, comparing them to their owners, as though Olivia hadn't lived opposite her for ten years. They went through this process every single month.

With a tut, Mrs Flynn swiped the cards through the machine, logging their attendance on the national insti-tute database. She scanned their online files and her face scrunched up as she read something on her tablet screen. That was new. Olivia peered over, trying to see what she was reading, but Mrs Flynn drew the tablet closer, block-ing Olivia's view.

'Those children of yours need to respect the noise curfew,'

Mrs Flynn tutted. 'It's nine p.m., not a minute after.' Mrs Flynn might be old but there was nothing wrong with her hearing.

'I know and they do, but they're children, they get excited sometimes.' Had Mrs Flynn reported them?

'All I'm saying is you can't afford another infraction.'

'Another infraction? What do you mean?'

Mrs Flynn harrumphed. 'I'm not at liberty to say.' She picked up her clipboard. 'Can I put you down to help at the summer fete?' She wrote their names down on the list as she spoke. 'Next.'

'Wait, I need to know what—'

Alice nudged her and made a small gesture in the direction of the stage. At the far end of the room stood pillar of the community and president of their Mother's Institute, Jenna Hook-Medwood. Tall, poised and with confidence oozing from every invisible pore, she surveyed the room from her elevated position. She was joined by an official-looking woman who seemed more intent on watching everyone file in than in listening to Jenna.

Alice steered Olivia towards two empty seats. 'Ignore Mrs Flynn, she's trying to make you paranoid.'

'She succeeded. Do you think it's a noise complaint? Or is it ...' She couldn't bring herself to mention the supermarket.

A loud crash made her jump; everybody fell silent and turned in the direction of the stage. A small, pale figure in a baggy cardigan knelt beside the President's table picking up shards of glass.

'Patricia! Do be careful.' Jenna turned on the secretary and Patricia hunched lower to the ground.

'Someone get her a dustpan and brush. I'm so sorry,' Jenna said, leading the dark-suited woman away from

Patricia and the mess. There was a long pause before the noise gradually picked up again, a burble of conversation about family drama, village gossip and the best Mother Mason recipes. Olivia lost herself in the chatter, giving herself a moment to regain her surface-level calm before the meeting began.

'You know they closed the supermarket.' The hushed conversation came from somewhere to her left and she homed in on the voices, holding her breath so she could listen closer.

'Yeah, and you know why that was,' a second voice whispered, 'it was obviously our one on the video; I recognised the ration dispensers.'

They had closed the supermarket? Thankfully, she had already got this week's rations, but what was she supposed to do after that? Was this because of the arrest? No, not the arrest, the video.

'We're all going to suffer. I don't know what I'll do if they cut our rations even further. If CTAS keep this up, Mother Mason is going to bring in stricter—'

'Have you decided what you're wearing to the Mother's Institute dinner?' Alice interrupted her eavesdropping.

'What?'

'The Mother's Institute dinner, have you decided what you're wearing?'

Olivia fought to refocus on Alice. 'Huh?'

'Your dress?'

'My dress?' Trust Alice to be more concerned with fashion. 'I've no idea, I'm sure I've got something that will do.'

A loud banging broke through the room's hubbub.

'Ladies. Ladies. Come to order please.' Jenna brought her silver gavel down on the President's table three times in quick succession, commanding everyone's attention. She

42

stood on the stage, flanked on either side by Patricia and the stranger. The visitor had a thin-lipped expression, though that might be due to how severely her hair was pulled back into a very high, very tight bun. Unsmiling, the woman stared out at the audience, her gaze moving from face to face. She paused at the only vacant seat, then looked to the open door and the Shame Box beyond; her lips twisted into a sneer of satisfaction.

'Good evening, ladies, welcome to our April meeting.' Jenna's voice easily carried to the back of the hall. 'In a change to our programme, tonight we are pleased to welcome Angelica Everly, our local liaison from the Department of Nutrition and Health.'

It was supposed to be a recipe demonstration from a government nutritionist, but Mother Mason had hijacked the schedule again. That was never a good sign.

'But first we have to sign off on the record of last meeting and I have a few announcements. As you know, next month is our annual, regional Mother's Institute formal dinner. We're so lucky this year to have Mary Vitasan, mother of the First Family, as our honorary guest speaker. It goes without saying that you must dress appropriately: you will be representing our Mother's Institute.' Here Jenna looked at Alice, who grinned back and gave her the thumbs-up sign. Jenna's serene mask slipped for a second and it took visible effort to restore it.

'We have the monthly Fittest Female badge to award. The member who has been most active, reached the highest number of steps and burnt the most calories is Lena Mazur.'

'Surprise, surprise,' Alice muttered.

'Congratulations, Lena, come and get your badge.'

'Might be nice if she let the rest of us win it sometimes,' Alice said.

'Really?' Olivia grinned. 'You think you stand a chance?' Alice only hit the minimum daily step allowance, her HealthHub barely reaching five figures, it was unlikely she would ever sport the small gold brooch that Jenna re-pinned to Lena's jacket.

'You never know,' Alice said, not convincing either of them.

'Diana Hugram, Kimlee Sun and Alice Evans, you are at the bottom of the group for general fitness levels and your numbers are bringing down the Bunham MI's total, I expect you to raise your stats before the dinner. We *will* win the Mother Mason award for healthiest MI; I won't accept any excuses. Do you understand?' Jenna waited for a response but when none was forthcoming. 'Emma Garrod?' She addressed a woman in a wheelchair on the end of the front row. 'I know you have special dispensation, but perhaps you could do a little more activity this month? Mother Mason has some special exercises designed for people with your . . . physical needs. There's really no reason why you can't help us reach our target, and you wouldn't want to be the one holding us back, now would you?' Emma shrank down in her chair, as Jenna turned to her second in command. 'Patricia, give your report.'

Patricia shuffled forward and fumbled to unfold a piece of paper.

'This month, the village—'

'Speak up,' Jenna said.

The piece of paper in Patricia's hands shook.

'This month, the village standards team has been kept busy. The good weather has meant a sudden increase in lawn height. Members are reminded that grass should be no higher than two point five centimetres, that's one inch. Official tape measures are available. Spot checks will take place and residents face a fine of five hundred pounds.'

'Remember when you fail, you fail us all,' Jenna said. 'Why are these measures so important, Patricia?'

Patricia looked at Jenna and then at her piece of paper.

'It is ...' Jenna prompted.

'It is?' Patricia turned the paper over to stare at the blank side, before turning it back.

'It is our duty ...' Jenna rolled her eyes.

'Oh yes. It is our duty and honour to care for the country we live in. We must do our very best to preserve this great nation. Nurturing it as Mother Mason nurtures us,' Patricia intoned in a flat voice.

'Very good. Sit down, Patricia.' Jenna took a step forward and adopted a solemn expression. 'Someone who has not been fulfilling her duty is Sasha Nowak,' she paused to look out of the front door. Olivia felt the draw to turn and look too, but she, like everybody else, remained frozen, staring straight ahead.

'Sasha is in the Shame Box tonight because she missed two exercise classes this month and, as you're all aware, this is not permitted.'

'Her mother's having treatment for cancer, what was she supposed to do?' Alice muttered.

'I'm sorry, did you say something, Alice?' Jenna glared across the room.

Alice drew herself up but Olivia squeezed her hand: with their government visitor, tonight was not the night to take Jenna on again. Alice remained stiff and upright for a moment, then she let out a sigh and sank back into her seat. Nobody else in the room said a word; instead, they perfected their art of statue impersonations.

Jenna gave a nod of satisfaction. 'Sasha will learn from her mistakes or her case will be escalated to a trial, and none of us want to see that happen. Our Mother's Institute will not be known for having rebels and rule-breakers, is that clear? I expect all of you to ensure that Sasha is at each and every exercise class for the rest of the year. Call her before you go, offer to give her a lift, do everything you can to support her in her fitness. We're doing it for her own good, as Mother Mason works for our own good, to keep us healthy and happy. That leads us perfectly onto our speaker for tonight. Ladies, please welcome our very special guest, Angelica Everly. She's here to tell us about Mother Mason's exciting new SmartShop directive. We no longer have to waste our precious time and energy on food shopping. Mother Mason's specially trained Customer Service Agents will do that for us and deliver it straight to our doors. Won't that be wonderful? Angelica, over to you.'

Chapter Five

'I want toast,' Mia said, as they came in from their morning jog around the village.

'You can have some, but there's no more butter, remember? You finished your ration yesterday.' Olivia braced for Mia's reaction. 'I'm going to have porridge with a big spoonful of strawberry jam,' she told Mia. The big spoonful was a slight exaggeration, the level teaspoon of her homemade sugar-free jam was all Mia was allowed: fructose was almost as deadly as sucrose, after all.

'All right,' Mia said in a dejected voice, sounding far too grown-up for the tiny person in the rainbow headband and matching dress.

'Porridge again?' Danny asked in an equally disappointed voice.

'Yes, lovely, yummy porridge.' Olivia sounded as enthusiastic and demented as the shop assistant at the supermarket, and she glared at him over the kitchen island.

'Right, porridge, my favourite.' He elevated his tone as she handed him two bowls and he adopted a pleasant smile as he delivered Mia her breakfast. Matthew was already halfway through his, shovelling it down without complaining.

'What homework have you got this weekend?' Olivia asked him as she served up the last of the porridge for herself.

'We have to write about somebody successful.' Matthew scraped the bottom of his bowl and licked his spoon clean.

'That sounds interesting. Who are you going to write about?' Danny sliced a banana over the top of his porridge, disguising the grey, watery oats.

Matthew shrugged. 'You, of course. I don't know anyone else successful.'

Olivia's first mouthful of porridge burned as it went down.

'I think there was a compliment in there somewhere,' Danny said. 'Although, your Auntie Alice runs a very successful web design company and your mum—'

'Mummy doesn't do anything.' Mia picked out the last of her strawberry jam, leaving the porridge behind.

'Yeah, she just stays at home.' Matthew drained his glass of milk.

Was that really how they saw her? Well, why wouldn't they? That was all she did, all she was now. She abandoned her breakfast, unable to force down another mouthful of the hot, gloopy mass.

'That's not true, your mother runs a company almost single-handedly. It's called the Pritchard Family and we'd be completely lost without her. She's CEO, administrator, caterer, transport, educator and counsellor. Your mum does more in a morning, before you even get up, than the rest of us do all day. We'd be lost without her.'

'That's just what mums do,' Matthew said, a perfect little 1950s' husband-in-waiting, right here in her kitchen in the twenty-first century. She was truly winning at parenting this morning.

'Matthew! We've brought you up better than that,' Danny said.

'I'm just saying, Ben's mum looks after him and runs the Mother's Institute.'

'Hayley's mum works in a bank. Could you work in a bank, Mummy?' Mia asked.

'She could, if she wanted, your mum can do anything; she's amazing. You know before you were born, Mum was incredibly successful, she—'

'Danny, don't.' She had no desire to revisit the past; it was nothing but pain and grief, layered with a good dose of social guilt and shame. Besides, there was nothing he could say that wasn't potentially incriminating, even now. She had worked hard over the past few years to disassociate herself with the bakery, hoping people would forget who she was and what she used to do, she didn't want her children to have to do the same.

'No, it's okay, they should know how proud I was of you and your success.'

Proud? It hadn't felt like pride when the world turned against her. Even Danny, who wanted her to accept things gracefully. Quietly. Like he had. Not that it mattered: his reputation was tarnished along with hers. The expected promotion, the business contacts and the social invitations all dried up. He became as tainted as her. It took a long time for people to forget, to move on; and for the sake of their marriage, they tried to pretend that nothing had ever happened. So why was he bringing it all up again now?

'Mum ran a business making—'

'Danny!'

'—*food* for other people. She baked lots of things people had at weddings and parties. Her creations looked amazing and tasted even better.'

'Really, Mummy?' Mia sounded disbelieving and that set something burning within Olivia. Why shouldn't her children know about her life? Her achievements? She had been so proud of what she used to do. This small, pathetic version of herself wasn't the person she ever imagined being; she certainly didn't want her family to see her that way too.

'Really. I even made . . . food, for a couple of TV shows and some celebrities paid me to bake for their weddings.'

'What did you make?' Matthew asked. 'Can we see pictures?'

She took a shaky breath. There had once been photos, pictures all over her website, on her social media accounts, around her house, but after the forced closure of Sweet Temptations and the online abuse, she deleted or destroyed everything. It was safest that way. It was also less painful.

'That was a long time ago,' she said.

'Before cameras?' Mia asked.

'It wasn't quite that long ago.' She didn't need photos to remember the tiered wedding cakes with the hand-crafted sugar roses, the chocolate layer cakes with the thick, glossy ganache and the birthday cakes in bright fondant and edible glitter. All of them works of art, made with love and served at perfect celebrations.

The magic of creating the tiered cakes took place in the back of the shop, but she only had to step out into the front of her bakery to be greeted by cookies and cupcakes, brownies and biscuits, pastries and pies, all laid out for the customers who arrived in a constant stream.

And the smell. The rich, sweet, buttery scent filled the shop and floated out onto the high street, drawing still more people in.

'Pics or it didn't happen.' Matthew brought her back to the small confines of her home kitchen.

'That's not nice,' Danny said.

'Dad, everybody says it.' Matthew gave the verbal equivalent of an eye roll.

'Still, if your mother tells you she did something, then I expect you to believe her. For the record, she was incredible at it. Mia, don't think I didn't see you picking out the jam. Finish your porridge too.'

'I want more jam.'

'Uh-uh, you know you get one spoonful, that's it.' No-nonsense Danny kicked in and Olivia felt a flutter of gratitude at his take-charge attitude; it was so refreshing when he was on her side and she didn't have to be the bad guy.

'It's so boring. Anyway, I'm not hungry.'

'Five more mouthfuls, please.'

Five was ambitious, but Olivia loved his optimism. Mia dipped the tip of her spoon into the porridge and took the tiniest of mouthfuls. Olivia had to suppress a laugh; her daughter was nothing if not inventive when it came to rule following. Maybe she'd spent too much time with her Auntie Alice.

Olivia caught sight of the row of cookbooks on the shelf behind Mia. The kitchen dresser used to hold her prized recipe books, but it now contained thirty different government cookbooks with titles like *Mother Mason and Me*, *Mother Mason's Meals in Minutes* and *Mother Mason's Family Fun*.

'Mia, if you finish your breakfast, we can have a treat later.' Bribery didn't make for Grade-A parenting, but it sure was effective. Both children perked up at the promise. 'Matthew, I might not have any photos, but we could bake something together.'

'Liv, what are you doing? You can't . . .' Danny sounded concerned.

'It's fine, there's a recipe for a Mother Mason cake we can bake in the newest cookbook. It looks good and it will give the kids an idea of what I used to do.' She hadn't bothered making any cakes since her first disasters after the ban came into place. The fat-free, sugar-free, taste-free monstrosities were a distant, if still slightly painful memory. Surely the recipe testers must have improved them by now?

'Danny, you get the cookbook out, and Matthew please can you look up the recipe. It's called a Celebration Slice.' It felt like a celebration, and a familiar surge of joy rushed through her.

'I want to do it,' Mia begged.

'You can help me get all the ingredients out.'

Matthew traced his finger down the list of recipes. 'Found it.'

'Great,' Danny read over his shoulder, 'tell them what they need.'

'Wholewheat flour, baking powder, bicarbonate of soda, salt—'

'Slow down, give us a chance. Here you go, Mia.' She took out the pots of baking powder and bicarbonate of soda. She really should check the expiry dates, very few recipes now called for these ingredients, but she would have to wait for the SmartShop delivery even if they were out of date.

'What next?' she asked, standing on tiptoe to reach into the cupboard for the small tin she kept their salt ration in.

'Eggs, milk, apples, dried apricots, ground mixed spice.'

Milk. Damn, she hadn't thought this through. That was okay, she could do half water, half milk, using up her ration. It would be fine.

'I'll get the eggs.' Mia advanced on the fridge.

'That's okay, you get the apples from the fruit bowl.' She intercepted Mia before she could get to the fragile ingredients. 'Matthew, can you measure out the flour?' She placed the heavy, pink ceramic mixing bowl in front of him, one of the few things to escape the baking amnesty. When Mother Mason announced the ban on sugar, all related activities and businesses became illegal. From home bakers to professional bakeries, they all risked the threat of imprisonment if they didn't surrender their cake utensils and baking ingredients during the six-week amnesty. Everything had to go, from jars of sugar to tins of golden syrup, piping bags to cookie cutters; she sent off hundreds, maybe thousands of pounds worth of kitchenware to be scrapped. Fortunately, the pink mixing bowl fell under the list of 'Approved Cookware – General', so it got a reprieve. For now.

'I want to measure the flour!' Mia reached for the canister but Matthew got there first.

'Hey, hey, no fighting.' Danny glanced up from typing on his phone. 'Listen to your mother, she's the boss.'

Olivia smiled at him but he had already returned to his world behind the screen.

'I could use your help peeling the apples.' He was too engrossed. Maybe if she threw in a few emojis and hashtags he'd pay more attention. 'Danny? ... Danny? ... Dan!' Her voice had risen to the nagging snappiness that she loathed and she hated him for making her do that.

'Sorry, what?'

'Can you put your phone away and help Mia with the apples?'

'I was only looking at it for a second.'

'Sure you were. I need you to – Mia, no, not the big knife. Put that down!'

Mia had managed to get the largest, sharpest knife from the block and had seized their distraction to start chopping the apples.

'I'm only helping.'

'I know you are, sweetheart, but let's swap that knife for

53

something a bit more manageable. Danny, do you think you can oversee this part?' Without getting absorbed in that bloody phone again. 'Matthew, if you find the measuring spoons you can do the other dry ingredients. I'll get the milk and eggs ready.'

'Can I break the eggs?' Mia begged, already bored with the apples.

'No, you help Daddy, leave me something to do.' The cake already lacked the majority of essential ingredients; crunchy eggshells would not enhance the taste experience.

It was weird making a cake without creaming butter and sugar. It felt more like stirring a bowl of mulch from the compost heap, but the smell, once the mixed spice met the liquid, was like Christmas in a bowl. She inhaled deeply, her eyes closed, remembering plum puddings and mince pies, celebrations with sprigs of holly, flaming brandy and thick, yellow custard full of sugar and cream.

'Can I put the apple in?' Mia begged.

'Sure. Matthew, Danny, can you purée the apricots in the food processor?' The recipe called for the rest of her precious packet of apricots; they were the only real sweetness in the bake. It would be worth the sacrifice.

By the time they mixed it all up, with each person having a stir, the brown gloopy sludge looked completely unappetising.

'It doesn't have to look good to taste good,' she reminded herself as much as them.

'Now what?' Matthew asked.

'We put it into a tin and bake it in the oven.' Except she no longer had any baking tins; she had surrendered them all during the baking amnesty and they had been melted down into scrap, along with her cupcake trays, her piping nozzles and her cookie cutters. She stood holding the bowl of cake mix. What on earth was she going to do?

'Liv?'

'I don't have a tin.' Frustration tempered with painful disappointment squashed her enthusiasm. 'I don't have anything to bake it in. I didn't think; I should have thought. How could I be so stupid?'

'It's all right.' Danny took the bowl from her. 'There must be something else you can cook it in. Matthew, do a search online for how to bake—'

'No! You can't type that into a search engine,' she snapped.

'Relax, Liv, it's one of Mother Mason's recipes, I'm sure it will tell you what to cook it in. Matthew, check the recipe.' Danny put the cake mix down and took both of her hands, smoothing his thumbs across her palms until her panic started to subside.

'It says to cook it in a glass bowl. Do we have a glass bowl?' Matthew asked.

She let out the breath she hadn't realised she was holding. 'Of course, I should have thought about that. I've done that a million times before, it was the perfect way to get a domed cake. I know this stuff.'

'I know you do.' Danny drew her to him, resting his forehead against hers. 'You've got this.' He kissed her gently and the children made gagging noises, so he kissed her again. 'Are the bowls in the bottom cupboard still?'

'Yes. Kids, get ready to scrape it all in – we can't leave anything behind, we don't want to waste a drop of this yummy mix.'

Twenty minutes later and the slice was in the oven; the children escaped outside to play, leaving her and Danny with clean-up duty.

'Who knew cake mix could go so far?' Danny picked up a blob from halfway across the floor.

'Not cake mix, slice mix, and yes, it goes further than you think, especially with an enthusiastic five-year-old.' She loaded the last spatula into the dishwasher. Humming to herself, she put the kettle on, getting everything ready for a nice cup of tea to go with their finished bake.

'I've missed seeing you like this.' Danny wiped the surfaces down with a dishcloth, moving closer until he stood behind her. She leaned back against him and closed her eyes.

'I've missed feeling like this. I know we all cook together, but it's not the same as baking. I don't know why we haven't tried this sooner. There are lots of new recipes on Mother Mason's site and they all have five-star reviews, I shouldn't have dismissed them so quickly.' She turned in his arms to find his lips with her own. Maybe she could finally get back the parts of her life she thought were gone for ever; maybe they could get back on track.

'Is it ready yet?' Matthew came running into the kitchen.

'Not quite, but if you get the plates out and I finish making the tea, then I'm sure it will be.' She reluctantly left Danny's embrace and looked through the window in the oven door. Unlike her old cake tins, she could see straight through the glass bowl to the brown mixture. It hadn't risen at all, despite the baking powder and bicarbonate of soda. It sat in the base of the bowl, a solid, uninspiring mass.

'Everything okay?' Danny stooped down beside her.

'Maybe.' It might be done and she didn't realise: the picture in the recipe book showed the dome covered in a spiral of fresh fruit, who knew what the cake was supposed to look like underneath the decoration? Resorting to her trusty cooking thermometer, she checked and rechecked the temperature, scanned the recipe again and returned to peering at the cake.

An hour later and several stabs with the thermometer, the cake was finally up to temperature and the end of the skewer no longer came out covered in raw gloop.

'Please say it's done.' Mia stood on tiptoe beside Olivia. 'I'm starving.'

'That's why you should have eaten your porridge this morning, isn't it? And yes, I think it's ready. Go and get your dad and brother.' She balanced a plate on top of the scalding hot glass bowl and inverted the cake. Nothing happened. She gave it a hard shake for good measure, to help release it from the bowl, but still nothing happened. The solid brown slice remained stubbornly in the bottom of the dish.

With desperation and determination as her motivation, she shook it again, harder this time, anything to get it out.

'Come on,' she muttered as Danny and the children came back in looking expectant.

'Is it meant to look like that?' Matthew asked.

'I'm not sure.' She ran a knife around the outside and tipped it up again. This time the slice fell out of the bowl and landed on the plate with a solid thud. Part had stuck to the side of the bowl and it left an ugly crater in the side of the domed bake.

'It smells funny.' Mia wrinkled her nose.

'I think it smells delicious. Sit down everyone, slices are better warm.' Danny guided the children over to the table and Olivia followed with the bake. It looked more like a miniature Christmas pudding than any cake she had ever made.

She sliced four small pieces, but the children didn't reach for their plates.

'Wow, Liv, thank you for this, it looks fantastic.' Danny pushed the children's plates towards them. 'I can't wait to try it.' His voice was overly enthusiastic as he picked up his spoon, but he hesitated before taking a mouthful.

Matthew bent over the cake, examining it. 'Did you really make this for TV?'

'Not this exactly, it was different, bigger and prettier. I decorated it with lots of colours and pretty flowers.'

'I want the pretty flowers.' Mia poked at the mush with her spoon.

'I can't make those any more, sweetheart.'

'Why?'

'Because they don't sell the ingredients.' She tried to stay smiling and serene.

'Why?'

'Because they aren't very healthy.' She moved past serenity and edged towards impatience.

'Why?'

'Just because!' She picked up her own spoon and dug in.

'Mia, Matthew, try your slice, it's really,' Danny swallowed hard, 'yummy.'

Matthew took a bite and his whole face contorted. 'Yuck!' He spat the mouthful straight back onto the plate.

'Matthew!' Danny put his own spoon down. 'Don't spit food out. It's not yuck, it's just a little different to what you're used to.'

Olivia took a bite of her own slice and had to resist the temptation to spit hers out too. The soggy, stodgy mass sat on her tongue. The dense flavours of the wholewheat flour mingled with the too sharp apples and the smell of the bran made her stomach turn.

'Mia, try some,' Danny said.

'No.' Mia pushed her plate as far away as she could reach.

58

'You're both being very ungrateful.' Danny pushed Mia's plate back. 'Your mother went to a lot of trouble, we all did.'

'It's disgusting,' Matthew said.

'Yeah, it's de-gutting,' Mia agreed.

Olivia forced her mouthful down, swallowing it along with the tears that threatened to spill over.

'That's very rude,' Danny said.

'I'd never pay for that,' Matthew said.

'Me either,' Mia agreed.

'That's it, everyone out, right now.' She stood up, her chair squealing on the tiles.

'Liv—'

'No, they're right, it's disgusting, a complete waste of time and ingredients.' She stacked up all the plates, one on top of the other, mashing the remains of the slice between them.

'Liv—' Danny reached for her hand but she wrenched away from him.

'Get out, all of you, get out.' She stomped across to the food bin and lifted the lid.

'Liv, it really wasn't that bad.'

'Yes, it was,' she said, her words only just escaping before her sob. 'Take them out, please.' She kept her back to her family and waited with her eyes closed until they left the room. Resisting the urge to throw plates into the bin too, she scraped the slice into the waste and slammed the lid. She sank down onto the floor, her hope and self-esteem in the rubbish along with the Celebration Slice.

Chapter Six

Olivia waited by the school gates on Monday afternoon, trying to tune out the humdrum conversations of the other parents. They were covering the same old topics: grades, school trips, the drama of the PTA. On good days she tried to join in, to be part of the group, but the effort to be included felt like too much today. She moved away from them, skirted the group of dads talking about the school's football team and found a quiet space on her own. Here she could wallow in her maternal guilt. Repeated apologies and a trip to the cinema, complete with buckets of natural, unflavoured popcorn, hadn't made her feel better after her meltdown. It had been a stupid idea: baking was in her past and trying to recapture that sense of joy, of achievement, was doomed to failure.

Why couldn't she just accept it was over? Maybe Danny was right. If she moved on with her life she might actually feel happy again. She needed to try a little harder, dedicate herself more to her family's health and happiness. That's what Mother Mason constantly told them to do. It's what Mary Vitasan showed them how to do. So why did *she* find it so hard?

'I'm not saying it was neglectful, I just wouldn't allow Ben to go out dressed like that.' Jenna must be talking about her again.

The woman held court with a cluster of Mother's Institute

members gathered around her in a respectful semicircle, her voice carried to Olivia as though she projected it on purpose.

'It's not difficult, after all, the Mother's Institute provides a perfectly accessible guide on appropriate clothing for children and young adults.' The other mothers nodded, their faces composed into suitably concerned expressions. 'With two daughters, she's got a responsibility to make sure she raises them as Mother Mason expects.'

Not talking about her then, not yet.

Trying hard not to get sucked in, she focused instead on the only sound that escaped the old school building: the loud, droning voice of a woman who sounded very much like Matthew's teacher, Mrs Miller. The same teacher she and Alice had when they were at school. Mrs Miller had seemed ancient then, but she would have been little older than Olivia was now. Her teaching style hadn't improved with time; she was more effective than a sleeping tablet. Olivia wished she could use her to try to combat her own insomnia.

Matthew deserved a treat after getting through a day of that, though definitely not a Celebration Slice. Her first SmartShop delivery had come this morning and she mentally reviewed her order to see if there was something suitable. She had to admit that it was a relief not to go through the stress of supermarket shopping, with no body-scanners or cameras and her weigh-in postponed until her next trip to the gym; it made her life much easier. They brought everything she wanted, all neatly packaged and delivered on time, straight to her door. Maybe not all the new changes were bad; this was certainly going to reduce her stress levels.

Now she just needed to think of something to make that

would be considered a reward for a hard day at school. If only she could bake him some chocolate chip cookies, the ones with three types of chocolate and two types of sugar. Her mouth watered at the memory. Of course Matthew and Mia didn't know what they were missing out on, but they never showed much enthusiasm for the snacks she made them. At least not the same level of excitement she remembered from when she was a child. Green juice and quinoa bars would never have the same appeal as milk and cookies, even if you didn't know what you were missing.

The buzz of the school bell triggered a cacophony of scraping chairs and thundering footsteps, announcing their arrival moments before the stream of small figures came running and tumbling out of the entrance. Matthew rushed out of the door with Ben and their little gang close behind. Mia trailed out at the back of the crowd, dragging her school bag.

Olivia waved and Matthew broke away, racing to greet her. 'Mum, look what Mrs Miller gave me.' He beamed as he thrust his chest out, showing off a large, shiny sticker. 'I got a gold star for speaking in class.'

'That's fantastic.' She reached for a hug but he stepped back.

'Mum!' He looked around to see if his friends were watching.

'Sorry.' She tucked her hands into her jacket pockets. It was hard to remember her little boy wasn't so little any more. There were 'Rules of Cool' now. 'I'm proud of you.'

Matthew grinned and straightened his shirt so the sticker shone in the sunlight.

'Carry me,' Mia announced, dropping her school bag at Olivia's feet.

'I can't do that, you're a big girl now, but I can carry your bag.' She shouldered the backpack, too heavy with homework for someone so small. They set off up the hill but only made it a few metres before the children started bickering.

'Matthew, are you going to tell us about your sticker? Was it for beating your personal best at the park run?' she asked, distracting him as they passed the local library, filled with only Mother Mason-approved books, and kept going down to the crossroads.

'No, it was for my Food Report.' Matthew walked a few steps ahead of them.

'That was today? You didn't tell me.' She stopped Mia at the curb and they waited for a car to pass.

'Didn't know. Mrs Miller just picked me.' Matthew waited for the road to clear and dashed across, jumping up onto the pavement. Olivia didn't move but Mia tugged on her hand until they followed.

'What did you tell her?' She increased her pace to catch up with him.

Matthew shrugged and kicked at a stone; it bounced and rolled along the pavement.

'What did you tell Mrs Miller we'd had to eat?' Tension crept into her tone but she did her best to sound light and breezy.

'I don't know, stuff. She said I was a good boy. Gave me my sticker. Ben was so jealous.' He polished the sticker with the sleeve of his jumper.

'I'm sure he was. Did Mrs Miller ask you anything special?'

'Nope.'

The squeak-squeal of plastic wheels from further down the road announced the presence of Mrs Flynn; she walked towards them, pushing her little wheeled shopping bag in front of her.

63

'Tell me what you said,' Olivia kept her voice low as Mrs Flynn got closer and closer. 'You made sure Mrs Miller knew you had lots of fruit and vegetables, didn't you?' They always had plenty, hidden in sauces, cooked into the crusts of their cheese-free pizzas, blitzed into juices and smoothies. The reality of her covert veggie smuggling settled in with a sickening lurch. The children didn't realise all the fruit and veg she gave them; that meant they wouldn't report back how much they had eaten. She thought she was being so clever, she should have just accepted the meal-time battles and made them eat their ten portions a day like every other parent did. Why did she have to think she was so smart?

'She didn't ask me much about last week. Not when I told her about the cake.'

The squeak of Mrs Flynn's shopping bag stopped.

'What the hell?' Olivia caught hold of him, pulling him close so she could find out why he had used the C-word. 'Why would you say that?' She looked past him to Mrs Flynn, who stood a few metres away, her bag clutched in front of her.

'We haven't had cake,' she said, for Mrs Flynn's benefit. 'We would never have cake. I don't know why he said that, where he's even heard that word. Tell her, Matthew, tell Mrs Flynn we haven't had cake.' She ignored his struggles to break free. 'Go on, tell her.'

'Mum, stop.'

Without pausing to look for oncoming cars, Mrs Flynn stepped off the curb and crossed the road.

'Please, he's just a child; he doesn't know what he's saying,' Olivia called after her.

Mrs Flynn didn't look back. She dragged her shopping case behind her, bumped it up onto the other pavement and rushed back towards her house. Towards the Department of Nutrition and Health who were just a phone call away.

'Ow! Mum, you're hurting me,' Matthew said.

She loosened her grip but didn't let go as Mrs Flynn's small form reached the end of the road and turned the corner.

'What cake?' she whispered, scanning the vicinity; the houses were quiet, no flickering curtains and no obvious street cameras either. 'You mean the Celebration Slice? That wasn't cake. I never said cake.' Or had she? When she was stressed and angry and completely unfiltered.

It wouldn't matter about Mrs Flynn; Matthew's teacher must have already informed DoNaH. Panic made Olivia light-headed and she swayed, bowing her head as if in prayer, as if there was somebody who could help her. She was going to end up in a Shame Box. No, worse – they would put her on trial; she'd be another terrible mother paraded for all to see, her crimes revealed on television for the nation's entertainment. Once she was found guilty – and you were always found guilty – she would enter the Societal Evolution Programme, and nobody came back from that.

'We have to go back to school, right now.' She turned around, pulling Matthew and Mia with her. 'You have to tell Mrs Miller you were wrong. It wasn't cake, it was Mother Mason's Celebration Slice. It's allowed; we didn't break any laws. We're not guilty.'

'Ow, Mummy.' Mia tried to prise Olivia's fingers off but she wouldn't let her go. She would never let them go.

'Did you at least tell her we used Mother Mason's cookery book?'

'I don't remember.' Matthew's voice wobbled and he took a gulping breath.

'Try, Matthew, it's very important.' They stopped at the crossroads and she bent to look at him as cars rushed past.

'I told Mrs Miller it was horrible, that we didn't eat it.'

'That's good, what else did she say?' The road cleared but Olivia didn't move. Mia started to cry, loud noisy tears and Matthew was moments away from doing the same.

'She asked if we had it a lot.'

'And?'

'I said no and that I would never, ever, ever eat it again.' His tears spilled over. 'I'm sorry, Mum, I didn't mean to say the wrong thing, it was a mistake. I'll do better next time. Please don't be cross.'

She released her grip on them and pulled them both into a tight hug, trying to hide her own tears. 'Matthew, you did nothing wrong, none of this is your fault. I should have explained things better. Shh, Mia, it's okay, Mummy's not angry. I will write to Mrs Miller tomorrow and tell her what we made.' There was still some in the food recycle bin, maybe she could send it in as proof. That had to be enough, they couldn't arrest her just for this, could they?

Of course they could. Over the past seven years people had disappeared all the time; at first everyone asked questions, fought back, but not any more, not when things kept getting worse. CTAS could make all the videos in the world, but they were still living in fear, terrified of the implications of a child's innocent words.

She glanced back towards the school. Mrs Miller's report would already have gone to DoNaH and Mrs Flynn was probably on the phone right now. It was too late, far too late.

'Mrs Miller said it was a good picture,' Matthew mumbled.

'What?' Olivia moved to see his face.

'Mrs Miller went online to see Dad's photos. She had them up on the screen for everyone to see.'

'Oh she did, did she?' Hope fluttered stronger than the outrage at the privacy invasion; there would be time for that later. 'Which photo did she like? Was there one of the Celebration Slice?' She tried not to sound too eager.

'I think so. There were lots of us.'

Of course there were, Danny couldn't go ten minutes without taking a picture to share online. Hope was like a drug, injecting her with life again. 'I'm sure it's fine, Mummy's just being silly. Look at the time, we had better hurry, the Captain Fit show is going to be on soon, you can't miss that. Let's run so we've got enough steps to make the TV work.'

Back home, with the kids settled in front of their favourite cartoon, Olivia opened Danny's photo feed and scrolled through the pictures. He'd posted one of the kids measuring out the ingredients, another of them stirring the batter, with flour all over the kitchen. She cringed at one of her looking dreadful with her eyes closed, they would have words about that, but there, the final post from the baking session, a picture of the Celebration Slice. He laid it out in true food porn fashion, with the Mother Mason cookbook and some artistically arranged spatulas. Thank you Danny and his social-media obsession. For once she didn't mind a bit.

Chapter Seven

'You didn't really take your food waste bin round to Mrs Flynn, did you?' Alice sprawled on Olivia's bed, with Kit curled up in her lap.

'Of course I did, how else was I going to convince her? I took the recipe book and Danny's photos too.' Olivia stared into her wardrobe at the row of neatly arranged clothes.

'What did she say?'

'Not much.'

If Alice hadn't insisted they pick her outfit for the Mother's Institute dinner, she would have put it off for another few weeks, probably until the night before the event.

'Do you think she already called the department?'

Olivia closed the wardrobe door again and flopped down on the bed. 'I expect so.' She stared up at the ceiling, fighting the panic that kept threatening to return. She hadn't done anything wrong, she had to keep telling herself that. 'She was on the phone when I went round, I think she was on hold, I could hear the annoying music. As soon as I showed her everything, she hung up pretty quickly, but who knows what she already told them.'

'With all the calls to DoNaH at the moment about the videos, she probably didn't get through. You'll be fine, they must be used to her overreacting. Although, if you want, I could go round and talk to her?' Alice lifted Kit off her lap and moved towards the door.

'No!' Olivia sat up so quick she felt dizzy. 'Please don't, you'll only make things worse. You're probably right, I'm being silly, ignore me.' Escalating the situation was the last thing she needed. 'Besides, you're meant to be finding something for me to wear.'

Clothes were the perfect distraction for Alice, and Olivia scooted back on the bed, relaxing as her own personal stylist took her place in front of the wardrobe set into the rafters.

'How can you have the same dress in five different shades of blurgh?' Alice flipped through the clothes on the rail.

'Why not? It fitted and passed the Decency Laws, that's good enough for me.'

'It shouldn't be, you deserve to wear beautiful things every day, not just on special occasions. You're always hiding in those baggy clothes.'

'I'm not, but there's no point wearing nice things, I'd only spill something on them, or the kids would wipe their hands on me. It's a waste of money.'

'Not if it makes you feel good. You can always stick it in the wash.' Alice pulled out a couple of dresses, held them up and after a fleeting glance dropped them onto the floor. 'Nobody could get excited about these clothes, but we could get you something gorgeous, that still fits within the Decency Laws.' She stroked her new peacock-blue jumper, the latest addition to her vast wardrobe. Nobody would ever ban Alice's favourite form of numbing, her comfort shopping was too valuable to the economy.

If they were searching through Alice's wardrobe it would take most of the evening, but Olivia's small selection needed barely three minutes. Alice removed each item, assessed and dismissed it in seconds. After a final flurry of activity she sank down onto the newly created clothes carpet.

'It's hopeless,' she pronounced, 'you've got nothing to wear.'

'Nonsense, there must be something.'

'I know you don't want to go shopping, but what choice do you have? You heard what Jenna said: "you're representing our Mother's Institute",' she mimicked. 'If we go to a boutique it will be much more relaxed than the high-street shops. Admittedly, they don't serve champagne any more, but we could still have fun.'

'I'm not buying a designer dress, it's a waste of money, Danny's money.'

'You know that's not how he sees it.'

'It's how I see it.' The heavy, leaden feeling sank deeper into her bones. How she missed having her own income, her own independence to buy what she wanted, when she wanted it. No guilt, no wondering if she should check in advance, get his permission.

'You could get a job, you'd be brilliant at whatever you did.'

'Nobody would hire me, they'd see *baker* on my CV and freak.'

'Then come and work for me.'

'Doing what? I'm rubbish with technology and you're not going to hire me for some pity job, like making tea and filing.'

'You do make a cracking cup of tea, but that's not the point, your creativity should be put to good use.'

It was. Her vivid imagination took up most of her time picturing horrifying situations that could happen to her family; her talent was definitely not going to waste.

'I don't know if I can do it, go back out there, be in the world again. I don't know how to speak to grown-ups any more.' And she was tired. From the moment she woke, to the last second before she slept, she was heavy with fatigue. This life was taking all she had, there was nothing left for jobs, or projects, or anything else.

'There's no pressure, I was just saying you have opportunities, if you want them, and if you don't want to buy a dress, you can always borrow one of mine.'

'Yeah, I'm sure one of your stunning size one, tall dresses would fit me perfectly.' She folded her arms across her stomach. Years of legally enforced exercise classes could only do so much; her body still bore stretches and scars, the price of motherhood. One of them, at least.

Guilt followed ingratitude, and she sought the gleaming silver photo frame beside Danny's side of the bed; two happy smiling faces beamed out at her.

'You looked so beautiful,' Alice said, following her gaze.

'I looked young and naive.' She reached for the frame and stared down at the half-forgotten strangers.

In the picture she stood smiling up at Danny. Her simple white dress was starkly contrasted against his dark suit. Light glinted off the raised silver fork, poised in the moment she fed Danny his first mouthful of wedding cake. If she closed her eyes she could still taste the rich, sweet, chocolate buttercream and feel the texture of the soft, moist cake in her mouth.

'It was a wonderful day,' Alice said.

'Yes, it was.' She set the picture down and turned to see Alice on her hands and knees, digging around at the back of the wardrobe.

'What are you doing?' She leapt up from the bed and ran over.

Alice had pushed aside Danny's clothes and crawled on all fours, deeper into the wardrobe. 'I'm just seeing if there are any treasures hidden at the back.' Her words were muffled.

'No!' Olivia caught hold of her.

'It's fine.' Alice pulled against her, stretching her arm further in. 'Just give me a sec.'

'Alice!' Her voice rose as she caught sight of the stack of brown cardboard boxes at the back. 'Don't! Come out now!'

'Are you worried I'll find some hidden dust? Maybe a cobweb or two?' Alice sat back on her heels, face flushed, breathing heavy.

'You got me.' She tried to laugh but the sound came out rough and fractured. 'Really, there's nothing there.'

'Of course there isn't, just your OCD organisation skills.' Alice pointed to the far box with the neat red lettering. 'Paperwork to sort. Why haven't you gone paper-free yet?'

'I like paper, you can rely on paper to tell the truth. I don't trust digital.'

'Maybe I should reconsider that job offer.'

'I think you should.' She grabbed Alice's hand and pulled her up from the floor. 'You know, you're right about the dress. I don't have anything to wear and it is a special occasion.' She steered her away from the wardrobe and shut the door.

Alice raised an eyebrow, eyes bright with possibility. 'You mean I get to take you shopping? You don't have to tell me twice.'

Chapter Eight

The little bell above the boutique door jingled as Olivia and Alice walked into Chique. It was the only welcoming sound, as dark-suited sales staff turned to greet them with unsmiling expressions. Alice didn't wait for their assistance; instead she led the way around the small shop, pointing out potential dresses.

'What about this one? Or this one? Oh, look this is gorgeous.'

Olivia smiled and nodded noncommittally, wishing she had managed to persuade Alice to go to one of the familiar high-street stores. But no, only designer would do for label-loving Alice.

They stopped in front of three Mary Mannequins positioned on a raised platform. Tall and elegant, Mary looked as glamorous in dummy form as she did on television. It was easy to see why Mother Mason had picked her and her family to represent the new regime. Olivia couldn't believe Alice almost convinced her to apply for the First Family competition. It had seemed like an exciting opportunity during Mother Mason's first year in government, but like a lot of things their leader had proposed, it now didn't seems so appealing.

'What about this dress?' Alice naturally picked out the brightest and most glamorous of all the outfits in the boutique: a long, flowing red gown that was as far from

Olivia's style as was possible to imagine. She'd rather go to the Mother's Institute dinner in her pyjamas than be seen in something that bold. It might fit with the Decency Laws, with the long skirt and high neckline, but the colour was far too daring for her taste.

'Nope.' She turned her back on the other two mannequins dressed in jewel blue and deep indigo, and went to the rack on the far wall where the clothes in black, brown and white hung. Their names would once have been chocolate, caramel and cream but they were now named beige, taupe and ash, much more mundane and less delicious.

'No way.' Alice dragged her back towards the brighter end of the colour spectrum. 'You're not getting anything that you already own. It would be a waste of money. We might as well go back to your wardrobe.'

'No, you're right,' she said a little too quickly. 'Pick some dresses and I'll try them on, just not the red.'

'Perfect.' Alice pulled three dresses off the nearest rail before Olivia had time to draw a full breath. 'I wonder where Deb is?' She peered around the store. 'She'll find the rest of the items we need.'

'Rest? I only came for a dress.'

'Good afternoon, ladies.' A woman in a dark suit advanced on them.

'Hi.' Alice nodded to the woman. 'Is Deb here? We want to get a dress for the Mother's Institute dinner and she knows what I like.'

'Deb no longer works here. Can I get your IDs, please.'

'Deb left? What about Louise? Or Sonya?'

'There's been a change of management.' Three gold stars graced the woman's name badge, identifying her as Laura, a senior Customer Services Agent. She raised the electronic notepad that hung over her shoulder and made a few quick motions on the touch screen. The device illuminated her in a blue-white glow that threw menacing dark shadows across her face. 'IDs, please.'

'Why do you need our ID's?' Alice asked, as Olivia immediately reached into her bag to retrieve hers.

'I need to take some measurements and then I can update your details on the system. Is there some reason why you don't want to give me your ID?' Laura spoke to Alice but looked up towards something in the corner of the room. Olivia followed her gaze to the camera on the ceiling, to all the cameras in fact, mounted around the small shop.

'Give her your ID,' she said, surrendering to the demand with weary resignation. With time and practice, it got easier to acquiesce.

'Why? Clothes aren't rationed, there's absolutely no reason—'

She stepped down hard on Alice's foot. 'Give the lady your ID card, she's just doing her job. We're all busy women.'

'It's not like you're hiding anything, are you?' Laura asked.

Olivia gave a nervous chuckle and passed her card across. 'Of course not. Right, Alice?'

Laura inserted the ID card into a slot on the side of the tablet and Olivia's details materialised on the screen.

'What size do you normally take?' Laura scrolled through pages and pages of information, more than Olivia knew the government held on her.

'Size two, sometimes three,' she said, not elaborating on her body's tendency to stubbornly cling to fluid during half of her monthly cycle.

'The permitted sizes have been recalculated. We no longer do size three.'

No, they couldn't do that, she needed size three, or her

jeans wouldn't do up before her period. What was she supposed to wear instead?

'That's insane, they can't do that.' Alice snapped, although she never needed anything larger than a size one. 'It's bullshit.'

'Language.' Laura sounded twenty years their senior when she looked much younger than they were. 'It's for your own good. Mother Mason wants to ensure that you're at your optimum healthy body size, and size three is too large. That's why I need to take your measurements today.'

'Surely you get enough information from our gym and workplace weigh-ins to calculate our BMI? You're not taking my measurements as well,' Alice stormed. 'I've got a right to my privacy.'

'Privacy won't keep you happy and healthy. Mother Mason is simply concerned about her citizens. Fat takes up more volume than muscle, we're only ensuring that you're as fit as you appear to be. Size three just isn't good for you.'

Olivia moved her handbag so that it covered her stomach. It felt as though her body had suddenly swollen. Her previously unnoticed waistband dug into her and she could feel the fabric of her T-shirt straining across her chest, and it wasn't even her time of the month.

'Is it the same for men?' Alice asked.

Laura laughed at the very idea of such nonsense. 'Of course not, men can easily reach size three with the bulk they put on during their body building, in fact they're going to add a size four, but you'll be pleased to know they're looking into removing size one. No man should be that under-toned.'

Alice smiled sweetly. 'I feel so much better.'

Olivia didn't. Danny wore size one trousers: his shoulders were broad and muscular, but he had a narrow waist and size two drowned him, despite hours at the Power Pro class. He was going to have to spend even longer at the gym, which meant even less time with her and the kids.

'Mrs Pritchard, come with me, I'll get you measured up and then you can start shopping.'

'This is outrageous, you can't expect us to do this. Liv, we're leaving.'

'You can leave, but I will make a note on both your files noting your refusal to comply; you can expect a follow-up from DoNaH within the week.' Laura said, puffed up with her own importance.

'If you think people are going to submit to this, you're in for a shock.' Alice pulled Olivia towards the door.

'Alice, wait.' She had to talk her down before they both got in trouble; this outburst was bad enough. 'We don't have a choice, we have to get it over with.'

'No, there's always a choice.' Alice turned a deeper shade of red as her fury rocketed.

'She's right, your other option is called the Shame Box. I'm sure I can make you an immediate appointment there.' Laura swung her electronic tablet off her shoulder and started to type.

'That's not necessary.' Olivia put her hand over the screen. 'We'll do what you ask.'

'Sensible woman. Follow me to the changing rooms.'

She led them to the back of the boutique, where the small space was divided up by heavy, hanging curtains. Laura dragged open the first one and motioned for Olivia to enter, but she couldn't bring herself to step into the narrow space, not with the large, unforgiving mirror watching her.

'Is there a problem, Mrs Pritchard?'

'No, of course not.' She drew on her mask of calm and her reflection did the same. It was pretty convincing as long as she didn't meet her own gaze, didn't see her wild animal panic so close to the surface, her visible terror, her need to run.

'Take your clothes off and I will be there in a minute.'

'Take off my clothes?' Her voice was hysteria high. 'Why do I have to undress?'

'You don't, if you think you can spare the extra centimetres.' Laura gave her a little shove into the cubicle.

'You can't expect us to do this,' Alice snapped.

'Please step back,' Laura said, 'you are infringing on my personal space.'

'Your personal space? What about our personal space? Our personal rights?'

'Mother Mason says I can and I must.' Laura squared up to Alice with the confidence of the indoctrinated.

'I don't care who you are or who you work for, this is unacceptable. I'm—' Alice was working herself up to a point of no return.

'Alice, stop. I'll get undressed.'

'Liv, don't.' Alice caught her arm, trying to pull her back.

'You can't protect me from this,' she whispered and stepped into the cubicle.

'I will give you one minute to change and then I will return.' Laura drew the curtain with a squeal of complaining curtain rings.

Alone, except for her reflection, Olivia hugged her arms around herself. This was all because of that bloody box. As soon as she went home she was going to burn it, and she was never, ever coming clothes shopping ever again.

She slipped off her T-shirt and unbuttoned her jeans, trying not to think too much and only venturing the swiftest of looks into the mirror, just enough to see that under

78

the artsy yellow bulbs of the store she looked horribly pale. The unflinching mirror threw her body back at her: sagging wrinkled skin, a map of white stretch marks that contoured her body and the sinking hollows of her neck, ribs and hips. Her greying bra hung down, barely filled by what remained of her breasts. She raised a hand and cupped the worn, bobbled fabric; she used to have a cleavage, curves she was proud of. They came with a rounded stomach and fuller thighs, but she had felt feminine and sexy in a way she could barely remember. The person staring back at her was a stranger, one she ignored at all costs.

Even her eyes seemed unrecognisable; they were the right colour but they were too far apart. Her face was shallower, her cheeks flat and sloping, the softness she knew had hardened out. No wonder Danny didn't see her any more, she couldn't see herself either.

Through the curtains she could hear Alice muttering as she stripped off. 'Civil rights ... disgusting ... illegal ... lawyer ...'

If her words were loud enough for Olivia to hear, Laura could too. 'Ready,' she shouted, desperate to stop Alice from saying anything worse.

Laura opened the curtain, allowing in a freezing blast of air. Instant goosebumps covered every millimetre of Olivia's skin and she started to shiver, her body shaking as Laura advanced on her with a yellow tape measure; it looked impossibly short, there was no way it could wrap around the vast expanse of her body.

'Stand up straight, arms out.' Laura smiled, a warped twist of her lips that conveyed no warmth.

Olivia closed her eyes as the cold ribbon of plastic snaked around her torso. Laura's hands touched her bust, lining the tape up, pulling it tight around her chest. She didn't dare breathe, didn't risk adding an extra few centimetres onto her measurements. The tape measure released and it uncoiled around her, as Laura's hands moved down to her stomach, her hips, her thighs.

Her panic crescendoed and then abruptly halted as mental and emotional distance settled in. She floated up, higher and higher, further away from the cubicle, her consciousness only barely connected to her body as the ordeal continued. It was somebody else's body being touched, measured, judged; they were somebody else's breasts and legs and waist. Somebody else was twisted and turned by rough hands with sharp fingernails that scratched soft, fragile skin.

Was it minutes or hours before she realised that Laura had finished, had left her alone in the cubicle? Just her and her dull-eyed reflection. She had stopped shivering but now she started to shake, tremors coming up from deep inside her, so intense that it was impossible to remain standing. The curtain hung open, but it was beyond her abilities to close it, to pull her clothes back on over limbs that wouldn't move properly, fingers no longer able to grip. Her strength left her and she fell down onto the hard wooden bench, the cold glass mirror pressing against her back. Everything was darker, closed down to the tiniest pinpoint of focus on the space in front of her. She leant forward as dizziness swamped her, her head between her knees as the room spun around her.

'No!' she cried, her hands raised in defence as someone touched her again. The action was more to ward off attack than to fight for herself; she had already submitted, there was no point in fighting back now.

'It's okay, Liv, it's me. Laura's gone.' Alice knelt down in front of her, not touching her again, not saying meaningless platitudes. Her presence was enough to soften the fog of numbness that enveloped Olivia.

'I want to go home,' she whispered.

'I've picked out some dresses for you both to try.' Laura returned with her arms laden. 'Who's going first?'

Chapter Nine

Olivia returned home with a new dress, a matching clutch bag and a vow to never be put in that position again. Danny and the children were still out and the house was unnervingly quiet. She took the ribbon-tied boutique bag upstairs, ready to shove it in her wardrobe and shut the door, but she was confronted with the devastation Alice had left behind. Clothes were everywhere, crumpled on the floor, thrown on the bed, while some still clung desperately to their hangers. The only upside was that it was far easier to get to the boxes in the back of the wardrobe. She shuddered at the memory of Alice rooting around in there. It had seemed like dress shopping was a small price to pay, compared to letting Alice continue her search, but with the feel of Laura's hands still fresh on her body, Olivia was no longer sure. The worst part was that it could have all been avoided if she had only been stronger seven years ago and done what she should.

Her upstairs duster was tucked in the top drawer of the dressing table, kept ready for just this purpose. She ran it over the top of the polished wooden table, swiped it across the mirror without looking at herself, then moved to the window, to polish the cleanest panes of glass in her house, maybe in the village. As she moved the soft cloth back and forth, she searched the blank windows opposite, looking for a flutter of curtain or a sway of blind. Her need for absolute privacy had never been so essential. Thankfully, Mrs Flynn's living-room window was vacant, her normal observation post empty. No cars passed along their quiet country road, no dogs barked. Nobody was watching her, for now.

Reflected in the glass she could see the open wardrobe behind her and the box with the big red lettering. It had seemed like the perfect disguise, Danny would never voluntarily open a box of paperwork, and it had worked. All these years and he never looked inside. He would have been so disappointed in her if he had. Disappointed enough to tell the authorities? She honestly didn't know.

Every time she went through this process, she promised herself it was the last time and every time she found herself back here, duster in hand. But today was different: things had to change, she couldn't put her family at risk any more. Even thinking about getting the box out was a betrayal. It was not the behaviour of a good wife, a good mother. Mary Vitasan would never do it. She wiped the glass once more, scrubbing at her reflection, and then with a swift motion she pulled the cord and lowered the blind.

As far as anybody knew, she was only dusting, that was all, there was nothing wrong with that, certainly nothing illegal. In the half-light she glanced towards the wardrobe and a familiar ache of desire flared up inside her, but she crushed it down. That part of her life was over, truly over this time.

She flicked the duster over the closed blind, bent low to run it along the skirting board and followed the pale yellow wall all the way to the built-in door frame of the wardrobe. Gliding the cloth up the grooved wood she hesitated. Was she really doing this? Was it really over?

Before she did anything, she ought to put her clothes away

first. Had there really been nothing she could have worn to the Mother's Institute dinner? If she'd refused Alice's help, none of this would be happening. Tears threatened to fall, but she only worked faster, gathering everything up, trying not to think about what she was sacrificing. She returned the clothes to their hangers, arranging the garments so they draped in front of the stack of boxes in the back of the wardrobe. For all appearances, her problem was solved. Except it wasn't. She couldn't pretend any longer that life would improve, that things would go back to the way they used to be. This was her reality and the contents of this brown box could bring everything down on her. It was time to get rid of it, she had no other option.

She dragged the box out of the cupboard, past the bed and towards the door, all ready to haul it downstairs and out into the garden. It slid easily along the soft blue carpet, retracing a faint path only she could see. The edge snagged on the corner of her bedside table and knocked the lid just enough for her to glimpse inside to the row of brightly coloured hardback books. Forbidden books with titles like *Love Cake*, *Best Ever Bakes* and *Cupcakes Galore*. The last of her treasured recipe books, the ones that didn't make it to City Hall.

It wasn't intentional, she had packed everything up for Danny to take away. Thousands of pounds worth of bakeware all sent off to be destroyed. It wasn't until a month after the amnesty ended she discovered the box of books pushed into a corner of Matthew's playroom, an island for his toys. It was too late to get rid of them, too late to tell anyone, so she did the only thing she could think of: she hid them.

She ran her fingers across the glossy spines, feeling the bumps and grooves of the titles, until she came to her favourite one: *The Ultimate Baking Bible*. It was her very first cookbook, the one that inspired a career and a passion that still burnt bright within her, even if she had to keep it hidden, locked up tight, along with her anger and resentment.

The books she could burn, create a bonfire in the garden along with the grass cuttings and the fallen branches, but her secret, unspoken hatred of Mother Mason and the world she forged was not so easily destroyed.

Baking had always been her solace, her escape from the world. If she was stressed, she baked; happy, she baked; bored, she baked. It was the best and easiest way to show people how she felt, and without it, she was lost, detached, without a way to express her feelings.

Her wedding photo on the bedside table was now at her eye level and she stared at her and Danny, at the joy in their expressions, the softness love brought to them as she fed him the chocolate wedding cake she made. The basis for the cake recipe came from the *Baking Bible*, the tutorial for how to perfectly ice a cake was in another; her skills, her success, her life, it was all here in front of her. A box full of love and memories. How could she destroy it? She needed time to say goodbye. Five minutes. That was all. She reached out and laid the silver frame face down on the bedside table.

Picking just one felt like an impossible choice, but she settled on the most worn and battered one, the one covered in spills and stains, with a hundred memories crammed between the pages. She took it out of the box and sat on the bed, curled up against the soft mound of pillows. She stroked the front cover and then traced the letters, caressing each one with her fingertip.

The tension in her shoulders eased but before she opened

it she paused to listen. The house was quiet, just the tick of the bedside clock and the distant hum of the fridge. A faint halo of sunlight seeped in around the blind but the rest of the world was shut out. Nobody, not even Mrs Flynn, could see in. She was safe: for this one last time, she could relax.

It had been like therapy for the past seven years; a quick flick through a few pages, and she could breathe again, the panic, the crushing weight of the world held back by a few pictures of cake. Who was it hurting? Really? Not Mother Mason, not her family, not her waistline. Nobody.

She glanced down at the cookbook in her hands; she was clutching it so tight that her nails had dug into the cover. Forcing her cramped fingers to release, she examined it for damage, feeling sick at the sight of the tiny crescent indentations. Laughter bubbled up, breaking the silence. What did it matter? Within a few minutes they were going to be nothing but ashes, a couple of scratches didn't make any difference. Except it did.

She opened the *Baking Bible*, smoothed her hand across the front page and scanned the list of recipes. It was like a scrapbook of her life, each one a memory of an event or celebration, better than a photo album; and there, like a bookmark, was her last remaining business card for Sweet Temptations. Alice had designed the pink logo that appeared everywhere, from the uniforms her staff wore, to the large sign that graced her store front, welcoming people to come in and try the cakes, cookies, pastries and cupcakes. She sighed and tucked the card away again, before turning to the first recipe. The white paper arced over to reveal a rich chocolate cake, so dark with cocoa it was almost black. Deep-brown glossy chocolate covered the cake, giving it a perfect, mouth-watering sheen. She ran her finger across the picture, imagining the trail she would leave behind in the smooth ganache.

There was a small dark spot on the white page and she scratched it with her nail, then lifted the book to her face. The faint smell brought back her wedding day. The four-tiered cake became one of her signature offerings at the bakery.

On the next page was a bright glossy photo of a Victoria sandwich. The golden cake was broken up by the sudden, almost shocking slashes of pale butter icing and bright red strawberry jam, the inner heart of the sliced-open sponge.

She reread her notes written in pencil by the side of the recipe: 'Buttercream too sweet, reduce sugar.' It was really code for 'Made it for antenatal group, Jenna hated it, pulled a face and made snide comments for two hours about feeding children healthy foods.' It was ridiculous, Matthew wasn't even on solids at that point. By the time he could eat one of her cakes, the baking ban was in place; she never even made him his first birthday cake.

The next page she always skipped over, tried to flick past it without looking at the picture of the pink, sparkly cupcakes. She baked them for the protest after Mother Mason announced the baking amnesty and the immediate closure of all sugar-related businesses. Alice didn't need to persuade her to join the Pink Apron Brigade on their march to Parliament. She carried the cupcakes, Alice brought the banners. The optimism in the crowd was electric; hundreds of thousands of bakers filled the streets of London, all clad in bright pink aprons, their placards held aloft: 'Save our Sugar'; 'Our food, our choice'; 'Food = Freedom'. They cheered and shouted until their throats hurt, passionate but peaceful, with men and women of all ages and generations marching together, taking a stand.

Until the men in suits appeared. The crowd of pink was dotted with darkness. Then the screams began. People were arrested, parents forced to the ground as their children were taken away. Everyone started to run, with no sense of direction. She and Alice got caught up in the panic and when they finally made it back to the train station, blood-ied and bruised, they ripped off their aprons and slipped in among the other passengers.

Sweet Temptations never opened again. The government sent in a team to strip her commercial premises, leaving only the oven and the empty fridges behind. That just left Olivia to pack up her home kitchen. She thought the hardest part was emptying the cupboards, letting go of her much-loved and well-used bakeware; but that was only the beginning.

The day after Sweet Temptations closed her parents in-vited her and Danny out to dinner. She didn't want to go but Danny persuaded her it would be good for her and that they needed to keep up appearances, prove they understood and accepted Mother Mason's decisions. Her mum and dad made a big show of going to their favourite Mother Mason-approved restaurant, the one where all their friends and business acquaintances frequented. The one they had never invited her to before. She thought it was meant to cheer her up, a misguided attempt to show her there was life after the bakery. She was wrong. Right there, in the middle of the restaurant, they announced in their loudest voices how ashamed they were of her and the damage she had done to society; how they couldn't, in good conscience, be part of her life anymore; that they hoped she had learnt her lesson and would raise Matthew to be a healthy and happy little boy, the way Mother Mason would expect. Olivia sat there in tears of rage and anguish, trying to find the words to finally speak back to her parents, while the other patrons looked on, enjoying dinner and a show. When she finally gathered her thoughts and emotions, ready to fight back, Danny stepped in, apologising to her parents for the situation and ushering her out of the restaurant. He tried to pacify her later, to explain that they couldn't risk causing a scene, but she saw which side of the line he stood on and it wasn't the same as her.

A distant awareness, a flicker in the back of her mind, nudged Olivia to pay attention. She stopped reading, ears straining to catch the sound. It was the noise of an approaching car. Not just any car though, this had a very specific, very familiar tone.

No, it couldn't be. They couldn't be back, not yet.

She got up and stumbled to the window. The simple task of opening the blind seemed impossible. With a wrench she dragged it up and squinted to see Danny's car pull into the drive.

'Oh no!'

She ran to the bed, threw the book back in the box and jammed the lid on.

'No, no, no.'

There was nothing to be done but to hide them again. She pushed the box across the floor, leaving a rough trail in the carpet, and thrust it back into the corner of the wardrobe. She dragged the clothes across, slammed the door and hurried downstairs.

Sprinting to the living room, she threw herself down onto the sofa, grabbed the television remote and touched it to her HealthHub. Please let me have enough steps to make it work, she thought.

There were muffled sounds from the front of the house, the jangle of keys, the clunk of the door handle. She didn't care what she watched, the number of steps she sacrificed, so long as she looked normal when they got in. Breathless from the rush, she ran her fingers through her hair, smoothed her skirt down and tried to slow her breathing. It was almost working until she saw what was on the television. A courtroom drama played out on the screen, a plump, middle-aged woman stood hunched in the dock, covering her face with her hands. Behind her sat a man and three teenagers, two boys and a girl. They all had their heads bowed, and a vein pulsed on the man's forehead, his skin pale and shiny on the high definition television. Their terror was contagious and it reignited her own panic, because this wasn't a glossy Hollywood drama, these weren't actors playing out roles, they were real people, with real lives: she had stumbled onto the live trials channel.

The woman didn't look like a monster, she seemed as normal as every woman Olivia had ever known. She certainly didn't look capable of the heinous crimes she must have been accused of, to get her to the point of a trial. It had to be bad, if your actions couldn't be cured by a stay in a Shame Box or a stint at the Re-education Programme.

The camera panned to Mary Vitasan, who presided over the court from the Judge's Bench. 'How do you plead?' she asked.

The woman spoke but it was inaudible. The gallery broke out into noisy murmuring and Mary raised the gavel and brought it down. The woman's lawyer hissed something at her and she dropped her hands. Her round, terrified face filled the screen.

'Guilty,' she repeated.

It wasn't the woman's expression that felt like a knife through Olivia's heart, it was the terrible anguish on the faces of her children, the grief and the loss that they could not escape now their mother had confessed. This was the last time they would see her before she joined the Societal Evolution Programme. It was the last time anybody would see her.

Olivia stared up at the ceiling. Was a box of cookery books enough to land her in the same trouble? She couldn't risk losing her family for something so stupid, so selfish. They were all that mattered.

Mia and Matthew burst into the living room, mid-squabble, and she reached to change the channel but she couldn't get the buttons to work before Danny walked in.

'You're early,' she said. It sounded like an accusation.

'It started to rain and the kids were tired. I thought it was best to come home.'

The children blocked her view of the television as they fought over a small plastic toy.

'That's enough! Put the toy down and go and wash your hands. Daddy won't take you out again if you come home fighting.'

They looked at her as if she had told them they were forbidden from having fun ever again. Behind them the father on the screen hugged his three teenage children as their mother swayed forward, moments away from collapsing.

'Please, just be kind to each other.' Olivia pressed her palms against her eyes, blocking out everyone's wounded expressions.

'Are you okay? You look a bit ... flushed.' Danny sat down beside her and placed the back of his cool, rough hand against her forehead.

'I'm fine.' She couldn't look at him or the children, who stood quietly now, the toy abandoned on the floor. 'Just tired. I've been busy cleaning, this is the first chance I've had to sit down,' she pulled away from him and leant forward to rearrange the magazines on the coffee table, 'but I guess I should start dinner now.'

'Don't do that, you look exhausted. We could go out? Try the new Salad Bar in the city.' He glanced at the screen. 'Why are you using up your TV minutes on this? You hate the live trials.'

'I do.' She snatched up the remote and tried to switch it off but only managed to increase the volume. The woman's sobs filled their living room.

'Let me.' He took the remote and turned it off. 'Are you sure you're all right?'

'Of course I am.' She forced out a little laugh.

He took her hand, stilling her frantic tidying, and brushed his lips across her palm. 'You really shouldn't watch these things, they always upset you. Let me cheer you up and save you cooking. The kids would love it, and so would I.'

'Yay, Mummy, please can we go out?' Matthew asked hopefully.

'Please?' Mia echoed, their petty fight forgotten at the promise of another outing.

Olivia looked from her children to her husband, the same hopeful expression mirrored in his dark eyes.

'Okay, okay. We'll go out.'

As they left the house, she glanced up at the bedroom window. The blind was still swaying. It had been close, too close; she couldn't do it again.

Matthew and Mia climbed into the back of the car, chattering about their trip to the zoo. She tried hard to focus on them, to listen to what they were saying, but there was a small fleck of dark brown under her nail. It released a faint sweet smell when she scraped it away. The scent undid some of the panicky tension that locked her muscles. She looked back towards the house. Getting rid of the books was her only option, she had to do it, just not today.

Chapter Ten

'Good morning, Mrs Pritchard.' The SmartShop delivery man stood on the doorstep, electronic tablet in hand. 'I'm here with your Mother Mason food shopping. How are we today?' The man might be wearing a hi-vis waistcoat and driving a refrigerated van but his gold-starred name badge clearly marked him out as Jeff from Customer Service.

'Good, thank you.' Olivia had her ID card ready before he could ask, trying to hurry the process. In fact, she had her whole morning planned out. As soon as she put her groceries away, she was going to light a bonfire and then this whole cookbook nightmare would be over.

'You can leave everything here,' she instructed Jeff.

'No can do,' Jeff said with a fake apologetic smile. 'There's new rules, I have to take the bags through to the kitchen.' He stepped forward with his plastic crate, barging her out of the way. 'This way?' He was already halfway down the hall, walking past the doors to the living and dining room, heading straight for the kitchen as if he'd been there before.

'Wait, stop!' Olivia chased after him.

'Can't, I'm on a tight schedule.' He pushed the door open with his foot, marched to the kitchen table and dumped the crate down among the chaos of empty cereal bowls, abandoned mugs of cold tea and crumb-covered plates.

'Somebody's not learnt that "a tidy house is a happy house",' he commented.

'Sorry, I've only just got back from the school run, I haven't had time to clear up the breakfast things,' she said, anger flaring at herself for apologising to this uninvited visitor, but her fury was tempered by fear. She felt very alone in this too-big house. Why hadn't she booked the delivery for when Danny was here? Because she'd had food delivered in the past, before Mother Mason, and it had never felt as intrusive as this.

Jeff stood back from the crate to look around the kitchen; his gaze scoured every surface and cupboard, taking in everything from the washing up on the draining board, to the knife block, her precious kitchen mixer and the spice racks on the wall.

Did he see anything incriminating? she wondered. Was there anything in the jar of utensils she should have got rid of in the amnesty? She felt the weight of the box of cookbooks upstairs and she forced herself not to look up towards the ceiling.

'You need to sign here.' He thrust the electronic tablet at her, but his attention was still focused on the room.

Half-watching him, she absentmindedly signed and he started unloading the shopping. Raw meat, fish, cans of tomatoes, baked beans, a bag of porridge oats. She peered over his shoulder, looking for her dried apricots, for any of the dried fruit, but it was missing from her order.

'Were there any substitutions?'

'No, but there's a few items we're no longer stocking. It's all listed on the receipt you signed,' Jeff explained as he retrieved the ration of butter and the bottle of milk and went to the fridge.

'I can do that.' She tried to take them, but he muscled

95

her out of the way and opened the fridge door. He stood looking in, scrutinising her neatly stacked shelves.

'What's in those?' He pointed to the pots of leftovers.

What right did he have to ask? To know? 'Pasta, vegetables, some cooked chicken,' she said, trying not to let her anger, or her fear, leak into her voice. It was supposed to be her lunch, but she no longer felt any desire to eat it.

Jeff bent closer to inspect them, barely refraining from opening the pots. 'Sounds like you have an issue with your portion sizes. Excess food means excess pounds.'

'Not if I spread it out over separate meals,' she said without thinking, losing her tight grip on her anger. Jeff's severe glare brought it back under control immediately, but this time she didn't apologise.

He returned to scanning the fridge shelves, never touching anything, but somehow contaminating everything, before he reluctantly turned away.

'See you the same time next week,' he said with an odious smile.

She followed him to the front door and as soon as he was back in his van, she closed and locked it behind him, but she could still feel his presence in the house: nothing felt safe. Least of all, the box of books upstairs. She had to get rid of them, now.

As she headed to the stairs, there was a knock at the front door. Please don't say he was back again. She peered through the spy hole at the distorted image of the postman; she'd never been so glad to see him.

'Hi,' she said brightly, almost throwing open the door, but the normally cheery man didn't smile back. He didn't look at her as he thrust a bundle of letters in her direction and hurried away. The tip of a brown envelope stood out from the stack of envelopes and colourful junk mail; she almost dropped the rest of the post in her rush to get to it. Cheap, rough paper, blocky font, it was an official government letter, with *her* name and address on the front. She tore into it; the sharp pain of a paper cut not slowing her. Had Mrs Flynn informed on her? Please no.

Hyperventilating, she took out the single sheet of thin, off-white paper. It was so light and flimsy that the breeze through the open door tried to snatch it away, but she held on, scanning the letter. Certain phrases stood out: 'Department of Nutrition and Health', 'Re-education', 'Rigby Hall' and 'attendance is mandatory'.

The world spun out around her, everything she loved slipping away from her, and there was nothing she could do to stop it. A high-pitched shriek made her scream, until she realised it was her mobile phone. Alice's name and face filled the display.

'Alice, I've got a summons for the Re-education Programme. What am I going to do?' She couldn't breathe, couldn't cope, this was too much.

'I got a letter too.'

'You did?' A strange sort of relief flooded through her. 'I thought it was because of the Celebration Slice. Do you think the woman at the boutique reported us?'

'Nah, it says it's because of the arrest at the supermarket.'

'It does?' She stared down at the letter, but through her tears and desperation, it looked like jumbled lines of black type.

'It says that due to our recent exposure to a known "extremist", we need to undergo a day's Re-education at Rigby Hall. A long boring lecture, a few frightening statistics and we'll all be home in time for dinner.'

A flash of light dazzled Olivia and she tracked the bright flare back across the road to Mrs Flynn's window. The nasty old woman stood with her binoculars out, a wide, cruel smile gracing her face. Olivia glared at her and slammed the front door, shutting her out.

'Liv, are you all right? It's going to be fine, I promise.'

'How can you be so sure?'

'We're not the first people to go on one of these programmes. I know plenty who've been through it and they all said it was fine, nothing more than scare tactics and emotional blackmail. We have to take our lunch, so we'll use it as an excuse to get out into the country and make a day of it. The kids will enjoy the adventure.'

'The kids? What do you mean?' She gripped the letter so tight the edges scrunched up inside her fists. This time she properly read the letter, taking in every horrifying word.

Dear Mrs Pritchard,

I'm writing to inform you that your presence is expected at Rigby Hall on Thursday 18th April for participation in the Re-education Programme.

It has come to our attention that you were recently exposed to an extremist arrest and as a result you must attend a one-day class.

You and all members of your household must attend the Re-education Programme, attendance is mandatory and rescheduling is not possible. Further action will be taken if you fail to appear.

Please arrive by 9 a.m., all attendees will need to bring their own lunch.

Yours—

'What am I going to tell Danny? How can I explain this to Matthew and Mia?' She retreated to the kitchen and collapsed onto a chair.

'This isn't your fault, you haven't done anything wrong; they'll understand.'

'Everyone is going to find out. I'm never going to live this down. I'll be shunned all over again.' Jenna would get the Mother's Institute announcement today too and it would be public news in under an hour, she'd seen it before, she knew the drill.

'No, you won't. Plenty of people go these classes. We'll be gossip for a few weeks and then they'll forget.'

That was what she said about the shunning.

'Just blame me,' Alice continued, 'tell them I led you astray. Jenna would totally believe that.'

Olivia struggled to focus for the rest of the day, she dropped her favourite mug, stepped on Matthew's school art project and worst of all, burnt their dinner to an inedible black crisp. Another way she was failing her family. No wonder they'd called her up for Rigby Hall; it was amazing they hadn't done it sooner.

Fortunately, she had enough unrationed food in the cupboards to throw together a quick meal of pasta and tomato sauce. Mia and Matthew didn't seem to mind, if anything they preferred her more basic meals, but she couldn't look at Danny as she set his bowl down in front of him, hadn't been able to look at him since he got home from work. Not that he had noticed, he was oblivious to anything other than the latest social media updates on his phone, posts from people he didn't know and would never meet.

She pushed the pasta around, unable to take even the smallest of bites, but hoping it was enough to convince the children to keep eating. With every non-mouthful, the weight in her stomach grew heavier; she had to tell Danny, tell all of them what was going to happen, but how could she explain it? How could she make them realise it wasn't her fault? She hadn't meant to get caught up in someone else's drama. It was so unfair, she hadn't done anything wrong.

'Liv?'

'Sorry, what?' Danny had taken enough time out of his busy online life to notice her.

The hot puffiness beneath her eyes made him look blurry and very far away.

'Kids, ' he said, 'special treat, take your dinner and finish it in front of the television. You can use my steps.'

She gave up all pretence of eating as he hurried them out of the kitchen

'What's happened?' He came back in and shut the door behind him.

'I . . .' None of her rehearsed speeches would reform in her mind. 'I . . .' The shame was unbearable, it surged up within her, accompanied by overwhelming nausea. She couldn't say the words, couldn't see the look on his face. Would he be angry? Upset? Worse, disappointed? The letter was folded back up in its brown envelope, but she'd read and reread it so many times that she knew it word for word. The folds in the paper were almost worn through as she handed it to him, unable to say it aloud.

'This incident, do they mean the arrest? The one in the video?'

She nodded, staring down at a small, shrivelled pea that had got stuck in the groove between the floor tiles.

'You didn't know the woman though, did you?'

She shook her head, emotion keeping her tongue still and her throat choked.

'So this is another scare tactic? They're shifting the blame. Bastards.'

His tone of anger and indignation drew her gaze up from the floor. He was mad, but not at her?

'It's unbelievable, how the hell do they think it's okay to make everyone suffer for the actions of a few? It doesn't matter what we do, how hard we try to follow their rules, they always find a way to blame us for something.' He scrunched the letter up and threw it across the room; it hit the far wall and rolled towards the bin. 'Come here.' He held out his hand to her and she went to him, relief taking the stress from her body as he wrapped her in a tight hug.

'You thought I was going to be mad?' he spoke, his face pressed against her head, so close that not even air could get between them.

'Yes.' Her pent-up tears released with that single word. 'Because I'm mad; I'm furious. With myself, with *them.*' Unfairly, with Becky. 'Why did this have to happen? I'm always so careful.'

'I know you are.' He stroked her back and she clung tighter to him.

'I've done everything they said, given up everything they asked of me. I was just doing my shopping and we're still in trouble. Danny, we have to take the kids. We have to take them out of school, everyone is going to know, the teachers, their friends, the other parents. What if my parents find out? It's going to be like before, we're going to be judged because of this. I don't want them to be shunned like I was.'

'This is not like before, we haven't done anything wrong.'

'I didn't do anything wrong,' she wailed. 'I was just running my business, but everyone acted like I was some hardened drug dealer, forcing them to buy my cakes. They all blamed me.' You blamed me, she thought.

'That's not true. It's just some people didn't want to take responsibility. That's on them, not you. Some of us could see how wrong the whole thing was and we didn't blame you.'

That wasn't how it felt.

'My parents did. Jenna did.'

'Jenna's evil.'

This forced her to pull away. Danny had never said a bad word about Jenna; his outburst was as shocking as it was refreshing.

'I'm sorry,' he said, 'I know I'm supposed to be the calm voice of reason but I can't stand her and that weasel of a husband. It's all I can do not to punch him when we take Matthew round to play.'

She started to laugh, a deep belly laugh that brought on more tears, but these were lighter and more refreshing. 'Me too! It might even be worth a stay in the Shame Box.'

'We'll go together, you take Jenna, I'll take Lewis.'

She wiped her tears away and leaned up to kiss him, feeling a pull of desire she only vaguely recognised. It had been so long since intimacy was something she wanted.

'Is it nearly bed time?' he asked.

'I think it's early beds all round.'

Chapter Eleven

Olivia wasn't remotely concerned about her weight when she went to the gym on Wednesday. The fast-approaching appointment at Rigby Hall had devastated her appetite and her sleep patterns. If anything she was more likely to be underweight and that would mean another brown letter. She was damned either way.

Writing to Matthew and Mia's teachers had been torture. How did you tell them that your children wouldn't be there because the whole family was being reprimanded for an incident she wasn't responsible for? She redrafted the letter twenty times before Danny took over and summarised everything in a single sentence.

'The children will be out of school on Thursday due to our attendance at a Re-education day.' He didn't apologise, didn't shift the blame, simply stated the facts. Mrs Miller and Miss Lewis would draw their own conclusions, if they didn't know already. Jenna had done a sterling job of one-woman public service announcer, ensuring the whole village knew about their punishment. Olivia power-walked the children to and from school, not stopping to talk to anyone, avoiding all eye contact and keeping her earbuds in to block out the gossipy whispers.

They had to get up early on Thursday morning for the long drive to Rigby Hall, but Mrs Flynn knew exactly when they were leaving; she was up before them, floral curtains pulled back to watch them all pile into the car.

'Hi, Mrs Flynn,' Alice waved at the old woman, who scowled, but kept watching. 'Nosy old bat.'

'She's that and worse, but don't antagonise her.' Olivia loaded their packed lunches into the car and slammed the boot closed.

Danny was fiddling with the radio when she climbed into the passenger seat. Matthew and Mia had already started bickering and they hadn't even left the house yet. The two-hour drive to the hall was going to be a nightmare. She didn't have the strength to turn around and placate them, instead she settled for twisting up the volume.

'—the vitamins you love.' A bright, chirpy voice covered the prickly atmosphere. 'Sponsors of Mother Mason's Morning Melodies. Now for "My Love, My Family" by The Purities.'

Alice clambered into the small space between the children and the argument ceased. Car-sharing brought more than the advantage of saving fuel.

The tension in Olivia's shoulders increased the further they got from home. The residential streets faded behind them and they sped out onto the open country roads. It will all be fine, she reminded herself, repeating the same mantra she'd been using unsuccessfully for the past week. We will go in, do the class and come home again. Simple.

The drive seemed endless, but after what felt like the hundredth round of I Spy they saw the large sign for Rigby Hall. Hidden behind the tall trees, a high wall ran parallel to the road, shutting the hall in. She wished Danny would keep driving, carry them far away and never look back, but he slowed the car and indicated left.

The swirling curlicues of a tall, black, iron gate greeted

them. It was ornate and apparently delicate, but there was little that could be done to disguise the raised spikes set into the tarmac and the cameras pointed at them from every possible angle. There was a squat, grey booth in the centre of the road and Danny pulled to a stop beside it. Not that he had much choice, the lowered red barrier and sharp yellow road spikes would halt their progress if they didn't. Danny left the vehicle idling until Olivia spotted a large red and white sign and pointed it out to him.

'Engines off. Phones surrendered. No unauthorised persons beyond this point.'

He turned the engine off and reached for her hand, intertwining their fingers. The rapid beat of his pulse moved in time with her own.

'ID cards.' A dark-suited man stood behind a large window in the security booth. It was like an old-school drive-through, except there would be no fast food here.

Danny lowered his window. 'Hi, we're here for the Re-education class.'

The man pointed to the slot below the window. 'ID cards and all phones.'

Alice leaned through the gap between the front seats. 'Why do we have to give up our phones?'

'It's the rules. I advise you to hurry up. Class starts in ten minutes; believe me when I say you don't want to be late.'

'Do as he says.' Olivia got out her and Danny's ID cards and phones, but Alice held on to hers for a second longer than necessary.

'I don't like this,' she said. 'Let it be known I'm surrendering my phone under duress.'

'Ma'am, your possessions will be returned to you on your departure. Make your way to the hall, follow the signs.'

The barrier lifted, the spikes retracted and the gates slid back. It looked like the entrance to a country estate, complete with a tree-lined driveway, bird song and squirrels racing around. Olivia glanced back in the side mirror, watching the gates close behind them.

Rigby Hall was one of many private estates Mother Mason had 'claimed' for her government Re-education Programme.

'Looks idyllic, doesn't it?' Alice broke the silence when it came into view.

The seventeenth-century stately home glowed a creamy gold in the morning sunshine. It looked beautiful, if you could ignore all the cameras mounted on posts around the grounds.

There had to be over a hundred people waiting in the large entrance hall. They stood huddled together, speaking in whispers, the words of fear jumbling together to echo around the vast room. Some people Olivia half remembered, like the old man with the walking stick, who stood alone, staring up at the architecture of the ornate ceiling, or the woman with pink braids who smiled at them as she held hands with her girlfriend. The anxious young man whose ID card wouldn't go into the ration machine was there with an older couple who Olivia assumed were his grandparents, and they looked as terrified as he did. As terrified as Olivia felt. Mia was really too big to pick up, but Olivia lifted her onto her hip and Danny kept his arm around Matthew's shoulders. Alice stood on guard in front of them, not as casual as she pretended to be. She glared at the agents who surrounded them.

The only person who was noticeably missing was Becky, but her presence filled the room, her plea for help resounding inside Olivia's head.

'Welcome to the Rigby Hall Re-education Programme.'

A man stepped in front of the group. 'My name is Lewis Hook-Medwood and I am a trainer for the Department of Nutrition and Health.'

Of all people, it had to be Jenna's husband. So this was what he did. He smiled smugly at them, his personal brand of creepy smarm emanating through the room of anxious attendees. He ran a hand over his slicked-back hair and adjusted his three-star name badge. 'You're all here because you witnessed an incident at your local supermarket and it's essential that we work through the implications of said incident together. Our aim is to help you process the trauma and move forward from a place of strength, health and happiness.'

'Please sir, there's been some kind of mistake,' the grandmother of the nervous young man spoke up. Her voice shook but desperation kept her going. 'We shouldn't be here; my grandson is a good boy. Rupert would never break the rules. It was just an accident that he was there during the arrest and he had nothing to do with the ...' her voice trailed off. She wasn't supposed to have any knowledge of the viral video, none of them were. 'He loves Mother Mason,' she said, stridently. 'He thinks she's a great leader, don't you, Rupert?' She nudged him and he cleared his throat several times before managing a strangled-sounding yes.

'We are not accusing anyone of any impropriety, the guilty culprit was arrested. Mother Mason just wants to ensure that the incident doesn't adversely affect her citizens. She's so compassionate and concerned for our well-being. We're truly lucky to have such a wonderful prime minister, aren't we?' He waited for a response. 'Well, aren't we?' he repeated and the whole room murmured their ascent. 'Good, now let's get back to the day's schedule. Can the children come to the front?'

Olivia kept hold of Mia and Danny didn't let Matthew go either. None of the parents were willing to release their children.

'It's okay, they are going to go and play with these nice ladies.' Lewis pointed out five severe-looking women who stood on guard by the exit. 'They'll have fun.'

He might have been convincing if any of the staff showed the faintest hint of warmth or basic humanity.

'Mummy, I don't want to go.' Mia wrapped her arms tight around Olivia's neck and Alice and Danny moved in closer, the three of them creating a shield around the children.

'It's all right, sweetheart, everything's going to be okay,' Olivia whispered.

Lewis sighed. 'Parents, do you really want your children to stay with you? We have a day's worth of presentations detailing the detrimental effects of your unhealthy life choices. Cancer, heart attacks, diabetes, is that really what you want to expose your children to?'

A little girl, barely eighteen months old, wriggled away from her mum, desperate to practise walking on her newly discovered legs.

'Ellie, no!' Her mother lurched after the tottering toddler, but her arms were full with a tiny newborn, and Ellie raced away from the group, running straight towards the only open space, the front of the room near Lewis.

'Ellie, stop!' her mother shouted and this woke the baby, who screamed his indignation. Keeping the baby clutched to her, the woman lunged after Ellie, who put on a burst of speed, but her tiny feet tripped and she stumbled forward.

Lewis caught her and handed her straight to one of the female agents.

'Ellie, you're a fine young citizen, thank you for showing

the other boys and girls how to be brave. You get to be the first one to meet Captain Fit.'

'Mummy! I want to meet Captain Fit!' Mia squirmed, trying to get down.

'Everybody gets to meet Captain Fit, he's waiting in the next room, but you have to come now or he'll fly away. You don't want that, do you?'

Two boys and a girl broke away from their parents and rushed to the front. Mia tried to follow but Olivia held onto her. She had no idea what would happen once the children were out of her sight; she couldn't just let them go.

'I'll look after Mia,' Matthew promised.

'I'm a big girl, I don't need looking after.' Mia huffed. 'Please, Mummy, I want to go.'

'You heard them, Olivia, they want to come and play,' Lewis said. 'Today will go a lot faster if you do as requested, without causing any more trouble.' He motioned for the other agents in the room to step forward, closing in on the children.

'They can't separate you if you refuse,' Alice said in a carrying whisper.

'Why would you refuse, *Alice*?' Lewis stressed her name, showing his knowledge of who she, who they, were. Jenna would love this, no doubt he'd report every detail to her when he got home.

Olivia leaned into Danny, their bodies forming a united pillar. The plan was to get through the day together, but it was already unravelling.

'What do we do?' he whispered.

She had absolutely no idea. All she knew was that it would be far worse if the children were as scared as she was, so ignoring every instinct, she gave Mia one last tight squeeze and lowered her to the ground.

'Have fun,' she smiled her biggest, fakest smile. 'Say hi to Captain Fit for me. Your lunch boxes are in your backpacks. Be good.'

The other parents had reached the same conclusion, they let go of hands and gave final hugs and kisses. Most children left their parents willingly, if a little reluctantly, but a couple of them howled, refusing to go. Their tears called to something primal in Olivia. She desperately wanted to protect them all. Two female guards left their posts and scooped the children up, carrying them out of the hall and away, the sounds of their tears getting quieter and quieter. The other children followed behind and Olivia had to hold onto Danny and Alice to stop herself from rushing after them.

'Finally.' Lewis checked his watch. 'Partners, relatives, house-sharers, anyone who wasn't directly exposed to the incident needs to go with Jane for your Re-education Programme.'

Not Danny too! She couldn't do this without him, but he was already in motion, giving her a quick kiss and pulling away before she could react. Alice stayed by her side.

The door swung shut behind the last relative and they were left with the other shoppers, all as pale and subdued as she felt.

'Follow me.' Lewis ushered them down a long, winding corridor, and Olivia lost all sense of direction by the time they reached their classroom. They entered to find rows of wooden benches and an illuminated screen with Mother Mason smiling out at them, her eyes following you wherever you sat.

'Some housekeeping before we begin.' Lewis took his place at the front of the class. 'Our morning session will run until one, you will have half an hour for lunch and we

110

finish at five. I hope you've used the bathroom, because we will not be stopping for any reason. If you leave this room during class I will fail you and you will spend twenty-four hours in a Shame Box.'

'He's making the most of being in charge. I guess with Jenna as your wife you'd have to take your power where you could get it,' Alice whispered, trying to lighten the mood.

'There will be no talking,' Lewis snapped. 'My voice is the only one that should be speaking, unless ...' He was drowned out by the sound of drilling that reverberated through the room. 'Unless,' he raised his voice to compensate, 'you are asked a question and then you will respond, immediately. No wallflowers, no shrugs, no "I'm sorry, I don't know." You will participate or—' The drilling stopped but Lewis continued at the same volume. '—you will spend twenty-four hours in a Shame Box.

'If you want to ask questions, you will raise your hand. If there's anything you do not understand, try harder.'

'This is going to be fun,' Alice whispered and a vaguely familiar man beside her exhaled a quiet, amused snort.

'You should know I have excellent hearing, in fact all my senses are superior because I strictly adhere to Mother Mason's health and happiness teachings. That means you cannot get away with anything, so don't try. I do not give out warnings, I do not give second chances and there is a van waiting to take you straight to your nearest Shame Box, the box all your friends and family will see.'

The rumbling groan of the drill started up again.

'As you may have noticed, there is building work going on in the north wing; please do not wander into any other areas. Any questions? Good. We'll start this morning with a message from our beloved leader.' He pressed a button on a remote control and Mother Mason was released from her frozen position on the screen.

'Welcome, welcome, I'm so pleased to see you all today, but I have to admit it saddens me that you are attending this class. I know you can all do so much better and that's what we're here for, to help you remember your lessons so you can go out and lead happy and healthy lives. After all, that's what we all want, isn't it?'

She paused, her hand outstretched to the group.

'Isn't it?'

'Well, isn't it?' Lewis demanded.

'Yes,' chorused the group, hesitancy in their forbidden voices.

'Health and happiness are the greatest rewards a person can achieve and, under my government, they are now available to everyone, no matter your class, race or status.' Mother Mason drew herself up taller, filling the screen with her beaming presence. 'Gone are the days when only the rich could afford to eat well or attend expensive gyms, now they are open to all.'

Behind Mother Mason a video montage of gyms around the country flitted across the screen. Men and women worked out at the Power Pro and Be Fit classes, grinning as they executed their routines.

'The obesity crisis is over, diabetes has been cured and the diagnosis rates for other conditions is down year on year. It is my aim that within the next five years all illness and disease is eradicated, and if you follow my Health and Happiness Programme, it will be. Won't that be wonderful?' She paused for the group.

'Yes,' they intoned.

'What will it be?'

'Wonderful.'

112

Alice's tone matched the bitterness Olivia felt, the words sharp and spiky, like broken glass in her mouth.

'None of this would have been possible without you.' Mother Mason spread her arms wide encompassing everyone in the room, and every room the video ever played in.

'Do you remember how awful life used to be?' Mother Mason's smile faded away and she bowed her head. 'So much sickness, so many deaths. Who did you lose to cancer? To diabetes? To a heart attack?' The video froze and Lewis stepped up to the front.

'What's your name and who did you lose? You.' He pointed to the old man who sat hunched over, his spine gnarled into a painful reversed question mark. He clutched his walking stick, as though it was the only thing keeping him upright.

'M-m-me?'

'Yes, tell us who you are and who you lost to an avoidable illness?'

'I, uh—' He rocked forward further, his body curving deeper with the weight of his grief. 'My ...' his last word was inaudible.

'What did I say about not answering questions?'

'I'm T-T-Tom. I lost my wife.' He bowed even further forward, curling in on himself.

'How?' Lewis demanded.

'She had lung cancer.' He whispered the words but they struck the room like a physical blow.

'An avoidable illness, prevented by Mother Mason's cigarette ban. You,' Lewis pointed to the woman with the pink braids.

'I'm Bronwyn. My father had a heart attack.' Her words were choked but she sat up tall in her seat, her gaze fixed straight ahead.

'Avoidable.'

A single, angry sniff was her only reaction to his cutting remark. He moved on to the nervous young man, who ran a finger around his collar as though it would make space for his voice. 'My mum had liver failure.'

'That's why Mother Mason banned alcohol. Next.'

My wife, my husband, my parent, my child, my sibling, my friend . . . everyone had a story, a loved one lost. They reached Olivia's row and the man beside Alice hesitated. He twisted the woven leather bracelet on his wrist, turning it round and around as though it held the answer.

'You. Who did you lose?' Lewis repeated.

He tugged at the frayed ends that looked so worn they might snap at any minute. 'I'm Dev.' He closed his hand around his wrist, trapping the bracelet beneath his fist. 'My brother had a hereditary heart condition. Genetics killed him.'

'Did he drink? Did he smoke? How was his diet?' Lewis fired off the questions. 'How can you know that his death wasn't caused by the choices he made in his life? Are you a doctor?'

'Actually, I—' The red hospital lanyard around his neck proved his credentials, but Lewis moved on before his argument could be called into question.

'Next.' He pointed at Alice.

'My parents, car crash.' She said the words with no emotion, glaring at Mother Mason's image on the screen. Olivia touched her arm, part comfort, part caution, and braced herself for what would come next.

'The end to drink driving is one of the greatest gifts Mother Mason has given us. Nobody else will lose a loved one in this way.'

'It was a fault with the car, they—'

'I'm Olivia and my grandfather had a stroke,' she volunteered quickly. 'Terrible thing, paralysed the whole of his left side. It was incredibly traumatic for everyone.' She could hear herself babbling but she continued to fill the silence. 'The hospital was fantastic, the doctors and nurses worked so hard but they were under-staffed—'

'That is no longer a problem.' Lewis capitalised on her endless chatter. 'Mother Mason knew changes had to be made after spending her working life as a nurse. I'll let her tell you more.' He pressed play and Mother Mason resumed.

'I'm so sorry for your losses, for the people who are no longer here; the people that should be, would be, if they had lived to see my government come to power. You all made wise decisions when you voted for me, this country changed for the better and we're now leading the rest of the world in our commitment to health and happiness.'

To accompany her words, a video of smiling, happy, healthy people passed across the screen: young and old, individuals, couples and families paraded their happiness for all to see. It made Olivia ache for Matthew and Mia. Where were they right now? What were they doing? She tried to picture them, reach out with her mother's intuition, but all she sensed was her own anxiety.

'I made a promise to you,' Mother Mason continued, 'to do things differently, to change the way this country was run. Thank you, you gave me the power to do that. You voted for me in a landslide victory, and we showed those lying, cheating politicians what we truly wanted.' Mother Mason didn't mention how she had commandeered the government and brought an end to democracy. That part didn't make quite such a good sound bite.

The camera zoomed in on her smug face. 'Everything I

do, I do for your best interests. The rules are there to protect you, to keep you safe and well. You are my children, my family, and this is for your own good.' The video stopped on a freeze frame of Mother Mason that remained on the screen.

'This is all for your own good, please remember that.' Lewis stepped back to the front of the room. 'We're now going to go through some workbooks.' He dumped a huge stack of printed booklets onto the lap of the woman nearest him. 'Take one and pass them along.'

Olivia flicked through her booklet, trying to skip over the graphic photos of overweight people, organs clogged with fat and bodies on morgue slabs. Beside her, Alice gagged.

'Think of them as parts of a machine,' Dev advised. 'It's how I got through medical school.'

'Thanks, I'd hate to throw up on you.' Alice moved her hand away from her mouth to smile at him. If she was well enough to flirt, Olivia didn't have to worry too much.

'You wouldn't be the first.' He loosened his grip on his bracelet and reached to shake Alice's hand, their grasp seeming to linger. 'I think we met before.' His gaze flickered to Olivia and back to Alice.

'Really?' Olivia couldn't remember him at all.

'Yeah,' Dev was fixated on Alice as she played with her necklace. 'I, uh, I was the one that crashed into your trolley. I'm so sorry, I—'

'No talking, remember?' Lewis snapped. 'Everybody turn to page one.'

Chapter Twelve

Three hours later, Olivia's brain felt like it had been thrown against a wall. Her eyes blurred as Lewis played another video, this one showing how the Department of Nutrition and Health calculated their individual dietary allowances, using their height, weight, BMI, age and occupation.

'Whose research are you using to calculate the personal fitness and intake requirements?' Dev asked.

'Yes!' Alice whispered under her breath.

Lewis had bombarded them with an unending stream of horrifying statistics, showing the grisly ways people had died, throwing in a few glory stats proving how many were living longer thanks to Mother Mason. Noticeably, he never gave any concrete figures or sources to back up his statements.

'You don't need to concern yourself with the actual numbers, the government do all that for you,' Lewis said sniffily. 'It makes everything so much easier. All you have to do is make healthy choices about what you eat and the way you choose to use your calories. There is so much freedom on Mother Mason's eating plan, especially if you use her delicious recipes, and that brings us to lunchtime. Get out your lunches.'

There was an audible sigh of relief from around the room. Most people had brought their lunch packed in boxes or paper bags. The old man, Tom, got his sandwich out of a battered plastic container that looked older than Olivia and Alice combined.

'You.' Lewis pointed to him. 'Come up here and show me what you're eating.'

Tom stopped mid-bite. 'Excuse me, young man?'

'I said bring it up here. And it's Agent Hook-Medwood. Hurry up.'

Tom placed the sandwich back in his container and leaning on his walking stick, tried to heave himself to his feet.

'Here, let me.' Bronwyn stood up in his place.

'No, sit down!' Lewis barked. 'Each person is responsible for their own lunch.'

Bronwyn remained standing, the beads in her braids clattering together as she seemed to vibrate with suppressed rage.

'Is there a problem?' Lewis asked.

'It's okay, my gal, I can get up.' Tom hauled himself upright and Bronwyn caught his elbow and helped him to stand. He shuffled forward with his stick in one hand and his lunch in the other.

Lewis took the sandwich apart layer by layer.

'Brown bread, excellent. Did you use butter? No, good. Filling? Ham and tomato, excellent. You could add in a pot of salad, it makes the lunch more filling and helps you reach Mother Mason's minimum of ten portions of fruit and vegetables a day.' He gave Tom back his deconstructed sandwich, but the old man seemed unsure what to do with it. Bronwyn reached forward and took the box, without leaving her seat, and Tom shuffled slowly back.

'Next,' Lewis demanded, but Bronwyn waited until Tom was safely in his chair before she took up her pitta breads wrapped in wax cloth.

Like a conveyor belt of lunches, Lewis inspected

sandwiches, salads and a couple of flasks of soup. Dev had a packet of pre-made sandwiches and a banana stuffed into the side pocket of his leather messenger bag. 'Bought sandwiches?' Lewis sneered at the packet. 'Doctor, I'm surprised you don't make your own, you know the health benefits of preparing your own meals, the engagement you get with the food, the appreciation of the ingredients. Studies show there is a far higher level of enjoyment from consuming your own creation.'

'I didn't have time, I was on call last night. It's a Mother Mason-approved sandwich, I imagine that would make it even better than anything I could do myself.'

Alice had to muffle her laugh and the rest of the group became very interested in their own lunches, hiding their enjoyment of the conversation.

'Everything Mother Mason approves is of the highest quality, of course. Go and sit down. Alice, your turn.'

'I haven't brought anything, I—'

'You must eat lunch, every day. Skipping meals is the fastest way to throw your metabolism out of balance and cause dangerous blood sugar fluctuations.'

'Olivia brought our lunch.'

Lewis's attention shifted and Olivia squirmed beneath his gaze. She reached for the insulated backpack at her feet, cursing herself for not throwing it all into a canvas bag like everyone else.

'Are you going on a five-mile hike?' Lewis asked sarcastically.

'I thought you'd be in favour of that,' Alice muttered under her breath. Lewis glared at her but did not reply.

'No, I just put some bits together. Aren't we eating with our families? I brought food for my husband.'

'Your attendance letter clearly stated that each person

was responsible for their own food. You won't see him until the end of the day.'

Olivia knew the letter off by heart and it hadn't been clear at all, but it was pointless to argue. Lewis snatched the backpack away from her and unzipped the front panel to reveal china plates, four glasses and compartments for each piece of cutlery; there was even salad tongs, a bread knife and a gap for where the cake slice used to be.

'My, you have come prepared. Where's the candelabra? The string quartet?'

'Doesn't Jenna pack a picnic like this?' Alice asked as Olivia blushed, desperately trying to re-zip the panel.

'My wife knows how to appropriately cater for the situation. Did you bring any actual food?'

Olivia couldn't speak through her mortification, she unzipped the inner compartment to reveal individual pots. Lewis took each one out and laid them in a long row across his desk. 'This is quite the feast. The letter said to bring your own lunch, not feed the whole class. What exactly have you brought?'

'They're all permitted recipes, everything is from the online recipe database.' With only a few alterations and substitutions.

'We'll see.' Lewis snapped the plastic clips on the first pot. It was a simple green salad, with a small pot inside containing a fat-free Dijon vinaigrette. Lewis opened the smaller pot and sniffed at the contents. 'Is there oil in this?'

'No! I mean no.' She lowered her voice. 'Dijon mustard, rice vinegar and garlic, that's all.'

Lewis dipped his finger into the pot and tried it.

'Hey!' Alice said, but Olivia nudged her.

Lewis scrunched up his face, searching for the oil that

120

wasn't there, then put the salad down and moved onto the next pot.

'Ah ha,' he held the Scotch eggs out triumphantly. 'These are forbidden. High fat, deep fried.'

'No, they're not. I used turkey mince and baked them in the oven. There's also a carrot salad soaked in orange juice and caraway seeds, beetroot hummus, some courgetti in lime and coriander, a black bean and sweet potato salad, and fruit kebabs with berry coulis for dessert.' The whole room was paying attention now, trying to see inside each pot as Lewis undid them. The mingled scent of the citrus and spices escaped as soon as the lids released, sending everyone's salivary glands into overdrive.

'It's not suitable to bring complex dishes to the Re-education Programme,' Lewis said once all the boxes were open on his desk.

'Surely she's found a high level of enjoyment from creating these dishes?' Dev asked and Lewis scowled at him.

'There's far too much food for two, even three, people here,' he said. 'Your portion control clearly needs a lot of work.'

'Aren't they all foods we can eat as much as we want though? Didn't you just say we were supposed to have ten portions of fruit and vegetables a day?' Bronwyn asked.

'That's what I heard him say,' Tom agreed.

'That's not what I, I mean, you're ...' The only colour more vivid than Lewis's face was the pot of beetroot hummus. 'You have half an hour for lunch, be back here by one thirty.' He stormed out, slamming the door behind him.

'That looks amazing.' Dev abandoned his pack of sandwiches.

'Did you really make all of this?' Bronwyn joined them.

'She did, Liv's an incredible cook. Good job, because I'm terrible, I burn water.'

'Your lunch makes my sandwiches want to hide in shame,' Dev said.

'No shame here, we'll leave that to Mama M,' Alice said.

'Feel free to help yourself. As Lewis pointed out, I tend to overcater.' Olivia offered them plates. 'I just hope someone shares with Danny.'

'I'm sure they will,' Alice said.

'Yeah, we're all in this hell-hole together,' Bronwyn agreed. 'Though I doubt anyone has brought a picnic as good as this. It smells delicious.'

'Tastes divine, I promise.' Alice loaded her plate up with spoonfuls of everything.

'If anybody else would like some, you're more than welcome,' Olivia addressed the room; several took her up on the offer, a few looked tempted but remained in their seats, while the rest kept their heads down, focused on eating their lunch and avoiding any possible association with her and her food. On other days that would have stung, brought back memories of her shunning, but seeing everyone tucking into her food allowed the past to fade into the background. She made up a plate for Tom then served herself some of the leftovers, scooping up the last of the salads floating in pools of dressing at the bottom of the pots.

Alice and Dev dragged seats over and they all sat together.

'Have you been on one of these before?' Alice asked Dev between bites of Scotch egg.

He glanced around the room but nobody was paying them attention. 'Yeah, when I worked in London. I was too questioning over the government plans to change the

National Child Measurement Programme and introduce more regular monitoring. I had to be reminded that Mother knows best. Which she does, clearly,' he sounded genuinely convinced but gave them a mocking smile.

'Of course she does, where would we be without dear Mother Mason?' Alice said and Olivia almost choked on her courgetti. 'Are you all right, Liv? Something go down the wrong way?' Alice smacked her on the back.

'Behave,' Olivia whispered, her eyes streaming with tears.

'Moi? Always!' Alice tilted her head and smiled at Dev.

'She's got a point,' Tom said in a not-so-quiet voice. 'In my day we made our own decisions on what was best for us. It's called self-responsibility. People today could learn a thing or two about that. Stop expecting everything to be safe and risk-free, that's not life, it's not real.'

'He's right, we all know what's best for us,' Bronwyn added. 'It's up to us to decide if we want to do that.'

Olivia shuffled in her chair, leaning back from the group. There was no way this room wasn't bugged.

'Don't worry, my gal. I'm old, no one listens to me. Even if they did, what are they going to do? Hurry me on my way to being with my Rita again? There's worse fates than that. I might even voluntarily sign up to the Societal Evolution Programme. Cheaper than going to Switzerland.'

'Does anybody want the last fruit kebab?' Olivia jumped up to collect the remains of the picnic, steering the conversation away from the subject with the distraction of food; a tactic that always worked.

'If you'll excuse me, I need to visit the facilities.' Dev gave her back his empty plate, collected his bag and slipped out of the classroom.

She cleared everything away, repacked the backpack

123

and wiped her fingers on a napkin, but they were still sticky from spilled vinaigrette.

'I need to go and wash my hands.'

'I'll come too,' Alice said a little too eagerly.

Olivia opened the heavy door to the gender-neutral bathroom and stopped at the sight of Dev standing in front of the sinks, an injection pen in one hand, his shirt raised to expose a well-defined torso.

'I take back every gym complaint I've ever had,' Alice whispered.

A drop of liquid hung suspended off the tip of the needle and a strong smell like metal and oil filled the air.

'I'm sorry.' Olivia stepped backwards.

'It's okay,' Dev said. 'Come in, I'm not getting high or anything.'

Alice pushed her way into the bathroom, dragging Olivia with her.

'I'm diabetic, it's just my insulin injection,' Dev explained

'I thought they said they'd eliminated diabetes?' Alice perched on the edge of the sinks, watching with fascination.

Dev snorted and pressed the needle into his side, Olivia looked away, catching sight of her paling reflection in the mirror. Were the day's horrifying sights never going to end?

'That's what they're telling everyone,' Dev said. 'Sounds good doesn't it? What they mean is type two. Anyone with diet-related diabetes has been *magically* cured. Take away their access to anything remotely sweet or unhealthy and their weight will go down, and hey presto, the diabetes goes away. Nobody wants to talk about us type ones, though. Going sugar-free does nothing if your pancreas has packed up and refuses to make insulin.'

There was a click-click-click as Dev depressed the button and seconds later he removed the injection pen, recapped the needle and put it back in its case.

'That's why they renamed it. Apparently, now I no longer have type-one diabetes, I have pancreatic fatigue syndrome. Great name, right? My pancreas is just a little tired, that's all. I'm sure with rest and some "Mother Mason Can Do" attitude it will perk right up and start producing insulin again for the first time in twenty-five years.' Dev shoved the kit back into his bag. 'I'm sorry, I shouldn't have said that, I didn't mean it. It's just after all our Re-education *I'm* a little fatigued.'

'Understandable.' Alice reached out and touched Dev's arm.

Olivia glanced around at the other bathroom stalls, checking for feet beneath doors.

'It's fine, there's no one else here,' Dev said.

There shouldn't be cameras either, bathrooms were meant to be off limits, but who really believed that?

Olivia washed her hands while Alice, who mysteriously no longer needed to use the toilet, went back with Dev.

As Olivia left the room, she was forced to stop for two workmen in dusty overalls. They carried a short metal bunk bed between them and she had to squeeze against the wall as they pushed past, grunting under the weight of the frame.

'Mind your back,' one of them said to her.

'What are you doing here?' Lewis shouted and she jumped.

'I was only—'

'Not you! Get back to class. You.' He pointed to the men. 'The beds go in the north wing, this is the east. Follow the signs, it's really not that complicated.'

The men muttered under their breaths but returned the way they'd come, pushing back past her. They were halfway down the corridor when another two appeared carrying a second child-sized bunk.

'Not this way.' Lewis waved them back. 'The dormitories are in the north wing. Do I have to do everything around here?' He stormed after them.

Alice and Dev were chatting when Olivia returned, but she didn't join them. Instead she stood by the window and looked out at the facing wing. The building was covered in scaffolding and white builders' vans parked in a long row outside. She counted five men drilling into the walls, fixing long metal bars over the window.

She didn't call out for Alice, didn't react in any way that would bring her or Dev over. Instead, she watched as more men retrieved bunk beds from a large lorry and carried them inside.

Lewis returned and the room fell silent. They retook their seats and focused on the next video of the presentation, but all Olivia could see were the iron bars and the beds, and the future rushing towards her.

Chapter Thirteen

The rumbling sound of the treadmill filtered into Olivia's dreams, and her already frantic nightmares shifted so that she was running through an endless forest, calling for Matthew and Mia, but never getting further than the one metre the treadmill allowed. All the time Lewis and Mother Mason were gaining on her, ready to drag her back to Rigby Hall.

She woke with the sound of the treadmill still haunting her, but reality dawned and the noise remained. Danny must be downstairs, already getting in his steps. He'd said little about his Re-education the day before and the children were equally uncommunicative about Captain Fit. Everyone was silent for the car journey home and they stayed close to each other for the rest of the evening.

Taking advantage of the warm space Danny had left behind, she rolled over to discover he was still there.

The only source of illumination came from the grey dawn light that seeped in around the blind and the glowing neon of her bedside clock: 5.09 a.m. What kind of burglar broke in to use a running machine when he could go to the gym for free?

'Danny.' She shook him hard but he slept on, oblivious. There was a beep as the runner increased speed. 'Danny!' she said louder but she might as well have used a loudhailer for the good it did her.

She flipped back the warm safety of the duvet and found the cold floor with her bare feet. Walking on tiptoe, she edged towards the door and opened it. A rectangle of light spilled in from the hallway, stretching across Danny's face, but still he slumbered on. With more courage than she knew she had, she stepped out onto the landing, the floorboards creaking under her weight. She froze, holding her breath as she waited for a change in the constant hum of the machine, but it continued on unabated. Mia's room was closest and she, like Danny, slept deeply, her Captain Fit doll clutched to her.

Matthew's room was across the hall and she edged her way to it, peering over the banister for any sign of the intruder. Maybe if she gave him her HealthHub he could get her steps up for the day.

Her fear shifted to one of a different variety when she saw Matthew's empty bed, his covers kicked back. Surely, he couldn't be the mystery runner? He knew he wasn't allowed on the treadmill. She hurried down the stairs and found him sprinting like he was being chased, his face flushed bright red, his hair dark with sweat.

'Matthew? What are you doing?'

His flush paled when he saw her and he stumbled, moments from falling; she threw herself across the room, snatched the red dead-man's cord and ripped it away. The treadmill stopped with barely enough time for her to grab him and they hit the ground together. She held him tight, their breathing ragged, both getting their cardio workout for the day.

'Baby, why are you on the treadmill?' she asked when her adrenalin subsided enough for her to speak.

Matthew's shoulders shifted into a shrug.

'You know it's only meant for grown-ups.'

He mumbled something unintelligible but two words stood out. Rigby Hall.

'What did they tell you at Rigby Hall? Did they say you should be using a treadmill? Because that's not true, you get plenty of exercise with PE and football, and now cricket club. Daddy uses this because it's often too dark when he gets home.' That and the fact he could run and watch TV at the same time.

'Talk to me. Tell me what they said.' She led him to the sofa and they sat down close together, her arms still tight around him.

'They said we had to help our families stay fit and healthy, that we had to make sure we reach our family steps every day, or else . . .' he pressed his face against her.

'Matthew, we always reach our fitness goals.' Even if it meant her or Danny staying up late on the treadmill. The way Matthew was doing now. Was this the example they were setting? 'Look at me. It is not your responsibility to keep anyone else healthy, do you hear me? The only person you need to think about is you and you don't have to do that on your own. Daddy and I are here to help you make good choices.'

He didn't look convinced.

'The people on the course might have said some scary things, but we can't let fear control us. That only makes us feel bad and it doesn't help anyone. How do you feel when you're playing football?'

'Happy. Especially when I score a goal.' His face lit up.

'How did you feel today on the treadmill?' She still had the red cord balled up in her fist.

'Bad.'

'Which do you think is better and healthier for your body?'

'When I'm happy?' He looked up at her with a painfully hopeful expression.

'Exactly.' She kissed his forehead. 'If you're feeling good and you're getting exercise at the same time, that's a winning combination, that's how you make a healthy, happy body.'

'I'm hungry.' Matthew's stomach gurgled in confirmation.

'I'm not surprised. Let's get you some breakfast and we'll enjoy the peace before your sister gets up for school.'

Chapter Fourteen

'Careful with the knife, Mia,' Olivia said as Mia hacked at a piece of celery.

'Mummy, I'm always careful.' Mia grinned at Olivia with her child's supreme confidence, not looking down as she cut another piece, the safety knife millimetres from her fingers.

'Just watch what you're doing.' She wanted to raise a strong, confident, capable daughter, she just hoped they would both survive the process.

Danny had taken Matthew out after school for a fruit smoothie and a 'father–son' chat as he put it, leaving her with some 'mummy–daughter' time. After hide and seek, card-making and jigsaws, Olivia had spent an exorbitant amount of time plaiting pink wool into Mia's hair so she could look like Bronwyn, her new style icon. Now, Olivia wanted a quieter option and cooking had seemed like a good idea; at least Mia was sitting down for a while, but even this was taking more patience than she had after a too-long day.

'Remember, cooking is fun but we have to stay safe; that means watch out for sharp knives and hot things.'

'I know, Mummy, I am five.' Mia rolled her eyes and Olivia had to fight the urge to do the same.

'Here you go, Kit, have a nice healthy piece of celery.' Mia dropped it onto the floor for the cat to nudge with her nose but it took less than a second for Kit to dismiss it as unworthy of her attention. She bumped up against Olivia, miaowing with a pitiful tone.

'No, Kit, I already fed you.' She shooed her away. 'If you keep this up you're going to get fat.' She stepped over her to fill a saucepan with water, ready for their pasta.

'Don't eat that, you'll get fat, you're gonna have a heart attack,' Mia chanted in a sing-song tone.

'Mia!' Olivia whirled around so fast she slopped water across the floor; Kit let out a yowl and raced out of the room. 'Where did you hear that?'

Mia gave a small, half shrug, not looking up from the celery.

'This is serious. Who did you hear say that?' She put the pan down and went to stand beside Mia, who refused to look up, chopping the sticks of celery into smaller and smaller pieces.

'Was it at school? Did you hear it in the playground?' With Mother Mason's new laws, the rhyme had become redundant, but apparently it didn't stop the kids repeating it. Would they still be chanting it like Ring-a-Ring-a Roses in four hundred years' time?

She marshalled her tone, now the first shock started to fade. 'You know it's not a nice thing to say to anyone, even Kit. I shouldn't have said she would get fat, that was a bad word and very unkind; I should have thought before I spoke.' They always had to think before they spoke, even here in their home.

Mia pushed pieces of celery around the chopping board with the tip of her knife.

'It's all right, I'm not cross.' She swallowed, forcing her misdirected fury back down to its normal simmering location deep inside her stomach. 'Our words have power, they can help people or hurt them, that's why we have to make good choices. Every day.' She stroked Mia's hair, wishing she could impart more, say more, find something to protect her from all this.

'Mummy, what's a heart attack?'

It was a relief that Mia was completely focused on the chopping board; it gave Olivia enough time to take a deep breath and compose her face into a neutral smile before she took the knife away. She prayed that by the time she moved the board of celery she would know what to say.

She didn't.

So like most parenting moments, she winged it and hoped not to mess her daughter up too much. 'A long time ago' – well, before Mia was born, so literally a lifetime ago – 'people used to get sick from eating too much and not doing enough. They put on weight and it made their bodies work really hard, sometimes too hard, and their hearts stopped working. But things are ...' Better now? 'Different. Since Mother Mason brought in the new food and exercise laws people are much healthier.' Lewis had reiterated that enough times. People weren't dying any more, at least not in the same way.

A frown creased Mia's tiny forehead. 'Is that why you and Daddy go to the gym?'

'Yes, it's meant to ... I mean ... it helps to keep us fit and healthy.'

'So you're not going to have heart attacks?'

'No, sweetheart, we're not.'

'And Kit? She doesn't eat any fruit or vegetables and they said we'd die if we didn't.'

Olivia couldn't breathe, she stared at Mia unable to form words that didn't allow her rage to overflow again; all she could do was shake her head, back and forth, over and over.

133

'Who said that?' she whispered, but she knew, of course she knew. Less than twenty-four hours after Rigby Hall and both her children were living in fear. 'Was it the people yesterday?'

Mia's eyes swam with tears and Olivia felt her own build up, but she blinked them back. This wasn't her time to break down; that could come later.

'No, my love, you won't die but you might not feel very well, and you wouldn't have enough energy to play and run around and make your brain work. Fruit and vegetables give your body special vitamins and minerals that make you strong and smart.'

'Like Captain Fit?'

'Exactly.'

'Captain Fit to the rescue!' Mia pumped her fist into the air. 'A healthy body is a happy body! Yummy, yum yum, this food feels good in my tum-tum-tum!' She rattled the catchphrases off like a good little indoctrinated citizen.

'Captain Fit and the people yesterday want to make sure everybody is eating well and you are, I promise you are. You like Mummy's green pasta, don't you? And stir fry and lasagne and rainbow soup? They all have vegetables in them and they taste yummy.'

'Green pasta is my favourite!'

'I know, and when you eat them you're getting all the vitamins and minerals you need.' She brushed Mia's fringe out of her eyes. 'You don't have anything to worry about. You focus on playing and having fun and I'll make sure you have lots of yummy things to eat. Deal?'

Mia clambered onto her lap, tiny arms wrapping tight around her neck. 'Deal!'

Chapter Fifteen

Olivia stood in the gym's shower cubicle, the burning jets of water attacking her already aching body, but she didn't care. If only she could turn the temperature up high enough to burn out the fear and fury she carried with her every day since the trip to Rigby Hall. The pressure of the water pulsed against her skin in time with the vibrating bass music that reverberated through the wall, as the next exercise class suffered the same punishing routine she'd just dragged herself through.

'Bronwyn knows the owners of this cute little restaurant, she arranged a table for me and Dev,' Alice called through from the next cubicle. 'They had this incredible lemon pasta dish that you'd love.'

'Uh-huh.' It was the most enthusiasm she could muster. Danny noticed the change in her straight away but Alice was lost in the haze of her new relationship. Didn't every iconic love story start at a government Re-education Programme? The couple that gets together at Rigby Hall, stays together ... at Rigby Hall ... the bunk beds, the bars. It was all Olivia could picture.

'Liv?'

'Sorry, what?'

'What do you think we should do?' Alice was too high on life to be annoyed at repeating the question.

'About Rigby Hall?'

'Rigby Hall? No, about Tom. He's all on his own and stuck at home, I thought we could go over sometime. Bronwyn's offered to help get his garden sorted, apparently he's had a formal warning.'

'Oh, right.' The five of them had exchanged numbers at the end of the Re-education day and the new friendships were the only good things to come out of it.

'Sounds good,' her voice was flat. She cared, really she did, and she wanted to help, but at the moment it took a superhuman effort for her to simply get through the day. Whenever her anger crumbled under her fear, all she was left with was immense fatigue and helpless frustration. Her desire to give up, to collapse where she stood, was only deterred by the cold, hard shower tiles beneath her and the black sludge that collected around the drain.

The changing room buzzed with the hum of women's voices and she hoped they would leave quickly; the only thing worse than Alice's cheery babbling was the inane conversations she heard everywhere she went. Didn't they realise how awful things were? That the world was falling apart and they were too busy moaning about the reduction in the butter ration, the intrusive SmartShop deliveries, or worse, trivialities like what to wear to the Mother's Institute dinner. Why wouldn't they wake up and see what was happening? If they thought things were as bad as they could get, they were very, very wrong.

'You're not listening, are you?' Something finally broke through Alice's happy delirium.

'I am. I'll bring my trowel.'

'To help Tom with cooking? I'm not the chef, but even I don't think that's standard practice.'

'You want me to cook?'

'Yeah, Bronwyn thinks he might be struggling with

preparing meals too. I told her you were the woman for that.'

'Fine, sure, message me the details.'

The voices in the changing room had faded, the slamming of lockers and the squeak-bang of the door had stopped. Her skin soft and prune-like, she turned off the water and retrieved her towel. With the fabric wrapped tight around her body, she left Alice singing to herself, and walked out of the shower room, gaze averted from the long stretch of mirrors that banked the wall of sinks.

She hadn't waited long enough. A group of women huddled in the corner, their backs to her. She sidled towards her locker, trying to stay invisible, but a distorted voice made her pause.

'Mother Mason wants us to remember the people we've lost, the people who died from preventable illnesses.'

'Preventable illnesses', there was that same damn term again, it seemed to be bloody everywhere. The only thing preventable was Mother Mason's election, everything after that felt out of their control and everyone just accepted that.

Except for the person making the videos: they were doing something. They kept releasing the videos online, kept putting themselves at risk to call attention to what was happening under Mother Mason's regime. If these women were anything to go by, it was working.

They were so intent on the screen that they didn't notice her edging a little closer, trying to listen in.

'What about the people who disappeared in the night?' The distorted voice demanded. 'The ones who went to the shops and never came home? The ones who pleaded guilty in court and were never seen again? Mother Mason, where are they? What did you do to them? We demand to know!'

'You heard anything about Becky?' one of the women asked, but she was shushed as they tried to watch the end of the video.

'Their disappearances were preventable and we can prevent more losses. Do you want to know how? We can do one simple thing: bring down Mother Mason. End her tyrannical rule. Cut The Apron Strings. Join the Fray. Down with Mother Mason!'

The voice stopped and the women broke apart. 'I told you it was good.' The youngest swiped across her phone screen and looked up to see Olivia.

'How long were you standing there?'

'Not long.' She backed towards her locker as the group advanced on her. 'I just, I wanted . . .' Where was her fury now? Her desire to fight back? She was just like everyone else, so weak when it came to making an actual stand. 'I just got out of the shower,' she spoke to the floor, unable to meet their gaze. 'I didn't hear anything, I won't say anything.' I'm with you, she added silently, I want to join the fray. Except she didn't say any of that. As usual she remained silent, her words, her outrage, locked up inside her.

'How would you know there was anything to hear?' A dauntingly tall woman asked as they closed ranks around her, forcing her to step back, and back, until she felt the cold shock of the metal lockers against her exposed skin.

'Dev's booked a table for us to go to Moeder on Saturday.' Alice came out of the shower room, wrapping her towel around herself. She stopped at the sight of the group. 'What's going on here, ladies? Did I miss a party?'

'You weren't invited and neither was she.' The youngest woman jabbed a finger into Olivia's chest. 'We don't like nosy intruders.'

'Then you probably should conduct your business in a private place.' Alice touched the space where her necklace normally hung and she glanced down at its unexpected absence.

'Back off, Tina, it's cool.' The taller friend nodded to Alice and the cluster of silver tassels at her ears jangled with the motion. 'Sorry, we should go.'

'Go? Why?' Tina demanded and her friend whispered something that made the group disband.

'Some people have no manners,' Alice said after the women gathered their gear and left the changing room. 'So, what do you think about Moeder?'

'Huh?' Olivia's chest still throbbed from where Tina pushed her.

'For dinner? I've only heard good things.'

She needed to get dressed, to get out of there.

'I know it's pretty fancy, but if you can't enjoy a good meal at a government-approved restaurant, then what's the point of dating, right?'

'Right.' She messed up her first two attempts to unlock her locker and gave up completely after the third. Shivering hard, she slumped on the bench.

'What's wrong?' Alice asked, doing up the last of her shirt buttons and coming to sit beside her.

'Nothing,' she said.

'And the award for most unconvincing lie goes to . . .' Alice wrapped an arm around her and pulled her in for a hug. The physical contact was like a key that released the tension that had kept Olivia functioning for the past few weeks. She started to cry, not small, lady-like tears, but full on, soul-shaking, desperate sobs.

'What happened?' Alice held her tighter. 'Is it Danny? The kids? Something worse?'

'I ... can't ... do ... this ...' she managed between gasping breaths.

'Do what?'

'Any of it, the rules, the fear, the stress, the expectations, the consequences.' She found her voice and now she couldn't stop. 'I'm so scared, all the time, it's only getting worse and I can't take it, I really can't. I'm not like you, I'm not strong or capable, I can't do anything. I can't protect my family and it's only going to get worse, they're putting beds into Rigby Hall, they're making it into a prison for families. What if we get sent there? I have to protect Matthew and Mia, but I don't know how. Oh Alice, I don't know what to do, but I can't keep doing this, not any longer. Please, don't make me do this any longer. I'm so tired, I want to stop, I have to stop.'

'Shh,' Alice hushed. 'It's okay, it's going to be okay.'

'How can you say that?' She pulled away from her. 'It's never going to be okay, not ever. It's going to get worse and worse until we die.'

'No.' Alice took her shoulders and squeezed. 'I won't let that happen, I promise I won't. Things are going to change, we're going to make this country sane again. You just have to hold on a bit longer.'

'I can't.'

'Yes, you can, you have to.' Alice pulled her in close. 'I'm working on it,' she whispered. 'You have to give me a little more time. Please.'

'What—' she moved to see Alice better but Alice pressed a finger to her lips.

'It's going to be okay, trust me.'

140

Chapter Sixteen

'Liv, you look beautiful,' Danny said, his hand resting in the small of her back as they made their way down the cobbled street. She moved closer into him, the warmth of his body welcome despite the warm spring night. Up ahead, the soft, golden glow of candlelight spilled out of Moeder's art-deco windows.

They stopped outside the restaurant and she ran a hand across his chest, smoothing out the soft cotton of his shirt and plucking some fluff from his tie. 'Thank you. You look very handsome.'

'You know we could change our plans, go somewhere that's just the two of us. I mean, how often do we go out on a Saturday evening?' He kissed her cheek, small fluttering kisses, moving towards her mouth. She leaned into him, inhaling the sharp tang of his aftershave, and felt the temptation to keep walking, to disappear into the night together.

'No, we can't. Alice organised this to cheer me up. We can't bail on her and Dev.'

Reluctantly, he let go of her hand to open the restaurant door, but a heavyset man in a dark tuxedo stepped out of the shadows to open it for them.

'Good evening,' he said in a low, deep voice. 'Welcome to Moeder.'

The entranceway was dimly lit, the art-deco light fixtures barely bright enough to see by, but that only added to the element of illusion and mystery that surrounded the Mother Mason-approved restaurant. The gentle sound of a piano came from further inside, the melody floating under the murmur of voices and the hushed clink of cutlery on china. The sounds triggered a flutter of memory and the awful scene with her parents pushed itself to the front of Olivia's mind. The deep shame and devastation felt as fresh and painful as if it had only just happened.

'Relax, it's okay,' Danny whispered in her ear. 'We're here to meet Alice, remember? It's going to be a good evening, I promise.' He squeezed her hand and she allowed him to lead her forward.

An older woman in a crisp, black suit seemed to materialise out of the darkness. 'Good evening. May I take your names?' The maître d' gave them a polite, professional smile from behind her welcome desk.

'Hi, I'm Danny, Daniel Pritchard and this is my wife Olivia. We're joining Alice Evans.'

The woman checked her computer. 'Ms Evans and Doctor Anand are already here, let me swipe your IDs and then I can show you through.' The maître d' took the cards and scanned them into the system. 'Lovely. Anton will show you to your table. I hope you have a wonderful evening.'

They heard Alice's easy laughter before they saw her; she sat at a table in the middle of the room, with Dev beside her, his arm across the back of her chair. He whispered something into her ear and she blushed, only noticing their arrival when Anton pulled out a chair for Olivia.

'You're here!' Alice leapt up to hug them.

Dev shook hands with Danny and leaned in to kiss Olivia on the cheek. 'It's good to see you again. I doubt dinner can come close to your amazing picnic. Your wife is a talented cook,' he told Danny.

'Yes she is,' Danny agreed.

Alice and Dev sat back down and Anton held Olivia's chair for her; she enjoyed the experience of someone waiting on her for a change. He picked up her folded linen napkin, opened it with a flick of his wrist and settled it across her lap.

'May I get you a drink?' he handed them menus.

'I'll get a near-beer,' Danny said and Dev chimed in his agreement.

'A glass of your house white no-cohol for me,' Alice requested.

'I'd prefer water,' Olivia said, deciding she might as well save the calories for the meal.

Anton lifted the electronic notebook that hung over his shoulder and made a note of their order. The names of all the guests would be listed on Anton's device, their menu choices would be recorded and added to their files.

'Just to let you know, the specials today are roast pumpkin soup, served with crispy sage leaves; artichoke risotto on a bed of wilted spinach and my personal recommendation is the venison medallions served with a redcurrant jus; it is one of Mother Mason's favourite dishes. I will give you a few moments to peruse the menu.'

Olivia needed more than a few minutes. The menu was long and elegant, with words like foam and smoke and, despite years of cooking, there were ingredients she had never heard of. She drew on her dusty memories of French lessons to translate as much as she could, but some remained a mystery. The only familiar things were the red, yellow or green dots beside each dish.

'Looks amazing, doesn't it?' Alice asked.

'It does. I don't know where to start.' Her mouth watered

at every description she read; she couldn't make up her mind.

Anton returned with their drinks and Danny took a long chug from his alcohol-free beer and wiped the foam from his mouth. 'Liv says you're a doctor,' he said to Dev. 'Where do you work?'

'I'm at the hospital.'

'He saves lives.' Alice squeezed his arm.

'Not really, not any more, there's no need since Mother Mason has reduced all illness rates and number of fatal conditions.' Dev trotted out the line they'd heard more than once during the Re-education Programme and Olivia's celebratory mood dissolved faster than the ice cubes in her drink.

'There must be work still do. People will always get hurt,' Danny commented.

'And sick,' Dev said so quietly Olivia wasn't sure he had actually spoken.

'Are you ready to order?' Anton never seemed to be far away. He stood with his electronic notebook poised. 'Ms Evans?'

'Can I please have the bruschetta, followed by chicken cacciatore, no oil and just a few olives?'

'Dr Anand?'

'I'll get the scallops, the steak, rare, with a jacket potato,' Dev said.

'Do you want to use some of your butter ration on the potato?'

'Sure, why not.'

'Mr Pritchard, what can I get for you?'

Danny stared down at his menu, lips pressed together.

'I'll have the terrine, then the monk fish with steamed vegetables and mashed potato, please.'

Anton slid the small silver stylus across the screen.

'The potato contains milk and butter; it will be deducted from your next week's ration.'

'That's fine.' Danny sounded resigned.

'And for you, Mrs Pritchard?'

How had everyone already picked what they wanted? It all sounded so good. She scanned the menu again, trying to choose something from the rows and rows of delicious dishes. Two stood out from the rest and her stomach gave an approving rumble. 'I'll have the crab salad and the sweet potato ravioli, please.'

Anton entered the order but a harsh beep sounded from his notebook. The diners in the room stopped talking and there was a pause of expectancy. This couldn't be good.

'I'm sorry, Mrs Pritchard,' Anton said with a quick, apologetic smile. 'The butter and cheese in the sweet potato ravioli exceeds your weekly allowance. You will need to choose something else. Something with a green dot, may I suggest?'

How could she have been so stupid? Ravioli was a ridiculous choice, it was full of fat. The red dot proved that. There was no way her calorie allowance would cover it.

'I, uh, I—'

Her face felt hot as she stared at the menu. She couldn't focus on anything other than the red dots, that stood out like drops of blood across her menu. The rest of the diners remained in an uncomfortable silence, the weight of their judgement made her want to shrink beneath the table. Why did she always mess everything up?

'Liv, you could get the chicken on wild rice, it's one of your favourites.' Danny pointed to a dish halfway down.

'That sounds delicious,' Alice said. 'Especially if you get a side of Savoy cabbage with nutmeg.'

'Perfect,' Olivia said, her voice too high, 'I'll have that. It's what I meant to order.'

'You know what, I think I'll get that too.' Alice closed her leather-bound menu and held it out to Anton.

'You don't need to do that.' She met Alice's gaze.

'It's okay, I want to. You know I always get dish envy, this way I won't.'

They smiled at each other as Anton tapped on the touch screen pad, the stylus making a loud click-click of judgement. 'Can I get you anything else? Crudités, bread sticks? No? Let me know if you change your mind.'

'A toast.' Alice raised her glass as soon as he left. 'To good friends and good food.' Her words broke the quiet and the restaurant resumed its pleasant ambiance of polite murmuring.

They clinked glasses. Olivia's water was the perfect cure to her horribly dry mouth. The addition of a slice of cucumber and a sprig of mint heightened the taste experience far beyond anything she could get straight from the tap.

'Alice tells me that the two of you went to school together,' Dev said.

'A lifetime ago.'

'Not that long.' Alice gave her a meaningful look.

'Right, practically yesterday.' Two kids, a marriage and a business ago, not long at all.

'What was Alice like at school?'

'A menace.'

Alice had terrorised the school and the teachers, questioning every rule, fighting every injustice, refusing to accept what she was told until she had proven the truth, the hard way.

'Um, no, I don't think so,' Alice countered. 'As I

remember it, you were the one with the big ideas, I just acted on them.'

'That sounds about right,' Danny said. 'Watch out, mate, when the two of them set their mind to something, there's nothing in this world that can stop them. Take it from a seasoned expert, get out of the way and let the storm pass, it's the only way you'll survive.'

'Hey!' she and Alice exclaimed, but she had the advantage of being close enough to swat his arm.

'Like it's not true?' he said, teasingly.

She felt her face warm; he might have a point.

'Where did you go to school?' she asked Dev, shifting the spotlight off them.

'London. I only moved up three months ago.'

'Oh? What made you decide to move?' Danny asked, voicing Olivia's concerns as her skin prickled with warning. It was hard to trust anybody these days, especially newcomers.

'They were reshuffling the hospital departments and I volunteered to go.'

'Why Norwich?' Danny asked. He said it as if he was casually interested, but Olivia could hear the hint of interrogation. Alice was family and they weren't going to let anyone hurt her.

'Honestly? Money. It's cheaper to buy a house here and I'd had enough of the city hustle; I wanted a slower life.'

Their starters arrived and conversation paused as everyone tucked into their food. Olivia's crab salad was divine, the sharp, spicy dressing combined with the natural sweetness of the crab in a perfect combination. She closed her eyes, trying to pick out each individual flavour: lemon, chilli, dill ...

'By the end of the week Olivia will have recreated her

meal at home.' Alice jarred her out of her contemplation and she blushed; it was true, she couldn't help it.

'I blame my grandmother, she's the one who taught her to cook,' Alice explained to Dev.

'Correction, she tried to teach both of us, I was the only one who wanted to learn.'

'Liv was brought up on a never-ending stream of microwave meals; learning to cook was the only way she got anything decent to eat.'

It was also the only way to get her parents to sit down with her for more than five minutes, ten if she was lucky. Most of the time it was Alice who benefited from her cooking and baking. Alice the actual orphan, as opposed to her, the work-orphan.

'Nana Ivy was the best cook ever.' Olivia couldn't think of her without remembering the warmth of the kitchen, the soft hugs, the delicious cakes and the tins always full of home-made biscuits.

'Tell me about it, I miss her apple—'

'Salad,' Olivia interjected before the word pie could venture into this public space. 'She was such a healthy cook.'

Alice raised an eyebrow and it was all Olivia could do not to burst out laughing. Nana Ivy had added butter to everything, literally everything. *There isn't a dish known to man that can't be improved by a bit of butter*. The words echoed inside her head as loudly as if Nana Ivy was still with them. Not that it did her any harm, she lived to ninety, staying busy and active in the community as the president of their old Women's Institute. It was her shoes Jenna now tried, and failed, to fill.

Tears came to Olivia's eyes. Other than Alice, Nana Ivy was the closest thing she had to family, until Danny. She tried to discreetly wipe them away, but Alice was in floods too and they sniffed and snuffled at the table, until they had to admit defeat and excuse themselves to the ladies'.

The toilets were more luxury spa than public convenience. The marble walls and floor should have been cold and echoey but there was a gentle warmth created by the soft lighting and tastefully decorated furnishing. With the sound of waves and the scent of pine trees and sea salt, it was like being on holiday. Olivia perched on the edge of the chaise longue as Alice rooted through the basket of complimentary toiletries, trying to find something to salvage their make-up. It was like having their own personal cosmetics counter, with lotions and potions, perfumes and even mouthwash, all from designer brands Olivia had only ever seen in magazines.

'I miss Nana so much.' Alice discovered a small packet of facial cleansing pads and held them out to Olivia.

'I know.' Olivia joined her in front of the washbasins and wiped away the remains of her mascara. 'I wish she was still here.'

'I don't, there's no way she'd cope with . . .' They glanced back in the mirrors to the toilet stalls and the sound of tinkling water coming from one.

'She would hate this place. "They're charging how much for a piece of chicken and a couple of carrots?" It's okay, Nana,' Alice looked heavenwards, 'we're making the most of the added extras.'

She squirted some of the expensive hand cream into her palm and held the bottle out for Olivia. The thick lotion was smooth and fragrant; it felt like a mini-massage, soothing her dry, cracked skin.

'She would have been a hundred and three this year.'

'And loving every minute.'

'More like getting herself into a heap of trouble,' Alice whispered and Olivia laughed.

'Like grandmother, like granddaughter.'

Alice drew herself up. 'I take that as a compliment.'

'You should.' She leaned over and gave Alice a quick hug, but they got tangled up, her dress caught on Alice's and as they broke apart, a button tore her blouse.

'No!' Alice lurched after it as it bounced and rolled across the tiled floor.

'I'm so sorry.' She bent down, following Alice's lead to search the floor.

'Where is it? Where is it?' Alice's voice was high with panic, an unusual emotion for her.

'It's okay, we'll find it, or I'm sure there's a spare inside your top. There must be a sewing kit in the basket, I can reattach it, you won't break the Decency Law.'

'I'm not worried about any stupid Decency Law.' Alice whirled around and they collided heads. The blow brought more tears to Olivia's eyes and she staggered back.

'Ow.' She clutched her forehead, but Alice kept moving, scrabbling across the marble floor, searching with her hands.

'It's just a button.'

Alice ignored her, only pausing when the woman in the cubicle came out.

'I can always put a small stitch into your shirt for now,' she said as the woman hurried out, having washed her hands remarkably quickly.

'I don't care about the shirt, just go back to the table. I'll be there in a minute.' Alice crawled to peer under the chaise longue. It was highly unhygienic and Olivia was about to stop her when she spotted a small black disc caught in a groove between the floor and the wall.

'Found it!' She swooped down and picked it up. 'No, wait, this isn't it.' The button had a small black square attached to the back and she peered closer, making out a tiny shiny lens in the centre.

'That's it.' Alice snatched it out of Olivia's palm and stuffed it in her bag.

'Alice—'

'We should go and sit down, the men will wonder where we've got to.' She pushed past, going straight to the door.

'But your top—'

'Forget it.' Alice rushed out, unconcerned about her partially exposed neckline.

Before Olivia could follow, three women pushed their way into the bathroom, delaying her long enough, so that by the time she reached the table, Alice was laughing and joking with Dev and Danny.

'Everything all right?' Danny asked, as Anton withdrew her chair for her.

'She's fine, just hungry. Dev was telling us about his family,' Alice said, a bright, brittle smile in place.

'When you come from a big family, there's always tales to tell,' he explained and Alice laughed more enthusiastically than the comment warranted.

'Are you sure you're okay?' Danny whispered to Olivia as Anton placed their main courses in front of them.

'I've got a bit of a headache.' That wasn't a lie, her forehead throbbed from the collision and her mind ached as she tried to arrange the information into an order that made sense. With all the viral videos, it didn't take a genius to figure out why someone wore a hidden camera. Alice was a member of CTAS and she'd kept it a secret all this time.

Chapter Seventeen

'I want in,' Olivia said, the moment Alice opened her front door the next morning.

'Of course you can come in, you can always come in, just not today.' Alice barred her entry. 'Sorry, I have lots of work to do.'

'That's not what I meant and you know it.' She pushed her way into the front hall she knew so well. Most of her childhood had been spent in this house, playing with Alice, learning to bake with Nana Ivy, escaping the emptiness and emotional void of her own home. The decor might be more modern now, but the smell of floor polish, freshly cut flowers and apple pie still seemed to linger in the air, if only in Olivia's memory.

'Please, after you ... do make yourself at home.' Alice closed the door behind them, shutting it harder than was necessary.

'It's you, you're—'

'Stop!' Alice caught her arm and dragged her down the hallway towards her office.

'What are you doing? I know you're—'

'Shut up. I have something to show you in my office.' Alice shoved her into the cluttered room, barely avoiding one of the precariously stacked towers of clutter.

'Stop stalling, I know—'

Alice closed the door behind them, flicked a switch on

the wall which didn't seem to do anything except allow her to relax.

'You're the one making the videos for CTAS,' Olivia said before Alice could palm her off again. 'I saw the button camera. It was you that recorded the footage from the supermarket.'

Alice laughed. 'Don't be ridiculous, of course it's not me, you saw the video, it was from about ten different angles. How can I possibly have filmed that? The camera is something I'm trialling for a client, they would be furious if I lost it. That's why I panicked.'

'I don't believe you, you're CTAS.'

'Don't be ridiculous, me? You know I can barely organise myself, let alone a rebellion. Are you feeling okay? How's your head? I think you must have hit it pretty hard last night, maybe we should get you checked for concussion.'

'Don't. Don't do that, don't make out that it's all in my head.'

'Not in your head, but maybe a head injury.'

Olivia crossed her arms and gave Alice the cold, hard stare she reserved for the children when they were telling white lies and half-truths. Alice sighed, deflating as her forced joviality left the room.

'Liv, leave this alone, please. You don't know what you're asking.'

'Yes, I do. Tell me the truth. Are you the one making videos for CTAS?'

Alice picked up a pile of papers from the desk, dumped them on the floor and leaned against the glass top. 'If I tell you this, then that's it, you can't go back.'

'To the way things are right now? I don't want to go back, I need to move forward.'

Alice held her gaze, assessing how sure she was. There

153

must have been something that satisfied her because she sighed. 'Yes.'

'Yes? You're the organiser of CTAS? You made the videos? Oh, Alice ...'

'Liv—'

She stepped forward and hugged her tight. 'That's amazing.'

'You think so?' Alice seemed surprised. 'I'm not the leader, though, I'm just one member of a very big, nationwide organisation, but that's all I can tell you, so please don't ask me anything else.'

'Don't ask anything else? Do you think I'll just go away and pretend I don't know? Alice, this is incredible, you're actually doing something, you're fighting back. I want to help.'

'No, that's out of the question. I don't want you involved.' Alice adopted the same forceful posture she'd had earlier, her arm crossed, unrelenting, as though the matter was resolved.

'Too late. You got me involved when you filmed a shopping trip we went on and then put it online.'

'I'm sorry about that.' Alice lost some of her determined stance as she worried at the pink threads on her necklace, shredding them so they became even finer. 'I didn't know Becky was going to be arrested, if I had I would have made sure you were nowhere near. Our informer let us down on that one.'

'I appreciate you're trying to protect me, but who's protecting you? If they catch you it's not going to be a trip to Rigby Hall or a spell in the Shame Box. They'll put you on trial for everyone to see and then they'll ...' *Kill you* hung silently between them.

'They're not going to arrest me. I'm careful, and the

footage from the supermarket was from a few CTAS members and our planted cameras. I know what I'm doing.'

'You have been doing it long enough.' It hadn't been meant as an accusation, not entirely.

Alice blushed and busied herself with moving more junk off her desk. 'I'm sorry, but Liv, I had to do something, I couldn't just sit by.'

'Like I did,' she whispered. She needed to sit down but there was no hope of clearing any of the chairs, so she kicked a box of computer leads to one side and sank onto the floor. It didn't make much difference, she still felt like she was falling. 'I should have helped Becky. She begged me to, but I just ignored her.'

Alice made more space and joined her on the floor. 'There was nothing you, me or anyone could have done at the time, not without being arrested too. I hate that we have to be so hands off, so passive, but when CTAS tried fighting back, we got arrested, or worse. We had to find another way to hit back and the videos are working, people are finding the courage to talk about how wrong this all is. Until recently they've been too scared to even do that. It's slow progress, frustratingly slow, but we're getting there.'

'What can I do?' Her pulse raced faster as she ventured out of her comfort zone, but the tingle of excitement and hope spurred her on.

'Nothing, we've got it covered.'

Alice's words shot her down and her enthusiasm withered, but she wouldn't be put off so easily.

'No, I'm serious; I meant what I said, I want in. I'll wear a camera, I'll share videos, whatever you need. I can't sit and do nothing any more. I hoped things would get better with time, that the world would wake up and start making sense again, but that hasn't happened, it's just got worse.'

She had to make Alice understand, to realise how much she needed this. It wasn't a whim or a distraction for a bored housewife, this was her only hope. 'I have to do this for Matthew and Mia. This is not the life I want for them and if I don't act now, maybe it will be too late.'

'I know you love them, that you want to protect them, but they need you. I can't let you risk it.'

'Their future is worth the risk. I know there's not much I can do—'

'That's not remotely the issue. Danny would kill me if I let you get involved.'

'Danny doesn't get to decide this, it's my choice to make. Alice, please, let me help.'

Chapter Eighteen

This had to be some kind of joke, Olivia thought as the sound of pounding dance music filtered out through the solid wood door of the exercise studio. The Fighting Fit Gym could not be home to CTAS, the Cut The Apron Strings rebellion group.

'Are you sure about this?' Alice asked for the tenth time. 'You won't be able to change your mind.'

'I know.' She was as sure as she had ever been, so long as she ignored the nervous flutter inside her stomach. It's excitement, she told herself. 'I want to do this.'

Alice reluctantly took out her ID, knowing exactly where it was for once, and with a quick glance around, swiped the card through the entry machine. The red light on the keypad remained bright but she pushed the door and it opened for her.

The music grew louder, the fast bass matching the speeding beat of Olivia's heart as she stepped into the brightly lit studio. She kept her gaze low to avoid making eye contact with anyone already exercising, but the room was completely empty, theirs the only reflections in the mirrored walls.

'Where is everybody?' she shouted.

'You'll see.' Alice headed straight to the far corner of the room, their images growing larger as they approached the mirrors. 'Last chance to back out,' she said, almost hopefully.

No, Olivia thought, she had come too far and her nerves had definitely shifted to excitement.

Alice sighed and pressed a spot on the reflective glass that was already covered in smeared fingerprints. For a moment nothing happened, Olivia stared at her own wide-eyed reflection, then the mirror swung back to reveal a doorway. They passed from the loud, bright studio into darkness and her senses were overwhelmed by the smell of strong, rich coffee. The hit of caffeine made a path straight to her brain, shocking her into greater alertness, as the door clicked shut behind them.

'Welcome to Barre Class.' Alice extended her arms like a game show host revealing a much anticipated prize.

The large, open space was lit by soft twinkling lights hanging from the ceiling, but the star attraction was the illuminated bar that ran the length of the room. Rows of glass bottles lined the back wall; the liquid inside them glowed in jewel-like shades of amber, gold, red, blue and green. Alcohol. So much alcohol. Tracksuit-clad men and women gathered in small groups, laughing and chatting with a casual air that Olivia could only vaguely remember, while a four-piece band played a relaxed melody from the raised stage.

Two men, dressed in black gym T-shirts and tracksuits, moved to block their path.

'Frank, it's all right, Liv's with me.'

The heavily built man frowned down at them, his arms crossed, T-shirt taut over tensed muscles.

'Has she been vetted?' he asked, not moving out of their way.

'Of course. I'm hardly a newcomer, am I?' Alice's voice held a surprising amount of authority and Frank instantly backed off.

'Yeah, sorry.' He held out a hand to Olivia. 'Welcome to the club. Has Ali filled you in on the rules?' He kept hold of her hand, his massive palm engulfing hers.

'Not yet, but I will, don't worry,' Alice said.

'Have a good time, stay safe.' Frank released Olivia and she discreetly flexed her fingers, returning the blood flow.

'Ali?' She queried as they stepped past him.

Alice shrugged and set off through the centre of the bar, but Olivia hung back. All the patrons knew 'Ali' and they were all desperate for her attention. She greeted them like old friends, shaking hands, sharing jokes, and they toasted her with fancy cocktails, glasses of champagne and pints of beer. From the overall merriment and good humour, it seemed unlikely they were saluting her with de-alcoholised drinks.

Olivia felt the world spin and she hadn't had a sip of alcohol. For the past seven years she had been sweating her guts out in the exercise classes, no more than a few metres away, and here they were downing drinks and laughing at the rest of the poor suckers who were too dumb, too poor or too cut off to know this was happening next door. How could she have been so stupid? So naive? How could Alice not have told her? Told her about this super-secret, super-illegal place.

A lurch of sickness hit her stomach, like a hangover acquired from simply inhaling the alcohol fumes. What was she doing here? Alice had been right, this was a huge mistake, she should never have come. If Danny knew she was here, if anyone knew, she would be in so much trouble, far more than hoarding a box of illegal cookbooks. She edged back towards the door, but collided with Frank.

'Is there a problem?' He loomed over her.

'No.' Her voice was supersonic high. 'I forgot something, in my locker, I should—'

'Liv, I lost you, I thought you were behind me.' Alice bounded over, a glass of champagne in hand, despite it only being eleven on a Sunday morning. 'Do you want one? Lucy always has my usual ready, but I thought you might like to pick your own.' Her enthusiasm dwindled. 'Everything okay?' She looked from Olivia to Frank and back.

'You sure you vouch for her?' Frank asked gruffly.

'Of course, Liv's just a little overwhelmed, you know how people get their first time.' Alice dragged her away from Frank and into a quieter space. 'What are you doing? I warned you about this, I told you there was no going back.'

'I know, but I didn't expect this . . .' she gestured to the revelling patrons. 'Alice, if anyone finds out—'

'Yeah, yeah, prison, trial, death. I know the speech.' She knocked back her champagne, then catching herself doing it, stopped mid-glass. 'I should have trusted my instincts, this is why I never told you.'

'Yeah, who knew you were so good at keeping secrets? Other than everyone in this room, of course.'

'Well, you're part of the secret now, so you'd better pull it together,' Alice snapped. She took a careful, considered sip of her champagne and softened with the bubbles. 'I love you, Olivia, I would do anything to protect you, but you've crossed a line and you can't leave. You're here because of me and we'll both get in trouble if they think you're going to the authorities. Important people come here, people you do not want to piss off. Do you understand?'

She nodded, unsure if words of anger or fear would launch from her mouth if she dared to speak.

'The bar is the perfect place for us to meet, *everyone* has something to lose.'

Including her, she heard the implication in Alice's words.

'I won't let anything happen to you, I promise.' Alice glanced over to the booths on the far side of the room where groups of patrons sat drinking. Most were lost in their revelry, but a few were paying close attention to her and Alice's exchange.

'You have to convince them you're on board, all right? Just remember,' Alice linked their arms together, 'we're doing good work here. Five minutes ago you were excited to be a part of this. Well, now you are.' She led the way to a booth where three people clustered together, talking in low voices.

'Orders are for the arrest to take place during their next Mother's Institute meeting.' A man sat in the curve of the U-shaped bench. He clutched a beer but was too intent on the conversation to take a drink. 'Apparently, with the loss of the supermarkets, she's looking for new venues to make public arrests. Kate's key to the operation, we need to get her and her family out of the country as soon as—' He stopped speaking the moment he noticed their arrival.

'You're here!' A woman stood up, her pink braids swinging as she enveloped Olivia in a hug.

'Bronwyn? You're in CTAS too?' Through the mass of vivid hair, she saw Dev greet Alice with a kiss. 'Dev!'

He gave her a small wave and slid along the long curving bench so Alice could join him.

'Alice?' Olivia whispered.

Her best friend was suddenly, uncharacteristically silent.

How could this be happening? Was everything a lie? She thought Alice was the only person in the whole world she could trust. The only person who stood by her, stood up for her, especially when everyone turned their backs; but all this time, Alice had been lying too.

'So this is her.' The man on the bench did not look happy. 'Ali, we have protocols for inducting new people. Just because you like to think you're in charge, doesn't mean the rules don't apply to you.'

'Ray, chill. You can trust Liv, she's cool.' Bronwyn dragged her down onto the seat.

'Hmm, we'll see.' He drank a slug from his beer. 'So, Olivia Pritchard, housewife, stay-at-home mum to Matthew and Mia, doting spouse of Danny, are you sure you're in the right place?'

No, she thought. I'm really not.

'Knock it off, Ray. You chose to be here, nobody forced you to reveal your involvement. You could have stayed away like the others.' Alice's voice held a hint of warning.

'Someone has to make sure she's legit. The two of you might have gone to school together, doesn't mean the rest of us can trust her. Especially now.'

'I'm aware of the risks, I was the one who vetted you. I don't make mistakes when it comes to CTAS, do I?'

Ray looked ready to argue back but he reconsidered and took another drink of his beer instead.

Alice beckoned to a waitress who hurried across. 'Lucy, can we get a round of coffees?'

'I'll have another beer,' Ray said.

'Good try, but that was your second,' Lucy said. 'You'll have to wait until your next visit.'

'Can we get some chocolates too?' Bronwyn asked.

'Chocolate?' Olivia couldn't possibly have heard right.

'Handmade truffles, smuggled in from Belgium,' Dev explained but she barely took his words in, as she stared at Alice, hurt overlaying her questions and confusion. Not only had Alice been sneaking off to this place on her own, but she had been having chocolate? That was their thing.

162

They had spent hours lamenting life without it, but apparently, she was the only one going without.

'I couldn't tell you,' Alice spoke quietly, the words meant just for her.

'There's been an awful lot of that,' she retorted and Alice flinched.

Bronwyn fished her cherry out of her cocktail glass and popped it into her mouth. 'You must have lots of questions.'

She laughed, but it was bitter and hollow and only tightened the band of pain around her chest. Lots of questions? That was an understatement, but she wasn't sure she wanted the answers any more.

'You're all CTAS?'

'We pronounce it C-Tas, but yes, we are. We're your friendly neighbourhood revolutionaries, fighting injustice and evil dictators wherever we go.' Bronwyn raised her fist in a superhero pose.

'Wow.' It felt like an understatement. Olivia's brain hurt as she tried to rearrange everything she knew, or thought she knew. 'Alice said there's more of you, that CTAS is nationwide. What's your role in it?'

'Why would you need to know that?' Ray asked.

'Ignore him,' Alice said. 'He works for the government, he's used to questioning people.'

'You work for Mother Mason? Were you at Rigby Hall too? Where's Tom? Or Danny? I'm surprised Matthew and Mia aren't here for the welcoming committee.'

Bronwyn laughed as if she'd made a joke, but the rest of the table sat in an uncomfortable silence.

'Tom and Danny aren't members. Danny doesn't seem the rebellious type and because of his age, Tom's exempt from attending the gym. It's difficult to find an excuse for

163

him to come,' Bronwyn said, 'and bless him, he's not the most discrete of people.'

'Is that why you didn't tell me? You didn't think you could trust me?' She spoke to Bronwyn but the shot was meant for Alice.

'No,' Dev intervened, 'Alice kept you out of it because she wanted to protect you.'

Alice didn't say anything in her own defence.

'I didn't know about this place either,' he continued. 'I joined CTAS when I lived in London. When I moved up, I tried to find the local group, but their security is tight, thanks to Alice. You need to know someone to be invited in.'

'You're in charge?' she asked Alice who sat, pale and rigid, opposite her.

'Nobody's in charge,' Ray said. 'We work together, it's a cooperative.'

'Sure it is, Ray.' Bronwyn rolled her eyes. 'Although, thanks to Ali's videos, Norfolk CTAS has a lot more clout with London, they actually listen to our ideas now.'

'How long have you been doing this?' Olivia tried to keep her fury to a suppressed, simmering frustration but she was struggling not to vent.

'Seven years, give or take,' Bronwyn answered for Alice, who was now completely focused on the champagne in the bottom of her glass.

'Seven years?' How could Alice have lied to her for all that time? She thought they told each other everything.

'Just because the original Pink Apron Brigade disbanded didn't mean the rest of us gave up,' Ray said. 'We've been risking our lives, sacrificing everything while you and everybody else tries to pretend this isn't happening. Just because you know now, doesn't make you one of us.'

'That's enough!' Alice snapped. 'I told you it was okay for you to stay, but not if you're going to make this harder. Would you prefer to leave?'

Ray glared at Alice but Lucy's return halted their conversation. She placed steaming cups of coffee in front of each of them and the smell wafted up in white trails of scented vapour.

Olivia leaned forward reflexively, unable to resist breathing in the heady aroma.

'First time?' Lucy asked.

'You can always tell, can't you?' Bronwyn said. 'Can we get some sugar too?'

Sugar? Of course they had sugar to go with the jug of cream and plate of chocolate truffles. Lucy beckoned to Frank, a small, subtle gesture. He left his position on the door and went behind the bar to a painting on the wall of a bowl of fruit. He had his back to them for a moment but when he turned around he had a small wooden box clutched to his chest. With a wire-tight alertness, he came over to their table and gently placed the box down. One hand still resting on it, he waited while Lucy reached into the neckline of her T-shirt and pulled out a silver key on a long chain. She unlocked the box and he lifted the lid to reveal two compartments. One held rock-like brown granulated sugar lumps, the other a mound of fine white sugar.

Olivia had never thought she would see sugar again but it was right there. For the taking. The tasting. There was enough to make a small sponge, or some cupcakes. Definitely enough for some scones, maybe even a batch of brownies.

'Hands on the table.' Frank's voice made her jump. Without realising it, she had reached for the sugar, wanting to touch it, to dip her little finger in and taste it. Just to be sure it was real.

'Sorry.' She moved her hands back, interlocking her fingers together, squeezing until her knuckles turned white.

Lucy used the pair of silver tongs to serve everyone. 'Any for you?' she asked Olivia.

No, that should be her automatic response. Absolutely not. There was a time delay between her brain and her mouth and by the time she formed the word, Lucy had acted on Alice's nod and dropped a lump into Olivia's cup. It instantly disappeared, swallowed up by the dark liquid. Automatically, she picked up her teaspoon, dipped it into the cup and stirred, hearing the gritty sugar scratch against the sides. The teaspoon struck the china and sent out a light, ringing, joyful sound.

'Cream?' Alice asked, already pouring the thick liquid in. The single stream rippled through the dark coffee, lightening the colour to a golden caramel. Olivia stirred again, but didn't pick up her cup.

'Oh, that's good,' Dev said.

'Only the best.' Bronwyn held her coffee close, cradling it to inhale the perfect scent. 'Life's too short for anything less.'

With this company, it very well might be, Olivia thought.

Bronwyn helped herself to a white chocolate truffle and stuffed it into her mouth whole, casually chewing as though the action couldn't get her sent straight to prison.

Olivia couldn't bring herself to drink; she had to distract herself from the glossy, round spheres in dark, milk and white chocolate. It was all she could do to stop herself from reaching across and eating every single one. Okay, not every single one, but she had dreamt of one perfect milk chocolate truffle every day for the past seven years. Alice had claimed to do the same.

'I don't understand, how can this place even exist?'

'We have well-connected friends,' Alice explained. 'They don't agree with Mother Mason's agenda, but they're unable to act, so they formed CTAS as a way to unite those willing to fight. This place was built as a safe space where we could meet away from prying eyes. The bar came later when we needed to raise funds. It took some doing; we have to use all our connections to "import" the items we need. Thankfully, it's proved popular, because it's an expensive business fighting the system.'

'What do you do other than make videos?'

'Not enough,' Ray muttered.

'Thank you, Ray, you've made your views perfectly clear.' Alice barely kept her exasperation in check. 'Our chapter of CTAS focuses on fighting Mother Mason's propaganda. She's painted us as dangerous terrorists, threatening the safety of the nation, when she's the biggest danger we face. On some level everybody knows that, but the consequences of acting against her are so extreme, people are too scared to get involved. That's where we come in. Each video undermines her, forces everyone to pay attention and see what's going on.'

'Yeah, and how long have we been doing this?' Ray asked. 'How many members have been arrested? We should be doing more.'

'And we are, you know things are moving forward with the next phase, you just have to be patient,' Alice said, not sounding remotely patient herself. 'If we're going to enact lasting change, we need the public to see that they have no choice but to act. It's a slow process.'

'You're doing what you can, Ray.' Bronwyn touched his hand but he pulled away. 'We've saved lots of people, thanks to you. If it wasn't for your tip-off, Kate—'

'Don't talk about that in front of *her*, you all might trust her, but I don't.' He glowered at Olivia and she shrank down into the seat.

'There are other chapters of CTAS across the country doing different things,' Bronwyn filled the awkward silence, 'hiding people—'

'Does she really need to know all this?' Ray demanded.

'—liaising with our supporters outside of the UK,' she continued as if he hadn't spoken. 'Securing the import supply chains, tactical planning for the next stages of the rebellion. We work together, but there's a certain amount of autonomy.'

'And all these people are members of CTAS?' Olivia asked, looking out at the forty-strong legion of drinkers.

'Hell no,' Ray said scornfully. 'Most are a bunch of amateur thrill seekers here for the booze, caffeine and chocolate. They like to think they're doing something dangerous, but they're a load of entitled rich kids, with no idea of the real purpose of the bar. As far as the majority are concerned, this is an exclusive speakeasy for those wealthy enough to break prohibition. As long as they keep their mouths shut, everybody wins.'

'How do you know who's in CTAS?' Olivia didn't know who to trust any more. Including Alice.

'We devised a secret code, like our own special handshake, but way cooler.' Bronwyn flicked her hair, the beads clicking together and making the tassels at the end of each braid flare out. 'Join the Fray? Get it?'

Alice touched her necklace and Dev held up his wrist to display his bracelet. Ray made no move, but a tassel hung from the pen clipped to his jacket pocket.

There was only one person Olivia knew who would think to use accessories as a political statement. 'Your idea?' she asked Alice, trying to keep the admiration out of her voice.

'This is for you.' Alice slid a small velvet necklace box across the table to her but she couldn't bring herself to take it. 'I've had it for years,' Alice's voice wobbled with tears. 'I've wanted to give it to you every single day, but I didn't want to put you in danger.' She coughed to clear her throat. 'I hated lying to you,' she swallowed 'but it was the only way I knew to keep you safe. I'm glad you found the camera, that you asked to come here, but I'm scared for you too, because we're risking our lives simply by being here.'

'It's a risk worth taking,' Ray interrupted their moment, 'so long as people don't chicken out and bring us all down. Olivia, do I need to worry about getting arrested the next time I show up for work? Will the bar be raided within the week? It doesn't matter what kind of deal you do, CTAS is nationwide. You betray us and someone will come for you and your family.'

'That's enough, Ray.' Alice leaned over the table, her face close to his. 'You don't threaten her, not ever, because if you go after her, you go after me.'

Olivia had seen this Alice before, the little girl who took on the biggest bully in the playground on her first day of school. The bully had stolen a doll and was about to throw it onto the school roof. After Alice had finished with her, she had retrieved the doll and reduced the bully to tears; making a lifelong enemy in Jenna and a lifelong friend in Olivia.

Olivia reached over and rested her hand on Alice's, shocking her into looking away from Ray.

'It's okay, he's allowed to have doubts, he doesn't know me like you do, but he'll learn. Worst mistake they can make is to underestimate us, right?'

'Right,' Alice smiled, relief lighting up her face. 'Ray,

Liv's granted you a reprieve. I appreciate your contribution to the group, but CTAS is bigger than one person, no matter how much they may do. Remember that.'

Ray scowled at Alice, fist tightening around his pint. Looking for a distraction, something to break the tension, Olivia reached for the necklace box. Inside was a gold flower necklace with a white tassel suspended from the flower, the twin to Alice's pink one.

'I love it,' she whispered, removing it from the box and fastening it around her neck. It hung against her chest, cool at first then rapidly warming to match her body temperature. She rested her hand over it and Alice copied the gesture with her own necklace; they smiled at each other.

'Welcome to CTAS, you've officially "Joined the Fray".'

'Thank you. Now, tell me how I can help,' she said, reaching for a chocolate.

Chapter Nineteen

'All in favour?'

Olivia raised her hand obediently but had to stifle a moan as pain radiated up her arm, tweaking muscles she never knew she had. It was the day after her visit to Barre Class and, post-indulgence, they all had to attend a two-hour gym session with a private trainer. Apparently, it was the "Cardinal Cardio Rule". All attendees had to burn off the calories before they left. Now everything hurt. Sitting on the small, hard school chairs for the monthly PTA meeting didn't help the situation.

Jenna counted up the votes, not that there was a single dissenting voter among the group: Olivia and the other members knew what was expected. The school's Parent– Teacher Association ran a lot like CTAS. One person was visibly in charge, a couple acted like they wanted to be the boss, and everyone else just showed up and did what they were told. With CTAS, Olivia was happy to fall into the latter group, especially if it came with chocolate but, like most committees, there seemed to be an awful lot of discussion and very little action. Not that she minded. Hearing the rebels say the things she had harboured for years, the thoughts she had been too afraid to voice, was like coming up for air.

She tried to focus on Jenna's next proposal but it was hard not to be distracted by the delicious memory of yesterday's truffles. The way the chocolate cracked with a sharp snap and then the smooth, creamy centre that melted on her tongue. She could still taste the sweetness of the sugar and the darker, almost fruity tang of the cocoa beans. Her mouth flooded with saliva as she remembered the sensation of the chocolate turning to liquid in her mouth and her extreme reluctance for the moment to be over.

Up on the classroom wall, Captain Fit stood with his hands on his hips, glaring at her with disappointment. 'Get Fit! Get Happy!' he shouted into his little white speech bubble. After her chocolate and intense exercise, she was both of those things.

'You don't agree, Olivia?' Jenna asked and the parents around the table twisted in their tiny chairs to stare at her.

'I'm sorry, I was ... thinking of new ways to raise funds.' It wasn't a complete lie. She had spent the previous evening trying to come up with ways she could contribute to CTAS. Alice seemed determined to keep her out of the action, wouldn't let the group discuss anything important in front of her; but if she could come up with some ideas to help, maybe they would trust her.

'We're not up to that part of the agenda,' Jenna said, 'don't skip ahead.'

'Of course not. Please carry on.' She smiled passive-aggressively, all her hatred of their chairwoman channelled into the simple curve of her mouth.

'In case you were too distracted to listen, we were discussing something I would have thought was of extreme relevance and importance to you and your family, considering your recent visit to Rigby Hall.' Jenna returned her smile with a far crueller one of her own. 'The extra measures of daily weigh-ins for the children and monthly checks with the school nurse aren't proving to be as effective as Mother

172

Mason had hoped. Some parents still fall short of the basic standards required to bring up happy and healthy children. It's very sad, no matter how hard Mother Mason and her government try to protect us, there are some people who continue to think they know best.'

For their children? Olivia thought. Imagine that.

'Lewis says how tragic it is seeing the families pass through Rigby Hall, knowing that it won't make a difference to those most in need of help.'

Everybody around the table sneaked glances between her and Jenna, the weight of their judgement was enough to make her want to shrink, but the physical tension stored in her body refused to let her; instead the hot pain forged her will into a steely inner strength.

'I suppose he and Mother Mason have a ten-point plan on how to address such issues?' she said, tone friendly, but wishing Jenna pain with an intensity that only fuelled her hardening fury.

'I shouldn't really say, it's not been announced yet, but since Lewis works at Rigby Hall, he knows everything that's going on. I'm sure he would understand me sharing this with you, especially if it helps those most at risk.' Jenna didn't look away as she spoke, waiting for Olivia's reaction. 'Mother Mason is introducing a residential programme, to see if that can get through to the most difficult cases.'

The building work, the bunk beds, the bars on the windows, she had been right but the reality was still terrifying. At least she'd had time to process the idea. The shock of the new information broke through the other parents' carefully constructed facades and horrified gasps rippled through the room.

'It's so sad that it's come to this, but it's necessary. I'm glad that I've never needed such strict measures. I hate to think what will happen to children whose parents have already refused to conform.' Jenna pressed a hand to her heart as though she were genuinely concerned.

Everybody openly watched Olivia now, measuring how well she contained her emotions. The sign of a good citizen was the person who could fake it the best, the one who knew how to take every hurt and fear and pack it away neatly inside themselves, but she was full, there was nowhere left to hide the pain. She couldn't do it any more. She wouldn't.

'What exactly do you mean by conform?' she asked Jenna, her mask still in place, but her tone snapping with anger. 'Follow the rules? Do what we're told without question? How does that make us happy and healthy? We're not teaching our children how to love and respect their bodies, we're training them to be obedient minions, forcing them to give up their own right to consent before they even know what that is.'

The room took a collective, audible breath. Fleeting looks of understanding and shared outrage crossed every face before most resumed their masks, physically shrinking back as far as possible from her, but a father she barely knew turned his wrist to reveal a tassel attached to his watch and the mother opposite flicked her hair back, showing off her fringed earrings. They were such tiny signs of rebellion, so easy to miss, but so reassuring, now that she knew. The solidarity loosened the tight gagging feeling around Olivia's throat.

'If you want to know what the PTA should be focusing on, then we need to start showing our children how to decide what's right for them and their bodies. Right now, they don't understand choice or balance, especially when it comes to food, and that's our fault. We should do something about that.'

'Be careful, Olivia, that sounds an awful lot like treason. People who talk like that end up in worse places than Rigby Hall.'

'Yes, and I'm sure you and Lewis would be happy to arrange it. It's fine, Jenna, I'm just being hormonal and irrational, time of the month and all that. I don't have a clue what I'm saying. Please ignore me. I forgot for a second that fear is the best way to motivate people to make better life decisions. Thank you for reminding me how damn happy and healthy I am.'

Absolute silence met her words. She shifted her body, the pain had lifted from her, and she stretched out her legs, uncurling from the confines of the tiny chair.

'I will have to report this outburst.' Jenna added a note to her record of the meeting.

'Go ahead. Make sure you note down the details of your disclosure about the upcoming plans at Rigby Hall. Remember, Hook-Medwood is hyphenated.' The words came from somewhere disconnected from her brain and much closer to her heart. The old, familiar voice inside her head whispered for her to be quiet, to stay small, but it was only a whisper, not the loud, screeching terror she was used to, and that made it so much easier to ignore. She smiled at Jenna with a real sense of joy and only the vaguest concern over what she had done.

'You'll pay for this.' Jenna looked ready to throw herself across the table and stab Olivia with her fountain pen.

'I already am, I have been for a long time.' She stroked the silky tassel of her necklace. 'I just think we'd be a lot healthier and happier if we worked together, supported one another, instead of looking for ways to tear each other down. My life would be so much easier without the burden of all this shame. Wouldn't yours be?' She felt genuine sympathy as she spoke to Jenna. As chairman and president, her public profile was greater than most of them: she must feel the weight of it.

Jenna swallowed, and maybe Olivia was kidding herself, but for a moment she swore she saw the faintest glimmer of tears.

'We're wasting time.' Jenna drew a line through the last thing she had written. 'We need to move on. What's next on the agenda? Ah yes, our fundraising at the summer fete. Who's got some ideas?'

Olivia was the first to raise her hand.

Chapter Twenty

'I can't keep doing this,' Ray said to Alice as Olivia approached the booth in Barre Class. 'You don't know what it's like working there.' He had two empty pint glasses in front of him and they clattered over onto the table as he leaned towards Alice. 'I don't know how much longer I can stick it.'

'I'm sorry, I know you're in a horrendous position.' Alice didn't flinch at his close proximity; her voice remained calm, her expression impassive. 'If there was anything more we could do, we would, but right now this is the best option. You have to keep going, we need you there, you're the only one who can do it.'

Olivia hesitated, not sure whether to step forward and intervene. Her indecision brought her to a stop a few tables away, unintentionally allowing her to eavesdrop.

'You're not the one having to stand by and watch, and your damn cameras don't count.' Ray kept his voice low, but he was barely containing his anger.

She ought to walk away, to leave them to it, but Olivia couldn't deny a part of her was curious. Alice had kept her out of the loop of anything related to CTAS's plan and it was hard not to feel snubbed. Alice said it was for her own safety, but it felt like being on the outside.

'You always get to be one step removed from everything that's happening, you don't know how hard it is. They're arresting more and more people all the time; more than we can ever help. And Becky—'

'Liv!' Alice looked up and spotted her lurking. 'I've been waiting for you. Ray and I were just rounding things up.'

'No, we weren't,' he said, still leaning in close. 'We're not done here. You can't expect me to shut up and go away. I won't do it.'

'What else do you want from me? There's nothing else we can do, it's just a matter of time and patience. We're nearly there, you just have to hold on a little longer. You can do this, Ray, I believe in you.'

'You believe in yourself,' Ray spat and stormed out of the booth. 'It's all about the Alice show,' he muttered as he pushed past Olivia and marched out of the bar. Alice signalled to Frank to follow him, then sat back in the booth, her eyes closed.

'Everything okay?' Olivia slid onto the bench opposite.

'I never knew organising a rebellion meant managing so many people, especially ones who think they can do it better than you. This is not what I signed up for.'

'Anything I can do to help?'

Alice opened her eyes. 'Thank you, but no. This will work itself out, Ray's just getting a little edgy.' She rubbed her temples and forced a smile. 'What did you want to talk about? You sounded pretty hyper on the phone.'

Olivia's excitement bubbled back up, but Alice looked exhausted. Her eyes were tired and dull, as though she had been staring at a computer screen for too long. Maybe now wasn't the best time to tell her.

'It can wait.'

'No, I haven't seen you looking this excited in ages. Tell me.'

She took a breath, gathering her courage. 'I want to organise a bake sale.'

'A what?'

'Like Nana Ivy used to do to raise money for charity. We were brainstorming ideas for the summer fete during PTA last night and I remembered how much money they make.'

'A bake sale?' Alice repeated as though they were conversing in two different languages.

'Yes, it's ideal, you've got the clients and the ingredients and I have the experience. It's the perfect partnership.' She knew she was babbling, but she was too excited, and a little too manic, to slow down. Jenna's confirmation of the Residential Programme and their PTA confrontation had strengthened Olivia's determination to do something to help CTAS and this was it. 'I could make all sorts of things, cakes, cookies, biscuits—'

'Wait, I haven't had much sleep and right now one or both of us is having a pretty vivid delusion. I need coffee.' She signalled to Lucy who interpreted her desperate miming and brought two cups over, already made up with cream and sugar.

'Just think about it, you could order a brownie to go with your coffee. Chocolatey, gooey, you know you couldn't resist them. Other people would be the same, we could make a fortune.'

Alice held up a hand to silence her while she fuelled up on caffeine. Olivia took a sip too, it was perfectly sweetened, the rich cream counteracting the first bitter, earthy taste of the beans, followed by subtle hints of citrus and chocolate. It would be the perfect ingredient for her coffee and walnut cake.

'We can do this, I can do this.' She couldn't keep quiet any longer. If she was silent for too long, her thoughts strayed back to Rigby Hall and the bars on the windows, the child-sized bunk beds awaiting their new occupants. The old panic threatened to steal her energy and drive, so she ploughed on. 'It would be easy. Barre Class already has access to chocolate and sugar, the cream can be made into butter, and there must be a way to get eggs and flour.'

'We've tried having food before. Importing anything fresh never works, we're limited by the complicated shipping routes and delays.' Alice dismissed her proposal without properly considering it. 'Everything went bad or stale by the time it reached us. That's why alcohol works so well, it doesn't go off.'

'This would be different,' she persisted. 'Basic ingredients last much longer, it's combining them that shortens their shelf-life.' She tried to keep the hint of frustration out of her voice, she did have some expertise in this area, after all.

'I don't think it's a good idea, the risk is too great. What would Danny say?'

'I'm not going to tell him.' He would never understand. If he couldn't, wouldn't, stand up for her during the shunning, there was no way he would be in favour of her plan. Best-case scenario, he would try to talk her out of it. The worst case didn't bear thinking about.

'What about the SmartShop deliveries? You can't have someone from Customer Services in your kitchen while you're baking cakes. It's a ridiculous idea, you'll get caught.'

This wasn't how the conversation was supposed to go. Alice was meant to be excited, enthusiastic and eager like she was. This was the answer to everything, the one thing she could do to help the cause, to help Alice. Telling her after the argument with Ray was a mistake, but it was too late now. Somehow, she had to find a way to get Alice to take her seriously.

'I won't bake the day he's coming and I'll clean up afterwards, no one will ever know.' She'd run a successful baking company, there was no reason why she couldn't do this. The getting caught part, that was trickier, but there had to be a way round that: CTAS were resourceful. Besides, this was about so much more than selling a couple of slices of cake. She needed this, why couldn't Alice see that?

'Just think about it, please. A good old-fashioned bake sale: cakes, cookies, cupcakes, scones, biscuits, flapjack, maybe even some sausage rolls.' She was playing dirty and she knew it.

Alice licked her lips, a tiny, involuntary flick of her tongue. 'No, we can't risk it, not at the moment, there's too much going on with . . . other plans. This would only complicate things.'

'You said yourself that CTAS is going to need all the money it can get for the next stage. You remember how much Nana used to make. That was before the food ban. We'd make a fortune and we only need to do it once, maybe twice.'

Alice drank more of her coffee, avoiding answering.

'Please, I want to help but there's nothing else I can contribute. This is my thing. Let me do what I'm good at.'

'There are plenty of ways you can get involved. You can wear a button cam or . . .' Alice cast around for something to palm her off with, a way to get her to go back in her box and stop being a nuisance. The rich coffee sat uncomfortably in Olivia's stomach and it mingled with a deep, exhausting sadness that replaced her fleeting excitement at the prospect of baking again. No, not just baking, but making a difference.

'It's fine, never mind.' She bit her cheek to keep her tears at bay and stared out across the bar. Hidden behind the partially closed curtains of one of the booths was a dark-haired woman leaning in close to whisper to a young man. He smiled and tilted his head just a fraction to kiss her. A kiss so intimate Olivia had to look away, but a nagging recognition made her turn back.

'Wait, isn't that . . .?' she whispered to Alice, her hurt forgotten.

'Our local member of parliament? Why yes, yes it is.'

'Didn't she vote for the bans?'

Alice laughed. 'A hypocritical politician. Who'd have thought it.'

'It's not fair, she shouldn't be allowed in here.'

'Her money is as good as anyone's.'

'So let's take more of it. Let's take all of it. Make them pay for the changes we desperately need. I know you're trying to keep me safe, but disaster is coming faster than you can protect me. Let me help you make a difference, not just for us, but for everyone. We can stop them, if we work together.'

Alice looked around the bar, and Olivia hoped she could see the potential, everything it was, everything it could be.

'We'll try it, but not until after the Mother's Institute dinner. There's too much at stake to draw extra attention before then.'

'Really? You mean it? Thank you!' She hugged her, but Alice didn't soften into the embrace. She was still reluctant, but that was okay, it would take time to win her round. She'd see that this was a good idea, they all would.

Chapter Twenty-One

Olivia had barely been able to think about anything other than her baking scheme for the rest of the week. Trying to look attentive during the next Mother's Institute meeting had been difficult, until she realised their speaker was a recipe developer for Mother Mason and her demonstration sparked a hundred new ideas of things she could bake. There were so many possibilities to choose from. She had to do the classics, obviously: Victoria sponge, lemon drizzle cake, coffee and walnut. Chocolate, of course. A Swiss roll would be a nice addition, and something gluten free, probably brownies; flapjacks were always a little boring. A vegan cake was trickier with her potentially limited resources but it was doable. She had already recited a long list of ingredients to Alice, not daring to write anything down, but as new recipes occurred to her, she kept mentally adding to the shopping list. While she washed clothes, put away toys, chopped vegetables and stirred stews, she was really thinking about creaming butter and sugar together, sifting flour, frosting cakes and decorating cookies.

Alice wouldn't commit to exactly when everything would be with her, but the thrill of anticipation made the wait deliciously exciting.

Vanilla, she remembered as she took her glass perfume bottle from her dressing table and dabbed a few drops behind her ear. Knowing she was going to get more soon had allowed her to be more liberal with her secret stash. She'd decanted some from the kitchen and started wearing it, but she couldn't wait to get a fresh bottle, some she could actually cook with.

For now though, it was the perfect finishing touch to her outfit for tonight's Mother's Institute dinner. There hadn't been time for her to get nervous about the event, not with all her exciting plans, but now she was dressed in her new sky-blue outfit, she hesitated as she looked at her reflection. The shop had checked the length with the modesty ruler twice and the neckline was so high it practically choked her, but there would still be scrutiny during the dinner and Alice's planned video wasn't going to make the night any more relaxing.

Not that she knew what to expect. It was all on a need-to-know basis and clearly, Alice didn't think she needed to know. It was hard not to feel a little offended, but she had her own plans to work on; she could let Alice get on with hers.

Humming to herself, she wandered downstairs, high heels in hand until the last possible moment.

'Mummy, you look like a princess!' Mia stared at her in shock.

'Why, thank you.' She gave a little twirl and the soft folds of the skirt swirled out around her.

'You're so beautiful,' Mia said, as though noticing for the very first time.

'Yes, you are.' Danny came out of the kitchen, her apron tied around his waist. He looked domesticated and surprisingly irresistible with a wooden spoon clutched in one hand and a tea towel in the other. She could get used to this side of him. Maybe she should go out more often.

'You look stunning.' He moved to kiss her but she

sidestepped the sauce-stained spoon, trying to protect her dress and her freshly applied lipstick.

'Later,' she promised.

'I hope the Mother's Institute arrange more fancy dinners if they make you this happy.'

'I don't need the Mother's Institute to be happy, just you and the kids.' And her top-secret baking plans. The news bubbled up inside her; how she wished she could share it with him. In the past he would have been as excited as she was. They had spent long nights planning her bakery, taste-testing her recipes. She thought he would always support her in what she did, but he hadn't and the risk that he wouldn't again was too much. Their marriage wouldn't survive another blow like that. Hopefully, one day she could tell him, could make him understand that she was doing this for all of them. Today wasn't that day.

'That's Alice,' she said at the sound of tyres crunching on gravel. She risked a quick peck on his cheek, leaving behind a perfect pink print of her lips. 'I've got to go.' She reluctantly stepped into her high heels, grabbed her shawl and clutch bag and headed for the door.

'Have a good time,' he called after her.

'I will, you too. Don't go too wild without me.'

'We will,' Matthew shouted from the living room.

'Bye.' She blew a kiss and headed out to Alice's little silver sports car.

'Whoa.' Alice let out a whistle as Olivia slipped into the low seat. 'Aren't I the luckiest woman tonight? I'm going with the hottest date.'

'Ha, ha,' she said, secretly pleased. 'Everything all sorted for later?'

The smile slipped from Alice's face. 'Yes, it is.' She was

unusually silent as they drove out of the village and onto the dual carriageway towards Norwich.

'Are you sure there's nothing I can do to help? I'm ready for whatever you need, I want to do what I can.'

'I know and you are.' Alice glanced across the car at her. 'You're incredibly brave and capable; there's nothing you can't do, you know that, right? I want you to remember that.' She returned her attention to the road but Olivia continued to watch her.

'Alice, is there something else going on? Something you need to tell me?'

'Only that you look stunning and tonight is going to be legendary. So let's promise to have fun, 'kay?'

The light, excited bubbles burst and a sickening anxiety returned to her stomach. 'Alice . . .'

'Let's put some music on, get us in the mood.' Alice turned the radio on and cranked up the volume until conversation was impossible.

The ornate City Hall building was illuminated by a soft golden light. It spilled out of the high, lead windows onto the crowd of women gathered near the entrance. Everybody seemed relaxed, voices loud as they chattered and laughed together, calling to friends, waving at acquaintances, but it belied the intense awareness each woman had of the Shame Box that sat across the road, illuminated with its own harsh floodlights. Unsurprisingly, Mother Mason was using the dinner to make a statement and a number of rule breakers had been rounded up for public punishment. Three women and two men sat with their backs to the crowd, and the Mother's Institute members turned away too, choosing instead to cast subtle glances over outfits, a quick flick of their eyes, up and down, a silent rating of approval or dismissal.

Olivia slid her hands over the soft silk of her dress, smoothing it out while pushing it down.

'Will you leave it alone?' Alice turned back from her scrutiny of a nearby group of women. 'Your dress is fine, relax.'

Olivia's anxiety in the car had settled in to a low-level panic that seemed to intensify by the minute. She spotted Bronwyn in the crowd, braids bobbing as she headed up the front steps and past the two lion statues that guarded the entrance to City Hall. Alice acted like she didn't see her or any of the other CTAS members waiting outside, and Olivia followed her lead. Not knowing the scheme allowed her imagination to spiral. Whatever they had planned, it was going to be dangerous, possibly for everyone attending the dinner, but it was too late to insist on hearing the details. Dark-suited agents milled through the crowd, corralling the women into groups before calling them forward to enter the hall.

'Come on, ladies.' Jenna pushed her way through the cluster of women from their MI; Patricia following in her wake. 'It's our turn to go in next: line up and make sure you have your ID cards ready. You do have your ID card, don't you, Alice?'

'Yes, Jenna.' Alice brandished her little white card.

Of course Alice had her card, Olivia had just handed it to her. She'd decided it was better if she took charge of it tonight and had kept their cards safe in her bag.

Jenna wasn't happy with Alice's response, but they were surrounded by women from other Mother's Institutes, so she couldn't say any more. 'Stop dawdling, Patricia,' she snapped and turned on her heel. She stalked up the steps to the grand front doors, Patricia running behind her as the other ladies fell into step.

They were stopped at the security checkpoint, where agents swiped their ID cards, then sent them through the X-ray scanners embedded in the carved wooden door frames. Checked for both weapons and excess body fat, they were captured in instant digital images that were uploaded to their personal files. Olivia stepped forward, tensing her stomach and holding her breath, trying to suck everything in until she got through the door. The very act made her ashamed and furious, and when she let out her breath, she let out her fear too. Mother Mason had done terrible things, was about to do even worse if the residential scheme was anything to go by; it was time somebody stopped her. Hopefully, CTAS's plan would bring her down, once and for all.

The Grand Entrance Hall deserved the title. From its polished marble floor to its carved wooden panelling and high vaulted ceiling, the room was spectacular. The chandeliers threw out blinding sparkles of rainbows, matching the equally dazzling jewellery that graced necks and earlobes. Everybody wore their finest, fanciest clothes tonight, as though the richer they looked, the happier they were, but it was all a lie. They were pretending as much as Olivia was, especially if their wealth also granted them access to Barre Class. That's fine, she thought. Once she started baking, she would take every penny they had and turn it against Mother Mason and her government.

She touched her CTAS pendant with pride, the gold flower warm against her skin. She wouldn't trade it for the biggest diamond in the room. Knowing what it meant, what she stood for, gave her a surge of confidence that made her walk with a little more sway to her hips, however wide or stretch-marked they might be, and added a bounce to her step, no matter how short she was, and she met the gaze of everyone who looked at her, both agents and Mother's Institute members, their equal in every way.

She smiled up at the large portrait of Mother Mason that hung opposite the door, the unfortunate focal point of the room. Their supercilious leader wore her usual haughty expression but it made Olivia want to laugh. The woman thought she was so much better than everyone else but she had no idea what was coming. Granted, neither did Olivia, but she knew it would be big. Mother Mason could look down on them from her gilt frame, but she wouldn't be up there for ever.

'Over here.' Jenna waved to them from the far side of the room. She stood in front of a large white board and pointed to three circles on the seating chart. 'This is us. Follow me.'

Olivia had been impressed by the entrance hall, but it was nothing to the magnificence and splendour of the ballroom. It was like walking into a room of golden light. It shone from the candles, sparkled off the chandeliers and reflected back from the fine gold detailing on the ceiling. The room was filled with row after row of round tables, each laid with crisp white cloths, sparkling crystal glasses and polished silverware, all mirror-bright in the candle-light. On the dais at the far end of the room stood the High Table, reserved for the bigwigs of the Mother's Institute. At the central setting was a throne-like chair, ready for Mary Vitasan.

Jenna led the way past the other Mother's Institutes, weaving through the attendees to reach their tables. She stopped to survey their position, her lips moving silently, counting the rows between them and the stage. They weren't at the back of the room, but they weren't that close to the front. At least, not as close as Jenna would have wanted.

Olivia searched for her place and found her name written

in swirling calligraphy among the other folded place cards. She pulled out her chair and Jenna made an exasperated sound. 'No one sits down until Mary Vitasan arrives.' Jenna stood tall behind her own seat, right next to Olivia's. No mention had been made of her PTA outburst, but she wondered if Jenna had arranged this on purpose, to make sure she didn't have any further breaches in etiquette. Jenna should really have known it was Alice that needed monitoring.

'Let's hope Mary gets here soon,' Alice said. 'I'm starving.'

'No, Alice, you are not starving. There's plenty of food in Mother Mason's country,' Jenna said.

'It was a figure of speech.'

'Not any more. Patricia, stand up straight, you're slouching. Did you really have to wear that cardigan?' She turned her attention to the rest of their group. 'Jody, your mascara's smudged. Fix it. Szara, pull up your top, your tattoo is showing. Roisin, bra strap. Kim—'

The regal blast of a trumpet cut her off and the chatter of hundreds of women ceased. A buzz of excitement started at the front of the room, a murmur that flowed back through the crowd, carried from table to table. Norwich didn't get many celebrity visitors.

Women peered over and around each other, stretching up, moving from side to side, desperate to catch a glimpse. Olivia felt conflicted. Mary represented every impossible standard she pushed herself to achieve, but she had started out like them, just a normal woman. If things were different, Olivia might have applied for the First Family competition. Could she have stood up to Mother Mason's twisted plans for the country? Considering how weak and defeated she'd been the past few years, it seemed doubtful.

The MI officials filed onto the stage, so far away they were merely small, unrecognisable figures, but a giant screen mounted on the wall lit up and the VIPs appeared for all to see. Mary wore an elegant dark blue dress that sparkled in the spotlight as she took her place at the centre of the High Table; she looked even more beautiful than she did on the posters at the supermarket, and Olivia felt a twinge of jealousy at her effortless charm and grace. The audience clapped for her, some more enthusiastically than others, but still they all joined in: they had to.

Mary and the local bigwigs stood poised behind the top table, smiling at everyone, until a waiter pulled back Mary's chair and she gracefully sat down. The rest of the select party followed but the audience hesitated, just for a fraction of a second, until Mary gestured for them to take their seats. As a collective group they pulled out their chairs and sat, but everybody's attention was still on the stage. A small, silver-haired woman stood up from her place beside Mary. It was Sylvia Buchanan, the chairwoman and head of Norfolk's Mother's Institute. There was a slight sigh, a soft sound of disappointment from the audience: Mary would not be speaking yet.

'Ladies of the Mother's Institute, it is my very great honour to welcome Mary Vitasan, spokeswoman of Mother Mason, and wife and mother of the First Family. On behalf of the Norfolk Federation I would like to say we are deeply grateful to have you here with us this evening.'

Mary sat poised and confident on her throne. Her expression on the big screen was one of pleasant engagement, but she might as well have been broadcasting from London, considering how distant she seemed.

'Do you think she's going to say anything?' Alice

whispered. 'If we're here we at least want some first-hand propaganda.'

'—recognition of the importance and value that the Mother's Institute has brought to our lives, as the ladies here tonight can attest to,' Sylvia said. 'We owe so much to Mother Mason and all that she has done for us, on both a local and national level. We ask that you pass on our deepest gratitude to her. Now, ladies, please be upstanding for Mother Mason's Anthem.'

There was a rush of movement as women hurried to get to their feet: no one wanted to be the last to stand. The trumpeter played the first few notes and the women began to sing.

> *Mother Mason good and true,*
> *We thank you, for all you do,*
> *With love and joy and family pride,*
> *We march together side by side.*
> *Mother Mason good and true,*
> *Mother Mason we honour you.*

The last words died away and despite herself, Olivia shivered as a tingle of goosebumps broke out on her skin. There was power in their collective voices. Women dabbed at their eyes and some openly cried, their heads held high, holding hands around the tables. Jenna reached out and took Olivia's hand in a clawing grip; she nodded for her to take Alice's. Alice rolled her eyes and had to let go of her necklace, clutched in her fist, so she could reach for Patricia. All twenty women smiled at each other, grins getting wider and wider as they tried to match the exact expression on the faces around them. Olivia was supposed to be happy and proud to be there, and like it or not, *they*

192

had to believe she felt it, truly felt it. A month ago it would have been easier to pretend, to fake it convincingly, but now she struggled to remember what passive obedience looked like. Her only memory was of shrinking and she couldn't bring herself to do that. She stood a little taller, held her head a little higher. Maybe they would take it as pride in her country, that was all she could hope for.

Not everyone looked as euphoric as Jenna. The light didn't reach all their eyes; on some faces there was a twitch of a muscle, a flicker of a pulse beating at their temples showing the real feeling behind the faux fervour. Now Olivia knew to look, she saw the tasselled earrings, necklaces and bracelets. There were more around the room than she had expected, dotted here and there among the masses, but the sight stirred her courage and she found the strength to smile along with the rest.

'Please be seated,' Sylvia said. 'We now have a wonderful meal produced with locally sourced ingredients and prepared to Mother Mason's specific recipe. I know we will all enjoy it very much.'

With that, waiters appeared, silently moving to place domed silver plates in front of each person. At an unspoken sign they removed the cloches to reveal steaming bowls of soup, carrot and coriander, if the vivid colour was any indication.

Olivia picked up her spoon from the array of sparkling silverware in front of her, and dipped it into the bowl. The soup was sharp and tangy, with too much pepper and not enough salt, but she swallowed and smiled.

Everybody else did the same.

The real question was how much was she supposed to eat? The menu would be carefully controlled, calories calculated to the last gram, but were they meant to eat everything they were given or leave a certain amount? Was it ungrateful not to clear your plate or was it a test of your self-restraint? She tried to match everyone spoon for spoon.

They had steamed salmon on a bed of leek and courgette for the main course. It was really rather boring; there was a million things she could have done with the same ingredients, but it was like the chefs hadn't bothered. Or they had wanted to make it patently clear that everything on the plate was 100 per cent approved by Mother Mason and the Department of Nutrition and Health. It still seemed like a wasted opportunity and one she would rectify at Barre Class.

Unimaginatively, dessert was a boring platter of fresh fruit. It had, at least, been artfully arranged to form a small, square tower of apple, mango and melon, with raspberry battlements. A little cream or ice cream, maybe a meringue, would have finished it off perfectly. Eton Mess, now there was an idea, she could easily get some fresh summer fruit to mix with whipped cream and crushed meringues. Pavlova was always popular too, or perhaps a roulade. They wouldn't keep long, but she had a strong suspicion that her bakes would sell the moment they reached the bar.

She wished she could share her plans with Alice, but when she turned to her, she saw Alice was struggling to finish her pudding. She pushed the pieces of fruit around her plate without lifting a single spoonful to her mouth.

'Everything okay?' Olivia whispered, Alice's nerves transferring to her.

Alice checked the time. 'Yes, it will be. I need to go the bathroom.' She pushed her plate away and stood up.

'Where do you think you're going?' Jenna demanded.

'I'm sorry, I didn't realise I had to get permission to take a—' Alice caught herself and stopped. 'Jenna, please can I be excused?'

If Olivia hadn't been concerned before, she was terrified now. Alice being polite to Jenna? Something was about to happen, something big. 'I'll come with you,' she said.

'Thanks, *Mum,* but I can go to the loo on my own.' Her tone was light and teasing, but Alice's expression implored Olivia to stay where she was. 'I'll be fine, I'm a big girl. I've got this.'

Olivia sank back onto her chair. Reluctantly, she watched Alice walk across the ballroom and disappear through a small side door.

'She had better hurry back,' Jenna said. 'If she gets in trouble we'll all pay the price.'

Olivia tried to laugh. 'She's going to the toilet, what possible trouble can she get into?'

'I'm not going to dignify that with a reply.'

Jenna was right: between here and the bathroom, Alice could get into a world of trouble. If she was even going to the bathroom. Great. Now Olivia needed the toilet, because just the thought of it sent her baby-weak bladder into overdrive. Could it really hurt to follow Alice? She might be able to help, or at least be a lookout. That was after she used the facilities, of course.

Chapter Twenty-Two

There were no guards to halt Olivia's progress as she followed Alice through the small side door and into a dimly lit corridor. That alone hinted at CTAS's involvement. It was refreshingly peaceful away from the chatter of thousands of women and the only sound was the echoing click of her heels on the parquet floor.

'Alice?' she hissed but there was no sign of her and with no one to ask, she picked a direction and hoped it was the right one. The hallway stretched endlessly into the distance and she passed door after door, each clearly locked, the red security light glowing brightly on the card entry machine. Her bladder reminded her of her more immediate need to search for the toilets; and the ladies silhouette sign up ahead was a welcome sight. Even better, there was a small dot of bright green light beside the door.

She entered the cold, echoing room to see Alice standing in front of the row of hand dryers. Sweet, welcome relief released Olivia from her mounting palpitations. Alice really had needed to use the bathroom.

'Liv! What are you doing here?' Her severe expression forced Olivia to take a step back. 'You shouldn't be here, you have to go. Now.'

The palpitations returned. 'Why? What's going on?'

'I can't explain, but please, you have to leave.' Alice took her arm and pushed her towards the door.

She'd never seen Alice this scared. 'I'm sorry, I only wanted to help. I'll go, but can I use the loo first? I'm desperate for a wee.'

'No, there's no time, you'll have to find another bathroom.' Alice opened the door a crack and the sound of voices filtered in. 'Shit!' She dragged Olivia back and shoved her towards a cubicle. 'You have to hide.'

'Hide? From who? Alice, you're frightening me.'

'Then you shouldn't have followed me. Damn it! I told you, I didn't want you involved.' Alice glanced back at the bathroom door. 'Get in and sit down, keep your feet up like we did at school.' She pushed Olivia into the cramped space and closed the door behind her.

'Alice—'

'Shh!'

Alice went into the adjoining cubicle and Olivia did as she was told, lowering the toilet seat lid and sitting down, just in time. The main door to the bathroom banged open and heavy footsteps entered the room, accompanied by the scent of a sharp, masculine aftershave. She raised her feet as a dark shadow passed beneath the door. It moved across the bathroom floor and back again.

'All clear,' a man said.

There were more footsteps on the marble tiles, the click of heels and the swish of a long skirt. Clutching her own dress tight to her sides, Olivia hunched down.

'You've reviewed the changes to your speech?' a second man asked, his words resonating around the bathroom.

'Yes, I read them in the car,' a familiar female voice replied.

'Emphasise the improvements in health, happiness and family values as a result of the Re-education Programme. You need to keep up morale before the Residential

Programme is announced. They're going to lose it when the news goes public. We're running out of places to install new Shame Boxes and the prisons are already full to capacity. At this rate, we're going to have to start doubling the number of trials we screen each week, just to get some free cells.'

'Great, more work for me,' the woman muttered.

'Not if you do your job properly. You're the one who's meant to keep them passive and compliant. If it's not working, you're not trying hard enough. You need to remind them this is all because of the health issues left by the previous government. If we forge ahead, everything will be on track to reach Mother Mason's target of absolute health and happiness within the next five years.'

'Fine.' A tap turned on and water rushed out, forcing the man to raise his voice.

'Your handkerchief is waiting, be sure to hold for the full thirty seconds after the children's future line. You rushed it on Monday.'

The running water stopped.

'Yeah, yeah, count to thirty. I know.'

There was a flurry of movement, shadows darted across the floor and the room fell very still.

'Ow, that hurts. Let go of me.' The woman's voice was tense. 'You're going to leave a bruise.'

'I'm sure that's not a problem, you've got plenty of ... padding. You've been skipping your gym sessions again, haven't you? She's noticed and we'll be dealing with it when we get back. For now you'll have to purge and hope it gets you down to your target weight.'

The single large shadow separated into two.

'You have ten minutes until your speech,' the man said, 'take care of business and get back out there.'

The door banged closed, but although Olivia's legs were burning with cramp, she remained very still.

'It's okay, Alice, you can come out,' the woman said.

A shrill squeak echoed around the bathroom as Alice opened her cubicle door.

'Are you all right?' Alice asked. 'Did he hurt you?'

'It's nothing I'm not used to. Did anyone see you come in?'

'No, Ray made sure it was all clear. How are you doing?'

The gurgling pipes were the only response to Alice's question.

'I know we're asking a lot of you and I'm truly grateful that you agreed to help CTAS. We couldn't do this without you.'

'Run me through the details again, I need to be sure you've thought of everything. What you're asking me to do is incredibly dangerous.'

'It is, but you're the only one who can do it.' Olivia recognised Alice's reassuring tone, she had heard it plenty of times. 'This is the only way to be free of Mother Mason. That's why you came to us, remember? You couldn't stand by any longer, not with her plans for the new children's health scheme.'

'I know, but what about *my* children?' The woman's voice wobbled.

'We've got people in place to protect you. I promise, they'll be safe.'

Olivia had been trying hard to remain still, to keep her legs tensed and tighten her core like Carrie taught her, but slowly, her heels started to slide down the door.

'Besides,' Alice continued, 'once the trial begins all the attention will be on me.'

Olivia's stomach flip-flopped and she hunched forward,

but in doing so, her clutch bag fell from her lap; she lunged for it, almost falling off the toilet, but the bag hit the tiles with a thud, rolled under the stall door and was gone.

The room became deathly silent.

'Is this some kind of trap?' the woman hissed. 'You're setting me up?'

A staccato of heels stalked towards the cubicle, carrying with it a waft of heavy, floral perfume.

'No, wait,' Alice cried.

The woman stopped on the other side of the stall, her shadow reached under the door towards Olivia as she bent to pick up the clutch.

'My friend followed me in here by mistake.' Alice moved to stand between the woman and the cubicle, her red shoes visible beneath the toilet door. 'She has no idea who you are or what we're doing. Please, this doesn't have to change anything.'

'It changes everything. I can't trust you, you're just like everybody else. I was an idiot to believe things could be different, that CTAS could help me. The plan's off, I want nothing more to do with you. I'm going to have you both arrested.'

'Please don't,' Olivia stood up quickly and opened the door, 'this is all my fault.'

Mary Vitasan, their honoured speaker, head of the First Family and Mother Mason's spokeswoman stood in front of her, looking as polished and perfect as she did on television. Her dark-blue evening dress glimmered with thousands of tiny, sparkling crystals that twinkled even under the yellow glow of the florescent lights; her make-up was immaculate and not a single strand of hair escaped the complicated style.

'You're working for *her*, aren't you?' Mary demanded.

'No, never!' Olivia cried.

'It's okay, Mary, she's a member of CTAS, you can trust her.' Alice stayed between them.

'I swear I'm not working for Mother Mason. I just needed the bathroom. Alice told me not to come, but I was desperate. I should never have followed her. I won't say anything, I promise.' She touched her tasselled necklace as proof.

'I'm supposed to just believe you ...' Mary opened the clutch bag and took out the ID, 'Mrs Olivia Pritchard of twenty-seven Meadow Road, Bunham.'

Olivia swallowed convulsively as the unspoken threat hung between them.

'You've put me in a very difficult position. I should call my guards. It wouldn't matter what you said, two rebels hiding in the bathroom, nobody would ever believe you.'

'That's not necessary,' Alice said. 'Please, you were the one who wanted to work with CTAS.'

Mary tapped the ID card against her hand, considering, then with a reluctant sigh, she handed it and the clutch back to Olivia. 'I don't know what I want any more,' she said in a weary voice. She moved away from them and went to wash her hands.

'Yes you do, you want to stop Mother Mason and free your family; it's what we all want.' Alice followed her to the basins. 'And we can, if we stick to the plan.'

'The plan that's already going wrong? If they find out about this, they'll kill me. I don't want to die.'

'Do you want to keep living like this?' Alice asked.

Mary looked at them through the mirror's reflection. 'You don't know what it's like, you're not a mother.'

'But I am,' Olivia said. 'I know how horrific it is to fear for your life, for the lives of your children. I was constantly

201

terrified of making a mistake. I felt so helpless and power-less, I sometimes questioned the point of going on.' She could feel Alice staring at her but she kept her focus on Mary. 'Joining CTAS is a huge risk, but it actually helps with the fear. Doing something, anything, to fight back feels so much better than being weak and passive.'

'I know that's what everyone thinks of me.' Mary cupped her hands under the soap dispenser and rubbed the bubblegum pink gel into a foaming mass, scrubbing at her skin until it looked like she might start to bleed. 'They say I'm a terrible person for supporting Mother Mason, for doing her bidding, but I don't have any other choice; I'm trapped.'

'No, it might feel like that because that's what *they* want you to believe, but you're not.' Olivia took Mary's hands before she could do any more damage to herself and gently held them under the tap, until the water washed them clean.

'Liv's right, you're the one with all the power,' Alice handed Mary a paper towel. 'It's why Mother Mason con-trols you so much, it's because she fears you.'

'You don't understand. The things I've done in her name, the women I've condemned. She'll do that to me too, to my children, she'll—' Mary tore herself away and spun back to the toilet, just managing to lift the lid before she vomited up their fancy three-course meal.

'Shh, it's okay.' Olivia followed her into the cubicle, stroking her back as the government spokeswoman sobbed. 'We don't blame you, it's not your fault.' She caught sight of pink skin behind Mary's ears, and the faintest ridge of a scar along her hairline. She wasn't as naturally perfect as she appeared.

Alice stood just outside the toilet and she helped Olivia to get Mary upright. They flushed away the evidence of

202

her fear and staggered back to the sinks. Mary wiped tears away from her face, trying to protect her perfect facade, but it was too late, her mascara was smeared around her eyes and down her cheeks.

'You shouldn't be seeing this,' Mary snuffled. 'I'm supposed to be perfect and beautiful all the time.'

'You're not meant to be anything all of the time, except human,' said Alice, 'and that's messy and complicated and beautiful in its own way.'

'You make it sound so simple.'

'It's not, but you don't have to do it alone.'

Mary seemed unconvinced. She sniffed, sucking up her emotions again, pulling together the broken threads of her composure. She retrieved a small clutch bag from beside the mirror and took out her emergency supplies: a packet of tissues, a tube of mascara, a lipstick, a roll of No Guilt sugar-free mints and a folding brush. It clearly wasn't the first time she'd had to redo her make-up in a bathroom.

'Mary, we don't have much time until your minder comes back. I want to run through what you need to do this evening,' Alice said.

'I'm going to be in so much trouble if they catch me like this.' Mary gestured to her ruined make-up.

'No, you're not, we can help you.' Olivia reached for the packet of tissues.

'Thank you, you're so kind. Alice hasn't mentioned you before; what is it you do for CTAS?'

'Nothing, yet.' Olivia dabbed at the tracks of tears, painfully aware she was touching the face of the most beautiful, most famous woman in Britain. 'I'm new, but I had this idea—'

'And now she's a fully fledged member,' Alice finished for her. 'Hold still,' she instructed Mary as she reapplied her mascara, doing a better job than Olivia ever could.

'What's your idea?' Mary asked, peeling the foil away from the roll of mints and offering one to Olivia.

'It's still in the early stages.' Alice recapped the mascara. 'There's lots to sort out.' She smoothed back the stray strands of Mary's hair that had escaped their proper place. 'Nothing will happen until after our plan comes to fruition. So, getting back to tonight, all you need to do is—'

'I want to know more about Olivia's idea.' Mary shook Alice off and smoothed her own hair down.

'I, uh ...' Olivia glanced at Alice who shook her head.

'Please, it helps hearing what other people are doing. I find your courage inspiring.'

'I'm not sure you'd call it courage. I used to have a bakery, before Mother Mason closed it down. I thought I could take those skills and raise some money for CTAS.'

'You're baking cakes?' Mary lost some of the hopeless look in her eyes and she actually smiled. 'What a fabulous idea, Mother Mason would hate it! But aren't you worried about what might happen to your children if they catch you?'

'Terrified, but that no longer feels like a reason not to act.' Olivia scrunched up the tissue and threw it away. 'Something has to change and I'll do whatever it takes to protect them.'

'Whatever it takes, huh? Well, a mother's love is a powerful thing,' Mary said thoughtfully.

'It is,' Alice agreed, 'so use it, Mary, use your love, use your power. Be the saviour we're waiting for.'

'Saviour.' Mary seemed to taste the word to see if she liked it. From her change in posture, the new way she looked at herself in the mirror, it seemed like she did. She crunched up her mint and swallowed. 'They're going to come looking for me, I need to get back.' With a final check on her appearance, her poise firmly back in place, she turned to go.

'Wait!' Alice glared at Olivia, as though somehow it was her fault Mary was leaving. 'We haven't been through all the details. You're going to—'

'It's okay, I know what I need to do. It was good to meet you, Olivia. I look forward to trying your cakes. Stay here for a couple of minutes after I leave, but don't be too long, they'll notice if you're not there for the speech.'

Chapter Twenty-Three

Olivia and Alice slipped back into their seats, trying to remain as invisible as possible, but everybody else was already sitting down, theirs the only empty chairs. Mary was in her place at the top table. She sat talking or, more accurately, listening to Sylvia Buchanan.

'Where have you been?' Jenna demanded.

'We got lost,' Alice said.

The waiters had cleared the tables, the plates replaced with white china cups of steaming, black coffee, the smell strong enough to overpower the scent of the floral table arrangements. Olivia took a sip, hoping to settle her stomach, but it lacked the zingy kick of caffeine that Barre Class coffee had.

'It's nice of you to grace us with your presence. You know you're here representing our Mother's Institute, you could try to act with some sense of decorum.' Jenna set her cup down with enough force to make the coffee spill into the saucer.

'It's fine, Jenna,' Alice said.

If only it was.

The crackle and pop of the speakers silenced the audience and they turned towards the stage. Mary stood on a podium, poised and beautiful beneath the spotlight, her face reproduced in high definition on the screen behind her. You wouldn't know that ten minutes ago she was a sobbing mess. The serene, confident woman was back in control as she looked out on the audience, smiling and waving as they clapped and cheered for her. The force of their applause was like a physical pressure in the room. Olivia brought her hands together, trying to match their enthusiasm.

When the clapping slowed, but before it became noticeably quieter, Mary cleared her throat. 'Ladies, thank you for your warm and wonderful welcome. I am so honoured to be here with you tonight.' Her gentle voice carried to the back of the hall, as clear as if she was standing right beside you, speaking personally to you. Gone was her weary, helpless tone, in its place was a honey-smooth confidence that eased your tension and made you want to pay attention.

'As you know, I have been travelling recently, visiting our sisters across the seas to share the success of our great country. But it is good to be home.' She paused as the audience clapped again but Olivia couldn't bring herself to join in with the lie. 'Mother Mason asked me to tell you how very proud she is of the work you are doing.'

Another pause for applause and a sweeping look around the room. It was as if Olivia could see the invisible puppet strings, hear her handler's voice speaking through her. None of it was authentic, none of it came from the heart.

'The women of the Mother's Institute are nurturing a nation. You are leading the way for a happier and healthier world. Mother Mason thanks you.'

More lies, more manipulation. She wished she could block up her ears, barricade herself against the propaganda.

'As you know, it's seven years since my family and I were selected to be Mother Mason's First Family. We are still truly honoured and deeply grateful to Mother Mason for this incredible opportunity.' Was there a slight waver as she spoke the final sentence? None of the other women seemed to have noticed: they sat with rapt expressions, eyes lit with a passionate enthusiasm.

'My darling Isabelle wished she could have been here tonight. She can't wait for the day she can join the Mother's Institute and I know that your daughters feel the same. It will be the proudest day of my life to see my child take her place beside me.'

This time there was a definite catch in Mary's voice and her eyes closed briefly.

'I know that Isabelle will learn to be the best woman she can be, surrounded by wonderful role models like yourselves. Together we can ensure a happier and healthier future, not just for our children, but for our children's children.'

There was a murmur of appreciation from the crowd. Mary reached for something on her lectern, and a moment later she picked up a small white handkerchief and dabbed at her eyes. Jenna and several other women took out their own tissues.

Alice took something out of her purse. She kept it held low, hidden amongst the folds of the linen tablecloth, but when the small screen lit up, Olivia could see it was a phone, not a tissue.

'PLAN OFF.' The bold black text flashed up on the phone and Alice cursed under her breath.

'Alice?' It felt like a slap when Alice looked up at her with anger bordering on hate.

'I told you not to come. You've ruined everything.'

Olivia didn't need to fake her need for a tissue and Jenna gave her an approving nod.

'One day our children will look back on all that we achieved and know we did it for them.' Mary stared down at the lectern. 'It is thanks to Mother Mason and all the mothers here today that we are a truly great nation, now and for ever.'

'Screw it,' Alice muttered and brought up an app on her phone.

'I know that—'

The screen behind Mary turned a blinding white and her face was replaced by flashing images of Shame Boxes from around the county.

'Mother Mason puts us in boxes, but we add the shame,' the distorted narrator's voice, Alice's voice, shouted out across the room. 'We judge others, criticise them for doing the things we're too afraid to do, the things we long to do.'

Mary shrank back from the video, she turned towards the audience, horrified and accusing as she searched the crowd.

'Turn it off,' she demanded, her microphone amplified voice competing with the video. 'Turn it off right now.'

Men in suits rushed towards her, forming a protective shield around her as the board of the Norfolk Mother's Institute scattered. Some left the stage, others searched for a way to end the broadcast, desperate for a lead to pull or a switch to flick.

'Mother Mason uses us. We are her willing soldiers, her guards, her agents without suits. Who needs spies when we inform on each other? Who needs laws when our own humiliation and shame will keep us in line?'

'What have you done?' Olivia whispered.

'What I had to,' Alice said, not trying to whisper

'This is unacceptable,' Jenna shouted above the noise. 'They can't get away with this.'

'We're hurting ourselves, our families and all the people we know and love. She's made us think we're the problem, that we deserve this, but this is down to her.

'We voted for Mother Mason because we thought she was one of us, a mother, a grandmother, a retired nurse. She was the promise of comfort and relief, a grown-up in charge. She isn't who we thought she was, she's not who we need. She destroyed our democracy and we let her, but now it's time to fight back. Now we must stop hiding and rise up and show Mother Mason we won't be ignored any more. I won't be ignored any more.'

The video of the Shame Boxes stopped and a woman in a pink apron and a fringed mask stood in front of the camera. She wielded a large pair of scissors. 'Cut The Apron Strings!'

'Cut The Apron Strings!' someone in the crowd shouted and the chant was taken up, the words thrown out around the room.

'Join the Fray! Join me!' The woman, Alice, reached up to remove her mask and ...

The screen went black.

Chapter Twenty-Four

Alice didn't need the radio to ensure they drove home in silence. She stopped the car outside Olivia's house, not bothering to pull up the drive. Olivia didn't move to undo her seatbelt, she was still reeling from the evening's events. After Mary was evacuated, they had to sit through a twenty-minute debrief from her adviser and were forced to sign non-disclosure agreements before they were allowed to leave. Not that Olivia wanted to talk about it with anyone. Except Alice.

'You wanted to be arrested?' If she could only understand the point of the evening, she might feel less hurt by Alice's anger.

'It doesn't matter what I want.' Alice stared straight out of the windscreen, her fingers clutching the steering wheel in a death grip.

'Why? They would have put you in prison, sent you to trial.'

'That's why!' Alice shouted. She switched on the radio and turned the volume up, but she wasn't done speaking. 'We've been working on the plan for a year, it was all sorted. Do you know how much hand-holding I've had to do to get Mary on board? I finally got her to commit, she was ready to help us and you show up and remind her of all the things she has to lose, of her "mother's love". All I asked of you was to stay at the damn table. Why couldn't you listen?'

'I was trying to help, I was worried about you. Rightly so. You can't get arrested, that's not a plan.'

'It is if we want a bigger platform, one that means Mother Mason can't pretend we don't exist. You don't understand, you've no idea what you're talking about.'

'Because you shut me out. Of everything. For *six* years.' Olivia's voice rose to match Alice's.

'That's what this is about? I was trying to protect you. How many times am I supposed to apologise? I'm sorry I didn't take you for coffee and chocolate, I'm sorry I kept a secret from you, I'm sorry I've spent the past six years doing everything I can to get your old life back.'

'I never asked you to do this, I never wanted you to put yourself in danger. In fact, I've been doing everything *I* can to keep *you* safe. Every shopping trip, every Mother's Institute meeting, every Be Fit class, I'm the one watching out for you, covering up when you say something stupid, when you voluntarily put us *both* in danger.'

'I'm not like you, I can't pretend I'm another one of Mother Mason's robots, just accepting the rules; anything for a quiet life.' There it was, the thing they both knew Alice had been wanting to say for a long time.

'I'm trying to keep my family safe,' Olivia's voice shook with angry tears.

'I was trying to keep your family safe, but that will never be possible with Mother Mason in power. That was supposed to change tonight.'

Mrs Flynn's taxi pulled up and they fell silent, watching as the driver helped her out of the car and up to her front door. Mrs Flynn went straight to her living-room window to watch them.

'It's over.' Alice closed her eyes and leaned her head back against the headrest.

'There must be more we can do, something else we can try. If the bake sale raises enough—'

'There isn't going to be a bake sale, there never was. It's a stupid idea that would have put you in the very danger I've been trying to keep you out of.'

No, Olivia couldn't believe it. She'd lied about that too?

'It's done,' Alice continued in a cold, dead voice. 'Go inside, kiss your husband, tuck your children into bed and forget tonight ever happened. In fact, forget you ever heard of CTAS, forget all of it. It's the best thing for everyone.'

Alice didn't wait to check if Olivia got into the house but sped off the instant the car door slammed shut. Olivia stumbled up the drive. Her heel caught on the gravel and she tripped, landing on the knife-sharp stones and scraping the palms of her hands. She dropped her clutch, kicked off her stupid shoes and left them where they fell.

Danny was running on the treadmill in front of the television when she walked in.

'Hey, how was the fancy food and fake champagne? Let me jump in the shower and—' He stopped at the sight of her face. 'What happened?'

She burst into tears, right there in the living room, as every hurtful thing Alice had said broke through her 'robot' persona. Danny punched the stop button and came to her, all strength and sweat, and wrapped her in an encompassing hug. She leaned into his embrace, her throat tight. It wasn't her fault, she hadn't ruined Alice's plan on purpose. How was she supposed to know if nobody ever told her anything? She was only trying to help. The thought only made her cry harder.

'The dinner was that bad?'

She swallowed against the words she wished she could say, the truths she longed to share with him. CTAS, the bar, Mary and now Alice. There was so much she wanted to tell him, but the knowledge would put him in danger and she couldn't do that. She had to protect him ... protect him the way Alice had protected her. Oh Alice! She couldn't control her sobs, deep, rasping cries, accompanied by sandpaper tears that scratched and burned as they dragged up from deep within her.

Danny held her up as she leaned heavily into him, remaining strong and steady long after her legs started to give.

His lips were only a small head tilt away and she kissed him until she couldn't breathe, couldn't think, couldn't feel.

'What's—'

She silenced him with another kiss. Moving her hands down his back, she searched for warm skin beneath his soft cotton shirt. He drew in a surprised breath, then reached for her, lifting her up. She locked her legs around him and he carried her to the worn, sagging cushions of the sofa.

She closed her eyes and images from the evening replaced everything else.

'Liv—' he stopped kissing her, but he couldn't stop, he must not stop, she had to forget. She held his gaze and with a small nod he surrendered to her need. She kissed him again, hard. Keeping her eyes open she focused on his face, his hands, his touch. His lips found the familiar place at the base of her neck and she wove her fingers deeper into his hair, holding on.

As the memories rose to the surface she pushed them down, replaced them with the solid strength of his physicality, the places where their bodies touched, the feel of his skin, the warmth of his body. She traced the sculpted curves of his muscles, the result of his time in the gym. Where she just had to be thin, he could be defined and toned.

His strength encircled her and she clung to him as the storm rose and fell within her. Until she found peace.

Afterwards she stayed close to him, close to the steady beat of his heart and the gentle hand upon her back. With her fingertips, she tried to trace every detail, commit every line, every curve and freckle to memory. How could she know him so well, yet feel she could forget his face in an instant?

'You don't have to tell me what happened.' His voice reached her as a rumbling vibration through his chest. 'I'm here though, if you need me.'

Chapter Twenty-Five

It was two weeks later and Olivia still hadn't spoken to Alice. This was the longest they'd ever gone without speaking and it was like someone had filleted Olivia's heart. She yo-yoed between devastated loss and boiling rage, but anger felt easier to live with. Maybe she shouldn't have followed Alice to the bathroom, but she was only trying to help. It wasn't her fault Mary freaked out and changed her mind; in fact, she'd worked hard to reassure and encourage Mary. Alice should realise that and stop blaming her. Now she was just acting like a stroppy child. Well, when Matthew and Mia threw tantrums, Olivia ignored those too.

That didn't stop her missing her best friend, missing their daily catch-ups and shared routine. There was a hollowness inside her where her connection with Alice used to be. Every mundane chore felt a million times harder and more soul-destroying, and she couldn't explain to Danny what had happened, no matter how many times he asked. She also couldn't admit, even to herself, that she missed the bar, missed the coffee and the chocolate, but mostly she missed the camaraderie with Bronwyn and the rest of CTAS.

The Be Fit classes were tougher too; Alice hadn't been to any since their fight. Hopefully, she had simply switched to another session, unless she was hell-bent on getting arrested. Not that it was Olivia's problem any more. She had other things to worry about, like her own potential arrest. What if Mary changed her mind and told her guards about their meeting? She'd broken other promises. Olivia still wasn't sure if it was a good thing or not that Mary had refused to go ahead with Alice's plan, but Mother Mason's strategy to target children continued unabated.

The school had just installed new weighing plates at the entrance and Olivia held her breath when she dropped the children off, waiting until they got safely inside before she left.

Feeling hyper-stressed and hypervigilant, she noticed the large white van the moment she rounded the corner. It was parked outside her house and the sight made her stomach flip. Her instincts screamed for her to run, but where would she go? Her whole life was in that house. She made herself take one step, then another, and as she drew closer, she saw the printed decal on the side door, an entwined heart, dumbbell and running shoe, the logo for the Fighting Fit Gym. Why would someone from the gym visit her? Except the gym meant CTAS ... and Alice. She felt a wistful flutter of hope, but she squashed it before she could get hurt again.

Mrs Flynn stood with her curtains fully drawn back, taking down the details in her Neighbourhood Watch diary. She scribbled even faster when the muscular, bald-headed delivery man got out. It was Frank, the bouncer from the bar.

'Hi,' he said gruffly. 'I was told you'd know what to do with these.' He climbed into the back of the van and re-appeared wheeling a large wicker basket. It was piled high with grimy, stained towels that reeked of stale sweat and body odour. Olivia took a step away as the warm spring breeze carried the smell to her.

'What are those?' she asked, her hand over her mouth.

'Towels, you know, since you're working for the gym now.'

'Working for the gym? I think there's been a mistake.'

'Not according to CTAS,' he whispered, glancing across the road to Mrs Flynn. 'The plan's a go. I'll collect everything late afternoon. Everyone's very excited about the new menu.'

The odour got drastically worse once Frank pushed the basket into her house and left it there. Who thought this was the best way to deliver ingredients? With her finger and thumb, she reached in and picked up the corner of one of the towels. It was cold and damp and she gagged. There was no way this was hygienic. The Food Standards Agency would have a field day. They weren't the only government organisation that would have a thing or two to say about it.

Did this mean Alice had forgiven her? As far as peace offerings went, Olivia couldn't think of a much better one. A heads up would have been nice though.

Taking small, shallow breaths, she manoeuvred the basket to the kitchen, banging into walls and scraping it through the doorway before she reached the laundry. She was desperate to get to the baking things, but there was no way she was touching the towels again without protection. She pulled on a pair of rubber gloves and, trying not to think about the moist, grimy fabric and the suspicious-looking stains, she scooped up the dirty washing and stuffed it into the washing machine.

As she neared the end, her hand struck a hard object; she swept the rest of the towels aside to reveal a steel box resting at the bottom of the basket. It took all her strength to heave the box out and she staggered back to the kitchen table. From the weight of it, Alice had got her everything she requested and more. She felt like a kid at Christmas, eager to see what Santa had brought her, but first she had to secure the kitchen.

The front of the house might have eagle-eyed Mrs Flynn to oversee it but the rear was blissfully private. Their garden backed onto fields and today they were deserted. There was no sign of the farmer inspecting his land or dog-walkers out for a stroll. Only the lone, headless scarecrow stood guard. Even so, she lowered the blind.

The stiff clasps on the trunk opened with a snap like gunfire and she raised the lid a fraction to peep in at the sacks of flour, cartons of eggs, packets of butter and most precious of all, three big bags of sugar. They'd remembered the tin of cocoa powder, the bag of ground coffee, and most exciting of all, a new bottle of vanilla extract.

Everything was unbranded and naturally lacked Mother Mason's seal of approval; so much the better. Baking tins lined the bottom of the box, gunmetal grey and non-stick: round, square and rectangular, eight, ten, twelve inches. All new, smooth and scratch-free. She felt almost giddy as she fell back into her baking routine: switching on the oven, turning on the radio and collecting up the utensils that escaped the amnesty. She hummed along to the music as she laid out her bowls, scales, sieve and mixer. Her aprons hung on the back of the door and she took down the pretty pink butterfly one, the one she had refused to put on since the baking ban. She tied it tight and pushed up her sleeves, ready to begin.

'That was "Every Day is Joy" by Divine Love,' announced the chipper DJ, 'brought to you by Vitasan Vitamins, the supplements you and the First Family love; sponsors of Mother Mason's Morning Melodies.' He transitioned into an equally upbeat pop song and the tune combined with

219

the white noise of the oven to cover the pounding beat of Olivia's heart. With a final look at the drawn blind, she picked up the first block of butter. It was so much larger than she was used to, heavier in her hand than the twenty-gram ration cubes. She unwrapped it, dropped it into the bowl, then reached for the sugar. A few precious grains spilled onto the worktop as she open the folded paper flap, bright white on the brown wood. She couldn't leave them there though; there must be no trace of her actions. Panic crept up again but she forced it down, this was not the time. Mary might be willing to back out on CTAS, but she wouldn't.

The sugar cascaded into the bowl, the numbers on the scales rushed upwards in fits and starts. For this cake she didn't need her recipe books. The all-in-one sponge was her favourite. She had made it so many times, she knew it by heart.

'That takes us to the top of the hour and now we cross over to Downing Street where Mary Vitasan is about to make a live announcement,' the DJ chattered in the background but Olivia was focused on measuring the self-raising flour.

'Good morning, citizens of Britain. Today, I'm pleased to be able to reveal to you Mother Mason's exciting new plans.' Mary sounded confident and self-assured, Mary the government spokesperson, not Mary the terrified woman breaking down in the bathroom.

'Mother Mason has become very concerned that not everyone is receiving the full benefit of the Eat Healthy Directive and the Exercise Hours. Therefore, anyone strug-gling to reach their maximum health and happiness will now be invited to take part in a wonderful new scheme.'

Olivia's hand jerked and she sent a cloud of flour bil-lowing up around her. She coughed repeatedly, unable to catch her breath, as the dry white powder filled her nose and mouth, stinging her eyes and burning her lungs. She abandoned the baking as she fought to keep breathing, concentrating solely on getting oxygen into her body. By the time she composed herself, the news had ended and the next song was mid-chorus. 'She's the greatest, the very best, I love her so, Mother—'

She slammed the radio's off button and clutched the edge of the worktop, needing its support. It was really happening, despite everything Mary had said. Despite the trauma and guilt she appeared to feel, she was still supporting Mother Mason and her hideous schemes. Damn her, damn all of them. Fear wasn't a good enough excuse not to act, to refuse to do what was needed.

Olivia released her grip on the top, straightened her shoulders and dusted the flour from her clothes. Mary could hide away and pretend this wasn't happening, but she refused to do the same. She returned to her mixing bowl and cracked the eggs in, shattering the shells one after another.

They were all cowards, all too busy protecting their own power instead of serving the people who elected them, who relied on them. She hated them for their greed and self-interest.

Sticky, gelatinous trails of egg white dripped from her fingers as she turned to dump the broken remains in the food bin, but she stopped at the sight of the flickering lights on the lid. The sensors monitored the items she threw away, all done in the name of 'eco-management'. Mother Mason wouldn't even let her dispose of her rubbish in private. If only her government had the same transparency.

Fine, the waste would have to be the bar's problem. She tossed the empty egg box back into the trunk and returned to the kitchen mixer. It made quick work of the process, beating the ingredients down, blending them into a nice, smooth batter, easy to manipulate and divide into three. She added cocoa powder to one, lemon zest to the other, and scooped the rest into the third tin, ready for the Victoria sponge. Three cakes, one mix, three times the money for CTAS. Perfect.

The hum of the oven changed, it became deeper, louder, and she knew it was ready. The wave of hot air assaulted her face as she placed the tins inside and closed the door with a thud. She sent up a silent prayer to the Baking Goddess. Don't let them burn, please rise, please be perfect.

Bang, bang, bang. Somebody hammered on the door.

It was a trap. Mary had told her guards about Olivia's plan and they had been waiting to catch her red-handed. They wouldn't need a trial, the evidence was all right there: the empty packets, the scattered grains of sugar and the white dusting of flour covering everything, including her.

Bang, bang, bang.

What had she done? Alice was right, she was an idiot and her family were going to pay the price. She grabbed what she could and stuffed it back into the trunk, her hands clumsy with panic. Dragging off her apron, she used it as a makeshift cloth to wipe the tops down, but it was pointless, there wasn't enough time. Her house must be surrounded, with agents ready to break down the door.

Bang, bang, bang.

Wait, why were they knocking? Surely, they would just raid the place and arrest her before she could run. Hope allowed her to take a calming breath. What if it was a co-incidence?

In fact, the knocking sounded more like Jeff, but she'd had her SmartShop delivery this week. Maybe it was the postman? If she ignored him he would go away.

He didn't, and the longer the knocking continued, the louder it got, drawing more and more attention. She would have to answer the door and get rid of whoever it was.

There was no way to completely hide the mess, but she threw a tea towel over the top of the trunk anyway. She wiped her hands on the back of her jeans and ran a hand through her hair, shaking out the last of the white flour.

Bang, bang, bang.

If she took the cakes out of the oven they would be ruined. How could she explain that to Frank? To Alice? Especially if it was just the postman. There was no alternative; the cakes would have to stay in. She closed the kitchen door, ran to the front hallway, only pausing for a quick check in the mirror. No smears of cake mix on her face, no cocoa powder blush on her cheeks. Free of any visible signs of criminality, she peeped through the spy hole and the angry, contorted face of Mrs Flynn scowled back at her.

She should have known.

'Mrs Flynn.' She opened the door a crack and twisted her lips into a passable smile. 'What can I do for you?'

Mrs Flynn tried to peered around her, to see deeper into the house. 'I wanted to make sure you were still making jam for the village fete.'

'Of course I am, we discussed it at the last Mother's Institute meeting.' She moved to block the doorway with her body.

'Saw you had a visitor this morning.'

'That's right, I've ... taken on a part-time job.'

'Things not going well with Daniel's work? I had heard rumours.'

'No.' It was getting harder to keep her fake smile in place. 'Things are fine, thank you. I just wanted something more to do with my days.'

'What is it, exactly, that you're doing?' Mrs Flynn took a step forward trying to enter, but Olivia held her ground.

'Just some laundry for the gym.' Might as well start her cover story now. 'I'm sorry, I've got a lot to do.' She took a breath and smelt the sweet scent of baking cakes, a vanilla perfume that carried out into the hallway. 'I'd better get back to it.' She darted backwards and slammed the door in Mrs Flynn's face. There would be trouble for that, but not as much as if Mrs Flynn smelt the baking.

She ignored the renewed banging and raced back to the kitchen. The delicious smell was stronger in there; the cakes had to be ready. She braved opening the oven and was rewarded with the sight of three perfectly risen sponges. The patrons at Barre Class were going to be ecstatic; she felt pretty delirious herself. The smell was mouth-watering, but she resisted cutting herself a slither. This was for CTAS, for a safer future; she couldn't squander it on a small slice now. Mary might have chickened out, but Alice would devise a new plan and the cake money would help her. Together they would be unstoppable.

Olivia did allow herself to run a finger around the empty tins, gathering the leftover flecks onto her fingertip. Very slowly she put it to her tongue and licked off the crumbs. They were delicious: sweet, moist and better than the chocolate truffles. The cakes were going to be a huge hit!

By three o'clock the towels were washed, dried and re-packed in the laundry basket. Soft, fluffy and neatly folded, they covered the steel box and the scent of fabric softener hid any traces of vanilla and sugar. A pot of coffee and two pieces of toast blackened under the grill took care of the smell in the house. It was a waste of food and the delicious fresh-baked cake smell, but what else could she do?

On her way to pick up the children, she wheeled the

basket back to the front hall and left it ready for Frank. Danny commented on it when he got back from work but she had her speech planned.

'You were right, I needed a new project, so I'm washing towels for the gym.' She kept busy stirring the pot of curry on the stove.

'Really?' He didn't sound as thrilled as she hoped. 'That wasn't quite what I'd anticipated, but if it makes you happy ...'

'It does.' She beamed at him. 'It really does.'

Chapter Twenty-Six

Olivia managed to wait until the end of her Be Fit session before she headed to Barre Class, but the anticipation was almost unbearable. The bar was fuller than she'd ever seen it. She squeezed past a crowd of people waiting by the door, not realising it was a queue until they started to complain, but Frank gave her a silent nod and let her through.

'You're here,' Bronwyn squealed, breaking away from a group devouring slices of lemon drizzle. 'Wow, wow, wow! People can't get enough, they've taken time off work this morning just to come, and they're already putting in requests for your next batch. The poor trainers are going to have to work extra shifts to keep up with the demand.'

'Next batch? No, I wasn't going to do this more than once,' she said, hearing the lie in her own words.

'You have to keep going now, people are going to want cake instead of alcohol, that's why the prices are twice as high and the portions are half as small. We're serving the most expensive cake the world has ever seen and it's worth every penny. You're a genius! Have you had a piece yet? No? You've got more restraint than me; we'll rectify that immediately.'

It was trickier to navigate around the room: the tables were closer together so they could fit more in. Each one was laid with a white tablecloth and a pretty china tea set. The clink of pastry forks combined with the up-tempo jazz number the band played. The other diners weren't simply eating her cakes, they were relishing them.

She heard words like 'delicious' and 'divine' as she followed Bronwyn to the CTAS booth. This was how she used to feel – confident, proud and happy to be alive. She was finally back to normal and it was all thanks to Alice. She couldn't wait to see her, to find out which cake she had tried first. Probably the chocolate brownie, she guessed.

Alice and Ray were in their regular places at the booth, but they were joined by other people, CTAS members Olivia had never met before. They all had slices of cake in front of them and they beamed at her when she arrived, all except Alice, whose expression killed Olivia's joy.

'So you found a way to get what you wanted,' Alice said. She was the only person at the table who didn't have a plate of cake.

'I don't understand. Didn't you organise the ingredients?'

'No.' Alice glared around the table. 'Someone else must have decided *your* plan was a good idea. All hail, Olivia, Queen of Cakes.'

'Queen of Cakes?' The tables were so close together that a women at a nearby table overheard. 'You're the baker?' Her voice put the bar's speaker system to shame. It carried over the hubbub of the rowdy patrons and seemed to echo in Olivia's head as everyone turned towards her.

'Oh my goodness, I think you're amazing.' Her friend stood up to give Olivia a hug. 'Thank you so, so much.'

'I'm going to have to do so much more exercise now.' A man at a nearby table rested his hand on his stomach. 'It's totally worth it.'

'Hear, hear,' his friend said and the bar cheered.

'A toast to the Queen of Cakes,' someone shouted and

everyone raised their cups and glasses. 'The Queen of Cakes!' they chanted.

'That's enough!' Alice shouted, puncturing the mood. 'Remember, nobody speaks about this outside the bar. If it goes public, we're all in trouble. Our safety depends on our silence. There's nobody coming to save you. Nobody who can stop Mother Mason now.' She glared at Olivia as though this was all her fault.

It wasn't a peace offering then, just another reason for Alice to be mad at her.

'I should go,' she said.

'No, stay.' Bronwyn shuffled up on the bench. 'You can't leave without having a slice of something. Your scones are gorgeous. How did you make them so light? Mine used to be dry and crumbly.'

'The trick is buttermilk, but I—' she stopped as Alice rolled her eyes. 'I'd better get back, it looks like I'll be getting anther delivery from Frank soon.'

Ray finished the last of his slice of carrot cake. 'Not bad,' he said, looking in her vague direction. 'Not as good as my mum's, but it's decent.'

'High praise,' Bronwyn said. Coming from Ray it really was.

'What are you making next? Can we get a red velvet cake?' Bronwyn put her hands together in supplication.

'I'll see what I can do. Alice, is there, uh, anything I can make you?'

'Nope. I'm good.'

Fine, if she wanted to stay mad, she could; Olivia had better things to do. As she walked back through the bar people stood up to shake her hand, to offer her a drink, a slice of cake, a hug. She brushed off their praise but she couldn't deny the swell of heady joy that blossomed through her. They weren't shunning her, they weren't acting like she was some kind of criminal, even though now she actually was one.

She could still feel Alice's furious anger, a cold weight on the back of her neck, but with all the praise, it didn't feel quite so hard to bear.

Chapter Twenty-Seven

The scones were out of the oven, hot, golden and cooling on the baking rack, the coffee and walnut needed five more minutes and the red velvet cupcakes were waiting to be iced. Once Olivia measured out the chocolate, the brownie ingredients would be ready too: another thing she could mentally check off her to-do list. Everything was on track for Frank to collect the cakes this afternoon. They had perfected their handover like a graceful dance. Frank showed up as she left to pick up the children, he wheeled the basket out, the fresh clean linen stacked on top, as she locked up behind him. The children and Danny had all commented on the new smells inside the house, but she palmed them off with excuses of new perfume, fresh flowers and jars of home-made jam for the fete. She was also burning lots of toast.

Baking was now a daily activity, except for weekends and between nine and ten on a Monday morning when her SmartShop arrived. Her little kitchen was turning out more baked goods than she thought possible and her poor dishwasher was working overtime; she knew how it felt. From the moment she dropped the kids off at school to when she picked them up, she was baking non-stop. She had to. Everything that went into the bar sold out within hours and she was getting special requests all the time. If only she could use her old bakery kitchen, she could have turned out ten times as many cakes. It would also be nice to have her staff back for a bit of extra help.

The saucepan of chilli was bubbling away nicely, so she turned down the gas just enough to keep clouds of spicy steam rising up to fill the kitchen. The mix of smells didn't sit well with her stomach, but needs must: she couldn't dare risk turning on the extractor fan and pumping the scent out to Mrs Flynn's waiting nostrils. Her nosy neighbour already knew something was up.

A tap on the back door made Olivia nearly drop the precious bar of chocolate. Seriously? The woman was coming round to the back of the house now? Good job Olivia still kept the blind closed, but the old familiar anxiety surged back up.

With time and practice, her nerves had faded away, leaving only the faintest unease at the risks she was taking. The reward of baking and the pleasure of knowing people loved her cakes was a great anaesthetic to her anxiety.

Mrs Flynn knocked again, a rather gentle tap, considering.

'Olivia, it's me, Dev. I need to talk to you.'

She was tempted to ignore him, to pretend she hadn't heard. What did he want? Alice was clearly still angry or she would be here. Olivia hadn't forgiven her either. Neither of them were willing to back down.

Except she missed her best friend. Alice should be here, sitting on the kitchen worktop, trying to lick the bowls, steal some chocolate or sneak a brownie, the way she used to.

She opened the door a crack. 'Hi, Dev.'

'Can I come in?'

'I'm really busy.'

'I know, I won't stay long.'

'I don't think there's much to say,' she said, closing the door behind him. 'Alice has made her position very clear.'

'She was upset. She worked hard to get Mary on board, but she knows it wasn't your fault.'

'Then she should say that.'

Dev laughed. 'That would be the right thing to do, wouldn't it? Admit the mistakes and make peace.'

Her own ping of guilt was an unwelcome sensation. 'I was only trying to help.' She picked up the bar of chocolate and snapped it, piece by piece, into the bowl of butter and sugar.

'I know, and I appreciate you looking out for her. If I could have been at the dinner, I would have done the same thing.'

She put the glass bowl onto the pan of boiling water, the heat rapidly melting everything together. This was how it always went. She knew it would come down to her being the grown-up, but why should she be the first one to say sorry? Why did Alice get to hold out for an apology?

'She misses you.'

It was a good job she had her back to Dev, so that he couldn't see her tears. A droplet fell perilously close to the melting chocolate and she sniffed quickly. Salt was her brownies' secret ingredient, but she preferred it in the granular variety. The chocolate, butter and sugar had formed a sweet, dark pool in the bottom of the bowl and it needed time to cool, away from the heat.

'Maybe you could both talk at the summer fete?' Dev suggested.

'So she's going to show up for that? She hasn't switched her shift to be with someone else?' She cracked the eggs one after the other into another bowl, satisfaction in the smack of shattering shell against hard china.

'She'll be there.'

'I guess I'll be there too. If she wants to talk then great, but Dev, I'm not taking all the blame. I'm done feeling like everything is my fault. We both made mistakes and said hurtful things. I'll take responsibility for my part, but she has to be willing to do the same.' She turned on the electric hand whisk, beating the eggs and drowning out anything Dev might want to say. She could sense him behind her, waiting, but she focused on adding the eggs to the brownie batter, mixing it for far longer than she should. They were going to be overworked, but she didn't stop until she felt a cool breeze as the back door opened then closed again.

She would talk to Alice, she wanted to be friends again, but things were different now, she was different. Alice needed to realise that, if they ever stood a chance of moving forward.

Chapter Twenty-Eight

The scent of freshly popped popcorn, sun-baked dirt and dying grass carried across the Bunham village fete, while the shrill tune of the merry-go-round lilted up and down, interspersed with children's screams and laughter, and the sudden shout of a stressed adult.

It was nearly lunchtime and the Mother's Institute stall was doing a roaring trade in sugar-free jams and chutneys. They had a reputation for their home-made produce and the crowds kept flocking to the stall. They formed a constantly changing barricade of faces that only parted briefly, allowing Olivia a glimpse of the village green. There were lots of stalls selling art, crafts and Mother Mason-approved food. A man two stalls down shouted for people to try their luck on the hoopla. He was getting louder as the day went on, competing with the barking dogs in the distance; the canine trials must have started in the arena.

'Hello, my gal, how's things?' Tom stood at the front of the crowd, leaning on his walking stick.

'Tom!' Olivia beamed at him. 'It's so good to see you.' It had been tough working alongside Alice and Mrs Flynn all morning; Tom's was the first friendly face she'd seen. 'How are you?'

'I'm very well, thank you for asking. I hear you've been busy. Which of these did you make?'

Which of them didn't she make? In between baking

cakes and making scones, she had been boiling oranges, simmering strawberries and straining blackcurrants. Jenna had looked begrudgingly pleased when she saw the boxes full of jams, chutneys and pickles, but she covered it well. She was less happy when she saw Olivia had five entries in the annual MI preserves competition. Alice would normally have enjoyed the moment but she had kept her back to them, arranging jars on the stall. She'd barely glanced at Olivia all morning, apparently not as eager to talk as Dev had made out.

'I can recommend the marmalade and the ploughman's pickle,' Olivia said.

'Sounds good to me.' He extended a shaky hand, a crumpled five-pound note clutched in his fist.

'I'd like a jar of the marmalade, two jars of strawberry and two raspberry.' A woman wearing an expensive linen suit and designer sunglasses pushed her way in front of Tom.

'Excuse me, I'm serving someone.' Olivia tried to sound polite.

The woman helped herself to Alice's display of precariously stacked jam jars, causing them to wobble and slide.

'Madam, I need you to wait a moment. Alice, can you see to this woman? Alice?'

'Uh-huh.' Alice didn't look up from her phone.

'Mrs Flynn, I could use some help, please.' Their treasurer sat stiff and upright on a folding chair, one hand resting on top of the cash tin, the other reaching out to claim the five pounds.

'I can't leave the money unattended.' She settled herself more firmly onto her seat and drew the tin closer to her.

'What's in the blackberry and apple jam?' The woman picked up a new jar and peered at the label. Women like

235

her came every year and bought up half the stock, allegedly passing it off as their own. From her general air of entitlement, she was probably no stranger to Barre Class, either.

'Alice, please could you see to this *lady*.'

The woman retrieved another jar of chutney from the bottom corner of the pyramid and the whole thing started to slide. Olivia lurched past Alice and grabbed the stack before they crashed to the ground. The woman tutted, pushed a crisp twenty-pound note in Olivia's direction, and left with her purchases.

'I'll take that.' Mrs Flynn held out her hand again.

Alice finally looked up from her phone as Olivia restacked the jars. 'Tom! I didn't know you were coming.' She leaned over the table to hug the old man.

'Bronwyn gave me a lift. She's off taking a phone call, so I thought I'd come over. I can't miss out on a jar of jam from the famous baker.' He winked at Olivia and anxiety, her old enemy, lurched back to life. How did he know?

'Does it have a *special* ingredient in?' He winked again.

'Of course it does.' Alice snatched up the nearest jar and thrust it at him. 'It's love. Everything Liv makes is full of love. It's what makes it so special.' For the first time she truly looked at Olivia and her expression softened. 'It's what makes her so special,' she said in a quieter voice.

'Don't 'spose you've got anything to serve it on, a nice—'

'No!' Olivia and Alice both said at the same time, loud enough to drown out Tom's tactless question. He might be willing to join the Societal Evolution Programme, but they had too much to live for.

'Olivia's recipe is top secret. In fact, it's highly classified, so don't mention it to anyone else.' Alice glared at him emphatically.

'Right you are, my gal, I take your point. Don't worry,

236

nothing gets past this trap.' He mimed turning a key in front of his mouth.

'Tom, there you are!' Bronwyn hurried up to join him as he took his purchases. 'Sorry, that call took longer than expected.'

'No worries, I was buying some jars of jam from Olivia. Maybe next time you're at the gym you could smuggle me a scon—'

'Right, we'd better be off.' Bronwyn's face was pinker than her hair and that was an achievement. 'You don't want to miss the best prizes on the tombola.' She took his arm and led him away.

'Cheerio.' Tom gave them a wave as he left, taking his volatile secret-keeping ability with him.

'Thank you,' Olivia whispered, wiping the sweat from her forehead with the back of her hand.

'Don't mention it,' Alice said, her tone still furious. 'Bronwyn and I are going to have words later.' She paused to take a deep breath. 'Not that I haven't been tempted to do the same.'

'Me either,' Olivia said. The number of times she'd almost held back a piece of shortbread or a sausage roll, but the risk was too great and Tom really couldn't keep a secret. She and Alice shared a tentative smile.

'Liv,' Alice's voice softened, 'I'm sorry ... I, uh, haven't been ... pulling my weight today. Is there anything I can do?'

'It's okay, I understand ... I'm sorry too.' Her eyes started to sting. 'Wretched grit, the dust from the playing field is covering everything.'

'Right?' Alice's eyes were watering too. 'Total nightmare.'

'Could you wipe the jars down?' Their fingers touched

237

as she passed Alice the soft cloth and they met each other's gaze again. It wasn't a full apology, but it was a start.

'So, you entered the jam competition again this year?' Alice rubbed at the top of each jar, wiping away the collected grime.

'I did.' She had entered the village fete competitions every year since Nana Ivy taught her how to cook; it would look suspicious if she stopped now. Every ounce of energy she wasn't channelling in to baking, she was using to keep up appearances, to both her family and the rest of the world.

'You deserve to win. Yours is always the best, no matter how much Jenna rigs it.'

Mrs Flynn harrumphed but they ignored her.

'I've, uh, I've been enjoying your *food* recently.' Alice was going to rub the ink off the label if she kept wiping it so hard.

'You tried some?' Olivia attempted a casual tone but failed dismally.

'Yeah, you've been making my favourites.'

She *had* noticed. Olivia had geared so many of her recipes towards Alice's tastes, but she hadn't dared to hope.

'They were amazing. You're amazing.' Alice bit her lip. 'I should have said something sooner.'

'No, I should have.' She wanted to hug her, but they were both clutching jars, so she settled on a smile that said more than she could.

'There's more customers,' Mrs Flynn snapped. 'You're not on a break yet.'

Trying hard not to cry with relief, Olivia resumed her welcoming shopkeeper pose as a group of young mums pushing prams reached the front of the loosely structured queue.

'Are they all sugar-free?' one of them asked.

'Of course.' There really wasn't any point in having signs all over the tent that said 'Sugar-free jam and chutney, Mother Mason's special recipe'. Apparently, big red letters were easy to miss. 'All the ingredients are on the label.'

A little girl in a rainbow stroller started to fuss, crying and kicking off her blanket.

'It's okay, sweetie.' Her mum leaned forward and cooed to the girl but stopped as two men in suits came up to join the group. She nudged her friends and they moved away from the stall, shoving their prams hard to get over the rough, bumpy ground.

Alice froze at the sight of the men and a jewel-bright jar of strawberry jam slipped through her fingers. Fortunately Olivia caught it before it could hit the ground and shatter into a hundred sharp, sticky pieces.

The other customers slipped away, joining the stream of passers-by, losing themselves among the crowd. The men stood, hands behind their backs, inspecting the home-made preserves. Obviously they couldn't read the signs either. One picked up a jar from the middle of the table and examined the small list of natural ingredients. It took him far longer than necessary to read it.

'Can I get you anything else?' Olivia asked but the man ignored her. He handed the jar to his partner, who took it without paying, and they walked away again.

Chapter Twenty-Nine

'Hurry up, Mummy, we can't be late.' Mia dragged Olivia across the village green, past the two agents at the entrance to the stage area and on towards one of the empty rows. A crowd had already gathered and all the seats on the front rows were occupied by ladies of the Mother's Institute. Jenna sat in the central seat, with an unobstructed path to the raised platform and the shiny trophies.

'You might get a prize,' Mia said.

That's unlikely, Olivia thought, trying to crush the tiny flicker of hope that sprang up every year. Jenna always won everything. It would be nice, though, to do some cooking that she could actually take public credit for.

Alice, Dev, Danny and Matthew trailed behind them, less excited by the competition and drawn-out ceremony.

'Whatever happens, you deserve to win.' Alice sat down beside Olivia and briefly squeezed her hand. 'You're the most talented person here.'

'She's right.' Danny took the folding chair on her other side and Mia climbed up onto her lap.

'Mummy's the best cook in the world.'

'Thank you.' She kissed the top of Mia's head. She might not be the best cook but she thought she might be the bravest. That was better than any silver-plated trophy they handed out today.

Sitting under the hot afternoon sun, the villagers were

growing restless when a woman in long black and gold robes and an ornate feathered tricorn hat took to the stage. Jenna loved having a touch of governmental dignitary at the fete, especially when she won. The mayor stepped up to the crackling microphone. 'Thank you ... welcome ... be here ... so many talented people ...' Her voice faded in and out over the whining squeal of the speaker system.

Mia cheered with delight, as the rest of the crowd applauded politely.

'The first ... goes to the best floral ...'

'This is boring,' Matthew said. 'When can we go?'

'Soon,' Danny said.

'Here, you can play on my phone.' Dev passed him the device and Matthew was instantly absorbed.

The prizes went on and on: best flower, best plant, best fruit, best vegetable, best photograph, handicraft, needlecraft, paper craft. So much produce. So many crafts. All with a multitude of different subcategories. The same people kept getting up to receive their prizes, Jenna strutted across the stage on more than one occasion. The crowd, like the entries, were wilting in the heat, but nonetheless, everyone stayed. It didn't hurt to be seen participating in local events.

Olivia was trying to entertain Mia by the time they got to the jam round.

'Now for the award for best preserve,' the woman's voice carried clearly enough to catch Olivia's attention. 'And the winner is ...' She paused, holding the requisite five seconds of quiz show silence.

Olivia mentally prepared herself: it wouldn't be her, it was never her. The woman would say Jenna, they always did. The increasing beat of her heart was a sad, whimsical hope that was about to get squashed. She couldn't possibly say—

'Olivia Pritchard.'

'What?' she whispered, her own name sounding like a foreign language.

'Mummy, you did it!' Mia bounced up and down.

'Go Mum!' Matthew high-fived her, his boredom evaporating.

'Congratulations!' Alice and Danny sandwiched her in a tight hug.

'Come and get your prize, Olivia.' The mayor beckoned to their little celebrating group and people turned to watch, smiling and clapping for her. She couldn't seem to move, couldn't process the information. She had actually won. It was like a waking dream, and she stood up as though sleepwalking, Mia still in her arms

'Mia, wait here,' Danny said but Mia clung on, refusing to let go.

'That's okay, Olivia, bring your daughter up,' the mayor's voice boomed out. 'Children are our future, after all.'

They slipped past the clapping spectators, past the agents at the end of their row and walked down the long grassy aisle to the stage.

'I knew you would win, Mummy.' Mia kissed her cheek.

They climbed the rickety metal steps up to the stage and everyone watched them cross the platform. The mayor stood holding a shiny silver trophy, her other hand outstretched for an expectant shake. She grasped Olivia, dragging her the last few steps, and turned her towards the audience. 'Smile for the cameras.'

The flash of light bulbs went off, the local press capturing the moment for all eternity.

'Have you anything to say?' the mayor asked.

'Thank you so much.'

The mayor held out a large silver cup to her. Jenna's

name was engraved over and over on the little plaque but there was a small space ready for her name.

'Mrs Pritchard?' A deep, male voice said behind her.

'Yes?' She turned into the shadow of two tall figures. The noise of the crowd ceased, a stillness fell over the fete, but the shrill tune of the merry-go-round continued on.

'Mummy.' Mia shrank close against her.

'Mrs Pritchard, you are under arrest for the possession of a Class A substance, and the illegal production and distribution of cakes and baked goods.' The first man spoke loud enough for his words to carry to the audience but the microphone picked up his voice and flung it out across the entire village green. The merry-go-round music stopped.

'No,' Olivia whispered. She took a step away, twisting to keep Mia safe, but the agent followed, his shadow retreating to reveal his face.

'Ray?' she whispered but he shook his head in warning. The second agent caught hold of her arm and he was familiar too.

'Hello, Olivia.' Ray's partner was Lewis Hook-Medwood. 'That belongs to my wife.' He dragged the silver cup away from her, then reached to take Mia, but she blocked him with her body.

'Get away from my daughter,' she bellowed, as Mia screamed, the sound echoing through the speaker system. She searched desperately for an ally, someone who could help them, but the mayor had slipped away, retreating down the steps on the other side of the stage, leaving Olivia and Mia all alone.

'No!' Alice screamed.

'Stop!' Danny shouted and they both fought their way through the spectators and past the agents at the end of their row.

'You've made a mistake; my wife's done nothing wrong.' Danny sprinted towards the stage but two more agents intercepted him.

'Nothing wrong?' Lewis sneered. 'You're a bigger fool than I thought you were. Do you have no idea what's been going on in your own home?' He took out a pair of hand-cuffs and snapped the cold metal hard across her wrist, he reached for her other arm, the one encircling Mia, and she fought against him; there was no way she was letting go. Mia screamed and clung tighter, and Olivia managed to pull away, almost dislocating her shoulder.

'Ray, no!' Alice shrieked. 'What are you doing? You've made a mistake, tell them you've made a mistake.' She tried to push past the agents but they stood immobile at the foot of the stairs. Ray ignored her completely as two more men came from out of the crowd and dragged her back. 'Let me go,' she screamed, 'let me go!'

Dev slipped past Matthew and ran to help Alice, while the other villagers looked on. He reached the brawl and took a swing at the man on the left, who ducked, released Alice and caught Dev's fist, deftly swinging him into a choke hold, one arm twisted up behind his back. Like an army of ants, agents flooded the area, converging on them. They wrestled Dev and Alice down to the ground, but Danny dodged as someone lunged for him and, avoiding the stairs completely, he vaulted up onto the stage. He tried to force his way to Olivia and Mia, but Ray stepped between them.

'There has to be some kind of mistake.' Danny held up his hands in surrender as three agents captured him. 'Please, my wife is innocent.'

Except she wasn't, she was as guilty as they said, and she had no defence. She looked to him with tears in her eyes. He would never forgive her for this.

'I'm sorry,' she whispered. 'I'm so sorry.'

'Don't, don't say anything,' he warned.

The crowd watched in silence: there were no flashes of cameras bulbs, no red dots of recording phones, they knew better than that; even the local press were packing up their equipment. The government would release official footage and a statement they were permitted to use.

Jenna sat in the front row, tall and proud, as her husband carried out Mother Mason's justice.

'Where's Matthew?' Olivia shielded Mia and searched for him. 'Matthew?' He had to be alone, abandoned by everyone in their bid to defend her, but she wasn't the one who needed protecting. 'Matthew?' she screamed, scanning the crowd of pale faces. They shrank back beneath her scrutiny, creating a void of space around her little boy. He stood small and alone in the middle of the aisle.

'I'm sorry, Olivia,' Ray whispered, 'but this can get a lot worse. Just do as you're told and everything will be all right.'

All right? She wanted to scratch his eyes out, the filthy, duplicitous traitor. She tried to tear away from him, to get down to Matthew, but she still had Mia to protect.

'Olivia's done nothing wrong.' Alice kicked out at the man who held her.

'Of course she has. Baking cakes, supplying a bar, leading an illegal organisation.' Lewis jerked Olivia back so she fell into him, close enough to smell the mingled scent of sweating flesh and sickly aftershave. Mia was dragged with her, flopping like a rag doll, but there was nothing Olivia could do to stop it.

'No,' Alice shrieked. 'I'm the leader of CTAS, I'm the one you want.'

'Love the spotlight, don't you, Alice?' Lewis jeered.

'Still trying to hog the glory, even when your friend's life is over. We know it's not you, you're a nobody. Olivia here, she's the prize Mother Mason has been waiting for. She's broken so many laws she might as well go straight to the Societal Evolution Programme. Her wardrobe alone contains enough items to get her convicted.'

'The cookbooks aren't hers, they're mine,' Danny said.

Wait – he knew? Olivia searched his face for judgement and scorn but found only compassion and understanding. I knew, his gaze said, I've always known; I don't care, I love you.

All this time she'd distrusted him, put up barriers between them, refused to believe he truly loved her.

'Danny,' she whispered, feeling the crushing weight of wasted love and missed opportunities.

'No, the books belong to me,' Alice shouted. 'Olivia was just looking after them. I'm telling you, none of this was her, it's all me, I'm the one you want. Ray, I'm the one who was meant to be arrested. Cut the Apron Strings! Down with Mother Mason. Down——' She let out an audible gasp and went silent.

'Alice!' Olivia and Dev screamed, but neither could reach her. Mia sobbed hysterically and Danny thrashed against the men who held him.

'Stop fighting!' Ray whispered into Olivia's ear. 'It's going to be okay, trust me, but if you keep fighting you're going to get everyone hurt, or worse.'

His words found the centre of her strength and the fight died within her. She stood still, no longer needing any restraint.

'Mummy, Mummy, Mummy ...' Mia sobbed, clinging tighter.

'It's okay, baby, go to Daddy. It's going to be fine.' She

kissed Mia's tear-drenched face and lowered her to the stage.

Alice was moving again, struggling on the ground while Dev sat handcuffed beside her. Matthew still stood alone.

'Alice, stop fighting. Please.' From her position in the dirt, Alice lifted her head up enough to meet Olivia's gaze. 'You have to take care of them for me.'

'Let's go,' Ray said.

'Not until my children are with their father.'

Ray signalled for the agents to release Danny. He pulled free and picked Mia up.

'I love you,' she whispered to them both as Lewis dragged her other arm behind her and locked her into the handcuffs. Pain tore through her shoulders as they pushed her past Danny, forcing her towards the side of the stage and down the stairs, not slowing as she stumbled and almost fell. They paraded her in front of the crowd. Some openly stared, while others became fascinated by the sun-scorched earth.

'It's going to be okay, Liv, I promise,' Alice shouted. 'I'll make this right.'

They rounded the corner of the arena and she turned her head to get a last glimpse. Alice had surrendered: she now knelt beside Matthew, her arms around him, both of them in tears.

What have I done? Olivia wondered. How could I have allowed this to happen? She had ruined everything.

The agents forced her on and her family were lost from sight. A waiting van came into view, the back doors open to reveal the cage inside. She struggled, twisting and bucking against the men. No, she could not go in there. If she went in she would never get out. She fought hard, trying to wrench herself away from them. Kicking out, she managed to connect with soft flesh, which elicited a grunt followed by a stream of curses. They twisted her arms until she screamed and went limp, then lifted her bodily and threw her into the van. Tumbling forward, she collided with the far wall and her head connected with the metal panel. She collapsed onto the floor, unable to react when they slammed the wire mesh gate and clicked the lock shut.

'You've been a bad girl, Olivia. I promise life is not going to be so sweet for you from here on out.' Lewis closed the van door, leaving her in darkness.

Chapter Thirty

Olivia huddled inside the dark van, attempting to brace herself against the burning hot metal of the sun-warmed walls. They rocketed around corners and jerked to sudden stops, but every sharp turn sent her scrabbling and sliding across the dirty, oily floor. At a particularly violent bend, she was thrown from one side of the van to the other and hit her head. A burst of electric white exploded across her vision, the only light in the darkness. The metallic tang of blood filled her mouth and she choked, unable to breathe. The surrounding darkness flooded her consciousness and she passed out.

She woke to a throbbing inside her skull and eyes so swollen it was almost impossible to open them. Not that it made any difference, it was still so dark she couldn't see a thing. How long had she been there? It could have been hours or days. Something was different though; it was quiet now, the van was stationary and thankfully so was she. She raised her head but nausea and dizziness quickly ended her attempt, forcing her to remain still.

Voices came from outside, laughter, a shared joke, then the back doors opened. The early evening sunshine chased away the dark and she cried out as the bright light hit her eyes. The pain almost matched the agony she felt inside, the sore, scoured feeling of her life stripped away. Black shadows moved to block her view. Lewis and Ray unlocked the gate and dragged her out into the fresh air. It was cool and the breeze dried the sweat that clung to her clothes, making her shiver.

She tried to look around to work out where she was but even the smallest motion brought on the sickening dizziness that seesawed the horizon, making it tilt and sway. The grey buildings blurred with the dark tarmac as the ground shifted beneath her feet, rising and swelling. It was like being at sea, with the seasickness to prove it. She giggled: seasick on land, that was funny. She giggled again.

'I'm glad you think this is amusing.' Lewis gave her a shake before propelling her into motion. She staggered forward, almost falling, but Ray caught her and set her back on her feet.

'Watch out, she's already a mess. I told you to drive slower. That cut on her cheek had better not leave a scar.'

'It's fine, Ray, you need to relax. Vera can cover it up.'

With one on either side of her, they half pushed, half dragged her towards the nearest building. She still wore the handcuffs but she couldn't feel the pain in her arms any more. Her fingers had an odd, numb tingling to them but it was better than the sharp wrenching agony from the arrest.

They stopped for Ray to retrieve his ID card and swipe it through the entry machine. He moved close to the silver plate set into the wall and a red light scanned his eye. She knew he was an agent, but this? This wasn't just providing inside information on upcoming arrests, he was the one taking women away. Had Alice known?

During the pause before the door swung open, he glanced at her but averted his gaze almost immediately. For a moment she caught the look of shame and self-hatred she'd seen before. Good, she thought, he should feel bad.

They thrust her over the threshold and she fought to get

one last look at her surroundings, but all she saw was the descending summer sun.

It was cold, grey and nondescript inside the building. The walls were painted the utilitarian colour of all government facilities. Beneath the flickering fluorescent lights she could make out scuff marks and dark faded stains on the linoleum that she didn't want to look too closely at. There were no signs, no markings, nothing to identify where they had brought her. Indistinct but uniform, it could be anywhere. How would Alice ever find her?

Lewis and Ray led her down a zigzagging maze of hallways. After the first left, right, right she gave up trying to remember the way; her head ached too much to hold more than the simplest thought. They passed many branching corridors and the distant sound of voices filtered up to them, but none of these were their destination. Solid metal gates constantly interrupted their journey; electronically locked, they only opened with a swipe of a security card and a scan of an eye or hand. The clunk, click, whir of the lock wasn't as bad as the solid thud when they closed behind her.

She didn't fight them, didn't even try to struggle. What was the point? It was all she could do not to throw up. The sharp smell of disinfectant was a constant, desperately trying to cover a heavy smell of stale air and something more ominous, but the further they went, the more she could make out a familiar delicious scent. It was impossible, she thought, the concussion must be worse than she realised. There was no way that here of all places she could smell freshly baked cake.

With a sense of finality, Lewis and Ray shoved her through the next gate into a large, high-ceilinged area. It looked like a regular lunch canteen, with long tables and benches and a serving hatch at the far end, but metal bars ran the length of each wall, dividing the sides of the room into individual cells. They led her past cell after cell and the resident of each one came forward to peer at her. There were no gaunt expressions or sallow skin, the women looked healthy, full-faced, with rounded, curving figures beneath tight grey jumpsuits.

'Aye-aye, who's the new girl?' A large woman leaned with her arms through the gaps in her cell door.

'New friend for you, Carol,' Lewis said.

'Watcha do, love?' the woman in the next cell asked, her round face pressed to the bars. 'Something bad? Were you wicked?'

'Tell them, Liv, tell them how you sold out your family so you could play the domestic goddess.' Lewis pushed her towards Carol who reached out a large, meaty hand and pinched Olivia's arm.

'She made cakes? How come she's so freaking skinny?'

Olivia cowered back but Lewis propelled her towards the rows of tables in the centre of the room.

'Practically skeletal,' a woman from the cell opposite shouted.

'Be nice, ladies,' an older woman called from the far end of the block.

'Sorry, Shawna, my bad.' Carol didn't sound sorry. 'All I'm saying is you can see her bony arse from here. Watch out, Louie Boy, or she'll escape through the bars.'

A couple of the women burst into raucous laughter and Lewis joined in. 'I'm not worried about that. She's not tasted Vera's cooking.' He pushed Olivia down onto the bench; she fell hard against the metal edge of the table and leaned forward, gasping for breath.

'Easy,' Ray warned.

'She's being a drama queen.' Lewis unlocked Olivia's handcuffs and her arms flopped by her sides. Pins and needles joined the shooting pains in her shoulders and the ache in her ribs.

'Vera, we've got a new one for you,' he shouted towards the long serving hatch set into the wall. This was the source of the baking smell. Two women dressed in chef's whites were busy in the kitchen. Despite the distant clatter of pans and the bubbling of boiling liquid, the older of the two turned at the sound of Lewis's voice and waved. She set a large glossy chocolate cake down onto the hatch counter, in full view of the prisoners. Moans and shouts of delight echoed from the cells and Vera smiled as she wiped her hands on her apron. She disappeared for a moment and emerged through a door in the far corner of the room.

'You must be Olivia, I'm Vera. I'll be your host for the next few months. You must be hungry. I bet you haven't eaten all day; you've come such a long way. Fancy a cuppa? The cake's ready to cut.'

Olivia looked from her to Lewis and back. She had no idea concussion hallucinations could be so real, so vivid. Surely she was back in the van, still lying on the dirty floor, because this place was insane. Or she was. She started to giggle again, but her laugh became a sob. This wasn't happening, it couldn't be, it had to be a horrible dream.

'It's a lovely chocolate fudge cake, your favourite, right?' Vera persisted.

Of course it was, but she wasn't going to admit it.

'She'd love a piece,' Lewis said.

'Thank you, but I'm not hungry,' Olivia said primly, but her stomach betrayed her with a loud gurgle.

'You're not lying to me, are you, deary? Nobody lies to Vera, do they, girls?'

The women pressed their faces to the bars as Vera cut a large slice and put it down in front of Olivia. Her stomach rumbled again, and she swallowed. She was hungry; she hadn't eaten since lunch at the fete ... today? Yesterday? Where were Matthew and Mia? Where was Danny? And why wasn't Alice here with her? She looked to Ray for answers, but he stared at the floor, kicking a dark stain with the tip of his boot.

A bitter taste filled her mouth and she leaned away from the sweet, sickly smell.

'No, thank you,' she said with more conviction, glaring at him and Lewis.

'No, thank you? How can you, the Queen of Cake, say no?' Lewis leaned over her, broke off a piece and held it in front of her mouth. 'You're being very rude.'

Vera sat down on the other side of the table and nudged the plate towards Olivia. 'I'll be very upset if you don't eat any. I made it especially for you; it's a treat.'

'Can we have a slice?' Carol asked.

'Yeah, we've smelt it for the last hour, it's been unbearable. Let us have it, we won't be ungrateful,' her neighbouring cellmate called. Her large, curvy figure pressed so close to the bars that rolls of fat bulged through.

'Don't eat it,' a woman's voice called, faint and breathy. Olivia saw movement in the nearest cell. A small figure lay on the bed, trying to rise. The effort made her even paler and she slumped against the wall. Painfully thin, her bones were so close to the surface Olivia could make out the shape of her skull, her skin stretched tight over it, her eyes dark concave spaces above sharp cheekbones. 'Whatever you do, don't eat anything.'

'Shut up, Nadine.' Lewis pushed the piece of cake towards Olivia's mouth. 'She's nuts, no one listens to Nadine.'

'Not if we can help it, right, Becky?' Carol guffawed and her neighbour joined in.

'Yeah, she might be a fussy eater, doesn't mean the rest of us are,' Becky said.

Becky? The name triggered something in Olivia's battered brain. It couldn't be, could it? The rotund woman looked like a complete stranger, but there was something about her eyes that sparked a memory of the supermarket. Was this where she ended up? Had she been here all this time and Ray had known?

'I told you to eat.' Lewis pressed the cake against her mouth. She could taste the chocolate on her lips but she tried to turn away. Nadine was staring at her, hunched over on the edge of her bed. The woman shook her head the smallest fraction, the movement seemed to take all her effort.

'Eat it already.' Lewis slammed his hand hard against Olivia's mouth, forcing the cake between her closed lips. His palm blocked her nose, cutting off her oxygen until she gasped for breath and he rammed the cake deep into her mouth. Her eyes watered and she choked, tasting blood and chocolate, salt and sweet.

'It's okay.' Vera pulled Lewis's hand away. 'If she's not hungry, she's not hungry. She will be soon enough. Put her in the cell near the kitchen.'

'Get up.' He wrenched her to her feet before she had a chance to move. She tripped over the bench and he dragged her across the floor to the cell opposite Nadine's.

'Home sweet home.' He pushed her into the small room. 'Enjoy your stay at Chez Mason.'

Chapter Thirty-One

Olivia fell forward into the cell, her body already bracing for the pain, but someone caught her and lowered her gently to the ground.

'It's okay,' a woman said. 'You're safe now.'

Olivia looked up into the kind eyes of a middle-aged woman. Streaks of grey shot through her dark hair and deep wrinkles etched sadness and worry into her face, but her voice was warm and her hands gentle as she helped Olivia to rise and move to sit on the bed.

'Olivia, is it? I'm Shawna. It looks like you're having a pretty tough day.'

'What gave it away?' Olivia asked.

Shawna reached up and touched Olivia's forehead, the lightest of caresses, but it still sent agonising waves of pain and dizziness through her skull.

'You must have really got under Lewis's skin; well done. Although, you might want to keep your head down while you're in here. This place is tough enough without making enemies of the guards.'

Fear and pain broke through Olivia's fragile defences and she started to shake, her whole body trembling as reality set in. How did this happen? How was she locked up in some godforsaken prison in the middle of nowhere? Nobody knew where she was, how would they ever come and get her?

'It's all right, you cry as much as you need.' Shawna held her hand, stroking it with the same soothing repetitive motion Olivia used to comfort Matthew and Mia.

'My children,' she sobbed.

'You'll see them again,' Shawna said, but the sorrow in her tone offered no comfort. 'For now though, you have to find a way to get through the day. Just one moment at a time. First, we need to get you cleaned up, wash off some of that dried blood and see if we can't take some of the swelling down.' She tore the seam of her grey jumpsuit and ripped off the cuff. 'Don't worry,' she said, seeing Olivia's shock, 'I won't be needing it after today.' She took the cloth to the tiny metal sink in the corner of the cell and ran it under the slow flowing tap.

Olivia tried hard not to flinch at the touch of the cold, wet fabric against her skin but it felt like her whole body was raw. Everything hurt.

'That's better,' Shawna said after a few minutes of gentle dabbing. 'You look less like a trauma victim; there's no reason to give Lewis the satisfaction of seeing the damage he's done. Take it from me: the more you act like he's not getting to you, the better. He thrives on making us suffer in here, so try to rise above it.'

'How can he get away with it?'

'How do they get away with anything now? People look away, they're too scared and too desperate to protect themselves. Don't worry, the women in here will look out for you. We take care of each other; we have to.'

Someone approached the cell and Olivia flinched, but Shawna smiled and stood up. 'Hi Ray, what can we do for you?'

'I've got a jumpsuit for Olivia, she needs to change.' Ray now at least looked at Olivia when he spoke, but he was more subdued than normal and he'd lost his usual air of superiority. So he should. Bastard.

Shawna stood to take them, but Ray shook his head. 'I need to give them directly to Olivia, new rules.'

'Of course there are.' Shawna sank back down on the bed but Olivia didn't want to get up, didn't want to go close to him, to accept the rough grey overalls that he held out to her.

'They're really not that bad.' Shawna nudged her. 'It's quite refreshing not having to worry about your outfit every day or do any washing. It's all taken care of in here.'

'Come on, Liv, Olivia, you need to put these on.' Ray extended the jumpsuit to her through the cell bars. 'Please, just get it over with.'

Please? He was asking her politely, like she would be doing him a favour? The traitor had just ripped her daughter from her arms and he wanted her to go lightly on him? She stood up and stalked towards the bars, snatching the jumpsuit and basic black trainers from him, and turned her back on his imploring expression. Did he want her understanding too? Or worse, her forgiveness? This had not been the plan, she was not meant to be in here. Alice was the one who wanted to get arrested, why wasn't she here? There was no way Alice had known what was happening. No matter what they had been through, how bad their fight, Alice would never have thrown her to the wolves like this ... But she had a plan, this was only the first step, if only Olivia could figure the rest out. She couldn't trust Ray, but he was the closest thing she had to CTAS and maybe there was a way to get him to reveal something useful.

She turned back to him and asked casually, 'What happens next?'

'You change into the jumpsuit and I take your old clothes

away.' That wasn't what she meant and he knew it. 'I need your jewellery too, except your wedding ring, you can keep that.'

'What about my necklace?' She caught it up with her finger, extending the white tasselled pendant out to him. 'Do I have to give this up as well?'

'For now, yes.' His tasselled pen was still in his pocket and she longed to rip it from him. How dare he corrupt their code, when he had been working against them all this time.

'I have to take everything away, you're a prisoner like everyone else.' He glanced up to something on the wall outside the cell. 'Just do as you're told and everything will be fine.'

'Fine? Really?' she laughed and there was a high note of hysteria running through the sound. 'I'm not sure how that's possible. Ray, I'm not meant to be here and you know it.'

'That's what everyone says,' Lewis strolled across to join them. 'Having problems? Need me to come in there and help you change, Olivia? You're no Alice, but ...' He leered at her, his gaze roving over her body. 'Man, I love it when we get the newbies in. Having to watch them feed you all up into ugly porkers breaks my heart, but that's the job.'

'I've got this, Lewis,' Ray said. 'You can help them set up for the party.'

'Of course. Shawna, you excited about tonight? Ready for your big send off?'

'I've been ready for a long time.' Shawna's voice was tired. 'Come on, Olivia, let's get you changed.'

Olivia felt more naked in the regulation prison jumpsuit than she had in the moments between getting undressed and pulling on the horrible outfit. Taking off her HealthHub was liberating, no longer worrying about how many steps she'd taken or calories she'd burned, but removing her watch, and worse her necklace, felt like stripping away the last of her armour. Her wedding ring was a small comfort.

Released from her cell, she sat on the edge of one of the benches, as far away from the other prisoners as she could get. Not that they noticed, they were all too busy stuffing their faces with the gluttonous feast of buffet food laid out on the long tables.

Everything looked and smelt repulsive, and Olivia had to fight to keep from throwing up. Instead, she focused on rubbing her thumb back and forth over the smooth, warm, metal band of her ring. Was Danny somewhere doing the same? The children must be so scared; they wouldn't understand what had happened, why she was gone. Why she might never go home again.

'You not having anything to eat?' Carol hefted her large bulk down onto the bench beside Olivia and the sturdy metal bowed under her weight. 'You refused the cake and now the party food, you're wasting perfectly delicious grub. Starving yourself in here isn't gonna help a thing, it certainly won't get you out any sooner.' She picked up a deep-fried chicken drumstick and took an enormous bite. The smell turned Olivia's stomach and she held her breath, wishing Carol would move and take her overflowing plate away with her.

Nadine was still in her cell, despite the door being open. She lay on her bed, watching everyone help themselves to the buffet.

'You don't want to take your life advice from her.' Carol pointed the half-eaten drumstick towards the cell. 'She's crazy, she'll drag you down with her and that's not a good place to be. Follow Shawna's example, she knows what she's doing.'

Shawna stood in the middle of a group of prisoners, all of them laughing and joking as they enjoyed their party food.

'Mmm, Vera makes the best damn coleslaw of anyone I know. You gotta try it.' Carol shovelled in a mouthful, drops of creamy mayonnaise splashing the table around her and dripping onto her jumpsuit. 'As far as final suppers go, Shawna has great taste. The last inmate wanted sushi. Sushi? If I'm picking a last meal it's gonna be deep fried with extra cheese.' She grabbed a fistful of chips, dipped them in a pool of blood-red ketchup and stuffed them into her mouth.

'Last meal?' Olivia felt the world spin around her and this time it wasn't because of the concussion.

'She didn't tell you?' Carol wiped her mouth on the back of her sleeve. 'Tonight's her last night, then it's off to court. Shawna's gonna be famous!' She made jazz hands, then licked the ketchup off her fingers.

Somebody made a joke and Shawna laughed, a little louder, a little harder than everyone else, but on the surface she didn't look like a woman about to go on trial.

'How can she be so calm?' Olivia asked.

'She gets to see her family tomorrow, her kids, her grandkids. She's waited eight months for this; you'll be excited too, when it's your turn.' Carol scraped together the last of her food. 'I'm getting some more chicken before it's all gone. You'd better hurry, but leave room for dessert. We've got cheesecake, thanks to Shawna, and you do not want to miss that.'

Miss out? How could anyone here have any kind of appetite? Especially Shawna. Surely a final meal should be sombre, with tears and desperate pleas, but from the women's excited chatter, this could have been any leaving-do, from any workplace across the country. Except this one ended in death.

They talked about the future as though it would be longer than twenty-four hours, wondering which of Shawna's family members would be in court and how many of her children and grandchildren could fit on the Family Bench. They never stopped talking for long; it was as if their upbeat tones and enthusiastic laughter could keep away the spectre of death, but it stalked among them, standing behind Shawna, following her through the room as she went to get more food, when she visited each prisoner to say her goodbyes, when she took time to go in to Nadine, who gave her earnest advice in hushed tones.

Nobody cried, nobody showed anything other than manic joy, but the arrival of dessert was the perfect excuse to take a step away, to turn their backs on Shawna, creating space between them and the future which awaited them all.

'Here, I brought you a piece of cheesecake.' Shawna came over to join Olivia who also remained alone. If Shawna reminded everyone of their future, Olivia reminded them of their past, of their arrests and their first losses. The present was the only safe place for them to inhabit.

'Don't worry,' Shawna said, 'you don't have to eat it. I just thought you might be getting hungry.'

Nausea was now Olivia's constant companion and the thick, claggy cheesecake looked far from appetising. Shawna didn't pick up her fork either.

'Are you okay?' Olivia asked.

'Why wouldn't I be? All my favourite foods *and* tomorrow I get to see my family.'

'I'm so sorry, I—'

'Don't.' Shawna was quick to cut her off. 'I don't want

your pity or your sympathy, that only makes things harder. I can't,' she swallowed, blinking back unwelcome tears, 'I can't think about ... My kids need me to be strong, one last time. I won't let my last moments with them be ones of grief and fear.' Shawna reached for Olivia's hand. 'You can spend your time in here getting angry and bitter, you can surrender to the fear and turn yourself inside out with anxiety, or you can focus on the people you love.'

A siren pulsed through the air, accompanied by a flashing amber light that made Olivia jump. Shawna froze and everyone turned to look at her.

'Back in your cells,' Ray shouted from the far side of the entrance gates, where he and Lewis waited. The women did as they were told, all except Shawna, who clung to Olivia's hand, her nails digging in.

'You too, Shawna, Olivia,' Ray said in a softer voice.

'I can't,' Shawna said, so quietly it was as if Olivia's own panicked thoughts had spoken aloud.

'Stop messing around and get in your cell,' Lewis ordered, his pleasure in his authority saturating every word. 'Your actions can still have consequences for your family, do you want that?'

Shawna stood immediately, but she didn't let go of Olivia's hand. They walked back to the cell together, but she stopped before the threshold.

'I can't,' she whispered.

The other prisoners were all in their cells, watching through their open doors. A sense of coiled anticipation, of muscles tight with suppressed energy, a desire to fight but a need to stay safe, electrified the atmosphere. It sent a cold shiver through Olivia.

'It's okay, just another step,' she coaxed.

'I can't. I can't do this.'

'If you two don't get in that bloody cell immediately, I'll be visiting both your families tonight,' Lewis warned.

Olivia tensed, ready to drag Shawna in if she had to, but she didn't need to. Shawna meekly stepped inside but she backed up as far as she could, dragging Olivia with her. Her breathing was loud and fast as their door slid closed.

'I can't, I can't do this. I can't, I can't, I can't.'

'It's all right, Shawna.' Ray reached them before Lewis. 'There's not much more to get through.' His voice was painfully sad as he unlocked their door. 'You can do this.' He had tears in his eyes but he blinked them away as Lewis caught up with him.

'We need to set off now,' Ray explained. 'Yours is the first hearing. You can change in the van.'

'Can't have you crushing your suit before your TV debut,' Lewis smirked. 'Got to look your best for Mary.'

'I can't do this.' Shawna clung to the wall. 'I don't want to die.' Her eyes held the same terror Becky's had.

'I know.' Olivia tried to keep it together as she wiped Shawna's tears but her own face was wet too. 'At least you get to see your family,' she repeated the phrase she'd heard so many times this evening, but it had lost its magical charm.

'I'm not ready,' Shawna howled. 'I was only trying to make enough money to live on. I didn't do anything wrong.'

'That's what you all say.' Lewis entered the tiny cell, making it feel like the walls were closing in. 'I'm surprised at you, Shawna, I thought you were going to do this with dignity.'

Olivia stayed between him and Shawna but, just like in the supermarket, she knew she was powerless.

'Ray, please ...' she begged, not knowing what to ask for, what to hope for.

He had his eyes closed as though none of this was happening. 'I'm just doing my job,' he said in a cold, dead voice.

'Hurry up, Shawna.' Lewis tapped his fancy watch. 'Time's a-ticking and you don't have much to waste.'

It took everything Olivia had not to turn on him and claw his eyes out, but she couldn't have moved if she'd tried. Shawna's grip was so tight around her, it was getting hard to breathe.

'Enough of this. Out. Now.' Lewis grabbed Shawna and dragged her towards the exit, pulling Olivia with them.

'Stop.' Ray tried to separate them, but Lewis was too strong. 'You're making it worse. Shawna, don't do this, you need to get it together. Please, you know the drill; this has to happen.'

Shawna was sobbing so hard she was hyperventilating. Lewis prised her fingers off Olivia one by one, but there was a horrible cracking sound and Shawna screamed and let go completely. Lewis shoved Olivia back towards the cell and she fell onto the bed in time to see the door slide closed, locking her in.

'What did you do?' Ray bellowed at Lewis. 'That was completely unnecessary.' His hands were curled into fists but he didn't take a swing. 'I'll report you for this.'

'Go ahead, I was just doing my job. She was refusing orders, so I did what I had to.'

Shawna cradled her hand to her, but she was no longer sobbing, instead silent tears coursed down her face as her last hope died, taking her fight with it.

'Are you going to walk or are we going to carry you?' Lewis demanded.

Shawna moved to the exit gate without any more encouragement.

The other prisoners stood by the doors to their cells, watching in silence until Shawna passed through the gate and was gone for ever.

Chapter Thirty-Two

Five paces by three paces, Olivia knew every centimetre of her stark, grey prison cell by the time her door unlocked the next morning. After Shawna left and the lights went out, she couldn't force herself to lie down on the bed, on Shawna's bed. Instead, she spent the night exploring the walls, the floor, even standing on the bed to investigate the ceiling with the tips of her fingers. There was nothing to find in the windowless room, no cracks or loose bricks, no broken wood or rusty nails, just paint-smoothed breeze blocks, a rudimentary toilet and sink, and the hard metal bed which was bolted to the floor. There was nothing to help her escape. There was also no sign that Shawna had ever been there.

Shawna who was on her way to London, on her way to see her family one last time. On her way to ... Olivia couldn't finish the thought. Exhausted and alone, she finally collapsed onto the bed, her bed, and surrendered to her fear.

She wasn't the only person overwhelmed by grief and panic. Among the rumbling snores of thirty sleeping women, there were muffled sobs and the sudden cries and shrieks of night terrors. The suppressed fears of the waking hours came back full force to haunt the prisoners while they slept. Unconsciousness allowed in all the things they tried hard to push away during the day.

'My babies,' someone cried out.

'No, please no.'

'Stop!'

Olivia cried until she crashed into exhausted oblivion and woke feeling sick and lethargic, her eyes puffy and sore to open. Her body ached all over from being thrown around in the van and she tentatively touched her forehead. A lump had formed and it sent needles of pain through her skull when she brushed her fingers against it.

'There ain't no breakfast in bed.' Carol walked past her open cell door, carrying a plate piled high with bacon, sausages, eggs and beans. 'You stay in there and you'll miss out on the best fry-up you've ever tasted. Take it from me, the fried bread is lush.'

'You're the lush, Carol.' Nadine shuffled out of her cell opposite. 'A few more pounds and you'll follow Shawna to the chopping block.'

'Piss off, Nutso.'

Carol put her plate down on the centre table and heaved herself onto the bench. She picked up her plastic cutlery, stabbed her fork into a sausage and took a large bite.

'It's your funeral,' Nadine said.

'Shut up, Nadine,' several women shouted. Shawna's trial was at the forefront of everyone's thoughts. They might seem intent on getting their breakfasts, but the atmosphere was subdued.

Shawna might not have left anything behind, but Olivia could still feel her presence. She kept picturing all the live trials she'd ever seen, all the desperate women and their families. Today, Shawna's suffering would become the nation's entertainment. If Olivia had eaten anything yesterday, she would have thrown up, but her stomach was an empty, gnawing cavern.

268

She wasn't ready to eat, but she forced herself to get up and join the other women, anything to escape the oppressive and lonely cell. Nadine and Becky stood at the back of the breakfast queue and she took her place behind them.

'How are you doing?' Nadine asked her.

She took a breath to speak but the tears she thought she had used up flowed once again. Badly: she was doing very, very badly and compassion only made it worse. The temptation to surrender to helplessness was strong and familiar, but beneath that was a flare of anger and defiance. Had she really done anything so wrong? Did she deserve to be treated like this?

No, the defiance said, no she did not. She tugged at the collar of her grey jumpsuit, finding the loose thread she had discovered the previous night, and worried at it again until she could pull another couple of strands free.

'It doesn't get easier but you'll get more used to it.' Nadine squeezed her hand, her cold, thin fingers digging into Olivia's.

'I don't want to get used to it.' Fury roared up within her, creating space beneath the foggy, drowning powerlessness. 'This is not okay, the way they took me from my children, the way everyone just watched.'

'I know,' Nadine said. 'I've been there. Hold onto your anger, it will keep you going when nothing else does.'

'Next,' Vera shouted from behind the hatch and the line moved up.

The smell of frying bacon, rich and smoky, triggered Olivia's hunger pangs. 'Don't let them bully you,' Nadine continued. 'You've got at least six months, although turnover's been faster recently. If you don't eat the food they serve, you can stretch it out far longer. I've been here years.'

'Years?'

'Yeah, Nadine likes the joint.' Becky turned around. 'Take my advice, keep your head down, do as you're told and get it over with. Protect your family the only way you can, save them from the shame and the long, drawn-out agony.'

Olivia stroked the collar of her shirt, the few frayed ends were the best she could manage at this point, but Becky didn't react, there wasn't even a flicker of awareness. Maybe it wasn't her after all.

'Why did they arrest you?' Nadine asked, as the queue shuffled closer to the hatch and the undeniably delicious smelling food.

'I—' Indecision caught her tongue, what was she allowed to say? Would it count as a confession? She didn't know who she could trust.

'My family owns a dairy farm, I got caught selling the cream.' Becky volunteered the information without concern.

'She was skimming.' Nadine laughed at her own joke but Becky ignored her.

'We needed the extra cash, there's no way to survive on the pittance the government pays for milk. Not that you can call it milk; it's so watered down now it's disgusting.'

'Next,' Vera shouted and they all moved forward.

A sheen of grease coated the piles of sausages and bacon; beside them were dark brown mushrooms, glossy tomatoes and bubbling baked beans. Vera used a giant spoon to ladle the breakfast out and as soon as one serving tray emptied her assistant replaced it with another. The food never stopped coming.

'Not that they serve mainstream milk here, we only get the good stuff.' Becky nodded to the drinks table beside the hatch.

'Why?' Olivia asked, watching as a woman poured thick cream into her coffee and added three spoonfuls of sugar.

'Because fat is guilty, no matter what you did or didn't do. Not that any of us are innocent. Carol made her own goat's cheese; Vicki,' she nodded towards the woman with the coffee, 'ran a ration exchange programme and Kirsty "imported" chocolate from Europe. We've each got tales to tell but they all end with us here, waiting for trial, and we all know how that ends. Guilty and gone.' Her voice was matter of fact, despite the events of last night. It contained none of the panic that choked Olivia, none of the panic she had seen during the 'other' Becky's arrest.

'There has to be something we can do. We've got rights, there are people who could help us.' It was as close as she could come to mentioning CTAS.

Becky laughed. 'Rights? Yeah, sure. We voted those away when we elected Mother Mason. Nobody's coming to save us, they don't care where we are, we might as well have ceased to exist the moment we were arrested.' Becky stepped up to the serving hatch. 'Some of everything please, Vera.'

'Good girl, that's what I like to hear.'

Becky took her plate and didn't look back as she joined Carol at her table.

'Nadine, what can I tempt you with today?' Vera asked, already dishing up double portions of everything. 'I saved you an extra piece of fried bread.' She winked at Nadine and passed the plate through the hatch. 'You're not going to be silly are you, deary?' Vera glanced meaningfully towards the guards patrolling the tables. Nadine stared down at the ground, not looking at Vera as she took her breakfast.

'Good girl. How about you? The same?' Vera didn't wait for Olivia's response either, just filled a second plate with an identical portion. 'There's more if you want it.'

The white plastic plate was hot from the warmer and so heavy with food that Olivia almost dropped it. The heavenly smell carried up on clouds of steam that made her mouth water. She took her overflowing plate across to Nadine who sat at the only empty table.

'There's one hundred and fifty five calories in one hundred grams of beans, that's seven tablespoons.' Nadine pushed the food around on her plate, making a space in the middle. She counted the beans into the gap and pierced a single one on the tip of her fork. 'I keep my intake to nine hundred calories every day.' She nibbled at the bean and then cut a tomato into eight precise segments. 'I'm following the guidelines Mother Mason set out, she is the expert in healthy eating.' She cackled at her own joke.

'How long have you been here?'

'Two thousand, eight hundred and ninety-seven days. I'll probably get a cake when I hit three thousand; not that I'd eat it.'

She was proud of it. Proud and probably a little unstable. Calorie deprivation would do that to you.

'Do you think they'll release you?'

Nadine laughed. 'I doubt it, I'm too important. Mother Mason hates me. She's keeping me alive until she needs to make a grand gesture, quell the rebels.' She lowered her voice and leaned in, holding eye contact with Olivia until she moved closer too. 'It's okay though, I've just got to hold on until my friends get me out; they won't let her keep me here for ever.'

'Your friends?' Could she mean CTAS? Nadine had been in here too long to know of Alice's plan, but Olivia desperately needed an ally, even if this one verged on the extreme side.

'The Pink Apron Brigade. I was one of the founders.'

Olivia's hope was short-lived and she struggled to hide her disappointment. The Pink Apron Brigade were the original protesters, before CTAS, the ones she and Alice had joined for the march to Parliament, but when Mother Mason cracked down, the group rapidly disbanded.

'They'll get me out, it's just taking some time to get a plan ready, but I can wait, as long as it takes.' Nadine pushed her plate away, hunched in on herself and started to rock back and forth on the bench. 'I'll wait as long as it takes,' she muttered over and over.

The breakfast smelt disgusting now. The congealed fat made Olivia's stomach churn, but could she really stay here like Nadine? The Pink Apron Brigade was over, barely a memory. When it disbanded, CTAS coalesced in the vacuum left behind, but what had they really achieved in six years? Were they coming or was she being stupidly, hopelessly deluded? Prison guards and metal bars felt a long way from secret bars and slices of cake. No one had come for Nadine, no one was ever coming for her, and if she could disappear so easily, what chance did the rest of them have?

Chapter Thirty-Three

'Right ladies,' Lewis announced, 'movie time. Everyone gather round, you know the drill.'

The inmates congregated around the large TV screen mounted inside a wire cage, high up on the far wall. They only had the hard metal benches to sit on, but Vera had laid out a spread of cinema snacks: popcorn, crisps, chocolate, sweets. One of her girls handed out huge tubs of ice cream to anyone who wanted one. The prisoners weren't showing as much enthusiasm for their evening treats as they had during their other meals. They took token amounts to pick at, but no one tucked in.

'You too, Olivia,' Lewis shouted up the room. 'You can refuse to eat, for now, but you're not too good to enjoy the show.'

The world tilted as she stood up from the dinner table, her untouched plate of lasagne and garlic bread still in front of her. Low blood sugar and mild concussion combined to undermine her balance, but Becky was near enough to catch her.

'None of that.' Becky pinched her arm. 'You pass out and they've got an excuse to stick a tube down your throat. Siding with Nadine is a mistake, but if you're going to do it, at least eat enough to keep you conscious. If you insist on waiting for CTAS, you need to stay alive.'

CTAS, finally someone had said the word she had been living for. 'It is you!'

'No, it isn't.' Becky let go of her arm. 'I'm not that woman any more, she might as well have died in the supermarket.'

'They've been trying to find you.' She clung to Becky, she couldn't lose the only connection to CTAS she had.

'And what good has that done? Nobody has ridden in to save me, Ray didn't tip them off to get me out of the country. They used me to supply the bar and then they cast me aside, just like they'll do to you. We're as screwed as everyone else in here.'

'I'm sorry I didn't help you at the supermarket.'

'Forget it, it's not like anybody from CTAS stepped in, they were all too busy filming. I'm sure Alice got a nice little video out of it. Got lots of people talking, right? CTAS loves to create drama, they're not so great with follow-through.'

'Hurry up, ladies. The show's about to start.' Lewis juggled the remote from hand to hand.

'They're working on something, they've got a plan.'

'Really? Have they told you what it is?' Becky laughed at her silence. 'See, they keep everyone in the dark, distracted with booze and chocolate, while nothing ever changes.'

'You can't give up on them. Alice won't let this happen.'

'It's already happened. Hundreds, thousands, of CTAS members have already died. What makes you think we're so special? You've only been here a day, you don't understand what it's like. I've been locked up for months and no one is coming to get me. Or you.'

'No, I won't accept that.' She couldn't accept that.

'That's your choice, but wait until you've seen our nightly screening before you decide.' Becky abandoned her and stalked down to the others, grabbing a handful of popcorn on the way.

Olivia followed at a slower, more wobbly pace. She perched on the end of the bench, beside Becky, who completely ignored her.

'Is everyone sitting comfortably? No? Good.' Lewis pressed play.

Olivia waited for the titles to roll. Please don't let it be Shawna's trial. She couldn't handle seeing it for real after spending the whole day imagining what had happened. Hopefully, it would be one of Mother Mason's propaganda features, the specially commissioned films that showed people how happy they could be if only they followed the rules. 'Aspiration porn', Alice called them.

The children that came onto the screen weren't actors though, this was no Oscar-winning movie and a Hollywood director hadn't orchestrated the action. The shot was filmed through a window, two children sat on a sofa, the little boy holding hands with his younger sister. The camera zoomed in, their faces grew to fill the screen; Olivia cried out at the sight. Matthew and Mia sat in their living room, silent and pale, frighteningly still.

'No!' She tried to stand but Becky pulled her back onto the bench.

'Stop,' Becky hissed. 'They're okay, keep watching.'

A moment later, Danny walked in and sat down beside them, gathering them into his arms. Alice followed him into the room, gesticulating wildly, ranting as she paced to the window, so close, Olivia felt like she could reach out and touch her. Her whole family were right there. It was ecstasy and agony, reward and punishment.

'Cute kids,' someone said.

'Hot husband.' Carol punctuated her comment with a wolf-whistle.

'Why?' It was the only word Olivia could form as heart-break shattered her.

'To remind you what's at stake,' Becky said. 'How far away you are, how close to them *they* are.' Right outside her house, close enough to capture the pictures on the walls, the tears on Mia's face. 'You thought your actions had consequences before? Wait and see what they'll do if you continue to disobey them. I didn't *just* give up, they made sure I had no other choice.'

The video moved on to someone else's family, someone else's home. The subjects of the film were oblivious to their surveillance, they were simply going about their daily routines. Different people, different lives, different backgrounds, but they all moved through the world with a subdued isolation, separate even when they were part of a crowd, at work, or school, out shopping or eating.

The impact of their incarcerations rippled out to touch everyone they loved. The women watched with rapt attention, eager and anxious, dreading seeing their family, then broken open by grief as the film moved on to someone else, tumbled dominos of hope and pain that travelled around the room.

Mia. Matthew. Danny. Alice. All in pain because of her, at risk because of her. They didn't know where she was. Couldn't help her even if they did. All they were left with was waiting: waiting for her trial, waiting for her confession, waiting for her sentence.

They reached the end of the video and the screen went black. Everyone had seen someone, except for Nadine who nibbled at a single piece of popcorn, working her way around the kernel. 'Bastards,' she said, encapsulating the sentiment of the room. 'I'm lucky I've got no one left, it means there's nothing they can do to me. I'm untouchable.'

'You're doing the torture for us, Nutso.' Lewis switched off the TV. 'Olivia has plenty to lose. How are your principles holding up now? Want the cameraman to move in closer tomorrow? Follow them to school? Watch them through the gates? Keep up your hunger strike and they will do more than film them.'

This wasn't supposed to happen to her. Alice was meant to bring everything down before she got caught. Now there was nothing she could do. Except one thing. She reached forward, snatched a handful of chocolate buttons and stuffed them into her mouth, chewing without tasting anything other than the acrid fear that threatened to choke her, a feeling that stayed with her long after she swallowed.

Chapter Thirty-Four

Olivia had never eaten so much. She filled her plate to overflowing, mechanically working through mouthful after mouthful. Ignoring all her body's signals, she kept cating long after she was full, long after her stomach hurt and she started to feel sick. She measured the days by the number of meals devoured and she was coming up to thirty-seven, not including snacks. Today's menu option was pizza and chips; the smell of the garlic and the orange sheen of oil made her digestive system rebel, clenching painfully, but she overrode her instincts and forced in another slice.

Foods she had craved for years tasted worse than medicine. There was no pleasure in her consumption, only the desperate need to end her time in prison. She had a montage of images of Danny, Matthew, Mia and Alice that played inside her mind, added to each day by the new surveillance footage. Through the gates at school, inside Danny's office, at the gym, the park, their house, all close up and in high definition. The videos were inter-cut with traffic cameras, security feeds and CCTV shots. There was nowhere they went that the government didn't follow them, nowhere they couldn't get to them.

Every bite of food she took, she used to push down the fear, numb the panic, but there was no comfort in her eating. She had no power here, no way to protect them, except to hope that she either bought Alice and CTAS some time, or that surrender kept her family safe.

The loud, reverberating cry of the klaxon jerked her to attention, the flashing amber light signified their immediate return to their cells. A tingle of fear cascaded through the other prisoners and Olivia felt her skin prickle. Mealtime was sacred, it must be important for them to interrupt it. She set down her cutlery, relieved to push her plate away, for an excuse to stop.

'Shift it,' Lewis bellowed from the other side of the security gate.

It was harder to hurry now. Her body felt stretched and swollen, the sharp curves of her hips and ribs covered in a layer of fat, quickly accrued under Mother Mason's new diet.

Once they were safely locked in, Lewis opened the security gate and stepped back for a tall, smartly dressed man to enter before him. Everything from the charcoal grey suit to the black leather briefcase screamed lawyer. He looked aloof and vaguely bored as he sat down at one of the tables and nodded for Lewis to proceed. Normally, when something happened in the prison block, everyone crowded forward, desperate to see, but today they all hung back, staying as close to the walls as they could get. Olivia followed their lead and retreated as far as she could from the man who should have been their saviour.

'Ladies, who will be today's lucky winner?' Lewis sauntered past the cells. 'Becky, will it be you? You're looking mighty huge.' She flinched and Lewis laughed. 'Nah, you've got a few more pounds to put on before you're ready for slaughter. Carol, my money was on you, I've seen smaller whales.'

'Good, I'm done with this place.' She strutted forward, but her usual swagger had a hollow feel to it. 'Why put off the inevitable? Give me the needle already and we can all move on.'

'Don't you wish.' Lewis walked past her and continued down towards Nadine.

'No! No way.' Carol banged her fists against the bars. 'Not Mad Nad. Look at her; she's the picture of neglect. You can't put her on TV. Take me. I'm fat and evil; I'm the one you want. *Please*, take me.'

'Sorry, love.' He reached Nadine's cell and she cowered back on her bed.

'No, I won't go. You can't make me.'

'Wanna bet?' Lewis reached to swipe his card and open Nadine's door then stopped. 'It's okay, Mad, it's not you either.' He turned, his leering grin vanished as he marched towards Olivia's cell. 'Mrs Pritchard, come on down. That's right, ladies, Olivia here has jumped the queue.'

'What?' Olivia's voice was lost beneath Carol's scream of rage.

'No. You can't do that!' Carol threw herself against the cell bars. 'Five months and sixteen days. It's my turn.'

'Trust me, this isn't my decision.' He opened Olivia's cell door, but she dug her finger nails into the cold breeze block wall, refusing to go.

'No!' Carol howled. 'I'm done, I can't do this any more. Please, I can't—'

'Get out here,' Lewis ordered Olivia, 'or I can come and get you.'

She was only just recovering from their latest encounter; she reluctantly left the cell, trying to stay out of his reach, but he grabbed her and dragged her towards the lawyer.

'Careful, Agent Hook-Medwood,' the man said in a bored tone. 'Can't have you leaving any more bruises; we don't have time for these ones to heal.'

281

Lewis dug his fingers into her arm before he pushed her towards the table, but she was ready for it and caught herself before she stumbled.

'What can I say? She's clumsy,' Lewis said. 'It's not my fault.'

'No, I imagine not. Sit down, Mrs Prichard. My name is Mr Rengar and I am your lawyer.' He picked up his electronic notebook and flicked across the screen. 'Your court date has been set for Friday.'

'Friday?' Carol slammed her fists against the door. 'How the hell is it so soon? You bitch, how could you? You stole my slot; I'll kill you, I swear I'll kill you.'

'Carol, that's hardly necessary, the Societal Evolution Programme will take care of that,' Lewis said. 'No need to get yourself into any more trouble.'

'Mrs Pritchard, you will be taken down to London for your hearing . . .' Mr Rengar droned on but she couldn't process what he was saying. Her body, her mind, nothing seemed to work.

'. . . you will enter your plea of guilty.'

Guilty, she was guilty, that should be her plea, he was right. This was what they expected of her, what she had to do to keep Matthew and Mia safe, but it was all moving so fast.

'What about a defence?' she heard herself say. 'You're supposed to be *my* lawyer?'

For the first time Mr Rengar looked up at her. 'Mrs Pritchard, we all have our parts to play in the proceedings. You do your job and I will do mine.' He stood up and repacked his briefcase.

'No, you can't leave, I still have questions. Damn it, I have rights.'

'Not any more,' Lewis said, enjoying the process immensely. 'You gave up your rights when you stopped making good choices. Now you need Mother Mason to take care of you, once and for all.'

What she wouldn't do to obliterate the sanctimonious smile from his face.

'What about my family?' she asked Mr Rengar.

'They will be fine, so long as you do what you're told. Everyone will be a lot safer once your trial is concluded.'

Carol gave a wail of agony. She shook the bars a final time before sinking down onto the floor, sobbing loudly.

Mr Rengar ignored her. 'They will attend your trial, of course. You must not speak to them, or even acknowledge their presence. You've seen the trials on television; you know what to expect. Behave, follow instructions; if you don't, you won't be the one to suffer the consequences.'

He signalled for Lewis to open the door.

'What happens afterwards?' she asked in a small voice, before he could leave.

'Nothing you need to concern yourself with.'

'But—'

Mr Rengar picked up his briefcase and walked swiftly away.

'Stop! Talk to me! I deserve to know what's going to happen.' She tried to follow but Lewis caught her arm and twisted it behind her back. The door shut behind Mr Rengar and he didn't turn, despite her scream of frustration.

'Don't worry, it will be quick, though I can't promise painless,' Lewis whispered into her ear, his breath hot against her face. 'You're no longer going to be a problem for this country and without the likes of you, our society stands a chance of becoming a truly great nation.'

Chapter Thirty-Five

Nobody spoke to Olivia after Mr Rengar left; even Nadine kept her distance. It was like a black hole had opened around her and nobody wanted to get too close.

'It's my turn,' Carol continued to wail to anyone that would listen, each time glaring at Olivia. Becky was equally furious; they both suspected why the trial had been moved up. CTAS. They had to be involved and were finally acting. The thought brought Olivia comfort as she continued to play out her prison role. She'd known Alice wouldn't let her down.

On Friday morning, she lay curled up in a tight ball when Vera and Lewis came to get her. Since her arrival, she spent every hour wanting to escape the prison, but when her door opened she didn't want to leave. Shawna's presence reasserted itself inside the cell, bringing with it a crippling fear. What if it wasn't CTAS? What if she was deluding herself and she was going to die like everyone else?

'Get up!' Lewis said. 'Mary won't wait for you to get your lazy arse out of bed.'

They escorted her to the cold, echoing shower block and she stood shivering beneath the freezing spray of water. She scrubbed at her matted hair and tried to remove the layers of grime and sweat from her skin. If she kept her eyes closed she could pretend Vera wasn't watching her every move, though what they thought she could do with a tiny piece of soap she had no idea.

Vera presented her with a cheap, grey suit that she struggled to squeeze herself into. The skirt cut into her stomach and the buttons on the blouse only just did up, the fabric constricted her lungs and increased her sensation of light-headedness. Breathing was a luxury they obviously didn't think she deserved.

The suit had to be at least two sizes too small. Surely she couldn't have put on that much weight? She ran a finger around the waistband, trying to stretch it out. Maybe they had intentionally given her the wrong size. They didn't have time to fatten her up enough, so this was the next best option. The jacket made an ominous ripping sound when she moved her arms, so she stood as still as possible while Vera applied a liberal amount of foundation and concealer to cover her latest bruises. They were starting to fade and didn't hurt any more, which was a small mercy because Vera pressed the make-up brush hard against them.

'Not bad.' Vera stood her in front of the mirror when she finished. Her reflection looked almost presentable; from a distance she might even be considered the picture of health, with her rounded face and cheeks flushed from blusher.

Lewis and Ray waited outside the shower block; they added the silver bracelets of handcuffs to complete her outfit and led her back through the prison. It was still early, long before their usual 7 a.m. wake-up call, but everyone was up, standing at their cell doors to watch her go. Nadine raised a hand in farewell and Becky smiled a small, sad smile but nobody said anything. Carol was the only one who remained on her bed, her back turned.

'I'm sorry,' Olivia said as they passed. She had wanted to say something since she found out and this was her last chance. Carol gave no indication that she heard and Lewis pushed Olivia on towards the gates.

The prison van they loaded her into was very different to the van they brought her in. Sleek, white and with tinted black windows, she climbed the polished silver steps and sat down on one of the benches. Ray leaned in as he chained her hands.

'Oliv—'.

'Make sure they're tight.' Lewis came to check, ratcheting the cuffs so the metal dug in and drawing the chains so short she couldn't move her arms.

'That's enough, she's not going anywhere.' Ray knelt down to anchor her feet. He glanced up, as though trying to catch her attention, but it didn't matter what he said. She couldn't possibly trust him.

'Don't let her timidity fool you, she's wild this one. Here,' Lewis tossed Ray the keys, 'you can drive.'

'No, I'm scheduled to be in here.'

'Someone has to make sure she doesn't do anything stupid.' Lewis took the seat next to her.

'I don't think that's a good idea, she has to be in one piece by the time we get there.'

'Don't worry, she will be.' Lewis leaned back with his legs spread out.

Ray hesitated, jingling the keys, wanting to say more, but after a pause, he climbed out of the van and slammed the door shut.

'Ready for your last moment in the spotlight? I hope it's been worth it,' Lewis said. 'What, no sparkling conversation? Alice was always the talker, wasn't she? Such a big mouth, it's amazing she didn't get into trouble years ago. You've no idea how many hours I've had to listen to Jenna complain about the two of you. She's been desperate to find a way to get rid of you. Hell, I was almost at the point of framing you myself, just to get her to shut up. Thanks for saving me the trouble.' He smirked at Olivia and settled back in his seat as the engine started.

The journey seemed endless. Every time the van slowed, Olivia braced herself, waiting for CTAS to intervene, but nothing happened and her faith began to dwindle. Was Becky right? Had she been delusional? What if there was no plan and they really were taking her to trial. This could be the last time she ever saw her family again.

Harsh, angry chanting and a volley of bangs against the side of the van announced that they had reached their destination.

'Your welcoming committee is ready.' Lewis smiled smugly at her. 'I'm sure they've got a lot to say to you.' The banging continued, each bang feeling like a physical blow and Olivia's panic intensified. This was a side of the trial they didn't show on TV.

'Doesn't sound like you've got too many fans, does it?' The chanting was growing louder. Some of the shouted words made it through the reinforced walls: 'disgrace', 'shame', 'die'.

'You've been waiting to be rescued, haven't you? Stupid cow. Nobody is coming to save you, you're on your own. Soon, your kids will be too. You've destroyed them; they'll carry the shame of your name for the rest of their lives. ' He leaned in, his breath stinking of bacon and stale coffee. 'They'll grow up hating you, blaming you for everything, and they should, you're a terrible mother, a horrible selfish woman who chose her own pleasure and glory over her children. You're all going to pay the price now.'

She bit the corner of her cheek, refusing to give him any kind of reaction.

'They're talking about sending your family to Rigby Hall, the first residents to live there. It's the only hope Matthew and Mia have of a happy, healthy life. They've got so many lessons to unlearn, so much of you that needs erasing from their memories. By the time they leave, they probably won't remember they ever had a mother. Other than Mother Mason, that is.'

She slammed her head to the side, connecting with his nose and he yelped, a spray of warm, sticky blood splattered across her as he leapt away clutching his face.

'Yoo itch!' His words were slurred through the stream of blood pouring from his nose. Bright red, it soaked into his nice, clean, white shirt. He threw himself at her but the van jerked to a stop and the motion propelled him forward so he crashed into the wall with an audible bang. He staggered back and stumbled towards her again but the rear door opened, flooding the interior with sunlight and the bright flash of camera bulbs.

'What the hell?' Ray stood in the open doorway. Taking in the scene, he moved to block the view of the cameras and climbed up quickly, shutting the door behind him. 'What did you do?' He came straight to her and she recoiled from him but he only searched her face for signs of injuries. 'I told you, our orders were not to touch her.'

'Wasn't ee.' Blood still gushed from Lewis's nose. 'Itch attac'd ee.'

'They're going to be furious.' Ray took out a handkerchief and gently wiped her cheek. 'She looks like she's been in a fight; she looks like *she's* the victim. They'll kill us.'

'S'wasn't my fault.' Lewis grabbed the handkerchief from Ray and wadded it against his nose.

'Well, it wasn't mine. If the press have got photos we're screwed. They might not be official but apparently that doesn't matter any more.' Ray frowned, scrutinising her face and spoke into his hidden mic. 'We're going to need help getting into the court.'

'I eed a octor,' Lewis demanded but Ray ignored him.

'It's going to be okay,' he said in a low voice. 'You have to trust —'

The banging on the van stopped all of a sudden and the back doors opened. Six men in suits stood outside; Ray unlocked her chains, but the handcuffs stayed on. 'It's going to be noisy,' he said, 'just keep walking. We'll get you inside as quick as we can.'

The men reached up and helped her down. Lewis followed but Ray blocked his exit. 'You stay here, you've done enough.'

Lewis glared at them over the bundle of bloody cloth but didn't try to leave.

Olivia's view of the street was blocked by the open door until Ray swung it shut and revealed the mob of people. At the sight of her they surged forward, reporters and demonstrators pressed towards her, all trying to get her attention.

'Olivia! Olivia! Olivia!'

The guards clustered around her, a small tight box of dark suits. They moved as one, a human shield that swept her towards the imposing white-stone Gothic arches of the High Court of Justice.

'Keep walking, look straight ahead,' Ray said.

'Bad mother! Bad wife! Bad mother! Bad wife!' The protesters stood to one side of the entrance. They held placards up; most were crude creations on bendy card with words scrawled in thick black marker pen.

'Shame on you.'

'You will be judged.'

'Death by chocolate!'

Some of the signs looked more professional, printed and mounted on wooden poles, they carried the slogans Mother Mason's marketing team used.

'Shame your family, pay the price.'

'Sugar is suicide.'

'Love your kids? Kill them with cake and kindness.'

One woman spat at Olivia as she passed, the warm globule landed on Olivia's cheek.

'Call yourself a mother?' the woman screamed. 'You're a disgrace. I hope you rot in hell.'

'Olivia, you should trust your mother's love!' a man shouted. Trusting Mother Mason's love was the last thing she would ever do. 'Trust your mother's love!' he repeated and there was something familiar about his voice. She scanned the throng of people for the source and spotted a banner with 'Trust your mother's love!' written in bright, neon-pink letters. Around the edges, a rainbow of coloured ribbons fluttered in the breeze, the frayed ends beckoning to her.

The man holding the sign wore a black hooded sweatshirt, the hood pulled down low so she couldn't see his face.

'Trust your mother's love,' he shouted again.

'Trust your mother's love!' A woman took up the chant. She stood a little further down, wearing a large floppy pink sun hat and brandishing a matching banner, but this one had a different slogan. 'Mother's Love = Power.' In seconds Olivia was past them, the ring of guards almost running her the final few metres, their physical bulk pushing back the crowd. She tried to keep the people in sight but they had vanished, almost as if they had never been there at all.

The guards marched her under the arches of the High Court of Justice and into the marble entrance hall, where they were greeted by a ten-foot-tall portrait of Mother Mason, the same one that hung in the Norwich City Hall building. The jeers and shouts of the public and press faded as the doors closed behind them, to be replaced with an eerie, echoing quiet. The hall was almost deserted except for Mr Rengar, dressed in a black silk gown and white horsehair wig. He waited on a nearby bench with a pretty young woman wearing a bright pink hijab.

'Finally.' Mr Rengar hurried forward, his gown rustling and flowing out around him. 'They've been waiting to start for twenty minutes; the court's full and they've had to push back the television schedule. Mother Mason will not be happy.' For the first time he took in Olivia's blood-splattered appearance. 'What on earth's happened to her? The bruises were bad enough, but this? You,' he waved over the young woman. 'Fix her.'

The woman came forward with a small beige sponge and a make-up brush. She dabbed at the blood spray on Olivia's cheek. Her motions were slow, gentle, but there was a stiff rigidity in her expression, a suppressed fury. Another angry stranger. Olivia flinched as the sponge touched a sensitive spot on her forehead.

'Sorry,' the woman whispered, her rage softening.

'Make it good, the cameras will pick up everything.' Mr Rengar peered over the woman's shoulder. Her eyes narrowed and anger hardened her features again. She shifted to block his view and took out a pot of foundation; with the lightest of touches, she swept the powder across Olivia's cheeks.

'That will have to do,' Mr Rengar said.

The woman lowered her brush and for a second she

cupped Olivia's cheek. 'Trust your mother's love,' she whispered, tugging at the frayed edge of her head scarf, then stepped away.

Olivia tried to catch her eye again but Mr Rengar and Ray hustled her towards the courtroom. Two armed guards stood on either side of the heavy double doors; at Mr Rengar's signal they heaved them open. The solid wood had held the sound of the packed courtroom at bay but now it overflowed into the entrance hall, a tide of shouts that grew to a crescendo the moment she stepped into view.

The court looked exactly as it did on television: the rows of press benches at the back, the public viewing gallery high above and, at the centre of the show, the judge's bench, the prisoner dock and the family platform, raised for all to see. Mary Vitasan's seat was vacant but the family platform wasn't. Danny, Matthew and Mia twisted in their seats.

'Mummy!' Mia screamed. Her high-pitched voice pierced through the crowd's chatter and pain twisted inside Olivia's chest.

'Mia.' She didn't fight Ray as he pushed her past the journalists, with their large mics and flashing camera bulbs.

'Steady.' He held her back, slowing her progress.

'Mummy.' Mia leant out over the platform, tiny hands stretching down and Olivia lifted her cuffed hands up to meet her. For a brief second she touched soft, warm skin, then Ray forced his way between them, knocking her arms down. The space between her and Mia opened up again.

'Don't,' Ray said. 'Trust your mother's love, just not yet.' Why did everyone keep telling her to do that? What was it supposed to mean? Her mother's love screamed at her to kill anyone who dared to come between her and her children. It seemed unlikely that this was what they meant.

'Mummy!' Mia threw herself forward but Danny caught her and held her tight. She struggled to get free, her face bright red and streaked with tears. Matthew sat beside them, pale and silent. He stared at Olivia with wide, scared eyes, so small and alone, while Danny tried to comfort Mia.

'Mia. Matthew. I love you. I love you, Danny.' She tried to push past Ray but he blocked her path and another guard joined him. They propelled her up the stairs into the dock and locked her in, but it only meant she was closer to her family. She went straight to the back of the small enclosed space, able to see them better, but the thin, bulletproof walls might as well have been a metre of lead: there was still no way to reach them, to touch them. She could hear Mia's sobs and Danny's soft voice as he murmured over and over again, 'It's okay, Mia. Everything's going to be all right. You have to trust your mother's love, it's a powerful thing.'

'Danny?' Olivia whispered. Not him too. 'Don't cry, Mia.' She pressed up against the cold glass, her hands against the same space hundreds of women had touched before her. Glass that Shawna might have touched.

Mia was inconsolable; her small body shaking as Danny held her.

'Matthew.' Olivia wished he would come closer.

Danny put one arm around Matthew's shoulders and for the first time looked directly at her, and she rocked back at the depth of his emotion: love, understanding, reassurance and something more, something she couldn't read.

'I'm sorry, I'm so sorry.' She tried to keep her voice low but it boomed out over the speakers, caught by the microphone that hung above her. An instant hush descended and she looked up to the gallery. It ran all the way around the room and a horde of people sat looking down on her. They craned forward in their seats, leaning over the balcony to get closer. Nobody wanted to miss a word.

Rengar snapped his fingers at her. 'Be quiet and face forward.' He stood at a desk to one side of the dock. 'Remember what we discussed.' He glanced at his watch and sighed. 'At this rate I'm going to have to push back my golf game. Stop crying, save your tears for the cameras.'

Big, black cameras stood in each corner of the room. Men and women in dark jeans and T-shirts hurried around, repositioning the tripods, adjusting lights and paying absolutely no attention to her. They were the only ones who weren't.

Somebody had left her a packet of tissues and a plastic cup of water, anticipating the props she would need to confess her guilt: how very considerate of them. She resisted the urge to drink, pushed the cup as far away as possible to avoid taking the nervous sips she had seen so many women doing. The liquid slopped over the rim, flooding out across the wooden ledge and cascading down onto the floor. She snatched up the pack of tissues and pulled a couple out to wipe up the mess. Sodden in seconds, she reached for another one but stopped at a glint of silver hidden between the soft white folds. She slipped her fingers into the plastic packet and withdrew a tube of No Guilt mints. Wonderful, minty fresh breath for her plea.

'All rise.' A deep, resonant voice reverberated around the room. The bailiff stood in front of the judge's bench silencing the crowd's hubbub. There was a scuffle of feet, the sound of hundreds of people standing up, and gasps from the gallery when Mary Vitasan entered. She looked very different to the glamorous woman at the Mother's Institute dinner, or the sobbing wreck in the bathroom. Her severe black robe swirled around her as she climbed the steps and took her seat on the Judge's Bench. Behind her hung Mother Mason's portrait overseeing the proceedings.

Mary brought her gavel down and the murmurs overhead ceased. She stared at Olivia, holding her gaze for a moment.

'Case number 29573 in session,' the bailiff said. 'Mother Mason versus Olivia Pritchard. Mary Vitasan is presiding. Take your seats.'

As one, the court sat down, all except for Olivia. She stood taller and stared straight ahead. This might be a show but that didn't mean she would give them any more entertainment than she already had: she would not cower, would not weep. If this was her final moments then her children would see her standing strong. She rolled the tube of mints back and forth between her fingers and thumb, channelling all her emotion into the small repetitive movement.

'Are you Olivia Pritchard of twenty-seven Meadow Road, Bunham?' Mary asked, using the same tone she had in the City Hall bathroom.

'Yes.' Olivia's voice sounded far too loud over the speakers.

'Mrs Pritchard, you are charged with the offence of the illegal production and supply of baked goods, the use of a Class A illegal substance and ninety-three counts of possession of banned items, including cookbooks and assorted bakeware.'

Mary held her gaze then looked down and back up. 'Under the benevolent laws of Mother Mason, these acts are crimes committed not only against the laws of this country but against the citizens of our great nation. You have let all of us down. Your behaviour is unacceptable. I hope you feel *sick* with guilt.' Mary frowned and repeated the quick flick of her gaze, down and up.

Olivia glanced down as well. Was she not looking contrite enough? Tough.

Except she wouldn't be the one to suffer. It was one last surrender, but this hurt the most, because this was how Mia and Matthew would remember her. She put the mints down and picked up the tissues but stopped at the sight of the black stains on her fingertips. She rubbed them together, trying to remove the marks. Where had they come from?

The tube of sugar-free mints sat on the ledge, the clean white paper also smeared in black. She picked them up and examined the packet. Two letters had been added to the name on the front, a T and a Y. New words ran across it: NoT GuiltY. She stared at the message, not able to comprehend it. Was this Alice's plan?

'You should have trusted your mother's love,' Mary said. 'For Mother Mason loves us all and would never do anything to harm her children. It's time to do what you're told.'

Olivia closed her hand into a tight fist around the mints. Nobody pleaded 'not guilty'. No one, not ever. The consequences to getting this wrong would be so much worse than she already faced, so much worse for her family. Could she take the risk? If only Alice was here, sitting on the family bench, or at least up in the gallery, she would tell her what to do.

'How do you plead?'

The silence drew out. What should she do?

Guilty. Not Guilty. Sorry. Not Sorry.

'Guilty,' Rengar hissed at her, and she was, guilty but not sorry, not really.

The people in the courtroom started to talk in low voices, a buzzing in the background. She squeezed the tube of mints until her hand hurt.

Mary brought her gavel down, silencing the room again. 'Mrs Pritchard? How do you plead?' She gave a firm nod.

Rengar banged on the dock wall, glaring at her, then turned a charming smile towards Mary. 'My client pleads guilty.'

'I need to hear that from her. Mrs Pritchard, you know what to say. How do you plead?'

Olivia opened her fist and stared at the mints. The black lettering was smeared but still there, she hadn't imagined it. She looked back up to meet Mary's intense gaze.

'Not guilty.'

The courtroom erupted. Voices shouted down from the gallery, bursts of angry noise, but there were cheers too, brief and cut off as soon as she registered them, but definitely cheers. CTAS was there, they hadn't abandoned her.

Bang, bang, bang. Mary hammered on her desk but nobody paid any attention.

'Mrs Pritchard, are you really not guilty?' A female journalist on the front bench shouted. Her question encouraged the other reporters and they stood up, pushing towards the barrier.

'If they found evidence at your house, how can you be innocent?'

'Why did you plead not guilty? Are you worried about the consequences?'

'Your honour,' Rengar shouted, trying to make himself heard. 'Your honour, my client has made a terrible mistake. Please give us, her, another chance.'

'Silence.' The bailiff's voice boomed out and quiet returned, but everybody remained standing.

'Your honour,' Rengar straightened his white wig and tugged at the cuffs of his robes, his air of disinterested

297

detachment gone. 'Your honour ...' he seemed at a loss as to what more to say.

'The defendant will be remanded in custody until a full trial can be arranged.'

'A full trial?' Rengar made a visible effort to reinstate his mask of composure. 'Please, your honour, that really won't be necessary.'

'Mr Rengar, it is not up to you to decide what is necessary. Prepare your defence. Mrs Pritchard, I hope you are aware of the seriousness of what has taken place today. In light of these unprecedented events, it is my decision that you will be held within the Trafalgar Square Shame Box until your trial date. If you want to be the centre of attention then I'm happy to grant it. Court is adjourned.' She banged the gavel one final time.

'But—' Rengar said.

Like that, it was done, Olivia had defied Mother Mason on live national television. They would kill her for this, and not in a quiet, injection-in-her-arm kind of way. It would be public and painful, and she wouldn't be the only one to die. Alice and CTAS had better know what they were doing; she was trusting them to keep her family safe.

'All rise,' the bailiff shouted although everyone was already on their feet. Mary left the room and there was a moment of shocked silence and then the court erupted once again.

'We have to get out of here.' Ray opened the dock and hurried her down. Her legs buckled and she would have fallen but he held her up. 'You're doing great,' he whispered. 'We've got you.'

'What now?' she asked, but he didn't reply as more guards surrounded them, pushing her through the crowd of press surging into the aisles. The pandemonium was terrifying as people tried to get to her, grabbing her, shouting questions. The world closed in around her as all the attention in the room, in the country, focused on her. This was supposed to be Alice: she would have known what to do, how to handle it. Olivia was out of her depth and sinking fast.

The only thing she was sure of was that she was being dragged further and further away from Danny, Matthew and Mia. 'I love you,' she shouted, managing to turn towards them one last time.

Chapter Thirty-Six

Nobody normally left through the front door, so the street was deserted when they bustled Olivia out of the court. The guards looked at each other with questioning expressions, unsure what to do. Their indecision did nothing to reassure her.

A black car with dark windows sped up the road and the men tensed around her, their bodies shielding her from possible attack; but the car stopped abruptly beside them. Ray ordered the agents to get her inside, then climbed in next to her. The car moved off before he closed the door and they raced through London, weaving in and out of traffic, moving fast despite the busy city. She sat rigid, still clutching the mints, not daring to let go.

'Get it ready,' Ray spoke to the person on the other end of his radio. 'I don't care, those are your orders.'

They pulled up sharply and Ray bundled her out of her seat and onto the pavement before she had time to adjust to the bright sunshine, so alien after her weeks in the dark prison. More agents waited to meet them and Ray took charge.

'We need to hurry, people are gathering and this has to be by the book, understand? There are lots of cameras on us, ours and theirs. We can't risk making a mistake, the situation is already out of control.'

They stood on the corner of Trafalgar Square as though

they were there for a sightseeing trip. Noisy, jostling tourists filled the square, milling around, trying to avoid the strutting pigeons; they took photos, clambered on the statues and generally made sure everyone on social media knew where they were and that they were having an amazing time. Olivia envied them.

The sun's glare reflected off the Shame Box, dazzling her as she took in her new cell. It squatted on the tarmac, beneath the shadow of Nelson's Column to the right and a statue of another long-dead white man to the left; both stood ready to guard her.

The locals ignored her as they walked past, heads down, eyes fixed on their phones, but she was more interesting to the tourists. A group of German women in tracksuits and comfortable trainers stopped taking photos of the fountains and monuments, and turned towards her, cameras raised. They muttered as a group of teenagers on scooters whizzed past them, ruining their shots.

'Get her inside,' Ray said as the guards closed ranks around her.

Three metres by three metres by three metres, the Shame Box was identical to the one at her supermarket. It looked equally inviting. She had always avoided inspecting it too closely but she never appreciated how exposed it was. There was nowhere to hide within the transparent walls, and the cameras mounted on lampposts around the Box ensured all could see her. The video live-streamed on the giant screen on the Fourth Plinth, just in front of the National Gallery. Below the image was a web address: now viewers from all over the world could watch her humiliation.

She couldn't do this. It was a mistake.

'You're going to be okay,' Ray said. 'Don't panic.'

She was beyond panic. It was hard to breathe with

the suit crushing her lungs and the waistband restricting her diaphragm. She struggled to catch her breath as they marched her past the people already lined up around the edges of the Shame Box, jostling for best position. They were only kept back by the red line painted on the pavement, a one metre boundary around the Box; she wasn't sure if it was for their benefit or hers. Two young mums watched her; one rocked a buggy back and forth, while the other held her small son close. Matthew used to be that tiny, an extension of her as he sat on her hip. Her arms ached to hold him again.

'I can't go in there, I can't,' she said as Ray drew her to a stop outside the Box.

'You have to, it's for your own good.' Ray's hand was vice tight around her upper arm. 'Trust—'

'My mother's love? Damn it, what does that even mean?'

Fear flashed across Ray's face and he glanced at his fellow agents. So, not all CTAS, not all there to save her.

'Everyone can see me.'

'That's the point: the more visible you are, the better.' Ray pulled her towards him. 'It's part of the plan, go with it,' he hissed in her ear. 'Mother Mason will try to get rid of you any way she can; you need witnesses.'

He swiped his card to open the door but she refused to cross the threshold.

'I can't. I won't.' Everywhere she looked people watched her. Staring, whispering, judging. She backed up a step but the guards were there, a wall of solid muscle. Ray didn't say another word but his expression implored her to do as he said, to be good and go quietly.

Lots of people had their phones out, bright red lights on as they filmed the spectacle. Some carried banners she recognised from the court, angry hate-filled cards, but the fluttering rainbow ribbons caught her attention: 'Mother's Love = Power'; 'Trust Your Mother's Love'. The woman and man stood together holding the banners up high. A pink sun hat and dark glasses hid the woman's face but she tilted her head to one side and moved the sign in a faint, beckoning gesture. She repeated the motion, this time more forcefully.

'Trust your mother's love,' Ray said.

The woman reached up to lower her glasses just a fraction. The chokehold of fear around Olivia's chest released and she stepped into the Box, walking straight to Alice. She got halfway across and Alice raised her hand, palm out. Stop. She halted in time to hear the clunk of the door locking her in. It was like entering a sauna; the air was hot and saturated with humidity from the midday sun. The light was brighter too, magnified by the bulletproof glass walls. Her previous cell felt like a luxury hotel in comparison and she longed for the dark solitude.

The guards took up position on each corner of the Box, but they stayed out of the way of the cameras, not blocking her, the star attraction. The crowd stared at her and her skin prickled under their scrutiny. They muttered to each other and the noise filtered in through the air vents at the tops of the walls.

'Pleaded not guilty,' the young mother with her son said to her buggy-pushing friend.

'No way.' The friend chewed on her gum and shook her head.

'She did.' An old woman and her husband sat in folding chairs, drinking tea from a flask. The woman spoke between bites of her sandwich, 'Stood there bold as brass, didn't she, George?' She turned to the small, hunched figure beside her.

George looked up from his newspaper. 'Yes, Nancy.'

'You think she is?' the young mum asked.

'Look at her, so fat her blouse barely does up. Of course she's guilty, isn't she, George?'

George stared at Olivia with watery, vague eyes and then returned to his paper. 'Trial of Bunham Baker' was emblazoned across the front page; the print was too small for Olivia to read but the large picture showed an old photo of her from the bakery. She stood in her chef's whites, holding a large chocolate cake. How had they found it? She had destroyed everything from before. No wonder everyone assumed her guilt.

'She pleaded *not* guilty,' Alice's voice carried above the chatter, cutting off conversation. Olivia turned to her then forced herself to look away, not wanting to draw any more attention.

'So?' Nancy folded her arms.

'So, maybe you should reserve judgement until you know the facts.'

Thank you, Alice. Finally, someone was speaking out in her defence. It gave Olivia strength, she was no longer the only dissenting voice.

'I know the facts,' Nancy retorted. 'Mother Mason tells us everything we need to know.'

If Mother Mason said it, it must be true. Why did people like Nancy blindly believe everything they were told? How could they not question one, single thing? That was all it would take for things to start to unravel.

'What about the video?' a teenage girl asked. 'Nobody deserves to be treated like she was, the way they arrested her, took her child away. That's not right.'

One of the guards stepped forward. The girl held her ground for a moment, then her friend slowly drew her back and they quickly disappeared into the growing crowd.

*

The sun traced a high path across the sky. No matter where Olivia sat she was flooded by the bright light. If she closed her eyes she could almost pretend she was at home, sitting in her kitchen, the room warm from the oven, but then somebody shouted her name or a camera flashed and her illusion shattered.

The temperature kept rising, the humid air felt dense in her lungs and the tight, synthetic suit constricted her chest until she couldn't bear it a second longer. She dragged the jacket off and dropped it on the floor. There were mutters of disgust and she looked down to see the cotton blouse was dark with sweat stains, the fabric straining at the buttons, revealing peepholes of skin and a new, deep cleavage. Her embarrassment was projected on to the six-metre high screen, just to make sure that nobody at the back of the square could miss out on her humiliation. It showed everything: her pink, flushed face, the sweat that ran down her forehead, her limp hair sticking to her cheeks. She tried to brush the damp strands away, to find a semblance of respectability, but she only succeeded in smearing the concealer, partially revealing her dark rainbow bruises. There were gasps from the crowd.

'Looks like she's been in a fight,' the woman with the buggy said.

'Must be painful.' Her younger companion touched her own face and winced.

The young mum frowned. 'You don't think *they* did it, do you?' She had lowered her voice but Olivia heard her and the guard nearest the woman shifted his stance. The mums fell silent but people further away continued to mutter.

'Covered in bruises.'

'Looks awful.'

'It's not right.'

The words passed from one to another, still whispered and hushed, but they flowed out through the gathering crowd.

'Probably deserved it, didn't she, George?' Nancy said.

Olivia raised her head and glared at Nancy. 'Who deserves this?' She scrubbed at the last traces of make-up, unveiling the full extent of her injuries. 'Is this the way a mother should be allowed to treat her children?'

'She's teaching you a lesson; you're the one who broke the law.'

'Really? You think everything she's doing is legal? The arrests, the trials, the Societal Evolution Programme? If you want to believe she's a saint, fall for her stories, that's your choice, but you'd better be sure you know what's really going on. Don't just believe what you're told because it's easiest.'

Rage felt good, hot and powerful, and Olivia sensed herself growing taller, standing prouder. Alice and Dev cheered and a burst of applause flowered out around them.

The crowd had grown substantially during the three hours she had been there. The original twenty or thirty people were joined by hundreds more. They filled the square, standing shoulder to shoulder. Some clambered up onto the backs of the giant lions that guarded Nelson's Column, while others squeezed onto the raised ledges around the fountains. Even the pigeons had been evicted from their regular scavenging ground, replaced by the exponentially growing mass of spectators.

A steady stream of people continued to arrive from every direction and more filed up from the Tube station. Most found places at the sides but some pushed their way through to get a better view; they were greeted with angry words and dismissals, shoved back to join the latecomers on the outskirts.

Photographers and vloggers weaved in and out of the people, seeming to be as interested in taking pictures and videos of the protestors as they were in Olivia. They kept out of the way of the guards, whose numbers had grown too. They took up positions around the perimeter of the square, hemming the crowd in. They didn't actively stop anyone from entering but they provided a dark presence that might once have deterred people, but now didn't have any effect.

Olivia closed her eyes, shutting everyone out, trying to block the pressure of their gaze. Nausea sat heavy in her stomach and an acrid taste coated her tongue, making her saliva thick and difficult to swallow. What she wouldn't do for a glass of water, a cup of tea, even a cup of Alice's awful coffee. Tiredness engulfed her, a deep fatigue that made it hard to sit upright. Slumped forward, she rested her head on her knees and found it helped with the foggy dizziness that wrapped around her brain. If only she could sleep for a little while; maybe that would make her feel better ...

What was she thinking? There was no time to sleep, she had to get the cake out of the oven, it must be ready by now. The kitchen was so suffocatingly hot, she ought to open a window but she couldn't find the strength to lift her head, let alone move.

'Danny?' she called. 'Danny, I don't feel so good. Something's wrong. Where are the children?' She opened her eyes but the glare of the sun was unbearable. 'Mia? Matthew? Danny, I don't know where they are.' She had to get up, had to find them. Why wouldn't her legs work? The children needed picking up from school, she needed to move, now. Danny would be home soon. He was ... where was he ...?

Somebody turned out the lights and relief flooded her. It felt safe to open her eyes, and she saw someone in front of her, holding a white tasselled parasol. It formed a halo behind the person's head, casting their face into darkness. They moved the domed shape so that its shadow fell across Olivia.

Olivia rubbed her eyes. 'What are you doing in my kitchen? Do you know where my family are? I need to find them.'

'Olivia, you need to have a mint,' the woman said.

'What?'

'The mints in your hand. Have one, please.'

Olivia stared down at the tube of mints in her hand. How did they get there? Black ink was smeared across her palm.

'I need to wash, I'm dirty.'

'No, Olivia, you're dehydrated. Eat a mint.' The woman's voice held such command that Olivia obeyed. She put a mint in her mouth and sucked on it. Within a minute her nausea eased and the cotton wool fog around her head started to lift.

'Have another one,' the woman instructed.

With her vision clear again, Olivia read the words across the packet. NoT GuiltY. Not guilty, but locked in the Shame Box. She ate a second mint and looked up at the woman. 'What happened?'

'You got a little confused but you're okay now. Just keep eating the mints.'

Olivia shifted forwards, leaning into the shade the woman's parasol cast; the throbbing behind her eyes eased and she uncurled and shuffled closer to the wall, deeper into the cool shadow. The woman tilted the parasol so the dark patch on the ground was as large as possible.

'Thank you,' Olivia whispered. If she squinted she could

308

make out some of the woman's features, bright eyes edged in thick, black eyeliner and a face contoured with so much blush it looked almost clown-like. Olivia glanced to her right. Alice still stood on the other side of the Box; her pink hat was a tall beacon above the crowd. Whoever this woman was, she was a stranger.

'She's not allowed to do that,' Nancy said, but people nearby hushed her. The guards were watching but they didn't seem to know whether to intervene, so they took their lead from Ray who stared straight ahead.

The sun didn't care about their plans; it kept moving across the sky, the angle of the shade shifting minute by minute. The woman readjusted the parasol every time the shadow slipped away and all too soon it was a long, thin line of darkness, impossible to hide in.

Bright light flashed across Olivia's eyes; the heat and light returned full force, a harsh slap against her face.

'I'm so sorry,' the woman said.

'It's okay.' Olivia tried to mean it.

'My turn!' A woman with pink braids reached for the parasol; she didn't bother with a hat or disguise, it was unmistakably Bronwyn. She flicked the tasselled ends of her hair, making the beads clatter and the tassels dance. The women smiled at each other and switched hold of the parasol; now empty-handed, the first woman kept her head down, tilted at an unnatural angle, so no one could properly see her face. She glanced up at Olivia from under her lashes and gave a small wave.

'Thank you,' Olivia said.

The woman placed a hand over her heart, bowed and walked away.

'Fancy seeing you here.' Bronwyn shifted the parasol shade. 'Out for a day trip?'

'Something like that.'

'It's all highly exciting, isn't it?' Bronwyn bounced as she talked, making the shade a little hit and miss, but having a friend to speak to made it worthwhile. 'You should relax, do some sunbathing; you've nothing to worry about.'

'Are you going to tell me to trust my mother's love?'

Bronwyn cackled. 'Hell no, what does that even mean? I'm telling you to trust yourself, you've got this.'

Ray cleared his throat and Bronwyn pulled a face, but she fell quiet and the parasol stayed still for a while.

When the sun moved again, Bronwyn turned to the elderly couple in their deck chairs. 'Excuse me, would you mind swapping places?'

'No.' Nancy settled herself deeper into her chair. George had fallen asleep beside her, snoring with his mouth open.

'Here.' A tall man moved up from behind them. 'Let me.' He reached for the parasol but Bronwyn recoiled.

'Please.' He smoothed down his grey tie; the woollen ends were shredded, the way they used to do at school.

Bronwyn looked to Olivia, raising her shoulders in silent question. The man met Olivia's gaze with a steady calmness. Her whole day was an exercise in trust, why stop now? She nodded and the parasol passed hands.

'Who do you think you are?' Nancy asked. 'You're encouraging a criminal. What would Mother Mason say?'

'Not a criminal, ma'am,' the gentleman said. 'Innocent until proven guilty. Technically, we still believe that in this country.'

Nancy harrumphed but Ray took a small step forward and she remained silent, her mouth pulled into a tight puckered frown. 'Wake up, George, we're leaving.' She elbowed her husband and he sat up with a snort.

'I've had enough of this disgusting spectacle! But you,'

she pointed at Olivia, 'you're in for trouble, missy, just you wait and see.' She marched off through the crowd, leaving George to fold up the chairs and trudge after her.

Chapter Thirty-Seven

The heat of the day broke as the sun moved behind the nearby buildings, spreading cool shade over the square. The man took down the parasol and set it on the ground, ready for tomorrow. He gave Olivia a slight bow and left too. She took advantage of the cooler weather to walk around. Her muscles and joints were stiff and she ached as she took her first, hobbling steps. As she did a circuit of the Box, trying to get feeling back in her limbs, she passed Bronwyn, who had remained in her original place on the perimeter. She watched as Bronwyn picked up a bottle of water and sipped. It looked incredibly good, so good Olivia had to hurry past, not stopping until she reached the other side of the Box, near Alice's space; but there was no sign of the pink sun hat. She stayed there longer than she should, searching the crowd, unable to move on, but Alice had gone. The urge to burst into tears was so overwhelming she had to bite her cheek until it hurt; she wouldn't let them see her cry. Instead, she stormed around the Box, stamping her feet hard enough to feel the shock travel up through her legs.

The sky was shot through with burning strawberry reds and candyfloss pinks that slowly faded to simmering oranges and lemon yellows. By the time the cooler, calmer blues settled in, the day's heat dropped to a comfortable warmth. The change in temperature brought more people out to see her and despite standing on tiptoe she couldn't see all the way to the back any more. Many of the faces that stared back at her looked hostile, but within the sea of anger and disgust, there were allies wearing frayed jeans, T-shirts and ties. They weren't signs of lack of pride in their appearance but garments that expressed integrity, strength and courage. With each fringed garment, shawl or piece of jewellery, she found a friendly expression, a nod of support, the occasional thumbs-up. She wished she still had her necklace.

A woman in a wheelchair managed to get to the front of the crowd. She wore a deep magenta apron over her clothes, the ends of the strings cut and left dangling. Her chair looked like it might float away with all the shiny helium balloons that floated above her, tethered by bright rainbow ribbons.

'I love your chair.' Olivia stopped to admire it; Mia would have adored it too.

'I decorated it specially.' The balloons bobbed every time the woman moved. 'How are you doing?'

'I'm okay, thank you. Better for seeing all the support.'

'Don't talk to the prisoner.' Four agents pushed their way through the spectators, Lewis in the lead. He wore sunglasses and a new white shirt but there were dark, black bruises leaking out along his cheekbones. Olivia felt rather smug.

'I'm taking over,' he told Ray.

'Those aren't my orders. You can stand over there.' Ray pointed to the far corner, away from the door.

'No, you need to—'

Boom!

The crowd scattered at the explosion; people ran for the exits, screaming and shoving each other, rushing to get away, but Olivia was trapped. She waited for the devastation, for the world to be torn apart, but instead something bright and sparkling fluttered down from the sky, catching the light of the setting sun. You could easily pick out the members of CTAS from the rest of the crowd, they remained where they were, barely flinching at the explosion and the ensuing chaos. They stood looking up, reaching out to catch handfuls of glitter, as the flickering, floating rainbow confetti drifted past them.

'We're under attack,' Lewis shouted. 'We have to get the prisoner out of the Box.'

'No, our orders are to keep her here, no matter what.' Ray pushed him back to his position. 'They're just trying to cause a scene; we can handle a little glitter.'

Lewis covered his ear and spoke to the control room. He gestured to the big screen and made a cutting gesture across his throat but the picture remained up, live-streaming Olivia and the CTAS protest.

Boom! Boom!

The next explosions came from opposite corners of the square and this time, along with the glitter were small, billowing parachutes, no bigger than a handkerchief, that caught on the evening breeze and glided across the square.

'Bombs!' Lewis shouted, ducking for cover behind the Box. Again Olivia braced herself as the billowing parachutes landed around her, but there was no further incident.

Ray laughed and caught one from mid-air. 'Relax, it's just a stunt, see ...' Attached to each cotton parachute was a small dangling package. He undid the little tassels and tipped three small, golden brown discs onto his palm. He thrust them towards Lewis and Olivia edged closer to see the tiny, perfectly baked, chocolate chip cookies. 'Not scared of biscuits, are you, Lewis?'

The woman in the wheelchair was covered in confetti; a parachute had caught on her balloons and she untangled it to retrieve her treats. She popped one into her mouth, her smile growing wider as she chewed.

'Delicious, but probably not as good as yours,' she said to Olivia.

Olivia looked up to the ceiling. There were several of the parcels on top of the box but none had made it through the vents.

'I'm sure we can get you some soon,' the woman said.

'No, you won't.' Lewis stormed around and knocked the cookies from her hand.

'Hey!'

'Leave her alone.' Olivia banged on the wall.

Lewis picked up one of the cookies and slammed it against the Box in front of Olivia's face. 'Is this your doing?'

'How could I do this? I'm locked in a box.'

He threw the crumbs down and ground them into the pavement. 'Seize the illegal items,' he instructed the other guards.

They walked around the Box trying to collect up the parachutes but the crowd were faster, darting forward to pick them up and hide them away. Ray slipped the rest of his cookies into his pocket. A small smile twitched at the corner of his mouth when he caught Olivia watching him, there for the briefest moment and replaced just as swiftly with his normal, impassive expression.

With a blare of music, the big screen grew brighter and the live-stream from the Shame Box was interrupted. It turned to grey and white static before a video started to play. A montage of Olivia and her family projected out across London, images that were painful and beautiful to see. Her wedding, Matthew's birth, their first Christmas,

Danny's birthday, her second baby bump, Mia crawling: the mundane and the momentous, their lives and love documented for the entire world to see.

'This is a mother's love,' Alice's voice broke over the music. 'This is a mother's love.' The images transitioned to photos of other women and their children. So many women, hundreds of faces, strangers and friends. Becky was there, Nadine, Shawna and Carol too. They flashed up one after the other, getting faster and faster, so many that it was impossible to take in. They were smiling, happy, together. 'These mothers love. These mothers *loved*.'

The music slowed, it became harder and angrier. Stark, sterile pictures from within the prison replaced the women. Ray had been busy. They showed the cells, the showers, the one long living space, then moved to other cell blocks Olivia had never seen. There was jumpy, grainy security camera footage of tired, pale, hopeless women, some she recognised but many more she had never met, would never be able to meet. They looked as lost and broken as she had felt.

'This is not a mother's love,' Alice's voiceover continued.

There were videos of the courtroom, the trials, women pleading for their lives, for their families, and then a small white room, a chair with restraints, a tray of syringes. A gagged woman was dragged in and strapped down, the video zoomed in on her terrified face. It was Shawna.

Olivia couldn't bear to watch, but she forced herself to look at the screen. Shawna deserved her suffering to be witnessed, for her life to be seen, right up until the very last moment when death stole the light from her eyes.

Pictures of other women joined Shawna on the screen, hundreds and hundreds of them, until it was impossible to pick out a single person in the collage of fear and despair.

The crowd watched in absolute silence. Nobody could pretend any longer, nobody could deny what was happening. Their shield of innocence and plausible deniability had been ripped away, once and for all. This was their reality, the consequences of their inaction, of their self-preservation. Olivia was the only person watching who felt relief as the truth was revealed. The burden of being one of the few who knew slipped away from her. She was no longer alone.

The music stopped and Mother Mason's face came up, one large, smiling image.

'This Mother does not love. Trust *your* mother's love. Trust—'

The video cut out and the screen went dark.

Chapter Thirty-Eight

Olivia woke the next morning from dreams of raining cookies and parachuting cupcakes. A scent of cinnamon lingered in the air but instead of fading away with sleep, it grew stronger the more conscious she became. She opened her eyes to the sight of cakes, cupcakes, brownies and pies laid out around the Shame Box. Pretty china plates, silver trays and wicker baskets piled high with baked goods had been pushed over the line to surround her on all four sides. Small gaps remained for the guards to stand in and they didn't look happy. Ray had left his post but Lewis was still there and he was clearly livid.

'You've had some deliveries.' The woman in the wheelchair sat in the same position.

'I think I might still be dreaming.' Olivia scooted over to the wall and inspected the offerings. Apparently, Vera wasn't the only one with access to contraband; CTAS had pulled out all the stops. Everything looked amazing and smelt even better. 'Where did they come from?'

The woman shrugged. 'Hard to tell when you've got so many friends close by.'

The early morning light whitewashed the square but the bright rainbow colours of the crowd uplifted the grey stone. The protesters had covered their frayed garments with aprons, all with the strings cut, the ends frayed and dangling at their sides. Some had customised theirs with

Alice's slogans, adorning them with beads, sequins and extra ribbons, while others wore the original pink aprons from the PAB; Nadine would be so proud. The dark-suited agents remained on the outskirts of the square, ringing the crowd in, but they and the protesters seemed resigned to ignore each other.

People waved at Olivia and a cheer went up when they realised she was awake.

'Mother's love! Mother's love!'

'I said you've got lots of friends.' The woman reversed her apron to show the words 'Mother's love!' written across it, just below the Pink Apron Brigade logo.

'Don't talk to the prisoner.' Lewis's broken nose gave him a strange nasal tone. He had lost the dark glasses but the blue-black shadows of bruises were still visible around his eyes, despite the obvious concealer. Jenna should have done a better job with his make-up.

'Morning, Lewis.' Olivia smiled sweetly at him. 'How's the nose?' For the first time the Box felt comfortingly safe.

He scowled at her but his face froze in a grimace of pain. 'You look hungry,' he said. 'Fancy a cupcake? No, a brownie maybe? Do help yourself.'

Her stomach rumbled, a gnawing, aching burn, made worse by the sweet, spicy cinnamon smell coming from the nearby apple pies. There was a plate of golden scones beside them that had to be fresh from the oven. A breath mint was not going to cut it, not with the baked treats just a piece of glass away.

She tried to ignore Lewis and the smell, and took a lap of the Box, walking slowly, bending low to look at everything they had baked for her. She couldn't remember the last time anybody had cooked anything for her. It was such a shame she couldn't eat any of it.

'Why is the food still here?' she asked the woman once she completed a full circuit. 'I thought they would have got rid of it.'

'They can't,' Dev's voice carried from the crowd, he and Bronwyn stood together but Alice was missing. 'The guards pick it up and they're on camera holding cakes. Not the image Mother Mason wants the nation to see, not now they've lost control of the video feed.'

'They smell so good. Lewis, doesn't it make your mouth water?' she asked, joy raising her spirits as he swallowed, a quick bob of his Adam's apple. Not fun being taunted, was it?

'She does need to eat,' Bronwyn spoke up. 'You're required to provide food, water and bathroom breaks for all prisoners. She's already suffered one health crisis, you're responsible if she has another.'

'What are you, her lawyer?'

'If only. If she'd had a real legal team we wouldn't be here. I'm just a concerned citizen.'

'One of many,' the woman in the wheelchair agreed. 'The world is watching, Agent Hook-Medwood. It would be in everybody's best interests if you looked after Olivia.'

'I'll take care of her, don't worry about that.' Lewis's gaze went distant, as if he was listening to something, and he looked up at the nearest camera. He shook his head, frowned, shook his head again, then grunted, before retrieving a brown paper bag from the ground beside him. He shoved it through the hatch in the door and it landed with a hard thump.

'Three minutes,' he said and pressed a button on the door panel. The walls around Olivia went opaque.

Within the bag was an apple, a small loaf of bread, a bottle of water and a roll of toilet paper. A hole in the corner of the Box opened up and Olivia didn't need to venture closer to know what it was for. Yesterday's dehydration was actually a blessing. She put the toilet paper to one side and opened the water. Her instinct was to drain it in one, but the gaping hole behind her, and the fear it might be the only drink she got today, forced her to take a few small sips and screw the lid back on. The bread was dry, tasteless and almost impossible to swallow but it was edible and filled up the gnawing hollow inside her stomach. She ate half and returned the rest to the bag, just as the walls turned clear again.

Time crept by, marked by the chimes of Big Ben ringing out over the constant hum of traffic. When the twelfth strike of noon died away, three black cars pulled up beside the National Gallery and a small group of people got out. A buzz of excitement rippled through the crowd.

'They're here.'

'Can you believe it?'

'They shouldn't be here.'

'What's he thinking?'

'It's not right.'

'I would never bring my children.'

Children? Olivia strained to hear what they were saying. She stood close to the glass, stretched up on tiptoe to try and see through the masses. Could it be? Were they here?

The crowd outside the gallery parted and a gangway formed down the stone steps and across the square. The group walked straight towards the Shame Box and the view on the screen changed from Olivia's battered appearance to a distant shot of a man in a dark suit holding the hands of a boy in a matching suit and a little girl in a white dress. They were flanked on either side by guards and a woman followed close behind them.

The camera zoomed in. It really was them.

'Matthew! Mia! Danny!' Olivia called.

Mia looked up and squealed. 'Mummy!' She tried to run forward, pulling on Danny's hand, but he held her back, refusing to let go.

'Mummy.' Mia struggled stretching Danny's arm to full extension, wriggling to be free.

Olivia pressed her forehead against the glass. 'Mia, baby.' She smiled at her, at Matthew and Danny, but Mia was the only one to smile back. Matthew kept his gaze fixed on the ground.

They were a few tuts and murmurs from the crowd but the majority clapped and cheered. Matthew ducked his head lower but Mia waved at the people, beaming when they waved back, the centre of attention and loving it. Matthew glanced up at the Box and Olivia tried to hold his attention but he looked away, stumbling forward. Danny reached to steady him and Mia seized the opportunity to break free. She ran towards the Box, her small feet racing over the paved square. A couple of people reached out to catch her and the two guards, acting as escorts, bolted after her.

'Mia, no!' Olivia and Danny shouted but Mia kept running, head down, the skirts of her dress flaring out around her. Tiny and vulnerable, and more determined and fearless than Olivia had ever felt, her baby girl ploughed forward through the vast crowd of strangers.

'Mia!' Olivia shouted, all her fear channelled into one word, making it snap hard and angry like a whip. That should have worked, it should have forced Mia to stop, but she kept running, straight towards Lewis who waited with hands outstretched ready to catch her.

'No!' Olivia banged her fists against the glass. 'Mia, no, stop.' She was ten metres away and closing the distance.

Danny ran, with Matthew a few steps behind him, but they were too far away. Mia darted under arms and outstretched hands; she had almost reached the front of the crowd, five metres, four, three. Lewis advanced on her.

'Don't touch her.' Olivia shouted through the glass. 'If you touch her I'll—'

'You'll do what?' Lewis asked, without looking round.

She slammed her hands helplessly against the Box. 'Mia!' she screamed, but Mia seemed to take it as an invitation to run faster. She was steps away from crossing the red line and Lewis grabbed for her.

'No,' Olivia shrieked, but Lewis's hand closed around empty space. The woman in the wheelchair had caught Mia and pulled her onto her lap. Mia howled her indignation, fighting to get away, but the woman held on.

'It's okay, Mia, I'm not going to hurt you,' she said, her voice gentle but firm.

'Mia, stop! Don't fight the nice lady. Please, she's helping you,' Olivia said, her legs almost giving way with relief. She felt as breathless as if she had been the one making the sprint across the square. She rested her head against the Box, not taking her gaze off her little girl.

'Hello, Mia. Looks like you're as naughty as your mother.' Lewis crossed the red line, looming over the woman's chair as he reached for Mia, but Danny and Matthew barrelled up to them and he backed off, retreating to his position.

'Thank you so much,' Danny said to the woman as he took Mia and held her tight against him.

'My pleasure, we have to protect our children. Olivia's already doing her bit, I'm proud to do mine. I'm Faye.' She shook Danny's hand and waved at Olivia.

'Mia, you're going to be in so much trouble. Dad told you not to run off,' Matthew said.

'I just wanted to see Mummy.' Mia lifted her chin and twisted in Danny's arms to look at Olivia.

'You know what we said about the red line.' Danny pointed to the ground. 'You're not allowed to cross it.'

'Why not?'

'Because it's the law,' Lewis said.

'Why?'

'Because it is.'

'Why?'

'Just because!'

The crowd laughed and Mia grinned.

'How can you resist a face like that?' Faye asked and the crowd laughed again, they didn't bother to try and hide or stifle it any more.

'Nobody crosses the line. You keep her in check or—'

'Or what?' Faye's shoulders stiffened. 'She's just a child. Surely she doesn't pose a threat to national security?'

'Nobody crosses the line.'

'She's just a child,' someone in the crowd shouted and others took up the cry.

'Mia, Ben's daddy is just doing his job.' Danny put her down but kept hold of her hand. 'I'm sure he'd do the same if it was Ben.' The frightening thing was Olivia didn't doubt it.

'Protecting the world from children,' a man in a fringed shirt said. 'What a great job; you must be so proud.'

Lewis didn't react but a pulse fluttered beside his clenched jaw.

'Mia, do as Daddy says.' Olivia pointed to the line. 'Talk to me from there.'

'But I want a cuddle.' Mia stuck her bottom lip out and her chin wobbled.

'I know.' Olivia leaned into the warm glass, her arms hung limp and empty by her sides. 'Me too.'

Mia edged forwards, until the tips of her shiny patent shoes were on the red line. She looked up at Lewis with an innocent smile, then grinned at Olivia; Alice would be proud. Danny shook his head; he kept hold of Mia's hand and reached for Matthew who stood a few steps away.

'When are you coming home, Mummy?' Mia asked, and Matthew jabbed an elbow into her side.

'You're not supposed to say things like that,' he said.

'Why not? I miss Mummy.'

'I miss you both too.' She bit the side of her cheek.

'Look what you've done,' Matthew said. 'You've upset her.'

'It's okay.' She tried to smile. 'I'm not upset. I just miss you all.'

'Huh-hum,' the woman accompanying Danny cleared her throat. She stood a little behind them, out of view of the cameras.

Danny's shoulders slumped and he ran a hand through his hair, forcing his neat style back into its usual unruly shape. He looked at Olivia, his gaze desperately sad and imploring. 'Olivia ...' He stopped, swallowed and didn't speak again.

'Olivia, we love ...' the woman said in a low voice.

He glanced down at the children, then took a deep breath. 'Olivia, we love you but what you are doing is wrong, your actions have consequences and it's only right and true that you face them, you did something bad and it's time you said sorry.' He recited the words in one long, rushed stream and when he reached the end his body sagged like it had been deflated. The woman cleared her throat again and Danny stroked the top of Matthew's head. 'It's your turn, son.'

Matthew shook his head, his hands balled up into tight fists at his sides.

'Go on, it's okay.'

'Matthew, it's all right.' Olivia looked over his head to the woman, wishing there wasn't glass between them. 'Say what you have to.' She knelt down so she was on his eye level. 'I love you. There's nothing you can say that will ever change that.'

He met her gaze and she worked harder to keep her tears hidden because his were ready to spill over.

'Mum,' his voice shook. 'We love you but ...' He looked up to Danny who nodded. 'But you have to do what's right. That's what you tell us. Lying is bad. You have to say you did a bad thing and that you're sorry. '

There was a long silence.

'Huh-hum.' The woman's cough was louder.

'Mia,' Danny said.

'No!' She stamped her tiny foot.

'Please, Mia.'

'I don't want to.'

Matthew shoved her.

'Ow.'

'You have to say it or they'll hurt Mummy too.'

Hurt her too? Olivia's heart felt like it tore away from her chest and she couldn't hold back an agonised cry. Mia burst into tears too.

'I don't want to,' she wailed.

Danny turned to the woman behind them and she shook her head a fraction. Rage pulsed from him, but he kept it coiled tight inside. Instead, he knelt down beside Mia, his movements sharp with fury, but not at her. 'Please, baby, it's for Mummy.'

'What have you done to them?' Olivia hammered on the glass and the woman flinched. 'Why are you making them do this? They're children.'

'I believe it's you who's making them do this,' the woman said.

'They're blackmailing your family,' Faye said, loud enough for the microphones in the Box to pick it up and enhance her words so the entire square could hear.

'That's not true, is it, Mr Pritchard?' the woman behind Danny said.

He gave Olivia a helpless look.

'How could you?' Alice shouted from the other side of the Box. 'You're using a mother's children to control her. Doesn't that go against everything Mother Mason stands for?'

'Alice?' Lewis scanned the crowd. 'I knew you'd be here. Find her,' he instructed the guards.

'Mia, say it,' Matthew urged her.

'No.' She shook her head, tears streaming down her face.

'Mr Pritchard,' the woman cautioned. Two guards moved up to join her, standing to either side of Danny, Matthew and Mia. Dev and Bronwyn pushed their way through the crowd but there were too many people in their way.

'No,' Olivia screamed. 'I did it. It's my fault. I'm guilty.' She projected her voice and the microphones did the rest.

'Liv, no,' Alice shouted. Lewis focused in on her voice and pointed her out to the nearest guard.

'Stop! Leave her alone, leave them all alone. It's me, I'm the one you want.' Olivia spoke directly into the camera. 'I did it. I did everything you said and more: I joined CTAS, I baked cakes, I rebelled against Mother Mason. What else do you want me to say? Tell me what you want and I'll do it, just leave my family alone.'

327

'Why did you do it?' Faye rolled forwards, almost over the red line and the whole crowd moved closer. 'Why risk everything just to bake a few cakes?'

'Because ... I'm a terrible person, I—'

'No, Mother Mason wants you to tell the truth. Do it, Olivia, tell the truth. Why did you join CTAS?' Faye's expression willed her to speak. 'Trust your mother's love, one last time.'

'Come on, Liv,' Alice shouted. 'You can do it.'

This was it, the final step in the plan, but this was meant to be Alice. 'I, uh ... it was never about the cakes ... I, uh, I couldn't accept the way things are any longer. I ...' she closed her eyes and remembered why she did it. Becky's petrified face, the arrest, Rigby Hall, the bars on the windows, Jenna, the PTA, Shawna ... 'I'm done being scared.' She opened her eyes and glared up at the camera. 'I've had enough of feeling terrified, of fearing the direction this country is headed in. I was frightened every day, for my children, for my husband, for myself, and I couldn't take any more.'

'It's not that bad, is it? You're just weak, you can't handle the pressure, everyone else is doing fine,' Faye said, gesturing for her to keep talking.

'Are they? That's not how things look to me. We're all stressed out and pushed to breaking point. Every single decision has consequences and the pressure is too much, nobody can be happy and healthy if they think they're going to be targeted for the smallest thing. Nothing we do is ever good enough, from what we eat to what we wear or how we live. It's impossible and I hate feeling so powerless.'

'What's any of that got to do with baking?' Faye's face was flushed, her eyes sparking with excitement and Olivia felt it too, her final chance to say everything she had ever thought but been too afraid to voice.

'Baking was all I had to offer, it was the only way I could help make a difference and support CTAS. It's a mother's job to protect her children, but for too long I did nothing. I had to find something that not just protected them, but changed the situation. I want a better future for them, so I did what I could with what I had to offer. It's all any of us can do.'

'What is it that you want?' Faye set her up for her final statement, it wouldn't be long before they shut her up. Permanently.

'All I want is for my children to be free to choose their own fates.'

'Even if that's fat and in a coffin?' Spittle flew against the glass as Lewis snarled at her.

'Nobody chooses that.'

'Really? History proves you wrong.'

Something inside her broke and everything she had ever felt but not said spilled forward.

'History shows desperate, angry, unhappy people who wanted to forget, to escape and find some kind of release. Before the ban, I baked when I was happy, sad, stressed, bored: it satisfied every mood. I shared the food I made with the people I love, to show them how much I cared.'

'Aww, boo-hoo, you couldn't make a cake, poor, sad Olivia.'

'How did you numb the pain, Lewis? How did you escape? Grab a beer? Go for a smoke? Place a bet? Or maybe it was something harder? Drugs? Sex? Life is tough and it hurts every day, in big and small ways. We all need some way to cope with that.'

People in the crowd nodded at her words and in their agreement she found strength.

'What do you do now? The pain sure as hell hasn't gone away; if anything the rules, the bans, the *protection*, have made everything a million times worse. So what do you do, Lewis? Do you spend hours on social media? Scrolling through posts that make you feel worse? Or maybe you go to the gym a lot? Nice and legal, that, but just as dangerous. Nobody talks about the increase in joint replacement surgeries, do they? Almost everyone I know is seeing a physiotherapist or waiting for surgery.'

'You're full of shit.' Lewis lifted his hand to his earpiece and muttered something into the microphone on his sleeve. Light glinted off his heavy, chunky watch.

'Oh, there it is. You get your high from shopping. I've seen the fancy cars and the designer clothes. Ben's always got the latest toys, the most expensive gaming gear, and Jenna makes sure everyone sees her new jewellery and dresses. We all have our vices and they feel good, right? When you click that pay button, when the parcel arrives with all the new stuff, it's like a release, a moment to breathe, really, truly, take a breath.' Her own breath sighed out of her and Lewis's posture reflected her ease.

'It's what we all need, so we're not constantly wound up with fear and pain. Everyone has a way to stop shrinking and feeling so small, so helpless against it all. I needed that so bad. Baking a cake, eating a piece of chocolate – it might not have lasted long, but damn, it pushed away the panic, the sense of drowning. It's all I wanted, to feel better, to not feel like I was overwhelmed by life.'

'How's that working out for you?' His voice didn't sound as angry as he intended and she laughed, more tension easing from her chest.

'Not so great, but isn't that proof that Mother Mason's way isn't the answer? I voted for her, I believed she was the solution, I truly did, but taking away our choices? Deciding for us? Reducing us all to children? That's not the way forward, because we're still desperate and broken, and in so much pain.'

She looked to Danny, who held their children close. Around him people had started to cry.

'We need help with the pain, in how to carry the parts that hurt, the broken pieces, the scared pieces, the sides of us we think no one will ever love. That's all I ever wanted.' She smiled at Danny and her own tears spilled over. 'And I had it, I just didn't realise.' She touched the glass and he reached out to her across the red line.

'Mother Mason is doing what she believes is right, but she's trying to solve the symptom, not the problem. It's not the way forward, pushing it down, ignoring it. Any doctor will tell you that never works.'

'Hear, hear,' Dev shouted and others in the crowd echoed him.

'So, *Dr* Pritchard, expert in all things medical, spiritual and emotional, what do you think Mother Mason should do?' Lewis asked.

'Focus on the pain, teach people how to be in the world and still feel. I never talked about my feelings, not really, not to my husband or my best friend, because I was so ashamed. I thought I was the only one, but I was wrong; being here, seeing how many people have shown up, it's made me realise we've all lived the same experience. We have to be able to help each other. We need to talk openly, share our lives, our struggles, and support one another. The solution can only come if we work together.'

'How exactly would that work?' For a moment he

sounded genuinely interested, his bluff and bluster gone.

'We need access to good food, healthcare, a decent living wage, *and* we need emotional support, to learn how to feel better, so we can do better, so that food, alcohol and all the other distractions are no longer crutches to get through the day. They become fun experiences, not numbing devices or routes to escapism. Heal the pain, solve the problem.'

'Yeah!' the crowd cheered. The sudden noise grounded her back in the Box and Lewis broke her gaze as the crowd reasserted its presence.

'Oli-vi-a! Oli-vi-a! Oli-vi-a!' The crowd chorused, energy surged through the square, a palpable thing that brought goosebumps up on her skin.

'That's enough.' Lewis stepped in front of her.

'It's not nearly enough!' Faye shouted. 'Mother Mason promised to protect us, to nurture us, and to help us be happy and healthy. Instead she's killing us and the people we love, all to protect her power.'

'We're done here. You need to leave, before there's any more trouble.' The anger in Lewis's stance returned, the moment of connection slipping away as he fell back on old habits. No, she wanted to scream, stop, this isn't the way, but nobody was listening to her any more.

'Disband or we will take action against agitators!' Lewis bellowed at the crowd.

'Are you going to put us in the Box too?' Faye shouted.

'Yeah, do you think there's enough space for me?' asked a man in a pink, purple and blue apron.

'And me?' Dev shouted.

'And me?'

'And me?'

The crowd moved forward, closer to the Shame Box and the red line. Lewis held his ground. 'Are you all really prepared to lose everything, for *her*? For her delusional fantasy?'

'This isn't about Olivia, this is so much bigger than her. It's time Mother Mason realised we've had enough, we won't be bullied or shamed any more,' Faye retorted.

Lewis reached up and removed his earpiece and dropped it into his pocket. 'You're so damn ungrateful, all of you. None of you have any idea the things we do for your own good. You need protecting from yourselves. Heal your pain? Why don't you have a group hug and kiss it better. That's not life. Life is hard, it hurts and you suck it up. Bunch of cry-baby, snowflake libtards. Join the army, see real pain, and then come back to me.'

'Isn't that the point?' Alice pushed her way to Dev and Bronwyn, and together they kept moving towards Danny. 'None of it is working, things keep getting worse. We have to do something different.'

'Lying politicians aren't the way. It's time we stopped Mother Mason, for the good of *our* children,' Faye shouted. 'We have to fight back, take what's ours and do whatever we must to end Mother Mason and her evil dictatorship.'

'Yeah!' People pushed closer to the action and anger crackled through the crowd. Olivia felt the open vulnerability around her heart replaced by a sickening fear, as the softness left people's faces and hardened into cold, ugly masks of rage.

'That's it,' Lewis said. 'You've had your visit, you need to leave.' He took hold of Matthew and Mia's shoulders.

'Don't touch them.' Danny stepped towards him but before he could do anything Lewis let out a strangled cry. Mia had her teeth clamped around his hand and he let go of Matthew to shake her off. Her little head flopped back and forth and he threw her from him.

'Mia!' Olivia screamed.

An angry buzz rose from the crowd, part gasps of shock, part growls of rage, and their indignation transformed into explosive fury in the seconds it took for Mia's tiny body to fall back.

'No,' Olivia screamed.

The people moved en masse, surging forward.

'Mia!' Danny tried to reach her but Lewis lunged for him. Danny reacted first; he drew back his fist and punched Lewis in the face. Blood gushed from Lewis's nose for a second time. He staggered back against the Box but too late: the crowd moved over the red line towards him.

'We need backup. Send reinforcements immediately,' Lewis choked out.

Olivia lost sight of Danny and the children, as the growing tide of people crossed the line and pressed up against the Shame Box.

'Danny? Matthew? Mia?' Where were they? There were so many people, all moving in confusion. She bent low, looking through the gaps between the chaos of legs, searching for small patent shoes among the trampled remains of the cakes and bakes.

'I order you to—' Lewis shouted but nobody listened to him. An old man came up behind him and hit him with his walking stick: it was Tom. Lewis turned on him with fury but three teenage boys dragged Lewis away. He let out a strangled cry and then was lost among the seething mass of protesters. The other guards had vanished too or had stripped off their jackets and joined the fray.

'Everyone move in front of the Box,' Faye shouted. She held a loudhailer and her voice carried over the crowd. 'Form a tight circle. No one gets close.'

'Matthew? Mia? Danny?' The roar of noise from outside

diluted Olivia's plea as though it were just a whisper. She ran along one side of the Box and down the other, ducking low and stretching high, peering between heads and closely packed bodies, bending to look for any sign of them. Some people tried to catch her attention, smiling, waving, taking selfies.

'Please, have you seen my children?' she begged them.

'Don't you worry, my gal,' Tom banged on the glass to get her attention. 'We'll find them. Have you seen her children?' he shouted to the woman beside him. She shook her head but turned to the teenage girl on her other side. 'Have you seen her kids?'

'Anyone seen Olivia's kids?' Tom hollered and others took up the shout. Over and over the question was repeated until it echoed over the loudhailer and the crowd grew quiet. The manic energy settled and instead of staring in at her, people turned to look outward.

'We're here,' Danny shouted.

Dizzying relief rushed through Olivia and she ran to the side of the Box nearest his voice. He came forward with Mia in his arms. Dev carried Matthew and Alice was a few steps behind. The children looked fine but Danny had blood seeping from a cut on his eyebrow.

'You're hurt.' She reached up and touched the glass near his head, tracing the path of blood that flowed down his face.

'Mummy!' Mia struggled to get down and Danny gasped, pain sharp across his face, but he held on tight.

'You're really hurt.'

'I'm okay. Now.'

'Mummy.' Mia struggled again. She reached her arms out to Olivia and pressed her small hands to the glass. Olivia rested her hand over them, trying to feel the warmth through the wall. Matthew, Dev and Alice came closer, they were just centimetres away.

'My loves.' Her voice echoed out over the speaker system but she didn't care who heard.

'It's okay, we're okay.' Danny had tears in his eyes. He wiped his face on his sleeve and leant his head against the glass, close to her. 'I'm so sorry for what they made me say. I never ... not for a moment ...'

'I know, of course I know. I love you.'

'Don't cry, Mum.' Matthew reached to touch her cheek as though the glass wasn't there.

'Did you see, Mummy? Did you see? I bit Lewis.' Mia gnashed her teeth as though they needed an action replay. 'He tasted yucky.'

'I'll bet he did.' Olivia laughed and wiped her eyes with the back of her hand. 'We don't bite people though, do we, Mia?'

'I think we can make an exception for Lewis,' Alice said. 'Hold on a moment.' She took out her phone and slid her finger across the screen. The live-stream image on the giant TV changed, the camera panned out from a close-up of Olivia, moving away to include the protesters clustered around the Box, then pushed further back still until the whole of Trafalgar Square was crammed into the picture. There were thousands of people pressed together but if Olivia looked closely she could still find herself, like a moving Where's Wally picture, the extreme edition.

'How's my rebel warrior?' Alice asked, her words staying between them, the microphones now switched off.

'Rebel warrior? Hardly. This was your plan, I've probably messed it all up.'

'No, you haven't, you're doing a great job.' Alice had tears in her eyes. 'Maybe better than I could.' She reached for her necklace but the pendant was missing and she balled up her fist instead. 'You managed to get through to them, even Lewis, he was listening to you. Until Faye took over.' She said the name like it left a vile taste in her mouth.

'You're not a fan?'

'No, I'm not.' Alice wasn't only missing her necklace, she didn't have a single fringed or tasselled item on; neither did Dev. They were among the few who didn't. 'She's one of the Pink Apron Brigade founders; they beat her so badly during the protest they put her in that wheelchair. Now she's the head of London CTAS and they have their own agenda, one that nobody bothered to tell me about. I'm so sorry they did this to you, I swear I had no idea they were going to twist my idea and use you. If I had, I'd have stopped them.'

'Why did they want me? You're the one who's good with words.' Alice would have taken this all in her stride and done it looking gorgeous.

'Absolutely no idea and no one will talk to me any more, they've shut me out of my own plan, but I'm going to get you out of here, I promise.'

'Good, because I'm ready to go home.' Never had her small village and little home felt more appealing.

Alice cleared her throat. 'Mia has escalated our timeline, so things are up in the air, but we're working on it.'

Mia looked up from instructing Matthew to pick up the pieces of confetti around their feet. 'I did not,' she said, stuffing the glittery foil into her pockets. 'What's excolated?'

Olivia looked to Danny for some semblance of sense but he shrugged.

'Don't ask me, they haven't told me a thing.'

'We couldn't, you know how hard they've been questioning you,' Alice said.

'They have?' Olivia pressed her hand harder against the glass. Danny wouldn't look at her but there were dark shadows beneath his eyes, exhaustion and pain giving his face deeper lines and hollows.

'How are we doing?' Faye wheeled towards them and people instantly shifted out of her way.

'I'm doing okay. Thank you for saving Mia,' Olivia said.

Faye shrugged off the praise. 'She's one of us. Fighting the system aren't you, Mia?'

Mia frowned at her and returned to picking up more glitter from the floor.

'When are we going to get Olivia out of the Box?' Alice asked irritably. 'She's been locked up for too long.'

'We're trying.' Faye gave them a neutral smile.

'Where's Ray? Surely he can get her out, he was the one who put her in here.'

'It's complicated. We have to protect Olivia and this really is the best place, nice and public, lots of witnesses. No one will try anything with her safely in there.' Faye's phone beeped and she typed a quick reply.

'Is that Mary?' Alice asked. 'What is she saying?'

Faye's phone beeped again and she read the message, ignoring Alice completely. 'Sorry,' she smiled at Olivia, 'things are moving fast and there are still some pieces we need to get in place. It's all good though. This may have taken us by surprise, but it shocked the hell out of them; that's excellent.' She raised the loudspeaker and it wailed and whined as it came to life. 'Everybody sit down. Make yourselves comfortable, we're not going anywhere. Link arms, they won't be able to move us if we unite. If you brought supplies, ration them out, but remember to share them with your neighbours. Mother Mason wants to see what a real family looks like? Well, we'll show her.'

Chapter Thirty-Nine

'Citizens must disperse immediately.' A man's voice carried over the speakers, silencing the crowd. 'Anyone who remains will be detained and prosecuted. Leave now and you will avoid punishment.' His orders were met with smirks and laughter; nobody believed that, so nobody moved.

The barricade of dark-suited agents fencing in the square had grown steadily larger all afternoon, but so had the crowd. They gradually pushed the guards back across the wide road, expanding to fill the area outside Trafalgar Square. Cars couldn't get through and the streets around the city were gridlocked. Drivers leaned on their horns and some got out to shout futilely at each other, but a surprisingly high number abandoned their cars and joined the protest.

Forced to retreat, the guards blocked off all entries into the square, keeping the rebels in and attempting to stop more from swelling their numbers, but people gathered behind the barricades, sandwiching the agents between masses of fringe-clad protesters. Mounted guards on sleek black horses arrived within the hour; this was one of the few forms of transportation that could still get through. The setting sun glinted off the shining bridles and the guns the guards carried.

'If you stay you will face the displeasure and disappointment of Mother Mason. This is your final warning.'

'Mother's love! Mother's love!' The protesters chanted.

'You have until the count of three.' Large numbers came up on the big screen.

'Here we go.' Faye took out packets of ear plugs and passed them round. A man by the door pushed a pack through the vent to Olivia.

'One ...'

'Alice?' Olivia took the small, green bullet-shaped pieces of foam.

'Put them in.' Alice bent over trying to get a pair into Mia's ears while she wriggled and squirmed away; Danny wasn't having much more luck with Matthew.

'Two ...'

'Mother's love! Mother's love!'

'You have to get the children out of here,' Olivia said.

'Three.'

The high-pitched siren screeched over the speakers. It sent needles of pain through Olivia's head. She clamped her hands over her ears but it did little to stop the penetrating sound. Matthew and Mia were both in tears, clinging to Danny. He wrapped his arms around them, using his whole body to block the noise.

'Make it stop,' Mia screamed.

There was nothing Olivia could do. She crouched close to the children, as if somehow that might help; she reached out a hand to them, but they were oblivious, eyes closed, their faces scrunched up with pain.

The noise went on and on, constant and unrelenting; there was nothing but pain and suffocating claustrophobia. There was no escape, the noise would never end.

When it did finally go quiet it was like coming up for air.

'Mummy,' Mia cried.

'It hurts so much.' Matthew said. 'Why are they—'

The siren started again. Dev took off his jacket and covered Matthew and Mia's heads. He leaned over them, joining Danny as a physical shield, and Alice and Bronwyn moved in closer.

'Stop!' Olivia looked up into the nearest camera. 'This isn't the way to get what you want. You're hurting people. I'll do whatever you want. Please.'

The sound continued.

The protesters huddled together, their arms interlocked, their ears covered; brought to tears, they rocked back and forth, keening with the pain, their voices drowned out by the siren. And yet, nobody left.

The siren stopped and started over and over again. Time had no meaning; all that existed was sound and pain.

Matthew and Mia cried for the first ten minutes, then they fell silent and that was worse; they lay between Danny and Alice, quiet and glassy-eyed. Nothing Olivia had been through so far was as bad as this.

Perversely, the hardest times were when the siren ceased: the respite was more painful because you couldn't relax and enjoy it. The waiting, the expectation, meant the quiet was as loud and painful as the siren.

'Mummy, I'm hungry,' Mia said during one of the breaks. It was getting dark and it had to be well past their bedtimes.

Faye instructed everyone to share out the emergency rations. Somebody posted a chocolate brownie through to Olivia and she nibbled it, not wanting food, but needing to eat. The low-blood-sugar fog lifted but she barely registered the taste. Mia and Matthew helped themselves to sugar-dusted shortbread. Matthew examined his, sniffing it, but Mia licked it without hesitation. Her eyes widened and she pulled a face.

'Yuck, that's so ... so ...' She didn't have the vocabulary to be able to describe the new flavour.

'Weird.' That didn't put Matthew off from taking a second bite.

'It's good,' Alice said, spraying a mouthful of crumbs. Her cheeks bulged and she closed her eyes to chew, reaching for another biscuit before she swallowed the first.

Mia picked at hers.

'You don't have to eat it,' Olivia said.

'But I'm hungry.'

'Here.' Faye took an apple out of her bag and gave it to Mia.

'You brought apples?' Alice asked.

'And? I can disagree with Mother Mason and still believe in healthy eating. It has never been about that.'

'Can I have one too?' Matthew gave the rest of his biscuit to Alice.

The sugar rush brought a new enthusiasm to the protesters.

'Bring it on,' some of them shouted the next time the siren wailed but the shrieking alarm only lasted a few seconds then cut out.

'Mother's love! Mother's love!' boomed through the speakers and the screen came back on, showing the wide shot of Trafalgar Square.

'They did it,' Faye cheered. 'They re-hacked the system. Mother's love! Mother's love!'

The crowd took up the chant but the image changed to another city, another protest.

'We've got demonstrations across the country,' Alice explained, 'all the CTAS branches united. Look, that's Edinburgh.'

'They're in Manchester there.' Dev pointed as the picture changed.

'Now Cardiff.'

As the cities came up, people on the screens saw themselves and they waved and cheered. The rebellion stretched across the country and it took an hour before the feed returned to London.

Faye wiped tears from her eyes. 'I knew they would come together.' She smiled at Olivia. 'We just needed a push, we needed you.'

Alice looked like she had swallowed a wasp.

'You didn't need me, this was Alice's plan, she's the one you should be grateful to.'

Faye swatted her words away. 'None of that matters now, it's almost over, we've nearly won.'

A flicker of orange flames sprang up in front of the gallery, bright in the gathering twilight. A group of people came out manhandling a large picture; they dragged it towards the fire and as they turned, Mother Mason's portrait beamed out at the protesters. They dropped her onto the flames and it looked like they had extinguished the blaze, but dark smoke crept up from underneath the canvas and slowly tongues of fire burnt through the painting. With the added fuel the flames reached higher into the sky, the thick black smoke billowed up to hang in a dense cloud above the city.

A high-pitched whine brought instant silence. Matthew and Mia pressed their hands over their ears, turning in towards Danny and Dev for shelter; but it wasn't the siren. The footage of the nationwide protest was interrupted by Mother Mason. She glared out of the screen, six metres tall and furious. Broadcasting from her office at 10 Downing Street, her usual sweet smile was gone, replaced with a thin, tight-lipped expression that emphasised the deep wrinkles around her mouth.

'I am appalled,' she snapped. 'These acts of disobedience will not be tolerated; it is unacceptable behaviour. I have never been so disappointed in my people, my children, in all my life. You have all let me down.' She shook her head and tutted. 'Go home. Think about what you have done and know that you will be punished. You need to be taught a lesson.' She drew out the pause so they could squirm under her disapproval.

'I expected better of you,' her voice grew shrill, her expression wild. 'I take care of you.' She pointed down the camera at them. 'I work every hour of every day to keep you safe, to keep you happy, and this is how you repay me.' She pulled a face as if she had tasted something nasty. 'How dare you.' She spat the words out and spittle sprayed onto the camera lens, visible on the large screen.

'You chose me. You voted for me.' Her eyes were wide and bulging, bright with fury. 'You wanted change. I gave you change. You wanted someone to take care of you. I did that. I gave you,' she stopped, swallowed. 'I gave you ...' she closed her eyes. When she opened them again she looked confused, her gaze unfocused. 'I gave you what you wanted.' Her voice was weaker; it had lost some of its biting edge. 'I made sacrifices for you, you ungrateful ...' She touched a hand to her forehead. 'You enjoy the peace and better health that I created and yet this is how you behave. I am so ashamed of you.'

'Ashamed?' Faye shouted. 'Ashamed of us? You should be ashamed of yourself, we trusted you.'

Her voice interrupted the cowed silence of the crowd, giving them back their voice. Boos and jeers competed with Mother Mason's next words, making it hard to hear her.

344

'All I ever did was love you. My people. My country. All I ever wanted was for your health and happiness, and ...' A fine sheen of sweat crept up under her smooth, powdered complexion; she blinked rapidly, staring to the left of the camera.

'And ...' her voice was breathless. She swayed and reached out an arm to steady herself. 'And ...' She wobbled, stumbled to the side of the screen. 'Mary——' she cried out and fell forwards, vanishing from view.

'Cut the feed,' somebody off camera shouted and the screen went black.

Nobody in Trafalgar Square reacted for several seconds, then a cheer erupted, flowing like a wave around the square and back again. 'Death to Mother Mason! Death to Mother Mason!'

Matthew and Mia danced around with Dev and Bronwyn, joining in the chant.

'Stop that!' Olivia snapped and the children fell still. 'What did you do?' she shouted at Faye and Alice.

Alice stood pale and motionless, shock silencing her, but Faye looked up from typing on her phone, a manic grin contorting her face. 'Do? I didn't do anything, I was here in my chair, you were in the Box, none of us did anything. Not guilty,' she mimicked Olivia's voice and her look of frenzied joy hardened into something cold and dark. 'Why aren't you celebrating? You of all people know what she's capable of. What we've lost, *who* we've lost. Mother Mason's taken everything from us.' She gripped the frame of her chair, as though her hatred could crush it and return the use of her legs.

'I know, but ...' Olivia wanted it to end, but this wasn't what she hoped for. Mother Mason was supposed to resign so that sanity could return. For seven years, her constant prayer was for the fear to stop, but she never intended it to come through death; not only death, but murder.

'We did what we had to do to end this once and for all,' Faye said, unrepentant. 'Mother Mason deserves this and far worse. I hope it hurt, I'm glad it's fatal.'

Olivia steadied herself against the Box, as the world shifted around her, and the crowd continued to celebrate. Alice remained uncharacteristically still and silent.

'You should be grateful they chose to make you the face of this or else you would have been another invisible victim, another dead mother. Kill one to save many, doesn't seem like a problem to me. Thanks Alice, it was a cracking plan.' Faye rolled away to join Bronwyn and the rest of the party.

'No,' Alice whispered, 'I never intended this, I swear. They were only meant to overthrow her, force her out of the government.' She started to cry. 'I didn't mean for this to happen.'

'They screwed everyone over.' Dev put his arm around her. 'It's not your fault.'

Except they were all part of this, they had all contributed. If this was supposed to be victory, why did it feel so awful?

Chapter Forty

Nobody else in Trafalgar Square seemed to have Olivia's scruples. They danced in the fountains and climbed on the statues. One idiot attempted to scale Nelson's Column, he got less than three metres up then slid back down to the ground; not that he seemed to mind, he just grinned and staggered off to join the revellers who converged around the bonfire. The same manic delight shone from every person Olivia saw; they looked gleeful and relieved, but all she felt was sick.

Forgotten by everyone now, Olivia huddled close to her family – or as close as she could get with the locked Shame Box still dividing them. Matthew and Mia fell asleep, curled up between Danny, Dev and Alice, who stayed up analysing everything until they crashed out too. There was no chance Olivia would sleep, because no matter what everyone else thought, this wasn't over, it couldn't be.

The only comfort was finally being unobserved. Even the cameras focused on the celebrations taking place all over the country. Big Ben struck 2 a.m. but all the cities remained packed with the celebrating masses, the curfew and noise restrictions completely ignored. Fireworks exploded over Edinburgh Castle, revellers celebrated at Stonehenge, people partied on beaches in Brighton, Newquay and Yarmouth.

City Hall in Norwich came on the screen. The door of their

Shame Box had been wrenched off and people sprawled on top of the Box, drinking and eating. A woman in a baggy cardigan, who looked remarkably like Patricia, sat singing Mother Mason's anthem between swigs of champagne. The words had changed since the last time Olivia heard it at the Mother's Institute dinner.

> *Mother Mason we hate you,*
> *We blame you, for all you do,*
> *You hurt, you shamed, until we cried.*
> *But now we all march side by side,*
> *Our future will be good and true,*
> *Mother Mason we've killed you.*

Gradually the people in Trafalgar Square passed out, falling asleep where they sat, leaning against the statues, or spread out on the pavement. Olivia kept watch over them all.

The next morning dawned with the arrival of more food; bacon or egg rolls with tomato ketchup and brown sauce, and flasks of hot tea, delivered by men and women on motorbikes. Barre Class couldn't be the only ones with access to imported items, Olivia realised. CTAS worked fast, when they wanted to.

When Big Ben chimed nine times, the live-stream of people making scones in the middle of Plymouth high street faded out and Mother Mason's office came back into view. Silence fell and anxiety returned as everybody stared up at the screen. The office was the same but it was Mary Vitasan, dressed in a white suit and pink shirt, who looked out at them, her expression sombre.

'I'm sorry to have to bring you such terrible news. I ...' She gave a little shake of her head and drew herself up.

'No, it's not terrible news, I will not lie to you. I know the pain and terror you have lived with for the past seven years, I experienced it too. I feared for my family every day because of Mother Mason.

'It is not with sadness but with relief that I bring you the news that her terrifying regime is over. Mother Mason is dead. Some of her advisers do not want me to tell you everything but you deserve to know the truth. You watched the moment she passed away, from what doctors believe to be a brain aneurysm. It was caused by a tumour she kept secret from everyone and the experts think this is what affected her decisions: it is the only thing that could explain the monstrous way she led this country. I, however, do not believe this excuses her actions. I am enraged by the suffering she caused and I want to apologise for my part in carrying out her wishes. After she threatened my children, I was too afraid to speak out,' Mary bowed her head, 'but I should have found the courage to stand up for you. I am deeply sorry I let my fear for my children stop me from doing what was right. I have let you down and I vow I will never let that happen again.'

The crowd cheered and the noise from Trafalgar Square was matched by everyone around London and out across the country.

'You have suffered deeply and my promise to you is that I will do everything I can to make amends, if you will let me. My first act of reparation will be to release the courageous woman who showed us all the way forward. Olivia,' Mary stared out of the screen as if she could see into the Shame Box. 'I'm coming to release you.'

Murmured voices came through the speakers, background arguments, sounds of disagreement from Downing Street.

'It is my decision,' Mary spoke to someone off camera and the arguments ceased.

'I'm on my way.' She smiled at the viewers and walked out of sight. The camera spun around the room, catching glimpses of worried-looking officials and Ray, who was giving out instructions, no longer a humble guard. The picture fixed on Mary's departing back, jolting up and down as the cameraman ran to catch up.

Mary marched out of the room, straight across a marble hallway, and opened the large wooden door herself. A mass of reporters stood outside Number 10. They gaped at Mary, then all at once they shouted for her attention, calling her name, pushing forward, firing questions at her. She waved at them but kept walking. The cameraman tailed her, showing the locked black metal gates up ahead. The picture wobbled as he put on a burst of speed and darted around in front of Mary, not to stop her but to capture her face as she reached the guards.

'Open the gates,' she commanded.

The two armed guards looked from her to Ray and the other advisers running to catch up.

'You heard her, do it,' Ray instructed.

They scurried to do as they were told and Mary thanked them, then walked out onto Whitehall. The journalists followed at a run; they crowded near her but men in grey suits moved into position, keeping the reporters back.

'What does this mean?' a woman asked, pointing a big, fluffy mic at Mary.

'I don't know,' Mary spoke down the camera lens. 'All I do know is it's time to put things right.'

The camera panned to show the mass of supporters blocking the street in both directions. A hush fell when they saw Mary.

'I'm going to release Olivia. Who wants to come?'

Despite the sealed box, Olivia could hear the echoing cheers in the distance.

The people parted, moving back to make a corridor for Mary to pass. They re-formed behind her and followed in her wake, a river of excitement and joy that flowed all the way from Whitehall to Trafalgar Square.

'Mary! Mary! Mary!'

The chant carried to the original protesters in the square.

'What happens now?' Olivia asked Alice, who was trans-fixed by the screen.

'Don't ask me.' She touched her palm to the Box and Olivia pressed her hand against the other side. 'Whatever happens, I'll protect you this time.'

'We both will,' Danny said.

It should be comforting, Olivia thought. She should have trusted that everything would be fine now Mother Mason was gone, but gnawing doubt ate away at her. The power and momentum carrying Mary forward felt like an overflowing tide coming to get them. Olivia wasn't sure she could withstand any more.

'Mary! Mary! Mary!' Matthew and Mia joined in with the shouts, their fists raised, copying the adults.

The screen followed Mary's progress. She had been forced to slow down, to greet her fans, who pushed their way forward, ducking under the arms of the security men. Everybody wanted to touch her, to shake her hand, to take a selfie. Ray and the guards tried to stop them, to keep them back but Mary rested a hand on Ray's arm and he stepped aside, allowing her to greet her public. She never stopped for long, ensuring she was continually moving forward towards the Shame Box. In the distance, Olivia could see a cluster of grey suits crossing the road. The scene repeated up on the screen. Mary was a small glimpse of white and pink, a bright beacon among the pressing throng.

'Mary! Mary! Mary!' The walls of the Shame Box vibrated with the crowd's cheers. The shouts were so loud Matthew and Mia covered their ears again. Olivia wanted to do the same but the image on the screen split to show her face beside Mary's advancing group. She tried to wipe away all traces of the past few days but with little success; she looked dirty and exhausted, while Mary glowed with passion, her cheeks flushed and full; she looked far better than Olivia had ever seen her. Gone was the hysterical mess of the bathroom, or the tightly controlled puppet on the stage; in her place was their future leader, self-possessed and strong.

'Whatever happens next,' Alice shouted to Olivia above the noise, 'just remember: *she* needs you.'

A corridor opened as the celebrating people separated and Mary seemed to float the final few metres towards the Box. Smiling wide, head high, she crossed the red line to reach Olivia.

'Hello.' Her smile encompassed Danny, Matthew and Mia, but she ignored Alice completely as she bent to speak to the children. 'I've heard a lot about you. My kids think you and your mummy are heroes. You should be very proud.' The microphones picked up every word and shared it with the rest of the square, with the rest of the world. 'I'm sorry for everything you've been through, but it's over now.'

Was it? Could it possibly be? Surely, that was too much to hope for. Mary seemed to expect a response but Olivia didn't trust herself to say anything, or at least not the 'right' thing, the political thing, so, since she couldn't say anything nice . . .

'My dear, are you ready to get out of here?' Mary took

Ray's ID card and swiped it through the key panel. The click-whir was familiar but this time Olivia stepped out into the waiting arms of Danny, Matthew and Mia.

Chapter Forty-One

'I don't like it,' Danny said, as their limo sped towards Downing Street the next morning.

Neither did Olivia, but she squeezed his hand, trying to reassure them both.

'I'm sure it's fine. Mary probably wants to say goodbye before we go home.' If only. From the Shame Box to a five-star hotel in the space of twenty-four hours, Olivia wasn't sure which was more surreal. The luxury hotel suite was gorgeous but it felt like switching one prison for another. All they wanted was to go home. Not that what she wanted seemed to matter: even now she had very little say in what she did.

Mary's request, or rather summons, arrived at breakfast. Delivered by the Royal Suite's private butler, he presented Olivia with a thick, cream envelope on a silver tray. The embossed card inside was emblazoned with the golden parliamentary crest and a confident, swirling script flowed across the page.

'Dearest Olivia, we did not get a chance to speak properly yesterday. There is much I want to discuss with you. When you are ready, Ray will bring you and your darling family to Downing Street. Yours affectionately, Mary.'

Nobody wanted to go, Olivia least of all. If she could have picked them up and swept them back to Bunham she would, but she was still trapped, still caught in the web of powerful people, with no car, no money and only a brand new, white linen suit to her name.

Ray was all smiles and polite chatter when he knocked at the door, but he was accompanied by three other guards and there was a ripple of tension when Alice and Dev insisted they were coming too.

'You want the Pritchard family, then we're it,' Olivia said, refusing to back down on this.

Ray calculated the odds of leaving the hotel without a fight and gave in.

It felt rather novel sitting in a car and not wearing handcuffs. The adults all turned down the glasses of champagne Ray offered and the children shunned the bags of crisps and chocolate biscuits. The food didn't hold any appeal for them, but if the snacks on offer were anything to by, it wouldn't be long before factories across the country restarted production; if they hadn't already.

Olivia stared out of the window at the remains of the street parties. The majority of revellers had dispersed leaving toppled barriers, scattered litter and abandoned aprons that the refuse workers now had to clear up. If only the mess in her life would be so quick to sort out.

The limo slowed as they approached the black gates of Downing Street; a large group of people, still wearing their aprons, gathered by the entrance and they cheered as the car turned off Whitehall. Four men in grey suits stood outside the gate and another four stood just inside, all armed and alert. One opened the large iron gate long enough to allow them to pass into the quieter side street, before closing it behind them. They drove a little further past the dark-bricked terraced buildings and stopped outside the famous black door with the silver number 10.

'Olivia! Olivia! Olivia!' The muffled shouts of the

journalists reached her through the hushed quiet of the limo. The sound intensified when Ray opened her door and she was greeted by camera flashes that exploded like a hundred daylight fireworks.

'Olivia, over here.'

'Olivia, how are you feeling?'

'Olivia! Olivia! Olivia!'

'Stay in the car,' she instructed Danny, blocking the children from getting out. 'I'll handle this, I don't want them any more exposed to this nonsense than they already have been.'

'I'm coming with you.' Alice pushed past Olivia to stand beside her.

'Olivia! Olivia! Olivia!' The press didn't let up. The camera flashes were seizure-inducing; she closed her eyes but they were still visible through her eyelids.

'Olivia! Olivia! Olivia!'

They didn't stop until they saw someone more important.

'Mary!'

Forgotten in an instant, Olivia could breathe again as the focus shifted to Mary coming out of Number 10. She wore a white linen suit and a magenta blouse, the twin of Olivia's outfit.

'You made it,' Mary hugged her like a long-lost friend. 'Where are your children? Isabelle and Alex are waiting to play with them.'

'They're tired, they need some quiet time.'

Mary looked to Ray who went round to the other side of the limo and opened the door.

'No!' Olivia took a step towards him but Mary caught her arm in a pinching grip; she smiled, but the intensity of her gaze was chilling.

'We're all going inside for a lovely chat,' Mary said, her

voice loud enough for the microphones to pick up.

Of course she didn't mean come straight in, she meant pose in front of the big black door, Mary in the centre, arm in arm with Olivia, Danny and the children beside them. Ray discreetly kept Alice and Dev back, while the photographers and reporters gathered enough footage for the next bulletin and broadsheet.

'Olivia, how does it feel to be out?' A balding man at the front of the group shouted. He stood with his microphone outstretched, leaning as far over the metal barrier as gravity would allow.

'What's it like to be reunited with your children?' an older woman asked.

'Are you angry about your treatment?' A woman in a fringed summer dress pushed her way to the front.

'Olivia has been through a traumatic ordeal,' Mary said, keeping a tight hold of Olivia's arm as she escorted her back a step. 'She will be available for interviews later, but right now we are going to enjoy a cup of tea together and maybe a slice of cake.' Mary waved at the press pack and steered the Pritchards through the door and out of the public eye. 'Sorry about that. As you can imagine you're headline news; we had to give them something to keep them happy.' Mary slipped out of her jacket and handed it to her waiting assistant. 'Come in, make yourselves comfortable. I meant what I said about the cup of tea. Mia, Matthew, my children are waiting in the garden to play with you, and they've got ice cream. Show Olivia's family outside,' she instructed the assistant.

'Mummy, can we go?' Mia asked.

The solid wood door and two armed guards stood between Olivia and freedom.

'Sure. Daddy will go with you.'

'Alice, I'm sure you'd like to try the ice cream, I know you've got quite the sweet tooth,' Mary said.

'I'm fine, thank you; I've had as much manufactured sweetness as I can take.'

Mary's smile set firmer. 'Of course, you may join us; I have afternoon tea laid out in the Lavender Room. Cook's been busy baking all morning, I've never seen her so excited. Gentlemen, please excuse us ladies, we've got lots to catch up on.' She linked arms with Olivia and Alice, like they were the best of friends, no longer the apparent strangers she wanted the rest of the world to believe. 'This is going to be so much fun.' They crossed the foyer, past two men struggling to take down a giant portrait of Mother Mason from the wall, and into an ornate room, painted light purple and embossed with cream and gold. Works of art in heavy gilt frames looked down on them, disapproving men and women who looked unamused by the coffee table laid with cakes and pastries.

'Take a pew,' Mary indicated the two long sofas either side the white marble fireplace. 'What can I get you to drink?' By *I*, she meant the butler who stood in the corner of the room, waiting for his instructions.

'I'm sure we could find some hot chocolate, if you would prefer? Nothing is off limits any more, thanks to you.' Mary beamed at Olivia, blanking Alice completely. 'I can't tell you how grateful I am, how grateful we all are. Doesn't the world feel so much fresher today? So full of possibility. Speaking of fresh, have a scone while they're still warm. I doubt they're as delicious as any you've made, but maybe you can give Cook some tips.'

The butler picked up the three-tiered cake stand and offered it to Mary; she helped herself to a scone and he brought the cakes round to Olivia and Alice, who sat close together on the opposite sofa. Olivia had no desire to eat, but Mary looked so excited, so expectant, it felt rude not to take one. Alice wasn't concerned with social niceties, she refused all refreshments, but on Mary's silent command, the butler ignored her and poured tea for them all.

'It's a special Downing Street blend, it's really very good. Mother Mason did love her tea.' Mary took her bone china cup and saucer and sipped her drink. 'Delicious. Olivia, you haven't had any jam or cream. It's not forbidden any more, so it would be a shame to waste it.'

'I'm okay, thank you, it's still a little early.'

'Of course,' Mary laughed, dolloping ruby-red strawberry jam followed by thick, white cream onto both halves of her scone. 'I forgot that not everyone's been up since five; there's just been so much to do. Not that I'm complaining, we've got a country to get back on track, haven't we?' She looked significantly at Olivia, but Olivia focused on her steaming cup of tea, trying not to spill it.

'It's been quite the adventure, hasn't it?' Mary continued between bites of her scone.

'That's one word for it,' Alice said.

Mary finally acknowledged her presence in the room. 'Alice, I meant to say, I'm sorry for my little panic at the dinner. You were counting on me and I let you down. Please, say you forgive me.'

Alice took a slow, controlled breath. 'I don't think *that* needs forgiving.'

Mary ignored, or missed, the inflection, as she helped herself to another spoonful of cream. 'It all worked out though, didn't it. People rallied around Olivia in the most wonderful way. It's so inspiring, don't you think? Like me, they recognised something in you, Liv. I can call you Liv, can't I?'

No, she couldn't, but Olivia just smiled. She was not here for friendship and tea parties, she just wanted to know when she could go home.

'I had some concerns, you see. I was worried about you, Alice, you're so beautiful, so dynamic, and your plan was excellent. I couldn't have come up with anything better, but we needed a downtrodden underdog. No offence, Liv.'

'How could she possibly take offence?' Alice bristled, her cup rattling in her saucer. 'This was never meant to be Olivia's fight.' She set her cup down so hard it spilled tea all over the table. Neither she nor Mary seemed to notice.

'It's okay, it's done now.' Olivia touched her arm, there was no need to antagonise the situation. 'It's over.'

'Over?' Mary laughed. 'It's not close to being over. This country has been through so much; people need our help, our reassurance that this is the right way forward. It's a wonderful opportunity. I, *we*, get to shape the nation into something better, something kinder and fairer. We both want that, don't we?' she spoke directly to Olivia. 'Your experience has made you a famous face, a beacon for the people. There will be great upheaval over the coming months and you're the best person to encourage everyone to move forward.'

Olivia shifted on the sofa, the cushions sinking around her as she adjusted her position.

'What exactly does this better nation need her to do?' Alice asked.

'It would only be a small commitment, attend a few meetings, speak with some of the Mother's Institutes, once they've been re-branded, of course. The women need to hear from you, Olivia. They need to know that things are changing for the better. You can use your own experiences to reassure them that everything will be okay.'

360

A faint wisp of steam snaked up from Olivia's cooling teacup.

'And will it be okay?' Alice asked.

'How could it not be with me in charge? Liv, I don't want you to feel pressured' — Mary leaned forward, her scone abandoned — 'we've both suffered so much under Mother Mason's regime, but now it's our duty and privilege to put things right. I just want to do what's best for the country. You feel the same, don't you?' Mary stared intently at Olivia.

'Hasn't Liv done enough? Unlike me, she didn't volunteer for this.' Alice moved closer to the edge of the sofa.

'Did any of us volunteer or were we called to act?'

Olivia broke Mary's gaze, focusing on her cup of cold tea. The full-fat milk had left a layer of scum that floated on the surface. 'Mary, thank you for thinking of me, but I'm not the right person. You're far more qualified than me.'

'Nonsense, you've already proven yourself. The people love you, they'll follow your lead and that means showing them the best way to live. Surely, after everything you've been through, you can see you're a remarkable woman. You and I are alike, I knew that from the first moment we met. You reminded me of myself, when I first set up CTAS.'

Alice's breath caught in her throat and she started to choke. 'You set up CTAS?' she gasped. 'How? Why the pretence? Why make me beg you to get involved? I had to convince you to act.'

'No, Alice, you had to convince me you were capable of doing what needed to be done, and you didn't. She did,' Mary pointed to Olivia. 'We have so much to offer the nation, it would be a crime to walk away.'

'I appreciate the, uh, compliment,' Olivia took Alice's

361

hand, getting ready to move, 'but all I want is to go home; my family have been through enough.'

'Of course, they have all been very brave. Your children especially.' Their voices filtered in from the distance, light with laughter and excitement, but they were too far away for Olivia to reach them.

'We both love our families and we want to do the best for them. That means creating a country they can be safe in.'

'I—'

'You'll be home soon enough. I'm not asking you to join my government, I only need your help during this transition period. Besides, if you don't do the interviews now the press will only follow you back to Bunham and camp out on your doorstep. That wouldn't be good for your children, would it? I can't protect you if you leave London.'

'That's okay,' Alice tensed, ready to stand. Or fight. 'I can protect Liv.'

'History has proven that to be false.' Mary gave Alice a smile sweeter than the bowl of sugar cubes. 'I see you're no longer wearing your necklace. That's a shame, you were such an enthusiastic member. But while you might be done with CTAS, Olivia's role isn't over yet.'

Olivia drank a mouthful of tea. The tepid liquid coated her tongue in a slick of fat and she swallowed again and again to clear it. It took for ever for her to find her voice but she wasn't about to lose it again. 'Thank you, Mary, I appreciate your offer, but I can't take you up on it.' Her words came out calm and confident. 'I've gone as far as I can; it's time for me to take my family home.' She put her cup and saucer down on the table with a resonant clang.

'I can't let you do that,' Mary said in a regretful voice. 'You may not have intended to become the face of the rebellion, but you are, and now we're counting on you. You have obligations to many, many people, and their happiness, their *safety* is in your hands. You are the only one who can do this and you will. I would prefer it if we were allies, but there are alternatives.' She sighed reluctantly. 'Defying me makes you a martyr to the cause and if you have no use, you have no value. I'd hate for you to follow in Mother Mason's footsteps. If you think this tea is special, wait until you try her final blend: it's to die for.'

Chapter Forty-Two

'You've lost more weight, haven't you?' Faye plucked at the side of Olivia's dress, pinching the extra caramel-coloured fabric together. 'We've told you that you need to maintain a certain body mass.'

'I am trying; it's not like I'm intentionally dieting.' Olivia shook Faye off, releasing the dress so the folds of the couture skirt swung back into place.

'Are you sticking to your eating plan? You need to model a responsible diet, show the people that they can have a balance. We have to re-educate them that there's no need to stick to Mother Mason's strict food rationing, but—'

'But they still need to practise moderation for a healthy body.' Olivia spoke to her reflection in the bathroom mirror, barely recognising the immaculately made-up woman looking back at her. Faye was right though: there were hollows in her cheeks she hadn't noticed before.

'If you know the objective, then you shouldn't be looking so thin, should you? I expect you to regain the weight within the next week.'

Somebody tapped gently on the bathroom door.

'Enter,' Faye instructed.

A man in a grey suit opened the door wide enough to peer in. 'The speeches will start in five minutes.'

'Very good. Olivia, remember that you need to emphasise

the increase in jobs now the food industry has re-established itself, and remind them that the higher prices are contributing to growth in the economy, money they will all directly benefit from. Try to sound a little more enthusiastic when you talk about your voluntary exercise programme: we want to keep everyone engaged in fitness; no one wants to see the health service bills increase again. At least not until the external investors are all in place. The Autocue will be directly in front of you. Your glass of water and handkerchief are already out; if you can't squeeze out a few tears of gratitude then pretend.'

Pretend: she could do that, she was an expert at doing that now. There wasn't a moment any more, even at their new Downing Street 'home', when she wasn't performing for the cameras, seen or unseen. It was exhausting.

Faye gave both their reflections a last look over, declared them presentable and escorted Olivia out of the private bathroom and back towards the Great Hall. They were sectioned off from the rest of the diners, but beyond the partition came the sounds of clinking china and the scent of rich coffee and sickly sweet lilies. Nine hundred women gathered for the inaugural meeting of the newly rebranded Unity Institute. After a fabulous five-course meal, crafted by the country's finest chefs to showcase the best butter, cream, cheese and, of course, sugar. Not that Olivia could manage more than a few bites; the scrutiny from the room, her upcoming speech and the live-stream television cameras killed her appetite. That had been happening a lot lately; maybe the weight loss wasn't so mysterious.

Her phone buzzed inside her clutch, and she turned away from Faye to scroll through the stream of photos Danny sent from their new apartment. Sandwiched between Mary and Faye's residences, they were perfectly located to ensure they were always on call for any public occasion or press conference.

'Looks good,' she texted back.

Seeing the few possessions he had brought back from Bunham made her homesickness intensify. She hadn't been allowed to return since her arrest; there was always another television interview or reporter she 'simply must speak to'. If she had taken Alice up on her plea to run, to leave the country, their lives might be very different. Or not. Alice's contacts had dried up the moment she left CTAS, so there was no guarantee they would have escaped safely, and Olivia was now far too famous to hide.

The phone vibrated in her hand and her children's faces lit up the display.

'Hello?' she whispered, answering the video chat. They filled her screen, feeling close enough to touch.

'There's no time for that.' Faye tried to take the phone but Olivia twisted away.

'Aren't you both meant to be in bed?' she asked Mia and Matthew in mock surprise.

'Daddy said we could watch your speech.' Mia sat on Danny's lap, dressed in her fluffiest, cuddliest pyjamas.

'We've got pizza, fizzy drinks and sweet popcorn!' Matthew held up the big bowl of popped white kernels.

'Sounds like bedtime is going to be fun.' She rolled her eyes at Danny, though she would rather be with him, wrestling their two overexcited, sugared-up children into bed, than facing an evening of propaganda dissemination. 'Save me a slice of pizza, it looks good.'

'Not enjoying your five-course meal?' Danny asked. 'Don't worry, you're going to do great.'

Public speaking didn't bother her as much as it used to. She, who hated talking in a group bigger than four, had lost her stage fright now that other things in her life were far more frightening. She'd had plenty of practice, giving interviews to every television show, newspaper, magazine, blog and radio station, though they all asked the same questions: 'How is life outside the Shame Box? Why did you rebel against Mother Mason? What are your hopes for the future? Have you got any baking tips?' She rattled off the same scripted answers every time, but nobody seemed to care.

'Are you sure you want to watch my speech?' she asked the children. 'Wouldn't you rather put a film on? I'm not saying anything you haven't heard before.' Many, many times.

'Olivia!' Faye wheeled closer, jamming her footrest into Olivia's leg. It would have hurt if it wasn't for the layers and layers of fabric encasing her body.

She ignored Faye and held the phone closer. 'I'll be home soon, I promise.'

'We'll be waiting for you,' Danny said.

A soundwoman in a black T-shirt and jeans advanced on Olivia with a microphone pack and an earpiece.

'I've got to go, I'm on in a minute.'

'Good luck with your speech.' Danny toasted her with his beer.

'Love you.'

'Love you too. Say bye, kids.'

'Bye kids,' Mia and Matthew chorused.

She kissed the screen, not caring about her smudged lipstick, and then they were gone.

'You have remembered—'

Olivia tuned Faye's voice out as the soundwoman discreetly unzipped her dress to slide the battery pack into place. An advantage of her weight loss was extra space inside the bodice, meaning the hard plastic box didn't dig in so much.

'—it really is very important. Olivia?' Faye's voice commanded attention. 'Did you get that?'

'Happier population, more freedom of choice, more hope for the future, yes I got it. I'm always on message, aren't I? I've never given you a second to doubt me.'

The woman ran the microphone cable up the back of Olivia's neck and threaded it through her intricately styled hair, seemingly deaf to the conversation.

'Your performance is passable, but we can both agree there's room for improvement.'

The hairgrips pinched as the woman slipped them into place, positioning the tiny microphone so it peeped out just below Olivia's hairline.

'I'm tired, I need a break. Maybe if I could get some time with my family, I could be a little more enthusiastic.' Olivia tried to keep her smile in place, but they both knew it was a lie. 'We missed Christmas; I've worked through both children's birthdays. I want to go home, just for a little while.'

'Home? You mean Bunham? Why ever would you want to go back there? London is your home now. You need to accept that your life has changed. It's not like you're in prison; you're going to glamorous events and doing great work for the country. You should be proud.'

Pride wasn't an emotion she was familiar with any more. There were moments in the Box when she connected with the crowd and she felt like she was soaring. Now all she felt was fear and shame for the betrayal she committed every time she stepped into the spotlight and spouted the contrived rhetoric that Mary and Faye constructed.

'The kids want to see their friends, I want to see . . .'

'Alice' was a dirty word and always instigated a fight. She and Dev had returned to Bunham under sufferance, after Olivia begged her to go; she couldn't submit to her enforced obligations with Alice raging and scheming in the background. Not that Alice ever came up with a way to escape; not one that would actually work.

Olivia missed her so much. Their stilted, filtered phone conversations – like two talking robots – had grown more and more infrequent, until they barely spoke at all.

'I want to see ... my house.'

Faye pursed her lips, for once taciturnly avoiding the anticipated argument.

'A month would be great ... or maybe a few weeks ... I'd settle for a long weekend.'

'I'm afraid that's completely out of the question. With the upcoming celebrations marking a year since Mary was voted into office, plus your speaking engagements at each of the Unity Institutes and all your other work commitments, you're booked up for at least the next six months. By the way, is your passport up to date?'

'My passport? Why would I need that?'

'Doesn't matter. I suppose you could have a couple of hours off when you visit Norfolk.'

'That's the last stop on the tour.'

'Of course it is. Their loyalty and support is unquestionable; it's the other Institutes that need your encouragement, we have to ensure their participation and dedication to Mary's goals. This really isn't the time to talk,' Faye glanced significantly towards the soundwoman. 'We'll discuss everything with Mary at our debrief tomorrow.' By discuss she meant dismiss.

The soundwoman handed Olivia an earpiece.

'Thank you,' Olivia said and the woman looked surprised at her acknowledgement.

'Hurry up now, and remember, the world is watching.' Faye propelled her forward onto the stage.

The public-speaking lessons, the social-etiquette training and the hundreds of speeches she had given in the past ten months allowed Olivia to step out onto the stage with only the smallest flicker of nerves. She had grown expert at covering that up too.

The applause from the Unity members carried her to the podium and she took her place in front of the Autocue.

'Thank you so much for being here tonight.' She paused to smile out on the crowd, her gaze travelling from the VIPs at the front of the room, all the way to the back of the hall. There was no possible way to make out the members sat in the cheap seats, the most provincial of the new Unity Institutes, but it was up to her to make them feel seen.

'I am honoured to speak to you on behalf of Mary Vitasan and her new government. We have all been through so many changes over the past year, but the launch of the Unity Institute is a symbol of our better future.' The words scrolled across the monitor, white on black, and she read them out as expected, trying to inject enthusiasm into her voice with the suitable vocal pitch, pausing where instructed. Literally instructed, they wrote it on the screen for her, along with when to laugh and when to cry. She might as well have an Autocue following her around every day.

'Our united future will allow us to lead our best lives, our happiest lives, our freest lives, thanks to Mary Vitasan.' 'Freest' caught in her throat and she stumbled through to the end of the sentence. Movement in her peripheral vision tugged at her attention but she stared straight ahead at the gothic arches at the far end of the room; there was time for Faye's remonstrations later.

She picked up the white pressed handkerchief, with Mary's now famous monogrammed logo embroidered on the corner. A thin object fell from the folds of fabric; it was a tube of mints, now full of sugar and eaten with absolutely no guilt.

'Use the handkerchief.' Faye hissed through the earpiece.

Olivia ignored her and picked up the mints, rolling them between her finger and thumb.

'Tears! Now!' Faye was right, this was the point on the screen that told her to cry, but she couldn't find it in her to even lift the flimsy piece of fabric. Instead she tore the silver foil open and took out a mint. She popped it into her mouth and sucked, the sweetness enveloping her in memories of another moment in the spotlight, another audience, another decision she made.

'Mary gave us . . .' Faye prompted.

Olivia looked up at the Autocue, the words laid out for her to say.

'Mary gave . . .' Faye's voice was loud enough that Olivia didn't need the earpiece to hear her.

'Mary gave us back our choices.' She read from the screen, the mint lodged against her cheek.

'Get it together. You're better than this.'

'I am better than this,' Olivia whispered, the microphone sharing her revelation with the room.

'Yeah, you are!' A raucous voice shouted from somewhere near the back. Nervous laughter rippled around the room but Olivia's full attention was focused on finding the woman who spoke, in finding Alice.

'Olivia, I'm warning you, get back onto the script,' Faye shouted into the earpiece.

She had a choice, she had always had a choice, but her fear made her cling to safety, rather than choose to be free. Mary had threatened to kill her, but this wasn't life, and it certainly wasn't the life she wanted for her children. Was choosing her own path worth the risk of death?

It didn't take a conscious thought for her to reach up and remove the tiny plastic earbud and drop it on the lectern beside the handkerchief.

'Mary gave us back our choices, she told us to choose what was right, for us, for our families, for our best friends.' She looked away from the Autocue and grinned out at the audience, at Alice. 'That's why I'm going home, today, right now.' She spoke straight down the camera. 'My family have all been through so much; it's time for us to get back to normal.'

Faye's gasp was audible.

Olivia kept talking before they could cut her off, the words tumbling out as if read from the Autocue; but they were unrehearsed and more genuine than a single thing she had been allowed to say up to this point.

'I'm so grateful for everything Mary Vitasan has done for me. She's shown me, shown all of us, that sometimes you have to be brave and do what your intuition calls you to do. You know what's right for you, even when you're too scared to admit it. I'm done being scared, done hiding and hoping things will get better on their own. I'm following Mary's lead and going after what I want. I hope she will be my first customer when I open my new café. In fact, I hope you will all visit me and we will have a cup of tea and share our stories, because we are all united. Our pain, our suffering, our joy, our hope, our every action has ripple effects on society, so let's choose actions of peace and community. We can be safe and free together.'

372

There was a stunned silence, but Alice was the first to break it with a loud whoop. Olivia could make out a small figure standing clapping, and her actions motivated the rest of the room to join in. Everyone except Faye, who glared at Olivia from the side of the stage.

'I look forward to seeing you soon. Thank you very much for your support. Good night.' She waved to the audience and breezed offstage.

'You're not going anywhere.' Faye caught hold of Olivia's arm, her fingers vice-tight.

'Yes, I am.' She grasped Faye's hand, applying an equal pressure. 'Come now, you don't want to make a scene, do you?' She gave an exaggerated look back towards the nine hundred guests.

Faye immediately released her hold but she didn't back off.

'I don't know what you thought you were doing but you can't just leave. You have responsibilities, obligations, remember?'

'You're right, I do. My only responsibility is to myself and my family, and threatening them won't work, not any more, because this is over, I'm done. We're leaving and you're going to let us.' Olivia took a step away.

'Why's that?'

'I disappeared when I was a nobody and people noticed. What do you think will happen now that you made me a somebody? Everybody knows my plans and as you like to remind me, the world is watching. Go back to your life, Faye, and leave me to go back to mine.'

'You mean go home and play house again? Disappear indoors and be the good little housewife? You were miserable before and you jumped at the chance of some adventure. Nobody forced you to bake, to join CTAS, that was all your

373

choice. You enjoyed the thrill, the platform, the power.'

'My life was never small, I just didn't realise how big it could be, and that has nothing to do with standing on a world stage. I'm done. Now get out of my way.'

'You can't.' Faye refused to move but she didn't sound as sure as she normally did.

'People have told me what I can't do my whole life. You know what I've learnt? There's pretty much nothing I can't do. Want to know what I can do? I can go and live my life, my way.' She took a deep breath, a breath that felt like her very first.

Chapter Forty-Three

Three Months Later

Olivia tipped the chocolate chips into the glass bowl and poured over the hot double cream. The chocolate started to melt, little flecks of dark brown rose to the surface and she added a pinch of sea salt to bring out the flavour. The bell above the café door jangled and she looked up to see another group of women walk in.

'I'll get this table,' Alice said, saving Olivia from coming out of the kitchen. She didn't want to leave the oven; the sweet, rich scent of nearly baked chocolate cake meant she couldn't afford to be distracted. The smell had already attracted a lot of pre-orders and at this rate she would need to get another one in if they were going to have enough cakes for this evening. Not that she minded; there were worse problems than being in demand. They hadn't had a quiet day since she opened Sweet Freedom.

While she waited for the timer to go off, she weighed and sliced the Victoria sponge, as per the official government legislation. Things had changed but they hadn't changed that much.

'I need two slices of that.' Alice darted back over to deposit her dirty tray and went back to clear a second table. The café was so busy it kept them constantly moving, and despite hiring Lucy from Barre Class and two other waitresses, Olivia had to occasionally venture out of the kitchen to serve the customers.

People came from all across the country, wanting to share their stories, their hope and now their frustration in Mary and her government.

The timer buzzed but Olivia didn't need it to know the cake smelt ready; she took the baking tin out of the oven and set it down on the wire rack to cool. There was a round of applause from the waiting customers and a few wolf whistles.

'That smells amazing.' Alice leaned on the counter and inhaled deeply. 'Save me some.'

'You've already had your quota for the week.' Olivia slapped her hand away from the hot tin. 'They'll take away my licence.' She risked leaving the cake unattended, to whisk the melted chocolate and cream together, the dark and light blending to form a glossy, thick ganache.

'The Queen of Cakes? Never.' Alice lifted the domed lid over the apple pie and placed two slices onto plates. Olivia watched to make sure she didn't take any for herself, didn't 'accidentally on purpose' cut an extra sliver to eat later; she was getting wise to Alice's tricks.

Lucy approached with another order and tore it off her pad. 'Four slices of the chocolate cake, when it's ready. Do you want me to start reserving tables for tonight?'

'No, anybody is welcome, they can all stay on if they want.' Olivia poured the ganache over the cake and it waterfalled down the sides, leaving behind a beautifully shiny mirror glaze.

The meeting was Alice's idea, a way to bring everyone together to talk about what they had survived, but Olivia hoped for more from the event than to just share their pain; there had been enough of that already. The support groups and prescribed therapy sessions that had sprung up after the leadership change were more than capable of working through the angst and anguish, all the while indoctrinating the attendees with the new agenda. Tonight was about something different.

By six the tables were almost full, by half past there was standing room only, and by seven people queued out the door and around the corner.

'Who wants tea?' Alice walked round with a teapot and a tray of cups.

'I've got coffee,' Dev called, following behind her.

Olivia carried plates piled high with slices of cake, fresh golden scones and chocolate chip cookies still warm from the oven. People helped themselves to the treat of their choice and settled in, waiting for the meeting to begin.

'Sorry, sorry,' Danny pushed his way through the crowd. 'Dinner took for ever, but we're here.' Matthew and Mia followed behind him, disappearing almost immediately to find their friends and play with the toy kitchen in the corner.

'Great turnout,' he said. 'You might need to hire the village hall next time.'

'You'll need to pick another night,' Patricia said from a nearby table, where she sat with Tom and Becky. 'Mrs Flynn's rather busy there with the Unity Institute, though I imagine it's a lot quieter this evening.'

'That's tonight?' Setting up the café had kept Olivia busy since she walked out of the Unity dinner. She had met up with Alice and they had called Danny on their way back, but he already had the children out of Downing Street and in a taxi. They reached Norfolk just after midnight and hadn't heard from Mary or Faye since. As Olivia had hoped, they didn't bother with her once she publicly stepped out of the limelight, but she remained in a bright enough spotlight to keep her safe, for now at least.

Jenna and Lewis were also noticeably absent from the village, with Mrs Flynn magnanimously stepping in to fill the breach; she also preferred to ignore Olivia and her family and that was just fine by them.

'I don't recognise half these people,' Tom said, 'they're not all local.' And none wore frayed or tasselled accessories.

There had been a clear parting of the ways between Olivia, Alice and CTAS, unsurprisingly. The group were fully behind Mary's radical methods for change. Olivia couldn't condone the lengths they were willing to go to and they were happy to move on without her.

She looked around the café at the familiar faces from the disbanded Mother's Institute. They were joined by husbands, partners and even their children, as well as people with accents that caught her attention as she weaved around the tables, carrying the rapidly emptying plates of cake. She picked out the sound of a lilting Irishman, the soft burr of a group of Scottish women, and the sing-song quality of a Welsh couple. There were people from nearer home too, with Londoners, Liverpudlians and Geordies adding to the blend of voices that were growing in volume, as strangers became friends and allies. This, she thought, was what it felt like to belong.

'Put this on.' Alice intercepted her with a lapel microphone.

'I don't need that.'

'You do for the people outside.' They were all clustered outside the plate-glass windows, peering in.

'I thought you said this would be a small gathering.'

'And you believed me?' Alice grinned at her.

'I don't know what they want.' Her new self-belief

wasn't a permanent fixture, it ebbed and flowed, sometimes at the most inopportune times.

'They want hope, and you're great at that. Tell them what you want, what you need, and see if they feel the same. You can do this.' Alice kissed her cheek and Olivia's confidence rose again.

She stared at all the expectant faces, could feel their desire for something she wasn't sure she could give, felt the faintest flutter of old anxiety, then she took a breath and smiled.

'Thank you for coming tonight. I'm honoured that you took time out of your day to be here. I want to start by saying I don't have the answers, I don't know how to change the world, I only know it needs changing. For us. For our children.'

Matthew and Mia played together, oblivious of the changes starting around them.

'I'm tired, so, so tired, of the way things are done, the way they've always been done. I thought, we all thought, the struggle was over when Mother Mason died. I hoped that life would get better, and everything did change but somehow it's stayed the same.'

There was no reaction from the crowd, they remained silent, watching her intently.

'I don't know where to start except for right here, where I am, hopefully with you.'

'Not just us,' an elderly Scottish woman on the table beside her said. 'I was at Trafalgar Square, I saw your speech at the Unity Institute dinner. You're what we've been waiting for. We heard what you said about doing things differently and that's what we want. We're all behind you, we're ready to support you in your bid to take over from Mary.'

A cheer went up from the room, full of passion and fervour that made the hairs on Olivia's neck stand up.

'No,' she waved them away. 'I've seen what government can do, the struggle for power, for control, and I don't want to be part of that. They're too far away, too out of touch to know what's needed, and they're all too concerned with their own lives. That's why it's time we started making decisions of our own, choosing what's right for us.

'I want to build a community, a place of support and connection. In this room alone, I see incredibly talented people. Each of you has your own gifts, skills and experiences, things you can share that would benefit so many.

'I believe we can build the life, and the world, we want for ourselves, our families, our friends and neighbours.' She swallowed as emotion threatened to overwhelm her. Everybody she loved, everything that mattered, was here with her in the café. She had found her joy and peace, if only she could help others do that too.

'We all want the same things: safety, love, connection. It's up to us to find a way to do that; we have to stop waiting for someone else to take care of us. I've learnt the hard way, no one is coming. The government won't save us, we're on our own, and that's not a bad thing. We'll save ourselves because we have to; this is a challenge we can't fail, because anything less is not an option. We each deserve to live the life we truly want, to have the freedom to pursue our dreams, and the support to get there. It's up to us to show our children it's possible for them too.

'I can't do this on my own. It's about more than just one person, but if we work together, I believe we can do anything.'

Read on to discover the inspiration
behind *The Choice*

Author's Note

I remember exactly where I was when I first came up with the idea for *The Choice*. It was January 2012 and I'd just been to buy cake decorations for some Valentine's cupcakes. On the way home we passed several fast-food drive-thrus and it reminded me of an article I'd read about sugar and fat potentially being as addictive as cocaine. If this was true, I wondered if they could be classified as drugs? What would happen if the government made them illegal?

I asked myself: how would I live in a world like that? I love baking – it's my favourite way to relax. Like Olivia, I bake when I'm happy, sad, bored or stressed. Cakes are the best ice-breaker at any gathering and the perfect way to start talking to strangers when you're feeling shy.

Originally, I intended my story to be a light, fun read about a young woman and her best friend baking secret cakes. That was the plan. The story had other ideas. The more I wrote about banning sugar, the more implications I discovered. It wouldn't just change the way people ate, the government would need a way to enforce the rules. Tougher laws would mean tougher restrictions on everything from diet to exercise, supermarket shopping to eating out. The impact was far reaching and Olivia's life became much scarier and harder to survive. It was a world that terrified me, but also one that seemed to be growing more real whenever I turned on the news.

The story might have started out about baking, but it rapidly evolved into something darker. It forced me to think about choices, mine and everyone else's, around what we eat, how we live and the role the government has in those decisions.

Instead of coming away with one clear answer, I realised that I don't believe there's a one-size-fits-all solution. I think it comes down to each individual choosing what's right for them. What do you think?

Questions for Readers

1. How would you survive in a world where sugar was illegal and baking was a crime?
2. Do you believe that sugar and fat are addictive? If so, should we limit access to them and introduce restrictions on how much people can eat?
3. How would you feel if you had to attend mandatory exercise classes?
4. What do you think the government's role should be in what we eat and how much we exercise?
5. Would you join the Cut The Apron Strings rebellion? If so, what frayed item would you wear?
6. How do you think peer pressure and shame impact the way we live today? Would a trip to the Shame Box stop you from breaking the rules?
7. What would you miss most if sugar, fat, alcohol and cigarettes were banned?
8. Which character in *The Choice* do you most identify with?
9. Olivia finds comfort in baking, Alice likes to shop and Danny goes on social media. What's your escape? Is it a form of relaxation or numbing?
10. If you marched on Trafalgar Square with CTAS, what would you bake?

Acknowledgements

The acknowledgments are my favourite part of a book. I'm honoured I get to write my own. That's all thanks to Joanne Finney, Clare Hey and Amanda Preston who picked me as the 2018 Good Housekeeping Novel Competition winner. You changed my life and I'm so grateful.

I've been really lucky to get Amanda as my agent. I truly appreciate your enthusiasm, support and guidance.

Orion is the perfect home for me and *The Choice*; everyone has worked so hard to bring my story into the world. A big thank you to Victoria Oundjian, my fantastic editor. You said you were going to push me and you did; it was completely worth it! It takes a team to publish a book. Thank you to Olivia Barber, Justine Taylor, Alainna Hadjigeorgiou, Tanjiah Islam, John Garth and James Nunn for all your work behind the scenes.

Writing can be a long, lonely process but I've had incredible support from some amazing friends. Deborah Globus, sharing the journey with you has made it much more fun; I'll see you on Skype. Debra Chapman, our cream teas at the Tea House have been a saving grace; they kept me going when things seemed impossible. Karen (KJ) Hawkwood, you helped me stay sane through the editing process, you always help me believe in myself. Alys Wilfred Earl, Heidi Swain, Jenni Keer, Rosie Hendry, Margaret Kirk, Kate

Hardy, Ian Wilfred, Moira Please, the lovely members of the RNA and the fabulous Savvies – your support, advice and friendship have carried me through the publishing experience. Melani Marx, thank you for telling me to write when I was worried I was wasting my time.

The Choice is about strong, amazing women and I'm lucky to have so many in my life, all thanks to Cake Club and the WI. A special mention for Vicki Bowden, Kate White, Jody Bicknell, Kim Greenstreet, Szara and Roisin Froud, my fellow founding Swallowtails. Your friendship means the world to me. I know you'd all be at the front of CTAS, guerrilla bakes in hand.

I wanted to write because I love to read. When I was a child, Mrs Gallaway was the local librarian and gatekeeper to the books. She was the first person I knew who published a story and showed me it was possible.

Thank you to all my book clubs, past and present: the books we read shaped the author I've become.

Ian Nettleton, Chris Armstrong, Yvonne Johnston and Susie Tansley, you finally get to read the whole story! It's changed a lot since I first introduced you to the characters, but the dark, twisty elements began with you.

Debi Alper and Emma Darwin were fundamental in teaching me how to take my writing to the next level. I'm so grateful for all the lightbulbs.

Thank you to the National Centre for Writing, TLC, Jericho, Writers' HQ and WriteNow who were there at the perfect time and helped me discover my writing voice.

For everyone else who has encouraged and supported me along the way, thank you for asking how the book was going even when I had no news.

Grandma, you were my first reader, thank you for sharing your love of books with me. Alice and Bronwyn, you are amazing. A, my "Alice" came into the world first but you share her spark and confidence. B, when a determined and cheeky character showed up, I knew she had to be called Bronwyn. Thank you to Simon and Fee for bringing you both into my life.

Finally, thank you to Anita Wade; I couldn't have done this without you. Mum, you're going to have to read the book now. x

Credits

Claire Wade and Orion Fiction would like to thank everyone at Orion who worked on the publication of *The Choice* in the UK.

Editorial
Victoria Oundjian
Olivia Barber

Copy editor
Justine Taylor

Proof reader
John Garth

Audio
Paul Stark
Amber Bates

Contracts
Anne Goddard
Paul Bulos
Jake Alderson

Design
Debbie Holmes
Joanna Ridley

Nick May
Helen Ewing

Editorial Management
Charlie Panayiotou
Jane Hughes
Alice Davis

Finance
Jasdip Nandra
Afeera Ahmed
Elizabeth Beaumont
Sue Baker

Marketing
Tanjiah Islam
Jennifer McMenemy

Production
Ruth Sharvell

Publicity
Alainna Hadjigeorgiou